BLESSED ARE THE POOR IN SPIRIT

ISBN: 978-1-967681-02-0
First Printing, 2025

Cover design: Pat Fultz

Blessed Are the Poor in Spirit

ASHLIE HAND

*To my life's greatest blessings -
Christopher, Thomas, Andrew and Maddy.*

"[The] first Beatitude is the source of all the others; it contains them all, as a seed contains a plant."
The Eight Doors of the Kingdom | Father Jacques Philippe

Prologue

Cate couldn't take her eyes off the photo. It was her favorite one of Charlie. He was smiling like he did just before letting loose his signature laugh, so loud and full of joy it never failed to make her laugh, too. His eyes were twinkling, his hair curling up just above his eyebrows, and the sunlight was bouncing off his shoulders. It was blown up to poster size and set on a flimsy easel that looked like it could topple over any minute.

She couldn't take her eyes off the photo because then she would have to look at the long, shiny wood box that was centered on the altar in front of them.

She knew it wasn't really her big brother in that long box, "just a shell that used to hold his spirit." That's what the man at the funeral home had said, anyway, when she and her parents saw Charlie for the first time all tucked into his casket. Still, it really looked like Charlie–only more waxy and pale. His face reminded her of her Ken dolls, so she had thrown them all in the trash when she got home from the visitation.

Cate idolized Charlie. At fourteen, he was tall, strong and handsome–the girls at school called him "dreamy," but that made Cate want to puke. He was built like an athlete, with the same straw-colored hair as her, piercing hazel eyes, and a nearly year-round suntan from all the time he spent outside. Charlie got to help out with everything–he had even started driving the tractor last summer. No one could make her laugh like Charlie. The worst was when he made her laugh so hard, milk squirted out of her nose. The best was when he called her "Kitty." The memory made her throat feel tight, and she tried not to cry.

It had only been a week, but the details were still so clear, like a movie she could replay in her head. She allowed her mind to wander back to that time just before everything changed.

She had been in the barn taking care of a tiny kitten meowing at her ankle. She picked it up, being extra careful not to squeeze too tight, protecting the little bones that felt like they were right under its fur.

She stuck out her bottom lip and blew a stray piece of hair off her forehead. She reached for the formula-filled water bottle with the tattered grocery store label. The kitten's tiny mouth and tongue slurped from the nipple, white, foamy milk catching in the thin layer of fur around its bottom lip and dripping onto her lap. Sunlight filtered through the gaps in the barn roof, and the fall chill burned her cheeks even though it was late afternoon. She slouched a little deeper into Charlie's thick Carhart jacket, grateful she had thought to grab it on her way out the door.

She didn't have any responsibility yet for the big animals, but her dad let her take care of the endless number of barn cats that turned up every year. She also had her own goat that she cared for and showed with her 4-H club at the Iowa State Fair every summer, but that barely took her an hour each day. She was marking off the days on her wall calendar in her bedroom because when she turned ten in February, her dad promised her she could have her own calf.

Cate loved feeling useful, and there seemed to be plenty of opportunities for that around the farm. Her mom let her help out in the garden, too. The tomatoes were her favorite. They came off the vine so easily when they were fully ripened, and her mouth would start to water as soon as she wrapped her hand around their smooth, meaty skin. She couldn't think of anything better than sliced tomato with salt and pepper–it was her favorite late-summer snack. Tomato season ended a couple of months ago, though, and now the only things to pick were yucky green and yellow squash.

The barn doors parted, and Cate looked up to see her cousin James running toward her. James was stocky and sort of lumbered along, his hair flopping around on top of his head.

"Catie! Where's your dad?" he asked breathlessly, stopping a short distance away from her, his eyes wild and scared. The bottom of his jeans were wet almost all the way to his knees, and dark brown spots were splattered all over his t-shirt. A big smudge of something that looked like mud was smeared across his cheek.

James was always playing tricks on her and making her think something was wrong when it wasn't. She hated being tricked.

"Knock it off, James." Cate tried to act nonchalant and didn't even look up when she spoke to him.

Just then, James let out a sound like nothing she'd ever heard before. It was a cross between a moan and a scream.

The sound startled her and she jumped, almost dropping the kitten and its bottle. She stared at James. It felt like her blood froze and her whole body went cold. She pulled the bottle from the kitten's mouth and set both on the hay bale as she stood up. Her heart was pounding, and her voice felt like it was caught in her throat.

"What's wrong, James–where's Charlie?" she croaked.

"Catie, please ... just tell me where I can find your dad!" James shouted, his voice now constricted with a threatening sob, tears springing into his eyes.

"I–I think he's on the back forty ... covering up the irrigation lines," she said, searching James' face for any clues to what he was so upset about.

"Where's ... Charlie," she demanded, her voice lowered and her hands balled up into fists.

James fell into a crouched position, his hands gripping the thick, dark hair on top of his head.

"Oh god oh god oh god ..." he whimpered.

"James! Tell me where Charlie is right now!" Cate screamed, standing over him, then crouching down to try to see into his eyes, her breath coming fast.

He just kept whimpering and fell onto his rear end, his head buried in his hands.

"Ugh ..." Cate groaned, popping up and racing to the door.

She exited the barn and headed toward the house. She spotted her dad climbing down from the cab of the tractor. He ran his familiar red handkerchief across his forehead, replacing the green John Deere baseball hat on his balding head.

"Dad! Dad!" Cate waved her arms as he turned away from her to fiddle with something on one of the tractor tires. When he finally heard her, he turned to her with a look of concern. Cate finally reached him and skidded to a stop.

"Dad, something's wrong–James is freaking out in the barn, and he won't tell me where Charlie is," she gasped.

Her Dad started toward the barn, and Cate followed. He turned to her as he picked up his pace and began to jog.

"Catie–go tell your mother to call 911."

Her heart jumped, and she spun around and sprinted to the house as fast as her legs would carry her. The sky was a crisp, clean blue, and the sun was like a yellow starburst in the cloudless sky. Bright red, yellow, and orange leaves still clung to the large mature trees in the front yard. None of it seemed to belong, like the world hadn't gotten the message that there was a crisis.

Cate's mom had driven them to where it happened, finding James and her dad standing on the shoulder of the road. They had been there for a while already, and they shielded Cate and her mom from getting too close to the ditch. Cate's mom had collapsed right there on the road, her legs folded and her hands planted on the rough, rocky shoulder.

It had felt like hours before they heard the wailing sirens coming toward them. Police cars, an ambulance, then the fire truck arrived last, lights twirling and flashing, kicking up a thick cloud of white dust. Cate had to shield her eyes and felt like she was biting down on sand when she tried to swallow. Her dad had thrown his coat over her mom's shoulders, and she was finally back on her feet, though he still wouldn't let her see Charlie. While they were distracted by the arrival of the emergency vehicles, though,

Cate snuck up to the edge of the ditch and looked down. That's when she saw it. The four-wheeler was on its side, and she could make out a pair of legs, perfectly still and strangely bent. Most of his body was under the murky, shallow water of the ditch, but she immediately recognized Charlie's work boots. She couldn't see his head, but she heard one of the paramedics say it was "submerged."

James and her dad had jumped into the ditch with the firemen and paramedics, and it took a huge team of them to move the four-wheeler away from Charlie's body. They got him onto a stretcher, and when Cate finally got a glimpse of his face, it happened.

Her head felt weird and floaty, and she thought she was going to throw up. Her face got super hot and tingly, and she felt like she was traveling through a tunnel. She couldn't remember much after that, at least not until she woke up in the hospital. She was confused, and alone, and she started to cry. A nurse came in and calmed her down and said she was going to get Cate's dad.

When her dad came into the small curtained room, his face was pale and his eyes were red and puffy. She immediately remembered Charlie and started crying even harder. Her dad came over and gave her a big hug, which made Cate cry so hard that she couldn't catch her breath. Her dad had to call the nurse back in, and they put a needle in her arm that made her sleepy.

The next time she woke up, her dad let her know that Charlie had died instantly when the four-wheeler fell on him. Cate hoped that meant Charlie never had a chance to be scared. She thought it would have been even worse knowing that Charlie had died scared and alone.

A doctor had come in and explained to Cate's parents that she had experienced a panic attack paired with a rare side effect that caused her to faint. He said she would have to be carefully watched, but it wasn't harmful. It had a long, funny name Cate couldn't remember and was too overwhelmed to ask him to repeat. She also just didn't care. All she knew was that now she was going to have to live without Charlie. She felt like she was floating out in the middle of the ocean, all alone and without her best friend.

The pastor was speaking from the altar now, talking about Charlie even though Cate couldn't remember him ever spending any time with Charlie. It made her mad to hear someone talking about her brother like he knew him. She crossed her arms and slumped against the back of the pew.

She looked across the aisle and saw James sitting stiffly in his suit and tie, his head bowed. She knew he felt responsible for what happened. Last night at the visitation, he was crying so hard about how it had been his idea to take the four-wheelers out that afternoon. He told Cate that he was driving faster than he was supposed to, and Charlie was trying to keep up with him. That made her more sad and angry, too, and she didn't want to look at James anymore.

She could feel the pew shaking gently beneath her and glanced over to see her mom's shoulders bouncing softly, her chin bent so far it was almost touching her chest as she rested a wad of tissue under her nose, tears rolling down her cheeks. Cate's dad put his arm around her mom, and she leaned into him. Cate knew if she looked at her dad's face one more time, she would start crying again and lose her breath. Instead, she let her mind wander to what Deacon George said to her during the visitation last night.

"You're going to have to step up and help your mom and dad a lot more now," he said, seated next to her at the round plastic table inside the parish hall. Her parents were standing by Charlie's casket while everyone came up and hugged them. Cate didn't want to hug anyone, so she had found an empty table where she could sit in a hard plastic chair that smelled like dirty feet and let her legs swing back and forth.

Cate nodded, her heart beating faster. Would Dad let her drive the tractor now? Take care of a whole herd of goats, plus milk the cows? She was only nine years old! It was scary, and she didn't feel like she was ready. Mom had been in bed for days now, ever since they found Charlie in the ditch, so maybe Cate was going to have to start cooking meals and make sure Dad had his lunch before he went out to the field in the morning. She might even have to quit school.

Cate had really tried to keep the tears from welling up in her eyes and spilling onto her cheeks, but it happened anyway.

"Dry those tears now," Deacon George had said. "You've gotta find that strength inside yourself." He poked his thick finger into the center of her chest. "Show your mom and dad they can depend on you. Don't give them another reason to be sad now," he added, dropping his chin and looking at her over his large, red nose.

Cate nodded, wiping the tears from her cheeks. Deacon George seemed to be the only person paying any attention to her, and she was desperate for any adult to tell her what to do. She wished her grandparents were there, but they were both sick and couldn't travel.

Cate had gotten to talk to her grandmother for just a few minutes the night before the visitation, and she had promised she would be praying for all of them. Her grandmother was the closest person to God she knew. She took Cate with her to church every time she was in town, told her Bible stories, and loved to share some of her favorite prayers–the ones about Jesus' mother were Cate's favorite.

Other than that, church wasn't really part of Cate's life. Cate's mom talked about God, but it was usually when she was telling her and Charlie why they should behave, and she didn't go to church regularly. Cate's dad said that the fields were his "church" and that he did his talking to God while he was out there. Charlie more or less followed her dad's example, so Cate was the only one who took up her grandma's offer to join her at Mass. Cate always treasured that time, and it made her feel safe in a different way than being at home.

The night before the visitation, Cate felt a strong urge to talk to God the way that she had seen her grandma do so many times. She kneeled down next to her bed, hands clasped together, and begged God to bring Charlie back, to show her that this had all just been a bad dream. The next morning, she woke up with hopeful anticipation, racing down for breakfast but finding the kitchen still and quiet. There was no breakfast prepared, no Charlie sitting on his side of the table. Her dad shuffled down the stairs and offered a half-hearted smile before patting the top of her head.

"Is that what you're wearing to the visitation?" he asked, his voice like gravel in his throat. Cate's heart shattered. Nothing had changed. Her prayer didn't work.

Her grandma always said that God and her guardian angels would protect her, but that hadn't worked for Charlie. Cate wasn't going to make the same mistake ever again. Everyone was counting on her.

~ 1 ~

In her remaining year of elementary school and all throughout middle school, Cate earned the reputation of the girl you could count on. Dependable, confident and steady. She picked up her chores on the farm with ease and became especially good at caring for the animals. By eighth grade, she had taken over all the jobs that Charlie had helped with and more. She was careful not to do anything that would upset her parents, and she relished the way they gazed at her with pride. She had just a few close friends, and other than her middle school cheerleading squad, she didn't have much time for outside activities.

She kept the darker part of her life secret. The sadness never really left their home after Charlie died. It was always there, at times quiet and soft, sitting like a well-behaved dog in its kennel, familiar and contained, and other times it was loud and obnoxious–like on holidays and Charlie's birthday. Those were the times Cate preferred to stay in her room where she could more easily control the panic building in her chest, turning her insides into jelly. She found she could usually breathe through the attack before it got so bad she passed out.

She had her first public panic attack in high school. It was the end of football season her sophomore year and her first year on the varsity cheerleading squad.

Charlie's birthday was coming up in a few days, and she had been going through one of her desk drawers when she found an old picture of him she had totally forgotten about. It was a polaroid she had taken a few days before his accident. She had asked him to make a silly face, so his eyes were crossed and he had pushed his tongue through his lips, tilting his head and raising both hands on top of his head like antlers. Cate initially smiled at the memory, recalling how hard they had laughed when the photo finally came into focus. He had written a note in the white border at the bottom: *To my Kitty, never stop laughing.* Cate's throat had tightened up when she read it again, and she had curled up on her bed, coughing through her sobs.

She had looked at the picture every single night before she fell asleep since then, and Charlie's memory had been hanging over her like a dark cloud all week. She could tell her parents knew something was off with her, but they never said anything. Charlie's birthday was just as difficult for them, and other than blowing out a candle for him each year, they didn't really talk about it.

It was almost halftime of their last home football game. Cate was a base for her squad, and they were preparing to lift their flyer. She turned to face her partner, joining her in placing their hands out for their flyer to step into. Normally focused and zeroed in on her teammate, Cate had been allowing her mind to wander throughout the game, thinking about how Charlie never really got to experience high school football games, hanging out with his friends in the student section, maybe sneaking under the bleachers with his first girlfriend. The unfairness of it all sunk deep into her bones, and she was fighting back angry tears. By the time she turned to face her base partner, the hot prickly feeling had already started in her forehead and chest, and her stomach was doing somersaults. She tried taking several deep breaths, but it seemed she had lost the ability to control the panic now rising from her belly.

They had gotten their flyer up with their arms extended when Cate's knees gave out. Her base partner was able to break her teammate's fall, which was the last thing Cate saw before she entered the tunnel and everything went black.

"Cate?" She heard a familiar voice calling to her, but it sounded far away. She heard it again, a little closer this time, and finally her eyes fluttered open. She was sitting up facing the football field, her back against the cold hard concrete at the base of the stands. She felt weak and lightheaded and wasn't able to stop the tears that came once she realized what had happened. Her best friend, Molly, was sitting next to her, holding her hand, and Cate saw her coach talking with her parents just a few steps away.

"Hey," Molly said softly. "Welcome back." She handed her a towel so Cate could wipe her tears and the snot now running from her nose.

She was able to focus on Molly's face and gave her a weak smile. "I'm so sorry ..." she whispered, and the tears came even heavier. She knew she had let her teammates down, and just hoped that her base partner and flyer didn't hate her.

Her dad came over and offered Cate his hand. "C'mon, kiddo, we're going to go get checked out and make sure you're okay. I was able to save you the embarrassment of the ambulance and paramedics rolling you out of here on a stretcher," he said with a small smile.

Molly helped her dad get Cate onto her feet, and though she wobbled briefly, she felt steady enough to walk holding her dad's arm. Her mom came over and tucked a piece of hair behind her ear that had escaped her ponytail. She laid her hand gently on Cate's back, and they made their way to their car.

There had been a barrage of tests of her heart, tubes of blood drawn, and a strange "tilt table" test that felt like a carnival ride. Eventually, the doctor had come in and told Cate and her parents that she experienced something called vasovagal syncope, causing her heart rate and blood pressure to suddenly drop in response to certain triggers. She could manage it with therapy, and he said lots of kids tend to outgrow it when they get to adulthood. Cate took

the news in stride, vowing to do whatever she could to avoid causing her parents any more distress.

She tried to ignore the sideways glances from her mom when
Charlie's birthday or the anniversary of his accident rolled around
each year, wordlessly checking on Cate to be sure she wasn't spi-
raling or masking her anxiety. Cate wished her mom would just
talk to her about it, but Cate's therapist helped her understand
that her mom was battling her own despair over losing her only
son and encouraged Cate to just give her time. Her dad kept busy
with farmwork and didn't seem to want to acknowledge Cate's
weaknesses. There were times when they would be wrapping up
something in the barn, the sun just beginning to set, and he would
put his arm around her shoulders with a nurturing squeeze. Cate's
heart would ache for him to ask her how she was doing, or acknowledge the loss they were all feeling, but he never did. It would
just hang silently between them as they walked back to the house
for dinner.

Thankfully, she was able to manage her panic attacks with
counseling throughout the rest of her high school years, and by
graduation Cate felt like she was in control of her body and her
emotions and was ready to embark on the next phase of her life.

Finally, the time came to take the leap to college and more independence than she'd ever had. She picked up the last box of knick-
knacks she wanted for her dorm room, but stopped when she got
to the doorway. She turned back for one final glance at her childhood bedroom, a bittersweet tug pulling at her heart.

"Don't worry, Charlie, I won't forget to laugh."

~ 2 ~

The doctor raised the squishy, slick infant over the drape, its tiny hands shaking like an angry old man's, its little face a frozen expression of pure shock.

"You've got a baby boy!" the doctor called out, then handed the baby off to a nurse. Cate closed her eyes as tears rolled down her temples and into her ears. Her husband, Anthony, leaned over and kissed her forehead.

"Wow! A boy!" he marveled.

"Joseph Charles ..." Cate sighed, wincing as the surgical team put her back together on the other side of the drape.

The weight of parenthood seemed to cover Cate like a heavy blanket now that her baby was on the outside of her body. She stared up at the bright fluorescent lights, listening to her baby's shaky cries as he drew his first breaths. She turned her head toward Anthony. His face was directed at where the nurses were weighing the baby and wrapping up his tiny body.

"Joey ..." Anthony whispered, a wide, joyful grin spreading across his face. He quickly turned back to Cate as if suddenly remembering she was lying there next to him and leaned over to place another soft kiss on her forehead.

* * *

Cate and Anthony met in their freshman year of college in the dorm building they'd been assigned, their rooms just a few doors apart from each other. Cate initially thought Anthony was immature and obnoxious, as she regularly heard loud music and what sounded like an entire crowd of voices coming from behind his

13

closed door. He was a typical jock, overly confident and aloof. He frequently had girls in his room and he had rushed one of the biggest party fraternities. She and her roommate would roll their eyes as they passed his room on the way to the next house party or sporting event.

Cate thrived in college. She was attending a major state university, and there were a million different ways to get involved, be active, and meet people. As a tribute to Charlie, she had decided to pursue nursing so she could care for other families facing tragic circumstances. Her classes were rigorous, and she spent long hours in labs and lecture halls. Eventually, she made her way to the university hospital, where she got to experience real patient care. She loved every minute of it and felt more whole and centered than she had her entire life. Life seemed to be playing out pretty much as expected.

Her affection for Anthony surprised her, however. She had seen him unexpectedly when she moved back into the dorm her sophomore year. He was leaning against the wall at the end of the hallway where she would turn to go to her new room. His gaze was focused toward an open doorway where he seemed to be talking to someone as Cate started down the hall. As she got closer to him, he stopped talking and turned to greet her.

"Hey," Anthony said, his face somehow softer and his smile genuine. He wasn't the cocky, aloof boy she remembered from the year before but seemed to have matured over the summer, exhibiting a different kind of confidence that Cate found comforting and attractive.

Cate's heart fluttered, and an unfamiliar feeling blossomed in her belly. "Hey," she said, returning his smile. She continued on to her dorm room, but a spark had developed, and it had her attention.

Over the next couple of months, Cate and Anthony gently and slowly established a friendship, though Cate chose to date other guys and would come home from one disappointing date after another and call Anthony.

"Hello?" Anthony would answer eagerly.

"Hey," Cate would say with an edge of frustration. "He's such an ass," she slurred.

"What happened now?" Anthony would ask with sincerity.

"He completely ignored me the entire night–it was like the night he kissed me never happened!"

"Sorry, Cate–you don't deserve that."

"I know ... I really don't. Who the heck does he think he is?"

"I wouldn't have any idea." Anthony would sigh and get quiet. Eventually, Cate would hang up, and the cycle would start all over again.

One afternoon, she was complaining to her roommate about the latest guy to disrespect her, and her roommate slapped her highlighter down on the textbook she was reading.

"Cate, why don't you just go for the one that's nice to you?"

Cate stared at her, the realization of what she was suggesting soaking in. Later that night, she walked up to Anthony's frat house and stood briefly on the large country-style porch. She'd been to the house many times, but this time felt different. She took a deep breath and pressed the doorbell. The house mother answered the door and flashed her familiar smile.

"Cate! Come on in. I think Anthony is up in his room studying." She stepped aside so Cate could come in, and Cate started up the carpeted stairs. Cate knocked gently on Anthony's bedroom door, and just a few seconds later, the door opened and he greeted her with a wide grin.

"Hey! What are you doing here?"

Cate stepped into the room and put her arms around Anthony's neck. He paused briefly, then wrapped his arms around her body.

"I'm so sorry, Anthony," she said into his shoulder.

"What? Why?" He pulled back and pushed Cate away so he could see her face.

"I've been whining to you for months now about these other jerks, and you never once made me feel like I was an idiot for falling for the same guys over and over."

"Well, you're not ... but you deserve to be treated so much better, Cate."

"I know," Cate said, looking at her hands. "Are you going to be studying for much longer?"

Anthony considered the pile of textbooks open on his bed before turning back to her. "No ... my night is wide open." His eyes twinkled, and he gestured for her to take the large saucer chair in the corner of the room. Cate folded herself into the matted fleece cover, and Anthony made a spot for himself on his bed.

They talked for the next several hours about their childhoods, their families, high school friends and experiences, and dreams for their future. Even though they had been friends for a while, Cate hadn't fully let her guard down in front of him so completely. That night, she finally told him the full story about Charlie, including how losing him had led to her history with panic attacks. Anthony listened with compassion and genuine interest, coming over and wrapping his arms around her when she began to cry softly, remembering how Charlie had always been her confidant. She began to sense the possibility that Anthony could be that person for her and realized just how much she had been missing that in her life. She fell asleep curled beside him and woke up with a sense that for the first time in a very long time, she was no longer alone in the world.

Their relationship evolved quickly, and soon Cate and Anthony were spending every possible moment together. Anthony was studying finance, so they rarely crossed paths during the school day, but they made time for each other whenever possible. They had picked up part-time jobs at the same casual dining restaurant and were regularly scheduled for the same shifts. After about a year, their relationship became more physical, and Cate gave herself to Anthony for the first time. He was her first, though Anthony had a couple of previous partners. He had been so gentle with her. Their relationship took on a new level of intimacy, and they were bonded even more strongly than before.

By graduation, their relationship had become comfortable, and Cate felt she could trust Anthony to always be there for her. They had discussed marriage a few times, but agreed they would wait until Cate was an RN so she could settle wherever she got her first nursing job. Their lives were steady and predictable, and aside from a few minor bumps along the road, about as perfect as possible.

The night after their graduation ceremony, they were celebrating with family and a big group of their college friends at a local sports bar. Anthony pulled Cate aside and presented her with a small felt box. She held her breath as she slowly lifted the lid, revealing a dainty gold band that twisted into a pair of hearts, the larger one framed with five diamond chips.

"Oh, Anthony," she breathed, looking at him with wide, affectionate eyes. She plucked the ring from the box, and he took it from her, sliding it onto the ring finger of her right hand.

"It's a promise ring," Anthony said softly. "My heart is yours, Cate. I know we're still young, but I can't imagine my life without you, and ... I really don't want to."

"Me either," Cate responded, wrapping her arms around Anthony's neck.

* * *

Cate shuffled into her apartment, closing the door behind her as quietly as possible so she didn't wake Anthony. She had been hired as a nursing assistant at a hospital in Kansas City after graduation and had just pulled her third overnight shift for the week. She was mercifully off now for the next four days. It was always a push to get through the grueling long hours at the hospital, but she had been able to get some more clinical experience and save up while she was studying for the RN exam. She would finally be able to take it after the first of the year.

Anthony had followed her to Kansas City and gotten hired pretty quickly with a financial services company downtown. Their apartment was in an overpriced converted cold storage facility along the Missouri River, but they loved the location and had even become dear friends with a few other couples in their building. They were generally living the charmed life of a young dual-income couple in an affordable Midwest city where they could spread their wings and begin to build a future.

Cate gently set her bag on the small dining table inside the door of the apartment, grateful Anthony had remembered to leave the light on above the stove so she could see her way to the fridge. She was exhausted but hadn't eaten anything since 7 p.m., and it was now just after 1 a.m. She opened the refrigerator door and smiled as she spotted the plate covered with aluminum foil, a large goofy smiley face drawn on the top in black marker. She pulled it out, quietly closing the refrigerator door. She pulled off the foil and moaned eagerly when she spotted Anthony's famous spaghetti and meatballs. It was his grandmother's recipe and one of her most favorite things he made for her. She threw a paper towel over the plate and popped it into the microwave to heat it up.

She poured herself a glass of red wine and settled with her plate of spaghetti on one of the barstools at the kitchen's breakfast counter. Once she had eaten to the point where she thought she might burst, she rinsed off her plate and gently set it in the sink with her empty wine glass.

Cate padded softly into the ensuite bathroom, careful not to turn on the lights until after she'd closed the door. She stripped out of her scrubs and turned on the shower. She let the water run over her shoulders, wrapping her arms around her waist and closing her eyes as the tension from the past three days finally melted away. She loved nursing, and her patients loved her. Her nurse manager said she had a strong command of patient care and a level of compassion that was rare in someone her age. Cate knew it came from experiencing loss and understanding the human desire to feel in control when it seemed like everything was falling apart.

She sensed another presence and opened her eyes just as the shower door clicked open. Anthony stepped into the shower, wrapping her in his arms and nuzzling her neck. She barely had the energy to hug him back but gave herself over to him, knowing how much he craved physical connection. These long stretches apart challenged him and their relationship, and refusing him would have been cruel. They toweled off, and Cate drifted to sleep with Anthony's arm curved around her, her fingers intertwined with his.

It was right before Halloween when Cate had a feeling something was up. She had been feeling nauseous off and on, and a kind of tired that rivaled the final day of her overnight shift schedule, only she couldn't shake it even during her off days. When she mentioned her symptoms to her friend and coworker, her immediate reaction was to ask if she could be pregnant.

Cate was on birth control but knew that wasn't always 100% effective, and it was possible that with her crazy schedule she had missed a pill here and there. Her cycle had been a little off, too, and she suddenly felt the icy-cold realization sink in.

"I mean, yeah, I guess it's a possibility," she answered with resignation.

"I think we have some pregnancy tests in the supply closet. I'll bring you one and you can take it when you go on break. Just take some deep breaths ... either way, it's going to be okay." Her friend squeezed her forearm affectionately and left to see to one of her patients.

Cate slipped into the private staff restroom so she could take the pregnancy test without fear of someone barging in at the wrong moment. She carefully followed the directions, setting the test on the edge of the sink to process. She gripped the other edge of the sink with one hand, her free hand resting gently on her belly. She wasn't sure if the nausea she was now experiencing was related to a growing pregnancy or the expectation of the test results. It had been a couple of years since her last panic attack, and she took deep cleansing breaths as she repeated her favorite calming mantra to be sure she kept her emotions in check.

"I am in control of how I respond ... I am not in danger ..."

She jumped when she heard the timer go off on her phone in her pocket. She quickly pulled it out and pressed the home button to stop the alarm. She dropped it back into her pocket and allowed her eyes to drift over to the plastic stick resting on the edge of the sink. Her heart dropped into her stomach as she saw the two pink lines glaring back at her with utter certainty. She picked it up with a shaky hand, unsure whether she should toss it in the trash or keep it as evidence. She decided to wrap it in a paper towel and dropped it into the other pocket of her scrubs.

Her brain felt like it was filled with static, and she couldn't determine her next move. She exited the bathroom and crossed the hall into the staff locker room. She gently placed the bundle of paper towel on the top shelf of her locker and quietly closed the door. She didn't know how to feel. She thought Anthony still wanted to get married, but they'd just been enjoying being on their own and hadn't talked about it seriously since they had graduated from college. She wore the promise ring every day, and as far as she knew, their plan was still to wait to get married until she passed her RN exam and had a permanent nursing job.

She felt the familiar prickly sensation in her forehead and chest and sat down on the bench, taking deep breaths. She needed a distraction. She knew she should just go back to work and face this with Anthony later when she got home. She still had a long night ahead of her, so she might as well put it on a shelf for now. She felt the tension ease, and she stood up and marched back to the nursing station to finish out her shift.

Anthony was sound asleep when she got home, but she already had a plan for how she was going to break the news to him. It was Friday, and she was off tomorrow, so they'd have the whole day together. She unwrapped the pregnancy test from its paper towel shroud and set it next to their shared sink. She knew he would see it the minute he went to wash his hands after using the bathroom in the morning, and then they could talk. She gently sunk into their bed and felt his arm come across her body and his mouth on the back of her neck. His breathing quickly returned to its slow, sleepy rhythm, though, and she fell into a light and restless sleep.

Cate's eyelids slowly parted, and she squinted at the sunlight streaming in through the open blinds of the sliding-glass door to the patio. She grabbed her phone off the bedside table and pressed the home button to reveal the screen. The numbers staring back at her read 9:30 a.m., and her stomach clenched, then roiled with a wave of nausea. There was no way Anthony was still sleeping, and sure enough, as she rolled over, she found his side of the bed empty and cool. She then heard him moving around in the kitchen, and confusion settled into her brain. He had to have seen the pregnancy test, so why hadn't he woken her up?

Just then, the bedroom door gently widened, and Anthony stood there with a small tray carrying a mug with steam slowly rising from it and a plate with scrambled eggs, toast, and fresh fruit. A small glass of orange juice completed the arrangement. Cate's heart swelled, and she pushed herself up to a seated position, running her hands through her hair and trying to blink the sleep from her eyes.

"Hey, beautiful," Anthony said, his voice deep and gentle.

Cate offered him a tentative smile, her eyebrows raised in expectation. He brought the tray over and set it down on the bedside table. Cate continued to watch as his hand went into the pocket of his sweatpants and he paused.

"This may not be exactly how I had planned this," he began, and Cate's eyes immediately welled up with tears. He brought his hand out of his pocket, and Cate saw the small navy-blue felt box. Her hand went to her mouth, and the tears spilled down her cheeks. Anthony went down on one knee, and Cate couldn't stop the sob that came up from her chest.

"Anthony ..." she whimpered.

"Cate, a little less than a year ago I told you that my heart was yours and that I didn't want to live without you. The last seven months have been the best of my entire life, and I couldn't imagine how it could be any better. Then I saw what you left on the sink and I think my heart exploded. There is nothing I want more than to build a family with you ... it may be happening a little faster than I expected ..." He paused and chuckled.

Cate laughed with him through her tears and melted into his deep-brown eyes.

"Cate Williams ... will you marry me?"

Cate slid off the bed and fell to her knees to join Anthony on the bedroom floor and threw her arms around his neck. "Anthony Elliot, Yes! Yes! A hundred times, yes!" she cried through her tears. She felt Anthony pull back, and he slid the ring onto her left hand. Cate stared at it in awe, the single round diamond simple and perfect set into a thin gold band. She placed both hands on Anthony's face and pressed her lips into his before wrapping her arms around him again and melting into his body. They were going to be a family.

$$\sim 3 \sim$$

Five years later

Cate stared at her hands lying helplessly on her lap. The exam room was bright and cold and too quiet. Anthony stood on the other side of the room, arms crossed, intermittently pacing from side to side, his designer sneakers squeaking against the polished linoleum floor. Their son Joey sat quietly, fixated on the matching game he was playing on Cate's smartphone. She turned toward him, tucking her hair behind her ear.

Joey had turned five just a month earlier and had grown thick brown curls that surrounded his round face. Long, dark lashes–the envy of all their family and friends–curled up from his chocolate-brown eyes. Despite giving him his uncle Charlie's name, Cate couldn't deny that he clearly favored Anthony's dark hair and olive skin tone. His rosy lips pursed in concentration. He was beginning to lengthen and thin out as he grew out of his toddler years, but his arms and hands still carried the last of his baby fat. Cate took in the outfit Joey had picked out this morning, his favorite t-shirt with the T-Rex on the front, sweatpants, and his Velcro sneakers.

Sitting here in the doctor's office made Joey seem even more vulnerable and fragile. Cate just wanted to scoop him up and hold him tightly to her chest like she'd done when he was a baby. She gently ran her fingers through his curls, which were so soft they didn't tangle. She smiled until he pulled away in irritation, and she tried to bury the feeling of rejection. She knew he rarely wanted to be touched or handled, no matter who the affection came from.

She thought about how much their lives had changed since they found out they were pregnant with Joey. She and Anthony had a civil wedding ceremony in November that year and a reception with their close family members around Christmas. Their parents had largely accepted their less conventional timeline and ceremony, though Cate had noted the disappointment in her mom's eyes when Cate had shown up to the reception wearing a festive red dress and sparkly silver heels.

Cate had passed her RN exam on her first try that February, her belly just beginning to harden and round out with her growing pregnancy. She was able to get one of the few full-time nursing spots at the hospital where she'd previously worked as an assistant, especially with the glowing review from her nurse manager. Joey arrived in June, and Cate had been granted a generous eight-week maternity leave. Anthony continued to move up the ladder in his firm and was knocking on the door of a director role just a year after Joey was born.

They had moved into their first home when Joey was two years old, a sweet four-bedroom, two-and-a-half-bath raised ranch in a suburban neighborhood filled with young families and lots of kids for Joey to play with. That was about the time things started to change. Cate knew something was different about Joey, but Anthony refused to see it.

It wasn't long before her panic attacks became harder to control. When Joey was about three years old, she was home alone with him and had one that got bad enough that she fainted. It had terrified her to think of what could have happened if she hadn't come to on her own. Her doctor started her on daily Prozac and instructed her to take lorazepam as needed to reduce the severity of an oncoming attack.

Anthony continued to deny that there was anything different about Joey, and it had all put a tremendous strain on their relationship. They were only at the doctor's office today by a small miracle. Cate's chest was tight, her forehead just slightly warm and prickly, but she had been practicing her breathing and slowly repeating her mantra under her breath. She had the lorazepam in her purse if it came to that, but that was always her last resort since it usually made her really drowsy.

She looked up to see Anthony standing still now, picking a piece of fuzz off the sleeve of his dress shirt. He seemed to be doing everything he could to avoid looking at her or Joey.

Before long, the pediatrician stepped into the exam room with purpose, her expression offering no clues. She raised her eyebrows and forced a smile in a clear effort to reassure them.

"Okay, guys," she began. "I have the report here from the psychologist. They *have* placed Joey on the autism spectrum."

Cate was surprised to find the tightness in her chest eased a little. At least they knew what they were dealing with now. Joey had been slow to talk, and at age five, he was just beginning to string words together. The diagnosis explained his outbursts at the grocery store and other places with loud noises, bright lights, and crowds. They'd delayed the evaluation, despite the urging of family members. But earlier that summer, parents of Joey's neighborhood playmates had approached her. They pointed out that a four-year-old should be able to ask for a snack, and that during birthday parties, he played by himself in a corner.

It had been a difficult, heartbreaking conversation, but it had finally ended the cycle of denial that Anthony had been stuck in. Cate knew she'd enabled it for way too long.

Joey was scheduled to start kindergarten in the fall, but Cate and Anthony were terrified of what he might do in a classroom setting. Preschool twice a week had been challenging enough for him. They had been called to the center multiple times to discuss

Joey's behavior. The school eventually suggested they have Joey evaluated by a doctor, but it had taken them months to build up the nerve to go through with it.

Anthony attached such a negative stigma to the idea that Joey might have a disability, believing that an autism diagnosis would mean he was somehow "broken" and unable to lead a fulfilling life. Even that morning, Anthony had resisted coming to the pediatrician's office, fully expecting that the diagnosis would be a simple case of stubbornness. He was always telling Cate that Joey was willfully holding back in his verbal development because she always spoke for him.

Cate looked wearily at the pediatrician, resigned to the fact that the life she dreamed of for Joey would be very different. "So, what are the next steps?"

"Well, there are a couple of different routes we can take," the doctor replied and went on to explain various strategies, how to work with the preschool and how to approach the administrators of the public school Joey would attend for kindergarten. She talked in general terms about what to expect from Joey, explaining that every child develops differently. When it comes to kids on the spectrum, there is no "normal," she said. She explained that they should follow Joey's lead in understanding his limitations and capabilities.

They gathered their things and walked out of the exam room as a family unit. After they checked out, though, Anthony seemed to drift ahead, unaware that he was leaving Cate and Joey behind. The car ride back to Joey's preschool was silent, and Cate kept stealing glances over at Anthony to gauge his mood. His jaw remained tight, and his eyes never left the road.

In the days and months that followed, Cate felt Anthony increasingly pulling away from her and Joey. Within six months, it was like they were living with a ghost. In the midst of the silence and tension, Cate found herself reflecting on the clear signs she shouldn't have ignored.

As much as Cate knew that Anthony loved Joey, there were times when she sensed he was struggling with sharing her with their son. Their time together as a couple had been so brief before Joey arrived, and she knew he felt there were things they had missed out on. As a first-time mom, Cate was protective of Joey and wanted to be his primary caretaker. That was easy when he was a newborn and an infant since Cate exclusively breastfed him and Joey never did take a bottle. Anthony was relegated to diaper duty and occasionally holding Joey when Cate was burned out. Anthony had just barely started to have the opportunity to engage with Joey through play when it became apparent that Joey was not developing like the other children in the neighborhood. It was just salt in his emotional wounds.

Cate really thought Anthony would pull out of it and step up to be the dad Joey needed him to be and to support Cate. She knew he loved her, but it was becoming increasingly clear that love might not be enough.

They had barely gotten through the holidays this year. Anthony kept his distance the entire time her parents were in town, even on Christmas morning. He had stayed in bed complaining of a bad cold over New Year's, and she had sat by herself in the blue light of the TV in the darkened living room, watching the ball drop, a coffee mug half full of warm champagne in her hand.

She began to dread the inevitable.

One Saturday afternoon that winter, while Joey was working on a puzzle in his room, she and Anthony retreated to their bedroom to talk as discreetly as possible.

"I can't do this, Cate," Anthony said, gripping the bedpost with one hand, the other balled in a fist by his side.

"What, like right now ... or ever?"

Anthony sighed and brought his hands together over his nose, eventually letting them fall to his sides before looking at Cate, his eyes dark and his lips firmly set.

"I'm not cut out to care for Joey, and I don't know how to support you, either. You never want my help, and nothing I do with him is right. I think you'll both be better off without me ... I've given this a lot of thought, and I just ... I need a fresh start."

Cate's stomach dropped into her knees. This was not happening. She sat down on the side of the bed, her back to Anthony. Every muscle in her body was tense, like she was bracing for a train barreling down the track, aiming for a direct hit. In some strange way, it felt like losing Charlie all over again.

"Anthony, how can you do this?" Her heart was beating fast, and she tried to take some deep breaths.

She sensed Anthony's movement behind her, and she turned around to face him. He didn't look at her. His hands were firmly planted on the dresser, his broad shoulders raised and his head bent. When he turned to face her, his face was blank, cold, and devoid of emotion. Cate felt her heart seize in her chest, and she braced herself for what he was going to say next.

"Well, like you always say ... you're his mom. This is more natural for you–I mean, you're wired to take care of Joey. I'm just ... not."

Cate felt the blood drain from her face. She stood up, her legs like watery Jell-O. She took several more deep breaths and closed her eyes as she repeated her mantra, and finally, the world seemed to settle again. Her eyes snapped open, and she saw Anthony throwing items from their dresser into a duffel bag.

"Anthony, stop. You had a choice when you married me, but we don't get to choose our kids–and we don't get to decide if we like what we were given. There isn't a fucking return policy! We are Joey's parents! How can you just turn your back on him? On us?"

Cate knew she was raising her voice and quickly tried to get control of the toxic emotions flooding her brain. She took another deep breath, tapping into the internal strength she had relied on for most of her life.

Anthony stared at the floor. "I don't know. Maybe this was all just a big mistake. Maybe we didn't have enough time to really get to know each other. To be able to handle a child with a disability. I'm just not cut out for this." He glanced up at Cate, and finally, something resembling pain … or shame … flashed across his face. The Anthony she knew was in there, but she had lost him somewhere along the way.

She took a couple of steps closer to him, lowering her voice to an aggressive, throaty whisper.

"We are a family. Don't do this."

Anthony's eyes darkened, and she could see his jaw muscles twitching.

She paused, swallowing hard and spoke in a regular voice. "You know what? Fine. Maybe you're right. I've got this all under control. Just go." Cate flung her hands at him, then quickly crossed her arms, her jaw clenched. Her mind was racing, and her stomach was twisted in a knot.

Anthony grabbed the duffel bag he'd packed and threw the long strap over his shoulder. Without looking at her, he turned toward the door. She watched him walk out and listened to his heavy footsteps go down the stairs to the first floor. After a short pause, she heard the back door open and shut, the garage door go up, his car rev to a start and back out. Slowly, the garage door made its distinctive grinding sound until it was closed.

Then … silence.

Joey appeared in the bedroom doorway, his face quizzical. "Da?" he asked.

"Daddy had to go," Cate said, and began walking toward him before falling to her knees, angry tears burning behind her eyelids.

She didn't know if Joey would be in the mood for physical contact, so she didn't initiate it. His eyes went to the floor, and he turned to go back to his room. Cate's heart shattered into a million pieces for the ten thousandth time.

Several months after Anthony moved out, Cate was staring down bumper-to-bumper traffic on the interstate, kicking herself for choosing this route during construction season. She replayed the last twelve hours, recalling the outburst from a post-surgical patient who she had to deny a third dose of pain medication, the coworker who didn't show up for the second time this week, and the family that learned their grandmother wouldn't make it through the afternoon. Her knee was still throbbing with what she knew was a developing bruise from ramming it into the side of the hospital bed while moving an overweight patient.

She looked in the rearview mirror, where Joey continued to scowl and grunt, occasionally kicking the back of the passenger seat. When she had arrived at the sitter's house, she'd said he had one of his hardest days all summer, requiring multiple "safe holds" just to make it to pick-up time.

To top it off, Anthony hadn't responded to a single one of her messages this week trying to arrange a mediation, so now she was definitely going to have to pay her lawyer to work out the divorce. Anthony's excuses had started as soon as Cate got a lawyer, and they had only become increasingly ridiculous. She was exhausted and discouraged, afraid of losing her reputation as a pillar of strength and disappointing everyone who had been supporting her.

She pulled into the garage and turned off the ignition. She stared blankly at the cluttered shelves on either side of the door into the house, desperately searching for the will to go inside.

"Mama?" she heard Joey ask from the back seat. His small, tentative voice gave her the motivation she needed, and she grabbed her purse and climbed out of the car.

She got Joey settled in front of the TV with a snack and stepped into the bathroom, quietly closing the door behind her. She pulled the mirrored medicine cabinet door open, her eyes falling on the prescription bottle tucked into a corner on the top shelf. It had been months since she'd resorted to medicating herself, but nothing else seemed to be working.

She grabbed the bottle, its familiar rattle immediately soothing her, and twisted open the lid. She poured one pill into her hand, hesitated, then let two more fall into her palm. She knew this was the max dose, but she just wanted to be numb. She put the bottle back in its place inside the cabinet, closed the door, and grabbed the small plastic cup Joey used to rinse his mouth out after brushing his teeth. She filled the cup halfway and tossed the pills into her mouth. Drinking from the side that wasn't coated with leftover toothpaste, she took a large mouthful of water and waited as the pills slid down her throat. She set the cup down on the counter, resting both palms on the edge, eyes closed.

"Just get me through the rest of this day and I'll start fresh tomorrow," she bargained with no one in particular.

Back in the kitchen, Cate set a pan of water to boil on the stove and threw a couple of hot dogs into the microwave. It would be comfort food for dinner tonight. The thick medicated blanket was already wrapping itself around her, cushioning her from the rest of the world.

Cate picked up the mail that had been pushed through the slot in the front door. She absently flipped through the small bundle as she shuffled back toward their small kitchen. A plain white envelope caught her eye, and she immediately recognized the handwriting. "Mom," she sighed and briefly closed her eyes. Cate had been avoiding her calls and emails for a couple of weeks now, overwhelmed by her questions about how she was coping and pressing her for updates.

She set the bills and junk mail on the kitchen table and opened the letter.

My dearest Cate,

Your dad and I are just sick over the situation Anthony has left you and our sweet Joseph Charles in. We would love for you and Joey to come to Iowa and spend some time with us here on the farm. Please think about coming for an extended visit, it could be just what you both need.

All our love,

Mom and Dad

Cate looked up from the letter and into the living room where Joey was sitting on his knees, legs splayed behind him. She watched as he stared at the television, his favorite cartoon characters chattering on about the letter of the day. Despite the familiar numbing, she had never felt more useless in all her life. A small, quiet, and distant voice was telling her, "Go home."

She knew it would be risky to drive, but she had done it once before, albeit after a much smaller dose of lorazepam. She thought as long as they got there before dark, she could stay awake. She glanced over at the clock on the microwave and calculated how many hours were left until sunset.

Then, once they had eaten, Cate packed a couple of overnight bags, called in sick to the hospital, and left a message with Joey's sitter. And they left.

$$\sim 4 \sim$$

Cate pulled into a small convenience store parking lot and eased in next to an available gas pump. Her mind had started drifting off as soon as they had hit the open road, and it was the ding of the low-fuel warning that had jolted her to attention. The August sun was now beginning its slow descent, but she guessed they still had another hour or so of daylight.

Joey was staring out his back seat window, taking in this new environment while Cate stepped out of the car. As the fuel flowed into her gas tank, she felt surprisingly clear headed and thought they were making pretty good time. She expected they'd be at the farm not long after dark, and she hoped her parents wouldn't be too startled when she and Joey showed up at the door.

She squinted at the sun's intensity and felt her skin dampen in the heavy humidity, but just then, a breeze lifted her hair away from her face, promising cooler, dryer fall days ahead.

The pump shut off, and Cate returned the handle to its place. She climbed into the driver's seat, pressed her foot on the brake, and pushed the button to start the ignition. All she heard was a hollow click. She tried again but got the same result. It was like the engine was mocking her with its silence.

"Damniiiiiit ..." she groaned. So much for making good time. She looked back at Joey, but he was still gazing out his window, oblivious to their predicament.

Cate unbuckled Joey from his booster seat, and they went inside to ask for help. The young man behind the register asked her to hang tight while he called his uncle who worked at the garage just a block away.

About five minutes later, a small pickup truck pulled into the convenience store lot. An older gentleman wearing denim striped mechanic's overalls stepped out and walked over to her car. The patch just below his left shoulder said "Fries Motor Service," and he had warm, friendly eyes.

"Hi, I'm Phil." He didn't offer his hand, which she noticed was mottled with dark spots of the stuff auto mechanics seem to always have on their hands. A wet toothpick was hanging out of the corner of his mouth, and he flipped it to the other side as he spoke. "What seems to be the problem?" he asked, looking down at Joey with a friendly wink.

"I'm not sure, I just couldn't get the engine to turn over after we filled up," Cate answered.

"Okay, let's have a look. Is this your car here?" Phil directed his question at Joey, trying to give the impression he was the man in charge. Cate smiled and looked down to see how Joey would respond. He turned and buried his face in her waist, and she felt his shoulders tense.

"Sorry," she apologized. "He's shy."

Phil nodded and moved toward her metallic-blue sedan. She stepped out of the way, giving him permission to advance.

Phil lifted the hood of her car, inspected a few hoses and caps, and pulled a wrench from his back pocket which he used to begin removing the protective cover over the car's engine. She decided to take Joey inside and wait in the air-conditioned convenience store rather than watch over Phil's shoulder.

Inside, she let Joey choose a drink from the cooler, grabbed an energy drink for herself, and paid the young man behind the counter.

"I'm Davis," he said. "It shouldn't be too long. Phil is a wizard with cars."

She gave Davis a tight smile and gently led Joey over to the magazine rack to flip through a comic book.

After about twenty minutes, Phil gently closed the car's hood and came inside, wiping his hands on the dingy blue towel hanging from his pocket.

"Well, kiddo, I can definitely fix this and get you back on the road, but it's gonna be a couple of days before I can get the part in. Do you have someone that can come pick you up?"

"Uh, no–we're just passing through on our way to my parents' farm near Denison. We still have a couple hours' drive ahead of us."

"Ah, I see. Well, there's a pretty decent motel just a short distance up the road that almost always has a room or two available."

Cate considered calling her parents but knew how difficult it was for them to leave the farm, even for a few hours. Since they weren't exactly expecting her, she didn't think they'd be concerned if she and Joey didn't show up for another couple of days. She would call the hospital tomorrow and let them know what was going on and use up a few of her vacation days.

"Can I drive you up there in the truck?" Phil offered, but Cate was uneasy about getting into a strange man's car.

"That's okay," she said with a smile and a soft hand on Joey's back. "We could use a little walk."

He nodded understandingly, turning to the counter where Davis waited at the register.

"I'll call a tow when I get back to the shop. Thanks, bud," Phil said.

He turned back to Cate. "I'll get you pointed in the right direction, at least." He pushed open the glass door, stepped aside, and held it open so Cate and Joey could walk out. She took Joey's hand and stepped into the convenience store's small parking lot.

Phil pointed them toward an intersection a half block away, then explained the hotel was just about a quarter of a mile up the road. He turned back to see if Cate was understanding his directions.

"I think we've got it, thank you," she said, giving him a warm smile.

"I'll get in touch with Davis here once the part arrives, so just check back tomorrow, okay?" Phil had a concerned look on his face, and Cate could tell he wasn't sure he should be letting a young mother and her child walk away.

"You bet, thanks ... again," she answered. She gently pulled Joey forward and began walking toward the sidewalk.

On the other side of the intersection, they found themselves on a gravel road, and the sidewalk gave way to a rocky shoulder, framed by tall grasses and weeds.

She made sure Joey was walking on the inside of the shoulder while she stayed along the roadside, though they didn't see a single vehicle. Grasshoppers crossed their path without warning, as if trying desperately to avoid being stepped on, their humming and clicking providing the soundtrack for the walk.

Cate briefly looked back over her left shoulder, the small convenience store and auto body shop still visible a couple of blocks behind her. With a sigh, she continued along the road toward the motel. They passed a pizza chain restaurant, and about a hundred feet away on either side of the road were some small WWII-era homes and a few steel-sided buildings. The cicadas were in full chorus, their signature mating call endlessly repeating from their hiding places among the trees.

Finally, she saw another building in the distance. It had a tall sign reading "Lighthouse Motel," and the word "Vacancy" was dimly lit in the fading evening sun. She paused, an uneasy feeling rising up from her gut when she thought about staying in a strange motel. Once again, she considered calling her parents. She laid her hand on her purse, comforted knowing that her cell phone was there if she decided she needed it.

Another breeze lifted her hair, and she sensed a presence she hadn't felt in years. The breeze shifted and was now coming from behind her, blowing her hair into her face and pressing against her back, almost as if it was urging her forward. The tall grasses bent forward in further emphasis, pointing the way toward the motel.

Still, she felt scared and uncertain. She didn't know if she could go through with this. The prickly sensation began to slowly spread across her chest and forehead.

She heard a voice inside her head: "Don't forget to laugh, Kitty. Think of this as an adventure!" She smiled at the memory of Charlie's voice. Her heart softened, and a renewed strength bloomed in her chest.

Joey began to fidget next to her, and Cate knew she needed to make a decision. She gave his hand a gentle squeeze and stepped confidently forward.

~ 5 ~

The L-shaped single-story building of rust-colored brick seemed sturdy, and the grounds were simple but well-maintained. The metal-framed windows and doors were painted a seafoam green, and thin metal blinds hung neatly on the inside of each window. There were only a few cars parked out front, most of them older models that had seen better days.

Cate approached a wood door with a plastic, brass-colored sign that said "OFFICE" and turned the simple round doorknob while pushing it open. The door made a loud scraping noise as it pulled away from its swollen frame. She took a deep breath as she guided Joey inside with gentle pressure on his back.

The motel's lobby was dimly lit with modern pine wood-paneled walls. A collection of small framed pictures of seaside scenes were scattered haphazardly on the walls around the lobby, and miniature lighthouses were carefully displayed on a shallow ledge just below the ceiling. A floor lamp lit a cozy brown leather couch and there was a wood-burning stove framed by large stones set into the wall. Straight ahead, a narrow hallway led to an outdoor courtyard where she could just make out a few tired patio tables and chairs.

Cate moved toward the motel's front desk. It was quiet, but cluttered. Holding gently to Joey's hand, Cate was scanning the desk for a bell or some other way to announce their arrival when she heard someone moving around behind a set of saloon doors hung in a narrow doorway.

"Hello?" She tilted her head to try to see through the crack between the doors. After a moment, a tall man in his early sixties with light-colored hair, dressed in a simple button-up shirt and khakis, gently pushed through the door. He flashed Cate a kind smile.

"Hello there, welcome to the Lighthouse Motel," he said, immediately putting Cate at ease. "What can I do for you two today?"

"We've had a little car trouble and need a place to stay for a few days while our car is being worked on up the road," Cate explained.

"Oh, sure! You're the young lady Phil just called me about."

"Yes, he was helping us at the gas station," Cate said, feeling a tenderness toward Phil for calling immediately to be sure they arrived and were taken care of.

"Phil is good people, he'll take care of you. Not to worry, not to worry. Let's get you set up with a nice room–just the two of you?" the man asked, glancing down toward Joey and giving him a wink. Joey buried his face in Cate's waist, then turned it just enough to have one eye on the man behind the counter. The man gently took the pair of eyeglasses hanging from the thin chain around his neck and placed them on his face, settling them halfway down the bridge of his nose.

"Yes, just the two of us," Cate affirmed.

"You're in luck, we're not too busy this week–do you prefer separate beds?" he asked.

"Just one bed would be fine–this little guy doesn't sleep great on his own," she offered.

The man's eyes shifted toward Joey again, and he peered over the top of his glasses, looking like he was going to ask another question, but instead he turned toward his computer and keyboard. He typed a few random keys, studied the screen, then turned to a series of small cubbies sticking out from the wall behind the desk. He pulled out an available key with a black plastic tag bearing the number 3.

"You two will be in Unit 3, which you can access from the court-yard. It's a little more private than the units facing the road ..." He trailed off, but Cate suspected he also felt this room would be a safer option for a single woman and little boy.

"That's very thoughtful, thank you," she said, offering her own kind smile.

"My name's Harvey if there's anything at all you need during your stay," he said, handing her the key.

"Okay, thank you ..." She hesitated. "I'm sorry, but when do I pay for the room? Do you need a credit card or anything?"

"We'll take care of that once your car is fixed," he answered, seemingly unconcerned that she could easily skip out without paying. He grinned and shot a wink in Joey's direction.

Cate was taken aback by his generosity and humbled by his trust in her. After a moment, she collected herself and once again took Joey's hand to head to their room.

"Do you have any luggage I can help you with?" Harvey offered.

"Oh." Cate's face immediately flushed with embarrassment. "We had to leave them with our car since we walked here from the gas station," she answered.

"Not to worry. I'll collect them and bring them to your room in a bit," he said. "You two get settled in and relax."

Cate tried to hold back the tears welling up in her eyes. Harvey reminded her of her dad and the way he was always bending over backward to make her feel safe and comfortable. She felt a desper-ation begin to build and again laid her hand over her purse. She would call them when they got to their room.

"Thank you," was all she could say.

Cate and Joey navigated the narrow hallway that led to the glass double doors and entered the courtyard. The entire area was completely exposed to the elements, and heat seemed to be ra-diating off the pebbled concrete tiles loosely set into the ground. Unit 3 was the first door on the left, its seafoam-green metal door and frame set into the same rust-colored brick she had seen on the front of the building. A weathered welcome mat rested just in front of the door on the concrete path circling the perimeter of the courtyard. A faded lighthouse looking out over a calm sea offered a weak "Welcome Home" in what was probably once a vibrant red.

Cate turned the key in the door lock and, after some effort, felt the lock catch and release. Joey looked up at her in anticipation of the new adventures this room surely held for him and his mom.

"New ... house ... Mommy?" he asked in his signature labored cadence, eyes wide and a smile spreading across his face.

"No, buddy, we'll just be here for a few days until our car is fixed." She pushed the door open and stepped into the room.

"Like ... Harvey," Joey added, beginning to scan the room and take in his new temporary living situation.

"Me, too, he seems like a very nice man," she said, again holding back the tears that threatened to fill her eyes. It had been so long since she had felt comfortable allowing someone to take care of her. She was finally feeling like her decision to leave was the right thing for her and Joey.

Her mind briefly wandered to all she had endured–her lost innocence following Charlie's accident and death, a lifetime of struggles with anxiety and panic attacks, Anthony's betrayal and all the suffering that had followed. It seemed like more hardships than one person should have to endure, and resentment simmered in her gut. She swallowed hard with pursed lips and pressed the door closed behind her.

She took in the simple room with its queen-size bed, matching bedside tables, and dresser. She was surprised to see modern amenities like a flat screen TV, USB ports in the lamps on either side of the bed, and a smart thermostat. She felt safe and comfortable, and that was exactly what she needed.

The light was beginning to change over to the amber hue of sunset, and she caught Joey in a wide-mouthed yawn. She got him settled on the bed with his iPad and stepped into the bathroom for a quick rinse before they started to wind down for the night.

She left the door open a crack and turned on the water before pulling the knob that would start the shower. She dropped her clothes into a pile on the bathroom floor and left the shower curtain open halfway so she could hear if Joey made any noise.

She let the water run over her shoulders briefly before wetting her hair. She was grateful to find a dispenser hanging from the wall with shampoo, conditioner and body wash, so she made a last-minute decision to go ahead and wash her hair as well. She finished up and turned off the water, pausing briefly to check for any sounds that might indicate Joey was moving around the room. All was quiet, and she hoped he had drifted off to sleep already.

She dried off and wrapped the thick white towel around her body. Harvey's gift for hospitality continued to impress her.

She glanced down at the counter where she had left her cell phone, the black vacant screen staring back at her. She took a deep breath and sighed.

If she called her parents now, they would feel helpless. In order to come to her and Joey's rescue, they would have to find someone to take care of the animals, and with the Iowa State Fair wrapping up, they would be preparing to leave for the Farm Progress Show in Illinois. They were probably just wrapping up dinner and planning to head to bed early. The last thing she wanted to do was give them something to stress about right before bed. First thing in the morning, she would call just to let them know the situation, reassure them that she and Joey were in good hands, and tell them that they would arrive in a few days.

She put her clothes back on and stepped out of the bathroom to find Joey still awake, but fixated on his tablet. She climbed into bed next to him, careful not to disturb his concentration and risk a tantrum. Her stomach rumbled quietly, and she wished she had thought to grab some snacks from the gas station. She leaned back into the soft pile of pillows, resting her head on the tufted headboard, and gently closed her eyes.

A soft knock sounded at the door, and Cate's eyes snapped open. She slid off the bed and went tentatively to the small peephole. She could just make out Harvey's retreat across the courtyard; then he was out of view. She undid the chain lock and deadbolt, pulling the door open toward her. Their suitcases were lined up neatly on the welcome mat, and the courtyard was quiet. She pulled the bags inside the room, pushed the door closed and made sure the locks were all securely back in place.

She brought Joey's backpack over to his side of the bed and handed him his favorite stuffed animal, a floppy rabbit he called Bun. He grabbed it from her and wrapped both his arms around its soft body. Cate saw his eyes almost immediately start to droop, and she clicked off the lamp by his side of the bed.

~ 6 ~

It had been a restless and fitful night's sleep. Cate had looked at her phone no less than half a dozen times, willing her brain to shut off, but the doubts and anxieties rolling over and over in her head were relentless. She pulled her hand out from underneath her pillow and tapped the glass on her phone, which immediately lit up with bold white numbers ... 7:24. She reluctantly lifted herself out of bed, gently shaking Joey awake. He rolled over, blinking his eyes in the morning sun shining through the narrow gaps between the blinds.

She considered her phone folded into her hand and what her parents might be doing right now. If she waited another hour or so, they would be nearing their morning coffee break before the farm hands showed up for whatever work Dad had for them today. She and Joey could get some breakfast and try to find a park, and she would call them.

She used the bathroom and ran her toothbrush through her mouth. She pulled the sides of her chin-length hair into a topknot and swiped on some deodorant before she stepped back out into the hotel room to grab some clean clothes.

Joey was sitting on the bed with his iPad, Bun tucked under his arm.

"Joey," Cate said gently, sitting on the edge of the bed closest to where he was sitting. "Joey, eyes on me, please."

Joey lifted his chocolate-brown eyes to Cate, his small round face otherwise expressionless.

"Would you like to go for a walk and find some breakfast?"

Joey blinked, then nodded subtly before turning his attention back to his iPad. She gently helped him transition from his game, put on a clean shirt and shorts, and brush his teeth, then put on shoes and socks. Cate breathed a sigh of relief that at least so far, taking Joey out of his normal routine hadn't backfired. He grabbed Bun off the bed and joined Cate by the door.

"Sure, let's bring Bun along," she agreed with a resigned grin. If nothing else, it ought to keep Joey comfortable while they explored. She grabbed her purse, making sure her phone was tucked inside, and they stepped out into the courtyard.

They approached the door to the motel office, intending to exit the same way they'd come in. Cate reached for the handle of the glass double doors, but when she pulled, they didn't budge. She pulled again, a little harder this time, and still, the doors were firmly closed.

"Why would these be locked?" she wondered, a wave of anxiety rippling through her chest.

She leaned in to peer through the glass door, cupping her hands around the sides of her face. No sign of Harvey or any of the other guests. Trying not to panic, she raised her head and ran her fingers through her hair. She looked down at Joey, who had a confused look on his face.

"In ... Mommy?"

"Well, it appears that this door is locked," Cate said, her throat desperately trying to close up.

"Harvey? Open?" Joey asked.

"It doesn't look like he's in the office right now," she answered. She decided to try knocking on the glass to see if maybe Harvey could hear from behind the saloon doors. She banged her knuckles as hard as she could stand against the glass, but nobody came.

She finally took a look around the rest of the courtyard, and that's when she noticed a second door at the opposite end from where they were standing. It was a rustic wood door painted a dark green, like you might see at the entrance of an old English garden. She hadn't noticed it earlier, set into the high brick wall that connected the two sections of guest rooms facing the courtyard. Tall leafy trees rose above the wall, creating a mysterious green veil across whatever lay on the other side of the gate.

A dark wood sign with faded words etched into it hung in the center of the door. Cate couldn't make out what it said from where she was standing, so she took Joey's hand and they crossed to the other end of the courtyard to get a better look.

"That ... Mommy?" Joey asked as they approached the wood door and sign.

It appeared to be some kind of poem, or song lyrics. As Cate began to read them, she realized she had seen it before. A fuzzy memory emerged, and she saw herself in her grandparents' living room, sitting on the couch with her grandmother as she read to her from her children's Bible, a story about Jesus talking to a large crowd up on a mountain.

"I think it's from the Bible," she said, partly to herself but loud enough that Joey heard her.

She looked down at him, his gaze locked on the door in concentration. She began to read the words out loud:

Blessed are the poor in spirit, for theirs is the kingdom of heaven.
Blessed are those who mourn, for they shall be comforted.
Blessed are the meek, for they shall possess the earth.
Blessed are those who hunger and thirst for justice, for they shall be satisfied.
Blessed are the merciful, for they shall obtain mercy.
Blessed are the clean of heart, for they shall see God.
Blessed are the peacemakers, for they shall be called children of God.
Blessed are those who suffer persecution for justice's sake, for theirs is the kingdom of heaven.

Blessed are you when men reproach you, and persecute you, and speaking falsely, say all manner of evil against you, for My sake.

"Mommy?" Joey had asked at least three times as she was reading the verses, pulling on her shirt and trying to get her attention.

She decided she might as well try opening the door and take the chance that it led them out of the courtyard. Maybe then they could walk around the building to the office to try to get Harvey's attention. Her stomach was starting to rumble with hunger, and even a greasy donut from the gas station sounded appetizing.

The gate's handle was a thick metal ring, and Cate pulled it down to unlatch it from the brick wall. The gate shuddered as she pulled it toward them, and she had to force it over a few bumps in the grass, but eventually she had pulled it back enough that they could squeeze out.

She took Joey's hand and led him out of the courtyard while he clutched Bun tightly under his arm.

They were standing on a well-maintained brick path and staring into another, much more narrow courtyard decorated with a few small ornamental trees and well-placed antique black wrought-iron garden tables and chairs. Some of the trees on the opposite side of the wall hung over the alley, creating a canopy of branches and rich, green leaves. The only light came through the branches, creating a dappled pattern on the brick walkway.

Cate's stomach was protesting loudly now, and she knew that Joey had to be starving, too. She hoped there was a restaurant or convenience store somewhere at the other end of this courtyard. Their only option was to keep moving forward and find out.

"Let's head down this way, buddy, and see if we can find a place to eat. Sound good?" she asked, more to drive herself forward than to truly get Joey's approval.

Joey looked at her, then nodded tentatively. She gave his hand a small squeeze to reassure him.

As they walked, Cate admired the fresh flowers spilling over the sides of expertly arranged flower boxes and planters hanging from hooks extending out from the wall. A small water feature gurgled peacefully, its sound amplified by the brick lining the alley. The courtyard offered a respite from the heat, and the temperature was noticeably more comfortable. After a short distance, they came up on an intricate iron gate. The scene on the other side of the gate filled Cate's heart with an overwhelming feeling of hope, and she felt immediately drawn forward. She squeezed Joey's small hand and approached it, taking in the action through the scrolling design.

Cate pulled the gate toward them and stepped through the opening, careful not to bump into one couple walking on the sidewalk. The couple glanced their way and offered friendly smiles. She didn't see any cars; all the activity was pedestrian. There was definitely more going on here than at the gas station and motel, and it had a distinctively different energy.

Cate looked down at Joey to see how he was handling the sudden increase in activity, but he was watching with wide eyes, taking it all in. As she looked up toward the opposite side of the street, she spotted a blue-and-white-striped awning and a large window with the words BAKERY AND DINER in simple lettering painted on the glass.

She instinctively looked both ways though there wasn't a car in sight, then led Joey quickly across the street.

Holding Joey's hand, Cate pushed against the thin metal bar to open the restaurant's glass door. As she stepped inside, small bells tinkled to signal that new customers had arrived. She spotted a long bakery case filled with pies, cookies, slices of cake and assorted pastries, a counter and two people behind the case serving customers. The smell of fresh baked goods–bread, cinnamon, melted butter and sugar–greeted them and immediately reminded her of her grandmother's kitchen. To her right was a simple hostess stand and a teenage girl with a long dark braid draped over her shoulder. She looked up as the two walked toward her.

"Hi, just two today?" the hostess asked sweetly.

"Yes, thank you," Cate answered.

The girl reached into a shelf inside the hostess stand and pulled out two laminated menus, a coloring sheet, a small bundle of crayons, and two sets of silverware wrapped in a white paper napkin and secured with a paper napkin ring.

"I haven't seen you two around before–are you new here?" the girl asked–rather boldly, Cate thought.

"Yes, just passing through, actually," Cate answered.

The girl flashed a small, knowing smile.

"I see. Follow me this way," she chirped, and Cate and Joey stepped into the main dining room.

The restaurant was bright, with large windows looking out onto the sidewalk. Blue-and-white gingham tablecloths were draped neatly over each table, the water glasses sparkling as they caught the sunlight. A small vase on each table held a single yellow rose. Every table was occupied, and she wondered where the hostess was planning to seat them.

The hostess led them up a single step and through a wide doorway into a secondary dining room with another group of simple square wood tables and chairs, just a few currently occupied. There was a large window at one end of the room, and two ceiling fans wobbled as their blades spun around just below the pressed-tin ceiling. The overall feeling was comfortable, almost cozy. A waitress burst through a swinging door at the back of the room that Cate assumed led to the kitchen.

The hostess seated them at an empty table and set their menus down in front of them.

"Your waitress will be with you in just a few minutes–can I get you something to drink while you wait?"

"Um, sure–I'll just take black coffee and an ice water ... and a chocolate milk for him," Cate answered.

"You bet–I'll be right back," the hostess said warmly and turned to go into the kitchen.

Cate got Joey settled with his crayons and coloring sheet, then took a few minutes to observe what she could see in the larger dining room.

Her eyes fell on a middle-aged man standing at one of the tables in the main dining room, visiting with the guests seated there. He was dressed in black, with creased dress pants and a button-down shirt. Cate noticed the familiar white collar and recognized immediately that he was a priest. She had met several priests as a child attending Mass with her grandmother, but they were always older, rounder white men or foreign men with dark skin and thick accents. This one was tall and trim, with an athletic build and chiseled good looks. His thick dark hair was neatly cut, short on the sides and longer on top, with strands of gray mixed in. He carried himself with an air of gentle authority, effortlessly commanding respect.

As she watched him interacting with the people at the table, she was struck by the abundant joy that seemed to radiate from him–he was so animated in the way he spoke, his bright eyes both kind and attentive, his smile wide and sincere. He stood casually with his hands resting on the back of one person's chair. It seemed that everyone at the table looked up at him with familiar admiration.

He seemed to easily transition from ebullient joy to attentive concern as Cate watched him turn to listen to one of the guests at the table. Those seated at the tables nearby had an air of eager anticipation, as if wondering which of their groups he would visit next. The entire room seemed to be observing him with heightened awareness.

Soon, he stood up straight and reached out to take the hands of those on either side of him. Everyone at the table bowed their heads and gently closed their eyes as he appeared to lead them all in prayer. This wasn't entirely foreign to Cate from growing up in a Midwestern small town, but she still squirmed a little in her seat with the feeling that she didn't quite belong here. After a brief moment, he let go and moved on to the next table.

She watched him for a few minutes more while Joey colored quietly, when finally their waitress appeared from the kitchen. She set down the drinks they had ordered from the hostess and pulled a small pad of paper and a pen from her apron pocket.

"Have you two decided what you'd like to order today?" she asked in a friendly but somewhat distracted tone.

"Um, yes, I think so," Cate said, quickly reaching over to touch Joey's hand so he would know she needed his attention.

"Eyes and ears on me, please, Joey. Would you like pancakes today?" Joey's dark-brown eyes stared briefly, then he nodded.

"Okay, we'll need a kid's stack of pancakes–"

"Chocolate chips or fruit cup?" the waitress interrupted.

"Fruit, please. And I'll just have the farmer's omelet," Cate continued.

"Toast?" The waitress was looking into the main dining room now, as if Cate was the only thing holding her from much more important activities on her agenda.

"Wheat toast would be fine," Cate answered as she folded up her menu and handed it to the waitress, who brusquely grabbed it from her, slid it under her order pad, and said with a tight, forced smile, "Great, that will be right out," before turning to go back into the kitchen.

Their food arrived surprisingly fast, and Cate leaned back slightly to allow the waitress to set down her plate. When the waitress set Joey's plate down on top of his coloring sheet, Cate braced herself. She watched Joey's brow fold and his two fists clenched tightly around the crayon held in each hand. She watched in horror as Joey's mouth opened, his fists vibrated with rage, and he let loose an ear-piercing, bloodcurdling scream. Cate immediately launched into action.

The familiar thrashing started just as she reached his chair, and she wrapped her arms around Joey in a safe hold, repeatedly asking him, "Are you done? Are you done?" loud enough to be heard over his screaming, as she had been trained to do. Joey was relentless, shouting and hurling angry screams, and violently trying to get out of Cate's arms.

Within seconds, out of the corner of her eye, she saw the priest approaching the table. Cate loosened her hold on Joey just slightly, but he continued to thrash around, howling. "What's your name, dear?" the priest gently asked her. "Cate," she grunted just before Joey threw his head back, smacking her in the middle of her chest and nearly taking her breath away.

"I'm Father Matthew. What is the young man's name?"

"Joey," she answered, struggling to keep a steady grip on Joey's arms.

Cate watched as Father Matthew crouched down next to Joey's chair and gently placed his hand on Joey's knee. His thrashing eased, and he looked down to see who had touched him. Cate braced herself once again, but Joey remained calm and stared intently at Father Matthew.

"Hi, Joey," Father Matthew said in a calm and soothing voice. "I'm Father Matthew. What are you having for breakfast today?"

Cate let go and stood up behind his chair, waiting to see how he would respond. Joey looked at his plate as if he was considering what to do. After a brief pause, he looked at Father Matthew, pointed to his plate and said, "Pan ... cakes."

Father Matthew looked up at Cate, then slowly stood up.

"Thank you," Cate was finally able to say, though it came out just barely louder than a whisper.

"Please, enjoy your breakfast," Father Matthew urged. "When you're done, I'd love to show you around."

Cate pressed down the humiliation that often accompanied Joey's public outbursts, the tears burning just behind her eyelids. She swallowed hard and took a deep breath. She appreciated the small-town hospitality, but part of her wanted nothing more than to find the fastest route out of here. She also found herself drawn to this religious man for reasons she didn't understand, and she couldn't deny that he seemed to have made a connection with Joey.

"Um, sure, we have a little time to kill. That would be great ... thank you," she said.

Father Matthew laid his hand on her shoulder and smiled. Now that he was looking at her, Cate noted his piercing blue eyes, kind and friendly, and the spray of freckles across nose and cheeks. She picked up on a sweet, woodsy fragrance mixed with spices that was distantly familiar and oddly calming. He nodded before turning to walk back into the main dining room.

She finally looked back at Joey as he was reaching with both hands for his glass of chocolate milk, his face relaxed and serene. She sat back down in her chair and finally dug her fork into her omelet. Her appetite had suddenly returned, and she was famished.

~ 7 ~

Cate and Joey waited in front of the bakery case while Father Matthew finished his rounds in the main dining room. There were pastries of every shape and color, including some with intricate designs, buttery flaky crusts, decadent rich and glossy frosting, and some that were beautiful in their simplicity.

"Can I help you find some dessert to take with you?" an older woman asked from behind the top of the glass counter. She had a round face, short, light-colored hair, and kind, friendly brown eyes.

"Oh, no thank you. We're just waiting for someone," Cate answered, feeling badly that she wasn't going to purchase anything.

"Okay, dear, just wave me down if you change your mind," the woman answered cheerfully.

At that moment, Father Matthew approached from the main dining room.

"You won't find a more delicious chocolate cake than those baked by Miss Henny." He turned toward the older woman behind the bakery case. "Would you bring us a couple samples to go, Miss Henny?"

"My pleasure, Father!" she replied and moved to the area of the case where there were some of the most decadent-looking cakes Cate had ever seen. Joey looked up at her with a huge smile, his Bun tucked under one arm.

Father Matthew crouched down, his face now level with Joey's. Sensing his presence, Joey turned to look at him with interest.

"How would you like to go for a walk after we have some cake?" he asked, speaking in a warm but direct tone.

Joey nodded, then turned to stare intently through the glass.

Father Matthew looked up at Cate, returning to his full standing position and bringing his hands together. Ms. Henny set two generous slices of cake on top of the counter, and Father Matthew took one in each hand. Cate thought Ms. Henny had an exaggerated idea of "samples" but swallowed her apprehension and gave her a grateful smile instead.

The trio sat at one of only a few small white wrought-iron tables against two large windows looking out onto the sidewalk and street. As Joey dug into his cake, chocolate frosting quickly collecting around his mouth and chin, Father Matthew turned to Cate just as she brought her first bite of cake to her mouth.

"So what brings you to town?" he asked her.

Cate quickly finished chewing, shooting Father Matthew an apologetic glance. "Sorry," she eked out around her mouthful of decadent chocolate. "We're actually having some work done on our car back in town and are staying at the Lighthouse Motel while we wait," she answered once she'd fully swallowed her bite.

"Oh, of course. I'm sure Harvey is taking great care of you?"

"Yes, he is so kind and thoughtful," Cate said. "Does he live in this part of town?"

"Harvey has a few different roles here–he's definitely a community staple," Father Matthew answered.

"You seem to have a lot of fans here, too," Cate said, taking a smaller bite this time.

Father Matthew nodded in acknowledgment. "I've had the honor of being a part of a lot of their lives. I try to be a guiding light for them and tend to be called upon during times of suffering. That creates a special bond."

He spoke confidently but humbly, and Cate believed he was truly grateful for the opportunity to touch the lives of the people in town.

"Are you a priest?"

"I am," he answered proudly. "My church, St. Ann's, is just up the hill."

"Is it Catholic, or ..." Cate let her question drift off as she struggled for some other faith tradition to mention.

"Roman Catholic, yes." Father Matthew regarded her more intently. "Are you Catholic?"

Cate swallowed another bite. "Um, no ... but I used to go to Mass with my grandmother when I was much younger. I always felt safe there."

Father Matthew's eyes twinkled, and he nodded subtly. "I hope you'll join us for Mass some time. We celebrate every day at 8 a.m."

Cate offered a tight, polite grin, again shifting uncomfortably in her seat. She had walked right into that and knew she would disappoint him when they didn't show up tomorrow morning.

Desperate for a distraction, she glanced over at Joey, who now had chocolate frosting smeared on his t-shirt up to his elbows and cake crumbs all over his Bun lying across his lap. "Oh, geez–I'm not sure he got much of that into his mouth," she said with a nervous laugh.

"The joy on his face says it all," Father Matthew responded. "We'll get a washcloth to clean him up. Then we can go for a little walk." He stood up and went over to Ms. Henny, who took a clean washcloth from a shelf behind the bakery case and ran it under the faucet, twisting it to release any excess water before handing it to Father Matthew.

"Joey, may I clean you up a bit so we can go for our walk?" Father Matthew asked kindly, again lowering himself to Joey's level and waiting for Joey to focus on him. Joey looked at him and nodded, showing a calm focus that Cate had rarely seen from him.

Joey allowed Father Matthew to gently wipe the frosting from his face, closing his eyes as the wash cloth traveled across his mouth slowly and deliberately, then watched as Father Matthew gently wiped off his hands, arms, and elbows and brushed the crumbs off his Bun, catching them in the washcloth and neatly wrapping them up with his hand. Cate watched the entire scene with awe and a slight tinge of guilt. How was it that this stranger had won Joey over so quickly?

"Are you sure you have time to show us around?" Cate asked, suddenly feeling like they were interrupting what must be a busy day for someone who clearly was in demand.

"Of course," Father Matthew answered matter-of-factly, looking up at her from where he was dusting the remaining crumbs from Joey's t-shirt. "I am exactly where I need to be today." He winked at Joey and returned the dirty washcloth to Ms. Henny, who smiled and tossed it into the sink behind her.

"Have a wonderful afternoon, Father," Ms. Henny called as Father Matthew turned back to Cate and Joey.

"Shall we?" Father Matthew said, opening his arms in the direction of the door.

Cate stood up and offered Joey her hand. He turned to Father Matthew, gazing up at him with soft, joy-filled eyes, and wrapped his hand around Father Matthew's two middle fingers. Cate tried not to look disappointed and offered Father Matthew a tight smile. Joey hopped down from his seat and followed as Father Matthew walked to the door. Cate walked behind them, fighting a sense that she had been, temporarily at least, displaced as Joey's source of comfort. She wrapped her hand around the strap of her purse, and the three of them walked out the glass door onto the sidewalk, the bells tinkling above them.

Father Matthew led Joey and Cate down the street, pointing out various shops and businesses–boutiques with colorful women's clothing, pottery, and glassware, a nostalgic candy store, a flower shop, a hotel, and a barbeque restaurant. They crossed to the other side of the street and passed a Mexican restaurant, a coffee shop, and another women's clothing boutique. At the corner, Father Matthew took a left and started up a new street.

As she turned to follow him, Cate spotted what appeared to be a festival taking place a couple of blocks away, and she slowed down to get a better look. She could hear the familiar sounds of a large crowd, their voices and movement punctuated by modern music blasting in stereo from a set of tinny speakers. She immediately recognized the smell of kettle corn and roasted nuts, calling up memories of the Iowa State Fair she had loved so much as a kid.

A memory crystallized at that moment, and she saw herself following Charlie down the main concourse toward the animal pavilions as he turned around to be sure she wasn't falling too far behind. "C'mon, Kitty, we're almost there–the horse show's about to start!" He reached for her hand, eyes twinkling ... then the memory faded. Cate was embarrassed to find that her eyes were misty, and she quickly blinked and turned to Father Matthew.

"What's going on down there?" she called to him, now several steps ahead of her. He and Joey stopped, and he turned back to face her, his eyes following her gaze.

"Today is the first day of the Graypourt Founders Day Festival," he answered enthusiastically.

Cate took in the activity for a moment longer, then turned back to Father Matthew with a polite smile. "Looks fun!"

"We can swing by there in a bit if you're both up for it," he offered, then began moving once again along the sidewalk.

Cate found herself in awe of Joey's quickly developing comfort with Father Matthew, the way he so confidently held on to his fingers while taking in the new surroundings. It was so uncharacteristic, and she couldn't put her finger on the nagging feeling that began rising in her chest. She quickly pressed it down once again, reminding herself that food had always been the way to Joey's heart. She rationalized that his affections would only last as long as his little belly was full of chocolate cake.

Cate's attention turned then to Father Matthew. He was movie-star attractive. He oozed with charm and a magnetic energy you couldn't help noticing, but with a humility that was unexpected. She could see how this would impact the way others responded to him, lending him an inner attractiveness that matched his physical characteristics.

They appeared to be in a historic neighborhood of older single-family homes, some clearly from an earlier era on her side of the street, and others built more recently on the opposite side. There were a couple of what appeared to be tiny one-room homes with wood siding, a brick and cinderblock commercial building, and a larger stone and brick home covered in ivy with a large, welcoming front porch. They were making a steeper climb at this point, and Cate worried that Joey's legs would be getting tired, forcing him into a meltdown. Thankfully, he held fast to Father Matthew's fingers, barely changing the pace of his steps, while Bun flopped along in rhythm.

Soon, Father Matthew slowed down and stopped at a black metal railing dividing a narrow sidewalk on their left. Cate glanced up to see a large stone church standing majestically at the top of the hill ahead.

The church had an impressive Gothic design. Its gray stone facade was flanked by two vertical spires, each with a single cross at the tip of its high peak. Each spire had a small arched opening, and centered below was a large arched doorway. A single rose window was set into the stone above the door.

Father Matthew started up the path as the church and its grounds rose above them. Water flowed gently over slabs of flat slate leading down the sloping hill next to the path as they turned to a set of concrete steps. Lush greenery and well-placed flowers dotted the side of the hill. The steps ended at a large decorative iron gate, spread open toward the church like a pair of out-stretched arms. Cate felt a wave of awe as she took in the impressive building and grounds.

"And here we are at St. Ann's," he said, turning to Cate with a proud smile. "The church dates back to the earliest days of Graypourt. The building over there that serves as the office and rectory is a bit more modern." He pointed to a single-story, vinyl-sided building that looked more like a repurposed single-family home.

"The office is in front closest to the church, and the rectory is on the back side," he explained.

Cate nodded politely. "It's a really beautiful spot. Who does all of your landscaping?"

"I do," Father Matthew said with another proud smile. "I was a master gardener in a former life."

Father Matthew seemed young to have already had multiple careers, and she raised her eyebrows in admiration.

He turned to face the tree line descending from their spot at the top of the hill, and he stretched out one arm gesturing to the landscape below. "I love that you can see nearly all of Graypourt from up here," he said.

Cate followed his gaze over the treetops to the buildings lining the main street, then to the rolling hills and pastures beyond. "It's really a beautiful setting. I've lived in Missouri for more than a decade if you include my college days, and I don't think I've ever heard of Graypourt."

"We're a little off the beaten path, but it's a wonderful place of rest and hospitality."

"How big is Graypourt?" Cate's eyes shifted toward Joey as he crouched down to get a closer look at the water feature bubbling and gurgling down the hill.

"It's a pretty small town, most of it is rural farmland. We get a lot of visitors passing through, though, and there's a wonderful sense of community pride."

"I can tell–the way that the downtown is so active and every storefront is occupied–you don't see that in a lot of smaller towns." Cate's mind wandered to her hometown, where many of the businesses had long since closed their doors as families and younger generations moved to bigger cities. She ignored the pang of guilt that poked her in the gut, realizing she had done the same thing.

Cate's hand went to her purse as she thought about her parents. She really should call them to let them know where she and Joey were and when they might be arriving.

"Father, would you excuse me for just a moment? I need to make a quick phone call to let our family know where we are."

Father Matthew smiled apologetically. "I'm not sure you'll have much luck finding a cell signal here ... we're a little too far off the beaten path for traditional cell towers. We usually have to rely on old-school landlines around here."

Cate pulled her phone out of her purse and tapped on the glass. Her screen came to life, but sure enough, where there should be a Wi-Fi signal and bars indicating cell signal strength, there was a bold SOS icon. Anxiety rippled through her chest, and she drew a deep breath. She glanced over at the office building Father Matthew had pointed out, but she didn't feel comfortable imposing on him. She had a signal back at the motel, so she just needed to get back there. She dropped her phone back into her purse and prepared to say goodbye to Father Matthew.

Joey stood up at that moment, flapping his hands in a familiar gesture of excitement and pleasure.

"He seems to like it here," Father Matthew said in an amused tone, his gaze fixed on Joey. Cate sensed he had some familiarity with Joey's gestures and looked at him with curiosity.

"Do you know many children on the autism spectrum?" she asked.

"Oh, sure–I've had experience with all kinds of children. How long have you known about Joey's special needs?"

Cate had never heard anyone ask about Joey's diagnosis this way, but it struck her as a kind approach. It was still new territory for her, and she hadn't yet gotten comfortable sharing it with many people. She swallowed her apprehension and cleared her throat.

"We've known for sure for just about a year, but he's had delays and challenges since around twelve months old."

"I'm sure that's been difficult for you and your husband."

Cate's stomach clenched, and a wave of humiliation washed over her. She really hadn't prepared to share the details of her life with this stranger, and she felt she was being forced to open up to him. She looked down at the ground and stuck her hands in the pockets of her shorts.

"My ... husband left us about six months ago," she said, her voice low and strained.

"Oh, I'm so sorry to hear that. Is he a part of Joey's life at all?"

His question felt bold and more than a little personal. It seemed to Cate like he was really prying now, and maybe even assuming Cate couldn't handle Joey on her own.

"I've spent most of my life being responsible for others and am surprisingly self-sufficient," she shot back, her voice clipped. Father Matthew blinked and offered a subtle nod. She averted her gaze back to Joey as an awkward silence settled between them.

"Would you like to see inside the church?" Father Matthew asked, bringing his hands together in front of him.

Cate was definitely curious about what the church looked like inside, but she could see that Joey was beginning to wilt in the rising heat and humidity, and she was beginning to feel like they were becoming a little too reliant on Father Matthew's hospitality.

"Father, really, thank you for this great visit and for showing us around, but I need to get Joey back to the motel," she said a bit more brusquely than she had wanted to.

"Of course," he replied. Joey calmly took Cate's hand when she offered it to him.

"I'll just get you back to Main Street so you're a little more familiar with the direction you'll need to go," Father Matthew offered.

As he turned to lead them back down the steps, he became oddly quiet, and Cate felt a pang of regret that she'd been so quick to dismiss him and his kindness. Maybe she was being too sensitive–Joey seemed to like Father Matthew, and she was still stunned at how quickly he had warmed up to him. She was eager to get ahold of her parents, but she was feeling guilty about snapping at Father Matthew and wanted to leave him on a good note.

Suddenly, Cate had a thought.

"Actually, Father, how about we stop in to that festival? It would be a great way to wear Joey out so he'll take a good nap," she said with a weak chuckle laced with resignation.

"Would Joey do okay with such a large crowd?"

Cate hesitated, a little irritated that Father Matthew seemed to be questioning her suggestion, but also not totally disagreeing with his presumption this time. She really wasn't sure how Joey might respond with so much stimulation. She looked down to gauge his reaction, and he turned to her with a look of expectation.

"Are you sure, buddy? You want to go see the festival?"

Joey nodded, pulling on Cate's hand. "Peese ... Mom," he pleaded.

"Okay, let's give it a shot." She nodded at Father Matthew and gave him a hesitant smile.

"Absolutely!" he responded enthusiastically. "Follow me!"

~ 8 ~

They turned onto Main Street and walked the couple of blocks to the festival entrance. A large crowd milled around a clean gravel lot, vendors and food trucks to their left, carnival rides and games spread across the wide open area. At the top of the hill looking over the lot was a historic coal house, river landing, and train depot. A large vinyl banner stretched across the main entrance to the lot, welcoming guests to the "Graypourt Founders Day Festival!"

It struck Cate as an odd spelling, hinting at an English or Canadian heritage Father Matthew had yet to mention. They walked under the banner and into the energetic and lively crowd. A couple of young boys ran across their path; one appeared to be chasing the other as they laughed unabashedly. A couple carrying a toddler crossed their path from the other direction, and Cate began to feel like they were swimming upstream. She kept looking down at Joey, checking his response, but he continued to calmly hold on to her hand.

Father Matthew led them over to a series of carnival games, and Joey pulled Cate toward the one with large stuffed animals hanging across its back wall. Father Matthew stepped up to the short counter and handed a $5 bill to the vendor. He waved Father Matthew off, and smiled, placing his hands together in a gesture of prayer. Father Matthew put the cash back in his pocket and accepted the four baseball sized balls the vendor handed to him.

Cate was amazed at his accuracy as he quickly knocked over four bottles and was soon accepting a large brown teddy bear with a bright yellow ribbon around its neck. She looked down to see Joey's eyes as big as saucers and laughed.

Father Matthew knelt down and gently offered the bear to him. Joey hesitated, but then turned to Cate to offer her his Bun. Cate was surprised at his willingness to hand over his favorite comfort item so easily, but she took it from him and watched as he quickly wrapped his arms around the stuffed bear, practically half his size. Cate laughed again, a feeling of affection washing over her as she witnessed Father Matthew's warmth and kindness toward her son.

Joey seemed content with this quick and early satisfaction, and they just wandered through the remaining game booths taking in the activity and energy of the crowd. The festival appeared to be a popular draw for families with lots of couples and young children, as well as older people she assumed were grandparents, all walking around in tight knit groups. She was struck by the wholesome nostalgia of it all, and felt a yearning for a simpler time–a time before she'd been forced to grow up without her big brother. She found herself once again transported back to her childhood and the Iowa State Fair, memories she hadn't given much thought to since leaving home for college.

She spotted a teenage boy up ahead turning down an aisle toward the food vendors and her heart jumped–his sandy blond hair and athletic build seemed familiar, and she wanted to get closer. She began moving toward him when a voice got her attention.

"Cate? Did you hear me?" Father Matthew gently touched Cate's arm and she turned to him. When she looked back in the direction of the boy, he had disappeared. Her heart sank and she turned back to Father Matthew.

"I think Joey is fading," he said.

Cate noticed Joey beginning to wilt once again, slowing his pace, small trickles of sweat rolling down his temples.

"I should probably get us something to drink," Cate suggested and Father Matthew nodded.

"Good call," he said, leading them toward the long row of food and drink vendors shaded by large trees at the far edge of the festival grounds.

Cate spotted a stand selling lemonade, Joey's favorite, and pointed it out to Father Matthew. She reached for Joey's hand, preferring to keep him close while she stood in line. Joey scowled, defiantly tucking his hand behind his back. Cate braced herself and crouched down next to Joey so she was eye level.

"Joey, do you want a lemonade?" He nodded vigorously, clutching his stuffed bear. "Okay, if you want a lemonade, I need you to stand with me in line." Joey now shook his head back and forth just as vigorously, his shoulders tensing.

"I would be happy to sit with Joey at a picnic table while you order the drinks," Father Matthew offered softly. Cate sensed that Father Matthew was picking up on the fact that Joey was dangerously close to another meltdown.

Cate felt her chest tighten with apprehension despite Father Matthew's connection with Joey. She knew it would be easier to let him distract Joey, but she also wasn't completely comfortable letting him out of her sight. On the other hand, she also wasn't feeling particularly up for a fight and possible tantrum.

"Okay ... sure," she said reluctantly, standing up again. "Joey, would you like to sit at that table over there with Father Matthew?"

Joey looked over at Father Matthew, focused on his chest. He paused briefly, then shifted the bear under one arm and offered Father Matthew his other hand. Cate's heart ached, but she ignored the feeling of inadequacy threatening to surface. She watched Father Matthew lead Joey over to the picnic table painted a garish kelly green on the other side of the paved walkway. He wasn't more than 15 feet away and so she turned and took her place in line.

The line moved slowly and Cate found herself turning back more than once to check that Joey and Father Matthew were still in sight. Joey was watching the activity around them, sitting calmly with his arms wrapped tightly around his prized bear. Cate tucked Bun under her arm and pulled her wallet out of her purse as she finally approached the window to place her order.

She handed over the remaining cash she had in her wallet, dropping the few coins she received in change into her purse. She grabbed the two plastic cups of lemonade and paper-wrapped straws and stepped out of line. The crowd had thickened in the narrow lane between the lemonade truck and the other vendors. She paused as the crowd shifted and the picnic table came into view. There was a young woman and little girl with stringy blond hair seated on one side, but Father Matthew and Joey were nowhere to be seen.

She turned toward the lane between the two rows of vendors. The crowd parted just enough and Cate strained her neck for any sign of Joey's familiar brown curls, or Father Matthew's black shirt and pants. Anxiety gripped her chest, and her vision wobbled. She briefly squeezed her eyes closed, bringing everything back into focus when she opened them again. She pressed her way through the crowd, faces and bodies melting together then coming back into focus. She came to the end of the row of food vendors, her eyes frantically searching the sea of people moving among the carnival games.

"Joey!" she screamed, choking and struggling to find her breath. A few of the people closest to her turned and looked at her, but no one approached. She continued desperately scanning the crowd, willing Joey to come into view. Oh, God–she'd really done it this time. She trusted a stranger and turned her back and now Joey was gone. This was her worst nightmare.

The familiar sensation of a developing panic attack washed over her. She wondered if she should return to the picnic table so they could find her if they came back, or if she should keep search-ing. She didn't think she'd be able to just sit there and wait so she kept moving through the crowd. Every time she thought she spotted Joey, the child would turn around and her hope would evaporate like smoke.

Eventually, she found herself back near the entrance to the festival grounds. She turned around still holding the two large Styrofoam cups, Bun tucked tightly under her arm, her eyes desperately darting from edge to edge of the large gravel lot. She felt her arms and legs start to go numb. She couldn't catch her breath and her head was throbbing. She thought she might be sick and she dropped one of the cups of lemonade as she moved to cover her mouth. She turned to try to find a trash bin or a patch of grass.

She pushed her way through the crowd, the sounds of voices becoming muffled as if she were sinking underwater.

'*No, no, no ... not now ... not here...*' She felt the darkness begin to close in as her field of vision narrowed. She felt her legs finally give out and everything went black.

~ 9 ~

When Cate opened her eyes, she was no longer on the festival grounds. She blinked several times to clear her vision as her surroundings slowly came into focus. The first thing she saw was a white curtain hanging from a silver track below a drop ceiling, one large fluorescent light glaring down at her.

There was a simple chair with a vinyl padded seat and basic chrome arms, a rolling cart with a few boxes of disposable gloves, unopened boxes of tissues, and several rolls of gauze. She was wearing a hospital gown and was covered up to her armpits with a sheet and soft flannel blanket.

She could hear muffled voices and activity on the other side of the curtain, but she couldn't make out what they were saying. She wiggled her toes and shifted her legs–all seemed to be in working order. She began to push herself up as realization materialized.

"Joey!" she croaked. She was pulling the sheet and blanket across her body and trying to get into a full sitting position when the curtain suddenly opened and a nurse rolled a small table into her room. Cate stopped, resting on her elbow, her other hand firmly grasping the edge of the sheet and blanket, ready to pull it back at a moment's notice.

"Well, look who's awake," the nurse said cheerfully.

"Please, I need to find my son," Cate croaked again, her throat painful and dry. "I lost him in the crowd down at the festival, and–"

"Don't worry," the nurse cooed, as if Cate had merely misplaced her phone. "You went down pretty hard out there, so we need to keep an eye on you for a bit longer. Let me just get a few vitals, then we'll bring someone in who can fill you in on what's going on, okay?"

"Wait, you mean you know where he is? He's okay?" Cate tried to push herself up to sit on the edge of the bed, but her head and legs felt like they were covered in heavy bricks.

"I need you to sit back and be still while I take your blood pressure," the nurse went on as if Cate hadn't reacted at all.

Cate could tell she was in no shape for a fight and closed her eyes in an attempt to stop the room from spinning. She had no choice but to comply. She relaxed her arm and lay back on the pillow while the nurse wrapped the flexible cuff around her biceps and fastened the Velcro. The nurse pushed a button on the electronic monitor, and the cuff began to tighten around Cate's arm. The nurse then reached back into the wire basket and pulled out the thermometer, pressing it into the box to apply the protective covering. Cate obediently opened her mouth, and the nurse pressed the probe under her tongue. She held the thermometer in Cate's mouth for just a few moments, cheerfully announcing, "98.6, perfect!" with a smile.

The blood pressure cuff finally loosened its grip on Cate's arm and the nurse pulled it off and checked her monitor. "BP's still a little low, but it's much better than when you arrived. Let me go get someone you can talk to about your son. Please try to rest."

At that moment, the curtain opened again, and Father Matthew entered the room.

Cate gasped at seeing a familiar face, and she tried again to push herself up to a sitting position.

"Oh, thank God!" she said. "Please tell me you have Joey," she pleaded.

Father Matthew caught the nurse's eyes and nodded, almost reverently. The nurse returned his nod, then turned to leave. He grabbed the rolling stool from the side of the bed and gently took a seat. He took Cate's hand and gave her a concerned look, and she was again struck by his confident good looks.

"How are you feeling?" he asked.

"I'm ... fine. I just want to see my son," she said as she felt tears begin to burn behind her eyelids. She felt her heart rate quicken as Father Matthew patted the top of her hand.

"He's safe," Father Matthew assured her. "I haven't left his side until just before arriving here at the hospital."

Cate sat up a little straighter, her eyes widening with anticipation. "Where did you take him? Is he here?!" she practically begged, looking over Father Matthew's shoulder, waiting for the nurse to appear from behind the curtain with Joey by her side.

"He's not here at the hospital, but he's safe and in good hands," Father Matthew explained, firm but kind. Cate's gaze snapped back to his face. "I can take you to see him as soon as you're feeling better."

Father Matthew's tone felt condescending. The memory of the way Joey had so quickly warmed up to him fed the self-doubt she couldn't ever seem to escape. She was done being polite. Cate felt her heart snap in half, adrenaline racing into her bloodstream. Her head was a balloon about to separate from her body.

"Where is my son?!" she screamed, her forehead, cheeks and neck suddenly on fire. Father Matthew stood up, his face darkening with concern. Cate swung her legs off the bed only to be hit with a pounding wave of dizziness and nausea. Spots danced before her eyes, and she gripped the side of the bed to keep from falling off.

She was squeezing her eyes closed, trying to stop her brain from free-floating inside her head and fighting to regain her balance when she sensed the movement of multiple people coming into the room. Hands were pressing her back onto the bed. Someone had her right arm, and she felt pressure where the IV was taped to the top of her hand. A warm, liquid sensation traveled up her arm and wrapped itself around her head and chest.

When Cate opened her eyes, she saw two female nurses by the curtain and a man dressed in scrubs standing next to the bed. She slowly turned her head toward the other side of the room and saw Father Matthew standing there, arms crossed, a concerned expression on his face.

"Cate, are you feeling a little better now?" the man next to her bed asked.

"Mmhmm," Cate murmured, feeling as if she were floating in a warm bath.

The male nurse looked over at Father Matthew, and he gave a small nod. The nurses all exited and Father Matthew approached Cate's bed. He gently laid his hand on her arm, the look of concern seemingly etched permanently onto his face. Everything seemed to be moving more slowly than normal, and her desperation had been dramatically watered down.

"Please ..." she whimpered. "Please don't hurt Joey ... I'll do anything." A sob caught in her throat.

"No one is going to hurt him, Cate. He is as far from danger as he can possibly get. He is in a wonderful place with people who are experts in caring for him." Father Matthew's face relaxed into a smile. "We will get you out of the hospital to a safe, quiet place where you can get your strength back. I promise I will reunite you with Joey as soon as you're feeling better."

Cate's gaze wandered to the other corner of the exam room as she willed her brain to respond, but it felt like it was covered in thick, heavy syrup.

She focused again on Father Matthew's face. How could she trust him? He had walked away from her with her son.

"Where did you and Joey go ... at the festival?"

"There was a runaway balloon and Joey took off after it ... I had to follow him to try to guide him back to the picnic table. By the time we got there, you were gone."

Cate closed her eyes and sighed remorsefully. If only she had followed her first instinct and returned to the picnic table. She and Joey might be napping peacefully in their hotel room.

"How can I ... prove to you ... I feel better?" she asked, her speech slow and halting. She pulled her arm away from Father Matthew and tried to fix her eyes on his face.

"You took a pretty nasty fall when you passed out. Let's just take this one step at a time," he answered gently.

Father Matthew stood up, sliding the rolling stool toward the curtain. He brought his hands together, fingers threaded. He gave Cate another smile before continuing.

"The nurse will bring you some clean clothes and release you once she believes you're ready. I'll be waiting for you outside." He gave Cate's leg one final pat and turned to leave, disappearing behind the privacy curtain.

Cate took a deep breath, searching for something that made sense. There had to be more to understand, but she was so tired now. She fought against the sedative that pulled her farther and farther down but eventually allowed her eyelids to fall and melted into the familiar cushioned sleep.

When her eyes began to slowly blink open, Cate sensed a renewed clarity. She had to find Joey. She slowly pulled back the blanket and sheet and slid her legs off the bed, trying to make as little noise as possible. Thankfully, she seemed steadier now and slowly stood up.

There was a small pile of clothes folded on the chair in the corner of the exam room. She quietly padded across the cold tile floor, pulling the hospital gown off, grateful she was still in her bra and underwear. She nervously glanced over at the curtain, expecting to see it move across the rod and for a nurse to burst in at any moment. She pulled on the tan scrub shorts and boxy V-neck top, feeling less like a patient than a prisoner. She slipped her feet into the white flip-flop sandals, then quickly changed her mind and decided to carry them and avoid their signature slapping noise.

She spotted her purse hanging from a small plastic hook on the wall above the chair and quickly threw it across her body. She pulled open the zipper and thrust her hand inside, immediately landing on her cell phone. She pulled it out and tapped on the glass, her screen coming to life just as she heard the curtain slide open behind her. Her heart seized in her chest as she turned to see the nurse standing just inside the curtain.

"Hey, Cate. Glad to see you back on your feet. Are you ready to go?"

Cate swallowed hard, discreetly sliding her phone back into her purse.

"C-could I please use the restroom before I leave?" she asked, desperately trying to keep her voice steady.

"Oh, of course. Why don't you put your sandals on, and then I can show you to the bathroom on our way out." The nurse held her ground, one hand gripping the curtain and the other resting authoritatively on her hip.

Cate obediently slid her feet into the sandals and followed the nurse out into the hallway, catching her first glimpse of the area outside the exam room. It was a typical emergency ward with a row of rooms like hers, humming with the sounds of medical equipment and of medical personnel moving with urgency or idly manning laptop stations. They passed a number of unoccupied rooms, but a few had the curtains pulled shut, and she could only see the shadowy outlines of people moving around on the opposite side.

Her eyes searched ahead, trying to anticipate where the nurse was leading her and whether there were any viable escape routes. They passed through a set of large, solid double doors that the nurse activated by flashing her badge against a sensor on the wall. Cate took note and began devising a way to get her hands on that badge. The activity on this side of the doors was instantly quieter, the energy less urgent. They entered a narrow hallway that felt more like a tunnel. It was flooded with fluorescent light, and there were no doors, windows or openings of any kind. An orderly passed them, flashing Cate a friendly smile, and she spotted daylight up ahead, which she assumed was the hospital exit.

The nurse stopped then and turned to Cate. "Okay, ladies' restroom is on the right. I'll just wait for you here, then I'll show you the way out."

"Oh, I think I can find it okay on my own, but thanks for all–"

"I'm to make sure you find your way to the exit, so I'll just wait here for you." Her light, friendly tone had changed and become tighter, authoritative.

Cate gave her a tight-lipped smile and pressed down on the handle of the door, pushing it open into a private bathroom with a single stool and sink. She waited for the door to close behind her and pushed in the button lock. She reached into her purse and pulled out her cell phone, quickly tapping the glass to activate her screen. The red battery icon briefly flashed before the screen once again went dark.

"Dammit!" she cursed quietly, shoving the phone back into her purse.

She turned and gripped the sides of the cold porcelain sink, squeezing her eyes shut to quiet the panic exploding in her head. She sensed she had already lost so much time. Joey could literally be anywhere by now. She had no idea where she was in proximity to the town of Graypourt and the festival grounds. She felt doors slamming all around her and desperately tried to hold on to hope that at some point a window would open.

She stood up, and her eyes darted around the small tiled room, searching for anything she could use to even briefly disarm the nurse so she could grab her badge. Just then, there was a knock on the bathroom door.

"Cate, are you okay?" The nurse seemed to have returned to her friendly, professional persona.

"Yes ... just finishing up," she answered, trying to match the nurse's tone, but her voice came out strained and shaky.

She tried to think. If she got the nurse's badge, she had no idea where she would go. Father Matthew had said Joey wasn't here in the hospital but had been taken somewhere else. If she was honest, she didn't even know if he was still in Graypourt. She could hide out for a while and try to sneak out a back entrance, but then what? Wander aimlessly around the hospital grounds hoping some clue dropped from the sky that would point her in the right direction? Who knew what would happen if she was caught–she might just end up in an actual prison cell.

Her best–and most efficient–bet was to press Father Matthew for information. He was the only person who seemed to know where Joey was. She didn't have any choice but to try to negotiate information out of him.

She pressed the lever on the toilet and turned on the faucet, pulling several paper towels out of the dispenser, trying to feign normal bathroom activity. She emerged to find the nurse standing patiently just outside the door and obediently followed her to the end of the hallway. They entered a small waiting room flooded with natural light.

Cate noticed an older woman seated behind a waist-high counter staring at a computer screen. Was this her window? She seized the opportunity and marched over to the counter.

"Excuse me, may I use your phone?" Cate tried to sound calm and confident though her entire body was trembling.

The woman looked up at her, then around her at the nurse who Cate sensed coming up right behind her.

"Okay, Cate, Father Matthew is waiting for you just outside the door," the nurse said, placing her hands gently around Cate's arm.

Cate turned to her, searching her face for any sign of camaraderie or compassion. She thought she noted a sympathetic light flash in her eyes, but the rest of her face remained calm, professional.

"I would like to make a phone call before I leave here. Even prisoners get that courtesy," Cate growled back at her. The nurse didn't flinch.

"I understand. Father Matthew will speak with you about that once he gets you settled."

The orderly who had passed them earlier now appeared in the doorway they had just come through, and Cate assumed the older woman behind the counter must have paged him. She felt cornered.

"Please ... can you tell me *anything* about where they took my son?" Cate pleaded, her voice catching in her throat. This felt like her last opportunity before she was back under the control of Father Matthew.

The nurse's face softened, and Cate's heart pounded.

"I'm so sorry, Cate. I don't have any idea." She rested her hand on Cate's back, and her heart crashed into her stomach. She felt a crushing weight on her chest and was afraid she might be sick. She took the deepest breath she could manage and tried to calm the anxiety flooding her brain.

"Come on ... I'll help you to the car." The nurse put her arm around Cate and applied gentle pressure. She couldn't help but feel she was a lamb being led to slaughter but couldn't think what choice she had but to follow. The only way to Joey was out those doors.

$$\sim 10 \sim$$

With a "whoosh," the double doors slid apart, and Cate stepped into the fresh air.

As he promised, Father Matthew was waiting there, standing next to the passenger side of a large black sedan idling quietly in the covered driveway. A late-afternoon breeze ruffled his hair, and he smiled warmly, opening the rear passenger door and gesturing for Cate to get in.

She gave Father Matthew a brief, tentative look, then quickly scanned her surroundings, her eyes searching for any possible escape route, but the nurse's grip on her arms had intensified as she continued leading her to the curb. Cate looked past the car and saw a parking lot, an unfamiliar, nondescript street, and a quiet highway beyond that. There wasn't another soul in sight, just an empty car and Father Matthew.

She took a deep, shaky breath, gripped the strap of her purse, and stepped into the car, sinking into the plush back seat. Father Matthew took the front passenger seat, and Cate noticed for the first time that someone else was in the driver's seat. He was tall, with broad shoulders and well-manicured salt-and-pepper-colored hair. It was hard to tell from behind, but she thought she noticed a short, well-trimmed beard. He wore a white dress shirt and black suit jacket and gave every indication of being a professional chauffeur. Father Matthew didn't introduce him, so Cate crossed her arms and watched as the nurse turned to go back inside. The car pulled away and the emergency room entrance slid out of view through her tinted window.

They pulled out onto the street and, after a short distance, merged onto the quiet four-lane highway. Cate could only make out a few industrial buildings in the distance, and every so often a farmhouse with grain towers and barns that reminded her of her parents' farm. Her stomach clenched at the thought that she was supposed to be there by now.

They drove for what felt like miles and miles in silence, the surroundings becoming increasingly rural the farther they got from the hospital. They exited the highway and pulled onto an even quieter two-lane road. Rolling fields dotted with large bundles of hay stretched as far as her eyes could see.

After a couple of turns, Cate saw farmhouses of varying size with large stretches of pasture in between. She tried to log landmarks into her memory but eventually lost all awareness of direction or proximity to Graypourt. They drove a bit farther, and the road became bumpier, and she could hear gravel crunching under the tires. Alarm bells were going off in her head, and she tried to calm the trembling that had picked up as they got farther and farther from the hospital. Finally, the car began to slow down, nearly coming to a complete stop before turning into a narrow single-lane driveway.

Ahead was a modest-sized, single-story home with white siding and black trim. The center of the home had a large picture window, set back under a covered concrete patio supported by two simple black posts. There was a small front yard, a large oak tree, and a few rosebushes. The home appeared to be unoccupied, and Cate felt her heart rate spike in anticipation.

Father Matthew got out of the car and opened Cate's door. She stared at the back of the driver's head, silently willing him to turn around so she could plead with him to take off, but he remained stoic, his gaze locked on the windshield. She sighed and gripped the strap of her purse.

"Come on out, Cate, and I'll show you around," Father Matthew said, offering his hand. She tentatively stepped out but avoided taking Father Matthew's hand. She could not process the fact that he alone was her only remaining connection to Joey.

She followed Father Matthew up a narrow set of concrete stairs onto a sidewalk that curved toward the covered patio. Cate took in the surroundings, noting a two-story farmhouse directly across the road and another smaller home a short distance farther. Both were set far back from the gravel road on large acreages that again reminded her of her childhood home.

There were no obvious signs of life at either residence, but Cate still found herself fighting the urge to bolt and at least try to find someone willing to help her. She had to remain calm. If she started acting like a lunatic, she worried Father Matthew would be forced to sedate her again. She would be no use to Joey in a constant medicated stupor.

Father Matthew reached into his pocket and pulled out a set of keys, which he used to unlock the outside aluminum screen door. Cate allowed herself to briefly peer into the large picture window, but thin white curtains were drawn, and she wasn't able to make out much detail inside. Father Matthew unlocked the second heavier wood door, which opened with a loud scraping, creaking sound, giving Cate her first glimpse into the house.

Up a couple of concrete steps and over the threshold, Cate stood on a laminate floor of brick-colored tiles of varying sizes. She stepped aside so Father Matthew could push the door closed. The air was slightly stale but cool and dry, and it smelled of old books and a mildly sour fragrance she didn't recognize. The small foyer was dimly lit and led into the main part of the home to the right.

The room ahead of her was cast in a dim sepia tone as if under a shroud, and Cate wrapped her arms around her waist, suddenly freezing cold. Father Matthew stepped around her to pull the cord that opened the thin curtains covering the large window at the front of the house. The room instantly brightened, and Cate's chest loosened just slightly.

She and Father Matthew were standing in a comfortable living area with a couch, two upholstered recliners, a few bookshelves of various heights and sizes, and a sturdy wood-burning stove atop a modest brick hearth.

"You are welcome to stay here as long as you need to," Father Matthew said, following Cate's gaze as she surveyed her surroundings. She had no intention of staying here any longer than necessary and tightened her crossed arms in defiance.

"I'll show you around and you can let me know what else you need." Father Matthew started toward the other end of the living room, past the wood-burning stove and recliners. Cate's eyes searched the room for evidence of her and Joey's bags, but she didn't see anything familiar.

Father Matthew led her into a small hallway. He flipped on the hall light, immediately washing the narrow space in a dull, buttery yellow. Directly in front of her was a full bathroom, and to the left and right were bedrooms. Father Matthew entered the bedroom on the left and pulled open the vinyl shade covering one large window. Cate looked around at the furniture–a double bed, a small sewing table, and a vanity. Father Matthew pulled up the second shade covering the window near the other side of the bed, letting a healthy amount of light into the room. Each window was framed by thin white curtains pinned back to the wall with delicate white sashes.

Cate let her gaze linger on the view outside each window, seeing only rolling hills and farmland beyond the immediate yard, driveway, and garage.

"There's a closet here ..." Father Matthew reached in front of Cate, twisting the small brass knob and opening the closet door. He then reached toward the ceiling and pulled down on a piece of sturdy twine. With a soft click, a single bulb came to life, revealing a shelf, a hanging rack, and Cate's backpack and suitcase, unopened and intact.

"... and I think you'll find your things have already been delivered for you," Father Matthew said, answering Cate's earlier question.

Cate turned to him, a bewildered look on her face.

"I called Harvey while you were resting, and he was very kind to come by and drop off your luggage."

"Thank you ..." she said, more out of habit than true gratitude. "But where are Joey's things?" she asked, again turning to Father Matthew with a pained expression, not quite sure she really wanted to know the answer.

"Joey has everything he needs–even Bun," he responded with a soft smile. Cate's stomach tightened at the mention of Bun, and tears immediately sprung to her eyes. It seemed especially cruel of him to mention something so sentimental. She narrowed her eyes in warning, but he didn't flinch.

Father Matthew pulled the string again to turn off the light and gently closed the closet door. "Let me show you the rest of the house."

Cate suddenly wished she had taken the opportunity to use the bathroom at the hospital since now her need was much more urgent.

"Actually, I could really use the bathroom," she said as they moved back into the hallway.

"Sure, it's right behind you." Father Matthew gestured to the doorway in the center of the hallway between the two bedrooms. Cate set her purse on the ground and stepped into the narrow room. There was a tub shower at the far end, as well as a stool and counter with a single sink and mirror. She quickly did her business, her mind racing.

She didn't need a tour, she wanted answers. She had to start asking questions about Joey's whereabouts. She steeled herself as she briskly washed and dried her hands, pulling open the door to find Father Matthew standing right where she'd left him. She picked up her purse and threw the strap across her body.

"How far is it to the place where Joey is staying?" she blurted out as they stepped back into the living room.

"Not too far," Father Matthew said casually. "I'll be able to check in on him anytime."

Cate's chest tightened, and she felt her cheeks flush with anger. She was not about to let Father Matthew see her son without her, but she tried to remain calm despite her pounding heart.

"So he's in Graypourt? Is he in town near the church?" she pressed. "Or out here in the country?"

Father Matthew turned around at this point, his back to the living room as Cate paused in the doorway.

"Cate, I'd like you to be able to focus on getting healthy and back to full strength. I know it's hard to trust me when I say that Joey is in the safest place he could possibly be, but I promise you that is exactly where he is. I will update you as often as I can, maybe even daily if that's what you want."

"None of this is what I want." Cate tossed her arms in the air, gesturing to the room they were in. "I don't have any idea where I am ... and I don't know you. So what makes you think I could trust you with the one person who is the most precious to me? Maybe if you were actually a parent, you could understand that hearing how he is doing is not enough ... I need to see him."

Father Matthew sighed, crossing his arms and looking down at the floor. Finally, he looked up at her with sympathy.

"I realize you don't know me very well–but I would like to change that." Father Matthew's eyes were almost pleading. "If you will just try to get to know me a little better, I think you will find that your stay will be much more meaningful for you."

Cate sensed that Father Matthew was sincere, but she didn't understand what kind of relationship he was after. Why her of all people?

He brought his hands together in front of him, "Let's see how you do overnight, and we can talk more tomorrow about seeing Joey."

"Please ... I can't wait until tomorrow. There's no way I can sleep here without seeing him," Cate felt herself whimpering and hated that she was losing control of her emotions.

Father Matthew stepped toward her and gently grasped her arms. Cate immediately tensed, but his face was calm, his eyes kind.

"I know this is hard. You've landed in this unfamiliar place, and you're scared. I'm sure you feel very alone ... but you're not alone, Cate. I, and many others you'll be meeting soon, are here to support you and help you get back home. You want to be at your best for Joey, right?"

"My best? I am all he has ... I don't care how experienced you say the people are that he's with. No one knows Joey like I do. He's a five-year-old boy, and he needs his mother." Cate's voice was strong now, unflinching. She was not going to allow Father Matthew to keep her from her son.

She stepped back, and Father Matthew let go of her arms.

"My cell phone is dead, but if you just let me call my parents, they will come pick us up. You don't need to do this."

"I've already spoken to them." Father Matthew put his hands in his pockets now, his stance firm and confident. Cate suddenly felt like he had injected ice into her veins.

"What? When? How did you find their number?" Cate's eyes were wide, and her heart was racing again.

"Their number was in Joey's backpack as an emergency contact. When they learned what happened, they were very supportive of you having this time to rest and focus on healing. They know how much you need this."

Cate froze. Her parents had been encouraging her for a while now to do something about her anxiety other than medicating herself. Would they actually consent to holding Cate somewhere against her will? Separate her from Joey? She'd never known them to be that cruel and couldn't imagine them agreeing to it.

"I don't believe you."

"How else would I know that your parents have supported the idea of getting help for your panic attacks ... that they've been asking you for months now?"

Cate thought back to the letter from her mom now sitting on her kitchen table at home. Had this been their plan all along? They couldn't have known that she and Joey would end up here. She pressed her fingers into her eyes, trying to process this new information.

"Your parents have entrusted you and Joey to me, Cate. You are safe here."

She couldn't make sense of it all, and she wasn't about to let her guard down.

"I thought the practice of forcing people into recovery went out of fashion a few generations ago." Cate held her ground, arms crossed.

"These are somewhat different circumstances." Father Matthew didn't elaborate and turned away from her at that point to continue his tour.

Cate gripped her arms, but relented and chose to swallow her questions for the time being, despite the heavy knot of frustration and dread in her stomach.

Father Matthew pointed out a third bedroom and office as they passed through the living room. They entered a dimly lit dining room with a banquet-sized table, antique buffet and another large window facing the backyard as they moved to the other end of the house.

"I'll show you the kitchen, then I'll be on my way so you can get a little more settled."

Cate followed him around a corner where there was an oak dining table and four chairs, a wall of white cabinets, and a small galley-style kitchen. A square window over the sink looked into the front yard and the country road beyond.

"There are a few basic items in the fridge and the cabinets, but I'll check in on you soon in case there's something we forgot," Father Matthew said gently as he moved toward the back door. Cate stood awkwardly in her same spot between the formal dining room and the kitchen, feeling like a caged animal.

Father Matthew hesitated, then turned to her with a look of gentle determination. "You can do this, Cate."

He pulled the door open and stepped out of the house. She turned toward the large window in the dining room and watched him walk along the sidewalk behind the house until he disappeared out of view.

The silence was painfully sharp, but she didn't hesitate. She ran toward the hallway and turned into the bedroom.

She had packed her laptop and chargers in her backpack and only needed a few minutes to charge her cell phone so she could make a call. When she got to the bed, she reached into her purse, feeling for her phone. She moved her hand around blindly, pushing aside the other items floating around inside the bag. She still didn't feel her phone, so she set her purse down and pulled it open farther, eventually dumping the entire contents onto the comforter.

Her wallet, a tube of lip gloss, a bottle of ibuprofen, a few receipts, and a small bottle of hand lotion stared back at her, but her phone was not there. She checked both inside pockets but already knew she wouldn't find that small black rectangle of glass and steel that was her lifeline to the outside world. Father Matthew must have taken it while she was in the bathroom. Her stomach dropped, and her heart was racing. *Think, Cate ... think!*

If she could find a place with Wi-Fi, she could fire up her laptop and might be able to get an email to her parents or to her supervisor at the hospital to send help. She threw open the closet door and pulled the backpack out of the closet, her heart sinking as she noted that it wasn't as heavy as usual, and set it down on the top of the bed. She unzipped the back pocket, and her chest immediately tightened. Her laptop wasn't there.

Cate frantically searched the other compartments, eventually dumping the entire contents of her backpack onto the bed. She stretched across the bed, spreading her things out across the comforter, her eyes searching every inch. There was no sign of her laptop or chargers. Dread threatened to consume her, but she pushed it away. Maybe Harvey had relocated it to her suitcase for safekeeping.

She pulled her suitcase out of the closet, laying it flat on the narrow space of floor near the bed, and opened it up to reveal its contents.

She pulled out each item of clothing, her makeup bag and styling tools, and several pairs of shoes. No laptop. No chargers. Defeated, she sat back on her heels, overwhelmed with an intense feeling of isolation and hopelessness. She really was a prisoner.

"What have I done ...?" she whimpered.

She allowed her head to fall back against the mattress, her eyes closed. She had to fight back, figure out where Father Matthew had taken Joey, and get out of Graypourt. She covered her face with her hands and drew in a deep breath, trying to string two cohesive thoughts together. Her hands dropped to her sides, and her gaze fell on the open bedroom door. Her mind went to the familiar instructions flight attendants always gave just before takeoff: "Place your own oxygen mask on before helping your child."

She would build up her strength, then set out to look for Joey.

~ 11 ~

Cate was suddenly aware of how thirsty she was. She lifted herself up off the floor and trudged across the house to the kitchen. She found a full cabinet of glassware behind the first door she opened, pulling out the largest glass she saw. She filled the glass with water from the kitchen faucet and brought it to her lips, emptying the entire thing in a matter of seconds. She refilled the glass and took another long swig before feeling like she had taken the edge off her thirst.

She set the glass on the counter, resting her other hand at the edge of the sink, and looked out the window into the front yard. Across the road and set back from an expansive grassy lawn was the farmhouse she saw when she first arrived. It was a simple two-story home with wood siding painted a creamy yellow with two rows of uniform windows. A wide set of steps led up to a comfortable wraparound porch, complete with two sets of large wicker armchairs on either side of the door. At the end of the long gravel driveway was a modern outbuilding for farming equipment, but she didn't see any cars or other signs of life.

She took another deep breath and one last drink before turning to try to get her bearings in her new surroundings.

She wasn't the slightest bit hungry, and she had no idea how long it had been since she last ate. She knew she needed to keep up her strength, though, so that when the opportunity came, she would be strong enough to grab Joey and run.

She opened the refrigerator and found a half gallon of milk, orange juice, a dozen eggs, and some deli meat and cheese. She saw a small bowl of fruit and grabbed an apple, its smooth, cool skin somehow soothing in her hand. Digging her teeth into the apple, she made her way back to the living room to sit for a minute, hopeful it would help her to think through her next move.

She stopped at the couch, taking a tentative seat on the edge of the cushion. She took another bite of apple, chewing slowly, acutely aware of the quiet surrounding her.

Gradually, she began to make out small noises–the ticking of a clock hanging on the wall across the room, the air conditioning kicking on with a gentle whistle as the air came up from the vent behind the couch, and the small creaks and twitches of an older home as it settles and bakes in the summer sun.

She shivered, her body cold and numb despite the sunlight on her back. She tried to ground herself, focusing on the way her feet felt against the carpeted floor, the coolness of the apple in her hand, the way the couch molded her to thighs.

She couldn't just sit here, waiting for someone to come and rescue her. She stood up and turned to look out the large picture window behind the couch. The farmhouse across the street was still, but she thought she saw something flash across one of the first-floor windows. There was someone inside. She set the partially eaten apple on the end table and moved apprehensively into the front hall.

As she turned the corner, she noticed for the first time a basic full-length mirror hanging on the narrow section of wall closest to the door. She dared to let her gaze linger long enough to take in the reflection staring back at her.

She grimaced at the shapeless silhouette of the scrubs that hung loosely from her body. She let her gaze slide down to her narrow shoulders and waist, the hips that had never quite returned to their pre-pregnancy tightness, and her long, athletic legs, which were decently toned from her semi-daily jogs around the park near the hospital.

Her straw-colored hair fell in a soft bob at her jawline. It had at one time had a clean, sleek look but was now a limp, greasy mess. There were dark circles under her hazel eyes, and without any makeup on, she looked ragged and pale and much older than her twenty-eight years.

This definitely wouldn't do.

She made a beeline into the bedroom, where her clothes were strewn across the bed and floor. She fished out a pair of shorts and a t-shirt and quickly changed out of the shapeless scrubs. She threw water on her face and ran her wet fingers through her hair.

Sliding her feet into a pair of leather flip-flops, she returned to the front hall. She took a deep breath and pulled open the solid wood door, sending a blast of August heat and humidity into the entryway.

She stepped out of the house, pulling the door closed behind her, and let the screen door slam shut as she made her way down the narrow sidewalk. When she got to the bottom of the driveway, she saw someone step out onto the front porch of the farmhouse.

A woman with a thin build held the storm door open with one hand and waved enthusiastically with the other. Thick blond hair framed her face, falling in loose stylish curls past her shoulders. She was dressed casually in a tank top and shorts, and from a distance Cate guessed she was about her age.

Hope suddenly bubbled up in Cate's chest, and she waved back, then stepped confidently into the gravel road and up the long driveway. The woman stepped away from the door and waited at the top of the steps, arms crossed, her expression warm and friendly.

As Cate approached, she suddenly realized she hadn't prepared what she was going to say at all, and she grasped for some way to explain what she was doing here.

Suddenly, the woman's face lit up, and her arms fell to her sides, a wide smile spreading across her face.

"Oh my gosh, you're Cate! I'm Maggie," she said, placing one hand on her chest. "Father Matthew called a little while ago and said a woman named Cate just moved in across the street."

Cate stopped at the bottom of the steps, and her heart sank. Of course this woman was friendly with Father Matthew. All hopes she had for finding a neighborly ally began to dissolve.

She wasn't sure what to say–and what might get back to Father Matthew. An awkward silence hung in the air between them, and Cate searched for some tiny glimmer of hope that she could win this woman over.

A cloud of concern passed over Maggie's face, and she crossed her arms again. "Are you okay?"

Cate willed herself to say something. Anything.

"Sorry... I, um, just got here and I ... just thought maybe you could answer some questions for me," Cate answered, forcing a smile. "It's been kind of a long day," she admitted.

"Oh, okay ... sure. Father Matthew seemed concerned, but maybe you need some time to get settled in." Maggie's face darkened, and she shifted as if she was thinking of backing away. "Maybe I could come by in the morning, just to make sure you have everything you need?" she added.

Cate had no idea how to answer that. Would she still be here tomorrow morning? She decided to go ahead and play along.

"Sure–that would be fine," she said, searching for an appropriate time for a hypothetical visitor. "Maybe around 10 a.m.?" she offered.

"Perfect! The kids will be at school, so my morning is pretty open–well, other than laundry–but I'm always looking for an excuse to take a break from that never-ending job." Maggie spoke quickly, adding a polite chuckle. "Have a good night, Cate. God bless!" she said.

Before Cate could respond, Maggie turned back toward the house and pulled the storm door toward her, stepping back inside.

She gave Cate a polite nod and pressed the front door closed. Cate's chest tightened, and she felt hot tears burning behind her eyelids. She reluctantly turned back to the driveway and trudged across the gravel road. She glanced back, and it struck her that she didn't see any toys, bikes, a swing–anything that would indicate children lived in the house. A chill ran down her back, and she wrapped her arms around her waist.

Once inside, she leaned back against the door, feeling its warmth through her shirt, and closed her eyes. She felt nauseous and wondered if she would be able to keep those few bites of apple down. Why hadn't she pressed Maggie for help?

She knew exactly why. If Maggie was somehow connected to Father Matthew, there was no way to know if she wouldn't just immediately turn her in.

How could she know who to trust?

She took another deep breath and let it out with a heavy sigh. She turned and went back into the living room, unsure what she was supposed to do. She felt hollowed out and like part of her body had been lopped off. She was used to being responsible for other people every second of the day–if she wasn't taking care of Joey, she had her patients. She was completely lost, as if she was drifting out in the ocean with no land in sight.

She picked up the half-eaten apple from the end table and went back toward the kitchen.

She found a small trash can in the cabinet under the sink and pitched the apple in, hearing it land with a soft thunk. She filled the glass with water once again, took a large gulp, and moved toward the kitchen table. She pulled out a chair, its legs scraping against the linoleum floor, and she took a seat on its thin cushion.

The intense isolation was like a heavy stone on her chest. She sensed the walls closing in, and a dark, heavy cloud of despair threatened to overwhelm her, expanding in her chest as her heart rate quickened. She rested her elbows on the table, cradling her face in the palms of her hands. Tears sprang to her eyes as a vision of Joey's face swam in front of her, pleading with her to come to him.

"Mama ..." he cried, tears rolling down his cheeks.

Cate couldn't restrain herself anymore. She released a loud, guttural scream that came from the very depths of her core; hot, stinging tears finally burst from her eyes and cooled as they ran down her cheeks. Sobs racked her body as she wrapped her arms around herself, pushing violently back from the table and folding over her knees. She couldn't stop the screams, like someone had flipped an irreversible switch. Her voice began to fail, growing hoarse with each new effort to expel the toxic feelings from her body.

Eventually, she wasn't making any sound. Her sobs slowed to a thick, heaving breaths. Her ribs ached, and her muscles trembled. She unwrapped her arms and put her face back into the palms of her hands, the saltiness of her skin stinging her raw cheeks. Her breathing began to return to normal, while quiet tears continued to leak from her eyes. Snot ran like a river from her nose, dripping onto her lap.

"Joey ... Joey ... Joey ..." she repeated through her tears, rocking back and forth. "I don't know what to do ... someone please tell me what to do ... please help," she whimpered. She slid off the chair and fell to her knees, then allowed her body to sink onto the floor under the table. She pulled her knees in and buried her face in the fold of her arm.

So far, she had failed at every attempt to take control of her situation. She had never felt more helpless and alone. She wished she was dead, wished the floor would just open up and swallow her whole. She didn't deserve to be here, to be Joey's mother, to be alive anymore. He was better off without her. She felt the familiar darkness expanding around her as her body relented and gave in.

~ 12 ~

A modest farmhouse in Iowa

Pam stood at the large ceramic farmhouse sink, her eyes focused on the pile of bubbles covering the plate she was scrubbing from lunch, but her mind was elsewhere. She had put the letter in the mail just over a week ago but had yet to hear any response from Cate. It wasn't totally unusual for her to take a while to respond due to her schedule and the heavy responsibility of caring for Joey all by herself. Pam's heart ached to help her daughter, to go to her and wrap her up in her arms. But she knew Cate better than anyone. She would have to come on her own, when she decided she was ready.

Pam ran the plate under the cold water and set it in the drying rack. She reached for the next dish, glancing up for a moment at the window directly over the sink. She was prepared to focus on the rolling hills she was so familiar with beyond the farmhouse, but something much more unexpected caught her eye. A butterfly, its delicate wings a bold, sunny yellow, fluttering persistently, hovered just outside the window. Something in her heart urged her to reach for the small crank that would push the window out toward the yard. The butterfly continued hovering now just outside of the screen, behavior Pam had never before witnessed from the typically skittish insect. She pressed the two tabs to release the screen from the window casing and slid the screen up, removing the final barrier between her and the outdoors. Pam stared in awe as the butterfly came into the kitchen, landing gracefully on the top of the faucet, gently tapping its wings together, then letting them open again. She felt her heart leap into her throat, and she was overwhelmed with emotion at the perfect beauty of the moment.

"Catie ..." she whispered, a primal instinct awakening with the realization that there was a deeper meaning behind this. The butterfly gracefully fluttered its wings once again, rising off the faucet and returning to its natural habitat. It was over almost as quickly as it began, and Pam stood there for a moment longer, absorbing the profound emotions she was experiencing. She knew this was not just a coincidence. This small, delicate and beautiful creature was a messenger ... and she knew without a shred of doubt that the message was one that would shatter her.

~ 13 ~

Cate finally began to stir from her place on the floor, blinking her eyes, which were gritty and swollen. Her throat felt raw, her ribs sore. She pulled herself up onto a chair, realizing that the room had begun to darken, the early evening shadows stretching across the table. She looked around for a light switch, flipping on the one closest to her. A warm, yellow light from above the table illuminated the room, and she took a deep breath.

Just then, she noticed the phone. It was a traditional landline phone, attached to the wall next to one of the cabinets, its curly cord hanging loosely above the counter. She quickly moved across the kitchen, lifting the receiver from its base and putting it up to her ear.

Silence.

She couldn't bear another slammed door in her face. Somewhere, there had to be a window.

She replaced the handset back into its cradle on the wall and turned toward the dining room. She could see through the large picture window that the backyard was shrouded in a dusky light, and the trees she'd noticed earlier cast long shadows across the lawn. She walked through the darkened living room and into the front hall, her shoulders and back aching. She found two more light switches. One light came on directly above her, filling the front hall with the same warm, yellow light. Cate pulled the heavy wood door toward her and pushed the screen door out toward the front porch. The porch light was already on, its glow reaching a few feet beyond the house.

The heat of the day had given way to a breezy, comfortable summer evening, and Cate took a large gulp of fresh air. She walked a few feet into the yard and noticed Maggie's house across the road with its wide front porch. The matching series of windows across the first and second floors emitted a golden glow from inside.

She imagined Maggie sitting down to dinner with her family. She could almost hear their happy conversation and the giggles from her perfect children, a delicious meal spread in front of them. She imagined dinner would end with an hour playing board games together as a family before the kids headed upstairs for their evening baths and bedtime routines. She felt her throat tighten at the profound unfairness, envy burning in her chest.

Cate took a deep breath as her eyes carried her gaze into the inky blue night sky. A single star caught her attention, its light powerful enough to overcome the light of any other stars around it. It had an almost orange glow to it and flickered like the flame of a candle.

"Surrender ..." a small, distinct voice whispered in Cate's ear.

Her head whipped around in the direction of the voice, but she didn't see anything but the surrounding yard, the front of the house, and the tall oak tree. Fear gripped her chest, and she wrapped her arms tightly around her waist. She walked backward toward the front porch and the security of the light, continuing to scan the front yard. Still not seeing anyone, she quickly went back inside, closing the heavy wooden door and turning the deadbolt.

Cate went through the entire house flipping on every light in an attempt to uncover every corner and possible hiding place. She returned to the kitchen and flopped down into a chair. Her heart was pounding so hard she could feel it in her throat and ears. She set her arms on the table and let her head fall to rest on them.

She heard the creaking of a metal spring coming from the back porch. Her heart immediately began racing, her intestines turning to jelly as her head popped up. Holding perfectly still, she looked across the kitchen table through the set of three small windows in the back door. The porch light came on, and a few seconds later, there was a knock.

Cate could see the top of a man's head. He seemed to be wearing a baseball cap, and his head was turned toward the dining-room window.

Cate moved carefully to the kitchen drawers, quietly opening and closing each one until she found what she was looking for. She pulled out the large carving knife and slid the cardboard sheath off, setting it down on the table. She jumped when the man knocked again and then he spoke.

"Hi, um, Cate? I don't mean to startle you ... Father Matthew asked me to come over. I promise, I'm safe." His muffled voice had a gentleness that put Cate's nerves slightly more at ease.

"Yeah, I'm good," Cate answered awkwardly from her side of the door, the knife still at her side.

"Would it be okay if I come in?" the man asked. "Oh ... I'm Peter, by the way," he added with a small chuckle.

"I'd actually rather you didn't." Cate's hand tightened around the handle of the knife.

"Totally understand–I realize it's getting late, and you don't know me. Father Matthew made me promise I would show you how to turn on the furnace–it can get a little chilly at night around here," Peter pressed.

Cate glanced down at the knife. So this guy was another one of Father Matthew's messengers. She knew she could defend herself if absolutely necessary and would be sure she kept her distance if he insisted on coming inside the house. She stepped toward the door and turned the knob, realizing it was already unlocked. She kept a strong grip on the handle of the knife as she pulled the door toward her.

Peter stood at the bottom of a pair of concrete steps leading down to the covered porch. It was attached to the house with two walls of particleboard and a roof angled away from the house, with another aluminum screen door leading into the back yard.

Peter smiled somewhat sheepishly, pulling a hand from his front pocket to offer a subtle wave. His eyes fell on the large carving knife and his hand quickly came out of his other pocket, both now raised in surrender.

"Whoa, I must have really scared you! I'm so sorry–I swear I come in peace," he said, his green eyes twinkling and an amused smile spreading across his face. He had a classic boyish face, but based on the healthy five-o'clock shadow and some faint laugh lines, she guessed he was in his mid to late thirties. He was just average height, maybe even a little short for a guy, with a mostly athletic build. He looked like someone who took care of himself, but with a slightly softer middle, indicating he probably didn't spend a ton of time in the gym. He wore a New York Yankees baseball cap with a curved bill, but she could see thick, dark hair with a little bit of curl peeking out from the sides. He was dressed in navy-blue golf shorts, a gray short-sleeved t-shirt and fashion athletic shoes–the kind that were just for looks. He reminded Cate of the preppy young dads that hung around her neighborhood bar back home, with his casual and confident stance.

Cate looked down at the knife, suddenly feeling ridiculous. Peter truly seemed harmless and might just be the ally she'd been waiting for.

"Oh my god, I'm so sorry." Cate hastily set the knife down on the kitchen table and turned back around to face him. "I'm just really jumpy tonight ... it's been a long day," she said with a sigh.

"Hey, I totally get it. I arrived here several months ago, and it's been ... an adjustment," Peter said, lowering his hands, a dark cloud passing over his friendly expression.

Cate's eyes narrowed as her interest piqued. The cloud passed, and his expression regained its friendly softness, his eyebrows raised in expectation. She continued to take him in, alert to any lingering alarm bells her intuition might be setting off. She desperately wanted to be able to trust him.

"Yeah, sorry, please come in," she finally relented, stepping aside as Peter crossed the threshold. She felt a brief wave of uneasiness and considered leaving the back door open in case she needed to quickly escape, but she dismissed it and pushed the door closed.

Peter's eyes fell to the knife on the table, but he chose to ignore it, focusing back on Cate.

"So, is it okay if I show you where the thermostat is and how you can flip it on to heat if it gets chilly in here?"

Cate nodded, and Peter moved toward a door set into a narrow section of wall between the dining room and the kitchen stove.

Cate wasn't sure about following a strange man into a part of the house she'd yet to explore, but she nodded, gesturing with her hand for him to proceed. Peter flipped a light switch just behind the stove, lifted a small hook from the metal loop in the door frame, then pushed the door open. A set of wood stairs led down into what Cate assumed was the home's basement. As Peter started down the steps, Cate stopped to see where he had found the light switch and was struck by his familiarity with the house. As she followed him into the basement, her curiosity demanded answers.

"So, how do you know this house so well if you've just been in town a few months?" Her tone was a little more skeptical than she intended.

As she descended the stairs, she noted the brightly lit, open area with simple, clean concrete floors and cinderblock walls. Crude wood shelves lined one side of the room, then the wall took a sharp turn into another area that was out of view.

Peter's voice came from across the large open space. He was turned away from her, focused on what looked like the home's water heater and furnace.

"Father Matthew has had me taking care of this place since I arrived, getting it ready for new guests, yard work, minor repairs, stuff like that ..." he responded, then turned toward her. "I just wanted to be sure the pilot was lit on this thing. It can be a little temperamental." He grinned and wiped his hands absently on the back of his shorts. Cate was struck by the sincerity of his smile, and her nerves began to settle.

"The thermostat is actually upstairs in the living room," he said, moving toward Cate and the stairs.

"Oh, sure ..." Cate turned around and followed him back up to the kitchen. She stepped aside as Peter pulled the door closed and secured the small hook. He reached in front of her to flip off the light, and Cate felt his arm graze her shoulder. She caught a whiff of his cologne, a fresh ocean scent that reminded her of an old high school boyfriend she'd long forgotten. She quickly stepped back to create some distance. Peter didn't seem to notice and instead turned away into the dining room.

Cate followed, hope beginning to flicker in her belly.

"So, what brought you here?" she asked, thinking she needed to warm him up before she started asking for his help. They came to the wall separating the living room from the bedrooms. His hand was poised over the small white plastic box attached to the wall, and he turned to face Cate.

The dark cloud passed across his face again, and Cate sensed something deep and painful just below the surface of Peter's friendly demeanor.

"Let's save that story for another day," he said, his voice suddenly deeper and more strained. Cate could see she'd been dismissed and had obviously crossed a line.

"Sure, sorry," she said instead, quickly focusing on her hands.

Peter turned back to the thermostat and briskly walked her through how to set the temperature and switch from AC to heat. Cate could feel that the energy between them had cooled, Peter's tone a little more clipped and businesslike.

"Okay, that's about all there is to it," he finished. "Any questions?"

Cate crossed her arms protectively, stepping back so Peter could head back toward the kitchen. "Nope, I think I got it," she said with a tight, polite smile.

She followed him to the back door, searching for some way to prevent him from leaving before she even had the chance to earn his sympathy. "Hey, I do have one question," she quickly blurted out as Peter was reaching for the doorknob. He turned back to face her, his expression a mixture of concern and hesitation.

"Do you happen to know how I can get the phone connected? I'd like to have some way to call out while I'm here ... you know, in case of an emergency?" she added, hoping to appeal to his sense of chivalry.

She noticed a subtle tension in Peter's stance, and he dropped his gaze.

"Sorry, you'll have to ask Father Matthew about that one."

He pulled open the door and moved down the steps. She watched him push the screen door out into the back yard, and he stopped, turning back to face her.

"Hey, sleep well, okay?"

Then he was gone. Cate lingered in the kitchen doorway for a moment, then pushed the door closed. She locked the deadbolt, her opposite hand sliding down the door frame. She crossed her arms again, suddenly feeling the chill that Peter had warned her about. The knife was still resting on the kitchen table. She picked it up and placed the cardboard sheath back over the blade, returning it to its drawer.

A sob caught in her throat as the weight of once again being alone in a dark and unfamiliar house settled over her. She was overwhelmed by the need to know where Joey was and who was with him. She wondered if he was scared and if they knew how to calm him down. She thought about how important his bedtime routine was and how he must be so confused about being in a strange place without her. She felt the weight of being forced to trust strangers with no way of knowing when she would see him again. All the doors that had been slammed in her face. There was only one way she was going to make it through the night.

There was only one window that she knew for certain would be open.

She began to shiver more violently now and shuffled back to the bedroom where her things were still spread out across the bed and scattered all over the floor. She pulled a sweatshirt out of the pile of clothes and slipped it over her head. She spotted the oval-shaped black cosmetic bag with its gold zipper and plucked it up by its handle. She brought it into the bathroom and rested it on the counter, opening the main compartment.

She breathed a sigh of relief at the sight of the familiar orange prescription bottle. She wasn't sure why it hadn't been taken from her, but she wasn't going to question that now. It had settled to the bottom, and she pushed her toothpaste aside to pull it from the bag. She felt its comforting cool solidity in her palm and sensed a tingling in her forehead in anticipation of the relief to come.

She threw back three pills with water, brushed her teeth, and wiped her mouth on the hand towel suspended from the towel ring on the wall. She flipped off the bathroom light and wandered into the second bedroom. She slowly settled onto the bed, the wave of numbness already washing over her. She felt herself sink into the mattress and allowed herself to float into oblivion.

~ 14 ~

Cate was standing on an unfamiliar front porch, a light summer breeze gently lifting her hair from her face. She was looking toward the opposite end where an older woman was sitting on a wooden bench swing that was moving gently back and forth. Next to her, Joey sat calmly, his legs swaying with the motion of the swing. The older woman was reading to him from a children's book, and he was listening intently, his hands folded and resting in his lap. Cate smiled, and she felt tears well up in her eyes.

Her body ached for the sensation of Joey's weight on her chest, the way he would fall asleep there when he was just a month or two old. Her favorite place to be was lying on her back on the couch with his infant body on hers, his little legs tucked up under his belly, their breathing synced as she drifted into a light sleep.

Cate became more and more aware of a chill spreading across her face, and felt her body curled into a tight fetal position. Her eyes fluttered open, and she was ripped away from the warm, sunny porch, finding herself in a strange room on a bed she didn't recognize. She allowed her eyes to travel around the parts of the room she could see from her position on the bed, noting the icy condition of her toes. Her arms were tucked in tightly against her body, but she began to shiver and sat up to find a blanket. The bedroom was still cloaked in a shadowy darkness from the vinyl shades covering the windows. Her head was mildly foggy from lorazepam, but her situation slowly took on a defined shape in her memory.

She ran her hands over her face, then through her hair. Her heart ached at the cruelty of seeing Joey and being unable to touch him, smell his hair, or kiss his chubby cheek.

The chill inside the house was like a sharp bite to her exposed skin. Sliding her legs to the side of the bed, she stood up and pulled the quilt she had been lying on off the bed and wrapped it around her shoulders, feeling almost immediate relief. She shuffled over to the window and pulled down gently on the vinyl blind, releasing it up to the top of the window. Sunlight flooded the room, and Cate had to shade her eyes. The sun was fully up, but yesterday's lush summer foliage had shifted, the leaves on the trees already turning various shades of yellow, orange, and red. Cate stared out in bewilderment. How long had she been sleeping?

She looked over at the alarm clock, waiting for the hands and numbers to come into focus: 7:30 a.m. She shuffled into the hall and around the corner to the thermostat. The current temperature in the house was reading 55 degrees, so Cate flipped the small arm to HEAT and set it for 70. She glanced out the front window and got a better view of the big oak tree and the bushes that had just yesterday been lush and full of roses, now empty branches clearly dormant for the season. She squeezed her eyes closed and buried her face behind the comforter around her shoulders.

Just do the next right thing, she told herself. Time to get showered and have some breakfast before Maggie's visit.

She leaned over her suitcase, still sprawled out on the floor of the other bedroom, and pulled out the one pair of black leggings and some athletic socks she'd packed for morning walks around her parents' property. Her heart briefly sank with the recognition that her plans had gone so horribly awry and her whole world had been turned upside down. She sighed and pushed away her disappointment, refocusing on the immediate task ahead.

The bathroom was a decent size and had delicate floral wallpaper. There was a small bath rug on the floor against the tub and a fresh towel hanging over the bar on the shower door. She slid open the glass shower door, noting the single frosted window on the outside wall letting in a soothing natural light. It took several minutes for the water to get warm, and Cate finally stepped into the tub letting the water run over shoulders, back, and chest, realizing how much she needed it. Her shoulders finally relaxed, and she wrapped her arms around her waist, bowing her head.

She took this moment of clarity to begin to devise a plan. She would find Joey, get back to their car, and get out of Graypourt for good. She would start with Maggie, quizzing her to figure out if she could be trusted. She hoped Maggie could at the very least help her find a working phone and, ideally, transportation. It wouldn't be easy, but she could rely on her intuition. She was determined to find a way.

She shut off the water and grabbed the towel to begin drying off. Out of curiosity, she pulled open a few of the vanity drawers and noted a hair dryer, an unopened toothbrush, toothpaste still in its box, a small container of dental floss, and a small bottle of hand lotion. She pulled open the mirrored cabinet door to find a bottle of ibuprofen, a travel-size bottle of mouthwash, and a small container of cotton swabs. Her cosmetic bag was still on the counter where she'd left it last night, the familiar prescription bottle resting on top of the other items, its lid haphazardly placed.

Dressed, her damp hair scrunched and taking on its natural wave as it air-dried, Cate hastily brushed on bronzer and applied a neutral eyeshadow, eyeliner, and some blush. She needed to present herself as a sane and devoted mother–not a desperate and deranged mental patient.

As she made her way to the kitchen, she passed by the large front window and noticed a school bus pulled up across the road. She couldn't see what was happening on the other side where passengers were loading, but she assumed Maggie was getting her kids off to school as planned. She felt a stab of resentment as she realized that she would be getting ready to send Joey back to school if they were still at home. Suddenly it occurred to her that this bus could be going to wherever Father Matthew was keeping Joey.

She ran back to the bedroom to grab her purse, but when she returned to the living room, she was horrified to see the bus was already moving away from Maggie's house and accelerating down the gravel road. A lump lodged in her throat, and tears stung her eyes.

"Damnit!" She felt her cheeks flush, and she threw her purse onto the couch. She turned away from the window and fell onto the couch, resting her head in her hands. She leaned back and squeezed her eyes shut. She felt a single tear roll down her temple, and she sat up, angrily wiping it away. She willed herself to move, stood up, and turned to walk through the dining room.

She glanced at the small analog clock sitting on the window sill between the two built-in cabinets. Only 8:30. She still didn't have much of an appetite but knew she needed to continue to fuel her body. She found a box of cereal in one of the cabinets and a stack of bowls near the water glasses. She found silverware in a drawer next to the dishwasher and pulled the milk from the fridge.

Finally seated at the table, she shoveled cereal absently into her mouth, staring out the large window at the opposite end of the table. A cardinal landed one of the small pegs sticking out from the birdfeeder just outside the window. Cate watched as he poked his tiny beak into the plastic container holding birdseed and marveled at the simplicity that was the life of a bird, never worrying about whether your basic needs would be taken care of.

The shrill ringing of the phone on the wall startled her, a spoonful of cereal halfway to her mouth. She dropped the spoon in her bowl and grabbed the receiver.

"Hello?" she answered tentatively.

"Hi, Cate, it's Father Matthew," the familiar voice responded, friendly and cheerful.

Cate was still processing the fact that the phone just rang after she had clearly determined it had no dial tone just twelve hours earlier.

"Oh ... hi," Cate stumbled. "Sorry ... but how did you call the house? I thought this phone was out of service," she continued.

"Yeah, I can see how that would be confusing." His tone was apologetic. "Your house phone can only accept incoming calls," he continued very matter-of-factly.

Cate shook off her bewilderment and seized the opportunity to ask about her devices.

"What did you do with my cell phone? And where is my laptop?"

"Cate, remember when I asked you to trust me?" Father Matthew responded, his tone still kind but firm.

An icy-cold sensation quickly spread through her chest, and her heart rate immediately intensified at the unexpected confrontation.

"You kidnapped my child–how am I supposed to trust you?" Cate snapped.

"It's true that you are temporarily separated, but Joey hasn't been taken away from you. There is nothing I want more than for you to join him, but you still have healing to do. He is not in any harm. He knows that you aren't feeling well and need some time to get better. He's doing really well, actually."

"Why are you treating me like I'm a prisoner here?" she pressed. "You've taken my phone and my laptop, put me out here in the middle of nowhere, and won't let me see my son. How is this supposed to be at all healing?" Cate felt her voice beginning to waver, and her hand was wrapped around the receiver with a vice grip.

"You're not a prisoner, Cate, but some of your choices are naturally limited by your circumstances. You are free to move around, leave the house, and interact with other members of the community here in Graypourt. In fact, I want you to make friends and connect with others."

Cate bristled at his attempt to characterize this situation as anything other than holding Cate against her will after kidnapping her son.

"Why do I need to be cut off from everyone and everything I know?" Cate asked, indignation and anger burning in her chest.

"This is all temporary. You're safe here, and I am here to help you get back to Joey. Look, I know you're only just beginning to get to know me, but please accept this gift of time and healing."

Cate scoffed. "You call this a gift? You won't let me see my son and are holding me hostage. What kind of sick idea of a gift is that?"

Father Matthew was silent on the other end of the line, but she could hear the quiet shuffling of paper. Her temper fumed as she searched for another insult to sling at him.

"I called to let you know that Joey did very well overnight," he said.

Cate's temper instantly cooled. Her hand went to her mouth as tears burned behind her eyelids and a sob caught in her throat. She swallowed hard then dropped her hand.

"Can I see him?"

"Yes, once you've fully recovered–"

"What am I recovering from?!" Cate shrieked, the despair and fear from the day before rising up in her chest.

"We discussed this yesterday, remember? You had a very serious panic attack, Cate. It's going to take time."

"Then let me call my parents to come pick him up." If she was going to be forced to stay here, that didn't mean Joey had to stay, too.

"We are working on connecting Joey with family members so he can go home. Your parents aren't able to care for him right now, but there are other options. Cate, I can't force you to trust me, but I'd like you to at least give us a chance," he finally admitted. "Everyone who loves you is pulling for you to take advantage of this opportunity. Can you just try?"

She let out a sigh and pulled out one of the kitchen chairs, sinking into its thin cushion. She heard papers shuffling in the background again and a distant female voice.

"I also just wanted to see how your first night at the house went, and make sure that your visitor was helpful to you," Father Matthew said, breaking through her despair.

Cate pinched the bridge of her nose as a headache began to spread across her forehead. She knew she needed to respond.

"Oh, yes, thank you. Peter was very kind."

"Okay, good. Well, please give yourself some time to get settled and used to the house. It's your space for as long as you need it, and I want you to feel safe there."

As much as Cate wanted to believe he was being sincere, she still was hesitant to believe that Father Matthew had her best interests at heart. She couldn't stop herself from trying one more time to appeal to him.

"Would it be possible for me to at least briefly see Joey and where he's staying? I'll stay hidden so he doesn't see me ... I just need to know that he's okay. That he's not scared," Cate pleaded, gripping the receiver in anticipation.

"Let's just take this one day at a time, okay?"

Cate fumed. She was not getting anywhere trying to reason with Father Matthew. She desperately clung to the dream she'd had just before waking up this morning as some small sense of control over her connection to her son.

Her grip on the receiver loosened slightly, though another question was still burning in her mind.

"How long was I asleep?" she asked, assuming Father Matthew had orchestrated some kind of additional sedative beyond what she remembered taking voluntarily.

"Well, I wouldn't know what time you went to bed last night, but I hope you had a restful sleep," he answered, sounding slightly amused.

Cate felt like he was mocking her, and she was tempted to snap back at him, but pressed ahead.

"This is probably going to sound crazy, but last night when I went to bed it was definitely summer, then when I woke up this morning, the leaves are changing and the rosebushes have gone dormant," she said, somewhat tentatively, unsure how Father Matthew would react to this observation.

"I guess the seasons do tend to change a little more abruptly here. I should have mentioned that to you yesterday," he said. "Okay, I need to run," he said with renewed urgency. "Take it slow today and give yourself time to get settled," he advised. "Feel free to explore around the house and get some fresh air. I'll check in with you again tomorrow."

With a soft click, the other line went silent. Cate held the receiver away from her face, staring at the numbered buttons as if they held some clue to what she was supposed to do now. Resigned, she replaced the receiver on its base on the wall.

Just do the next right thing. She pulled open a few drawers before finding a pad of paper and a collection of pens and pencils and settled into one of the kitchen chairs. Her only hope of finding Joey was to start asking questions.

~ 15 ~

Cate had just started brewing a pot of coffee when she heard a knock at the front door. She hurried to the front of the house, took a deep, settling breath, and pulled the door open. Maggie was standing there, holding open the screen door, a broad, friendly smile on her face. Cate noted the crisp, cool air and Maggie's much warmer clothes today–cable-knit sweater, jeans and suede boots.

"Mornin'!" Maggie chirped.

"Hey ... come on in," Cate said, opening the door wider and stepping back so Maggie could come into the front hall.

Maggie immediately peeked through the doorway into the living room. "Cute place," she offered, stepping into the next room as she waited for Cate to join her.

"Yeah, thanks ... I guess," Cate said flatly, still feeling awkward about welcoming someone into a home that wasn't hers.

"I'm really glad you stopped by yesterday. Sorry if I was a little distracted. What brings you to Graypourt?" Maggie asked, and Cate bristled slightly, anticipating where her curiosity might lead the conversation. She paused, debating where to start.

"Oh, um ... I had some car trouble, so I checked into the Lighthouse Motel while my car is being worked on," she offered. She regarded Maggie with caution and began gauging her demeanor, trying to determine if she could be trusted.

"Oh, okay ... but now you're staying here?" Maggie pressed, making Cate immediately more uncomfortable. Cate raised her eyebrows, offered her a tight smile, and nodded. The longer explanation would have to come later.

"Can I get you some coffee? I'm getting sort of a late start on caffeinating today," Cate said with a nervous chuckle.

"Oh, that sounds great, sure!"

Cate led Maggie through the dining room into the kitchen and gestured to her to take a seat at the kitchen table.

Maggie remained standing just inside the doorway between the kitchen and the dining room. She paused, looking around, a mildly nervous but pleasant expression on her face.

"I've been wondering what this little house looks like on the inside," she finally said, stepping farther into the kitchen and setting her hands on the back of one of the kitchen chairs.

Cate pulled two mugs out of the cabinet and filled both with the freshly brewed coffee. "Do you take anything in your coffee? I can't promise anything fancy, but I have skim milk and might be able to find some sugar," she offered, turning toward the table and setting the mugs down in front of the two chairs facing each other.

"No, that's okay, I'll just drink mine black," Maggie responded, still standing.

Cate pulled out a chair and took her seat, hoping Maggie would join her instead of looking like she was ready to bolt at any minute. Thankfully, Maggie followed her lead, taking the seat across the table.

There was a brief, awkward silence as Cate searched for where to pick up the conversation after yesterday's brief and somewhat unsettling encounter.

"So, I had a visitor last night."

Maggie was taking a first tentative sip of her coffee and gazed up at Cate, her eyes wide and eyebrows raised.

"Oh, I bet it was Peter?" Maggie guessed.

"Yeah, do you know him?" Cate asked.

"Mm-hmm, he's been here a little longer than I have, so he's come by a couple of times to help me with some things around the house." Maggie looked down into her coffee cup, and Cate wondered what she wasn't saying. Maybe there was something going on between them that she wasn't prepared to share.

Cate was too embarrassed to broach such an intimate topic right off the bat, and the awkward silence returned. She finally realized she was going to have to open up first. She stared into her mug, observing the oily surface of her coffee, steeling herself for what she was about to do. *Here goes nothing ...* she thought.

"I'm not here by myself," Cate started. "My son Joey is here with me, but I don't know where he is right now." She felt her eyes begin to well up, and her chest tightened. She sensed movement from Maggie's side of the table and glanced up to see Maggie's arm stretched across the table toward her, hand extended.

"I'm so sorry, Cate," she uttered softly and sincerely, her eyes becoming teary and her lip beginning to wobble. "I know how you feel."

Cate's eyebrows furrowed, and her eyes narrowed in alarmed confusion. "What? How?"

Maggie sat up straight and took a deep breath, "I've been separated from my Anna, too. I guess I'm on some kind of recovery plan, but so far it's not like any I've ever heard of before. Father Matthew just keeps telling me once I'm better, I'll be able to see her again." She lifted her coffee mug up to her lips.

Cate's head was spinning ... she hadn't even considered the possibility that there were others here in town like her trying to get back to their children. And if Maggie was in the same position she was in, surely she had information that would help her get closer to finding Joey.

"Wait, but I saw the school bus pull up to your house this morning," Cate said incredulously.

Maggie's eyes widened as she swallowed her sip of coffee, "Oh! That's just the supply bus. It drops off stuff I've let Father Matthew know I'm running low on or have realized I need ... toilet paper, warm clothes, food, laundry soap ... it's all provided for free."

Cate's heart sank.

"But yesterday you mentioned other children ... and laundry," she pressed, trying to understand why Maggie would have lied to her.

Maggie looked out the window at the end of the table. "I know ... I feel badly about that." She sounded contrite and turned to face Cate. "To be honest, I was embarrassed, so I just pretended like I actually live here with my family. I figured if you stayed long enough, the right time would come when I could tell you the truth."

Cate held still, her hands wrapped around her coffee mug, hopeful Maggie would continue.

"I haven't been here much longer than you," Maggie admitted. "My husband and other two kids are back at home in Chicago—we have a cute little bungalow on the south side of the city, and I walk the kids to school every day. We have an awesome church community, too, who have been amazing to us, especially in the last six years since Anna was born."

Cate tried to ignore the stereotypes surfacing in her brain as Maggie described what sounded like a perfectly idyllic home life.

"So, how did you end up in Graypourt?" she asked, bringing her mug up to her lips.

"I'm super embarrassed to admit it, but I'm not entirely sure. My memories of what happened just before we arrived are kind of fuzzy—but I do know that I had a really bad week of sleep because I was caring for some new issues that had surfaced with Anna's medical condition. She has a rare genetic disorder that was diagnosed when she was just a few weeks old," she explained.

Cate immediately felt a wave of humiliation wash over her as she realized how quickly she had judged Maggie. A child with a rare genetic disorder? She silently kicked herself for being so inconsiderate.

"I remember I was taking Anna to a new therapy farm that was about an hour and a half outside of the city. I got lost, so I pulled into a small town just off the interstate. We had left pretty early that morning, and I was really drowsy, so I thought I'd just rest my eyes for a minute before trying to get my bearings. So I pulled into a parking spot next to a big park under a shade tree and rolled the windows down. Anna was asleep in her car seat, so I knew I had at least twenty minutes or so. I let my eyes close, thinking I would just take a quick catnap, then we would get back on the road. I dozed off, and when I woke up, Anna was gone."

Cate immediately empathized with Maggie and could feel her heart rate rising with the memory of her own experience just the day before. She couldn't help but be encouraged to know Maggie was in the same position she was in, and she only hoped she could be convinced to join forces in tracking down their children. She swallowed hard, leaning in to urge Maggie to continue.

"I was totally frantic and screaming Anna's name, and Father Matthew came up to my car. He tried to calm me down and told me that he knew where Anna was and that she was safe. He took me to the church office, and I assumed he was going to give her back to me.

"When we got there, he took me into this side room with chairs and couches and explained to me that he noticed that I could use a little break. He offered to let me stay in Graypourt to rest up and said that Anna would be cared for by the best experts on her condition. That was really hard to believe at first because her condition is so rare, but he brought in one of the nurses–I think he called her a guardian–and I was shocked at how knowledgeable she was about Anna's specific needs. She honestly knew more than I did.

"She also said she'd spoken to my husband, Greg, and that after she had explained what happened, he totally supported me getting a break. It was hard for me to believe that Greg would just take some stranger's word–he's usually more protective of Anna than I am–but the nurse was really convincing."

Maggie paused to take a sip from her coffee mug. Cate set her mug down, a look of skepticism on her face.

"How did Father Matthew know how to reach your husband?"

"His cell phone number is printed on the inside of Anna's backpack with all of her medical supplies ... Father Matthew had taken it when he got Anna out of the car while I was sleeping."

"You didn't hear him getting her out of the car?"

"No ... I guess I was sleeping a lot more soundly than I even realized."

Cate brought her mug to her lips, still unsure she was totally buying this story, and Maggie seemed oddly calm about it all. Maggie cleared her throat again and continued.

"Believe me, I was having a hard time trusting him, but when I protested, Father Matthew said that Greg mentioned how much of a toll Anna's care had been lately and there was no other way he could have known that. Greg is the only one who truly understands how difficult the road we are on is.

"Father Matthew said that he would update me regularly during my stay on how Anna was doing so I didn't miss a thing. He said that he would personally make sure that she was content and safe, but I really didn't like not knowing exactly where she was. He just said she wasn't far, and that as soon as I was ready, it wouldn't take long to get to her.

"I pressed him to let me just see where she was staying, but he said it wasn't open to visitors at that moment. Of course, I screamed that I was her mother and that visiting hours didn't apply to me, but he said it wasn't possible.

"I guess he finally wore me down because I was so tired ... I just felt like I didn't have any choice but to comply since he had Greg's blessing, and I didn't even know where I would begin if I tried to figure out where he had taken Anna. If I'm being totally honest, the opportunity to rest and know that Anna was cared for was hard to pass up.

"Father Matthew promised to keep Greg updated on how we were doing, too. I really thought it would just be a day or two. I even handed over my cell phone so I could completely unplug." Maggie sighed and covered her face with her hands.

The similarities between Maggie's story and hers were too numerous to ignore, and as much as Cate hated to admit it, Maggie's experience began to legitimize everything that Father Matthew had told her. Cate softened toward Maggie and started to believe she just might be able to trust her.

"So, how did you end up out here ... have you been able to see Anna?" Cate held onto a shred of hope that Maggie had been reunited with her daughter at some point, even briefly.

Maggie's body language immediately answered the question. She rested her hands on the table, her shoulders drooped, and she stared into her coffee cup.

"Father Matthew brought me out here from the church the day we arrived. And no, I haven't seen Anna since that day in the park," she finally answered, looking up with eyes that revealed a deep, painful sadness. "I miss Greg and my other kids ... until you arrived, I felt completely isolated and alone."

Cate's heart broke for Maggie, and she sensed an opening.

"Hey, you're not alone anymore, okay," Cate offered, in her most soothing voice. "We'll do this together. We'll get them back."

"I've had a few dreams about Anna," Maggie said with a hopeful lilt in her voice. "I know they're just dreams, but it does help me to feel like she's safe ... and maybe even happier." Maggie's face crumpled as a sob escaped her throat, and she buried her face in her hands.

"Hey, hey, hey ... don't think like that," Cate said, leaning into the table. "Anna needs you just like Joey needs me. We're going to figure this out," she added, trying to muster up her own strength as much as she was trying to encourage Maggie.

Cate sat back in her chair and remained quiet while Maggie calmed down, eventually regaining her composure. Maggie straightened up in her chair, wiping her fingers across her cheeks and dabbing the back of her hand under her nose, sniffling loudly.

"Oh my God, I'm so sorry," Maggie choked out through her labored breathing. "That was humiliating. I have no idea where that came from."

Cate offered Maggie a small, gentle smile. "I imagine you've been holding that in for a while," she said, understanding more than Maggie probably realized.

"Yeah," Maggie responded with an amused smile and a small laugh she was able to get out in between the sharp inhale of breaths as she continued to recover. "So much for a nice, composed neighborly visit."

Cate stood up and got Maggie a glass of water, setting it down gently in front of her. She still had so many questions. It was clear Maggie hadn't seen Anna, but had Father Matthew allowed her to speak to her husband? How were her other kids coping? She didn't want to traumatize her any further this morning, though. She figured those details would come out soon enough.

The two women sat quietly together for a few more minutes, and Maggie's breathing returned to normal. She was slowly turning her coffee mug in her hands, eventually letting out a long sigh.

"I think Father Matthew placed me in this house for a reason," Cate started, gently and quietly attempting to reengage Maggie. "Maybe he thinks we can support each other and get through this a lot faster."

Maggie looked up with a half-hearted smile, "Yeah, maybe," she offered before turning to stare out the window again.

"Okay, so what else do I need to know?" Cate asked, thinking she would start with an open-ended question and see what Maggie would offer willingly.

"Um ... oh! The supply bus is for us, too. We can take it into town or to another resident's home."

Cate's heart jumped ... a bus that would take her wherever she needed to go?

"Wait, seriously? Can I ask the driver to take me to Joey?" She couldn't fathom why Father Matthew hadn't mentioned this before.

Maggie gave her a defeated look. "No ... I asked about that after my first few days here. Father Matthew just said that the driver was limited to specific destinations, and he's not allowed to leave Graypourt."

Finally Cate had something to grab on to. She would get on that bus the very next time it pulled up and demand that the driver take her to where Joey was staying. Her mind flashed to the knife she had found the night before, and she realized she wasn't above using force if necessary.

"So, why are we all the way out here, anyway? Is it to distance us from our kids?" Cate was convinced that the kids must be in town, but she braced herself, anticipating an answer she might not want to hear.

"Well, I think it's meant to be restorative. It's quiet out here, so there's lots of time to reflect and recharge. The town is mostly rural, actually, and most of the people live in country homes like this on big pieces of land. There are a few neighborhoods in town, too, I guess for those who recover better with more people around them," Maggie explained, though it was clear from her tone of voice that she was still trying to piece things together herself. "I guess maybe it's possible the kids are staying somewhere near the church ..."

"Okay, that's great! What time does the bus come by again?" Cate was on the edge of her seat. She began to believe she would be reunited with Joey before lunch.

"It comes at random times–since it was just here this morning, I probably wouldn't expect it to be back until closer to Noon."

Cate's enthusiasm briefly deflated, but she would be watching the road like a hawk until she saw that bus pull up again.

"So ... is everyone here recovering from something? Like some kind of rehab town?" Cate was energized by this discovery, and she was hungry to understand as much as possible.

Maggie just shrugged, and her gaze moved back toward the window. She seemed to be shutting down, and Cate realized she was going to have to take it slow. Maggie was traumatized, and the rapid-fire questions weren't helping.

Cate shared what she had observed the day before while walking up the street to the church and taking the short walk to the festival.

"What do you know about the hospital?" Cate asked gently.

"Not much ... I've never been there. Have you?"

Cate wasn't sure she was ready to relive the full details of the previous day, but she had sort of walked herself into it. She stared down into her coffee cup and sighed.

"Yes. I ended up there yesterday after Joey went missing."

Maggie's expression changed to a sympathetic frown. "Are you feeling better now?"

"I guess that's why I'm here ..." Cate shrugged and Maggie just nodded.

"Besides Father Matthew, the nurse, and Peter, who else have you met here?" Cate asked, thinking there might be others who could answer her questions.

"I haven't left the house much, honestly. I just can't seem to bring myself to feel like going anywhere."

Cate felt a wave of pity for Maggie that quickly gave way to a jolt of fear that she would be in the same boat soon if she didn't figure out how to get out of Graypourt.

"I've been thinking a lot this morning ... about how I might be able to find Joey and get out of here." Cate spoke softly, unsure how Maggie might respond to the idea.

Maggie looked at her with a pained expression.

"I'm not sure that's a great idea." Maggie stared down into her coffee cup again, taking a deep breath. "Father Matthew has made it pretty clear to me that ignoring my own recovery is only going to extend the time I'm separated from Anna and my family."

Cate felt her heart sink again. Maggie seemed to be totally defeated, but Cate wasn't about to let her give up.

"Don't you want to get back to your family?"

Maggie looked up, her eyes dull and sad. "Of course I do. I felt like you when I first got here," she started. "I asked where Anna was every chance I got, but the most I ever got out of Father Matthew was that Anna was safe. When I would ask to call Greg, he would tell me that he was keeping him updated. It's useless, Cate. We are totally dependent on Father Matthew, and everyone else I've met is pretty much in the same boat we are. We just have to wait it out."

"But you said you haven't really left your house, so maybe there's someone here in town who can help. You just haven't met them yet."

Maggie nodded but didn't look up.

"Well, I'm not ready to give up yet, and I don't think you should, either. I'm going into town today, and I'm going to start asking some questions."

When Maggie looked up, her mouth broke into a half-hearted smile. Maybe Maggie didn't feel like she could tackle this on her own, but now that they had each other, she saw a glimmer of hope come to life in her eyes. Cate could feel hope start to blossom in her own chest, too. She wasn't alone anymore.

~ 16 ~

Cate watched Maggie as she traveled down the driveway and crossed the gravel road. She let the screen door close and pushed the heavy wood door into its frame. She hadn't been able to convince Maggie to go into town with her, but she had taken down a couple of additional questions and promised to get her some answers.

It was almost noon when she heard the squeaky brakes and the loud hissing sound as the bus came to a stop at the bottom of her driveway. The large carving knife wasn't going to fit inside of her purse, and the more she thought about it, the less she felt violence was going to get her anywhere. If she was caught, there was no telling what Father Matthew might do to her, and she didn't want to lose what little freedom she currently had. She was going to have to rely on her intuition and negotiating skills, both of which had served her well before arriving in Graypourt.

She grabbed her purse out of the bedroom, checked the deadbolt on the front door, and decided to exit through the back porch. She hoped the bus wouldn't leave without her as she followed the sidewalk around the back of the house, down a small set of concrete steps, and down the driveway. There was a crispness to the air, but the sun still felt warm, and she noted the gathering yellow leaves on the front lawn. She reached the bus and the narrow folding door opened. Cate was astonished to see Harvey seated behind the wheel.

"Afternoon!" he said cheerfully.

"Harvey!" Cate exclaimed, relieved to see a somewhat familiar face.

"Hey, darlin', how's it goin'?" he asked with his broad, friendly smile.

Cate wasn't sure how to answer that. Since she'd last seen Harvey, Joey had been taken away from her and she'd been told she would need to prove that she was fully recovered (whatever that meant) before she could be reunited with him. She was exhausted and distraught and had no idea what would happen next. She bit the inside of her cheek and tried to keep the tears at bay.

"Harvey, I need your help ... please, tell me where they are keeping Joey," Cate pleaded, her hands gripping both her arms, a sob catching in her throat.

Harvey looked up at the rearview mirror, and Cate followed his gaze. The bus was only about half full, but every set of eyes was on her, observing her like some kind of zoo animal. Harvey turned his head to look at her directly.

"I'm so sorry, kiddo, I really don't know. I haven't seen him since you two checked into the motel day before yesterday. When I'm not asleep in my bed, I've been here running my bus routes."

Cate considered his face, searching for any sign of dishonesty or evasion, but she only saw those soft blue eyes, and an expression that told her he desperately wished he had the answer she wanted. Her hand went to her mouth as she felt tears spill onto her cheeks.

Harvey looked down and nodded, raising his eyes again with a kind, knowing look on his face.

"Hang in there," he said. "Have a seat. I'll get you safely into town."

Cate paused for another moment and thought about her list of questions, neatly folded and tucked into the outside pocket of her purse. She considered asking Harvey to help her get back to her car, but she knew there was no way she could leave without Joey.

She needed to get back into town so she could start from the last place she knew Joey had been. She reluctantly turned away and made her way down the center aisle, taking the first available seat in the second row.

The ride into town was mostly quiet aside from the occasional crunching of gravel under the bus tires, the groaning and squeaking of the aging suspension, and the high-pitched whirring of the engine as they accelerated.

They made several stops along the way, each one pretty much the same as the last. Harvey would pull up to the end of a long gravel or paved driveway, and someone would be waiting there with a wagon or wheelbarrow. The driver would walk to the back of the bus, grab a box, and bring it out to the person waiting. Sometimes there was a familiar greeting or a polite thank you, but it was mostly transactional. Cate found herself carefully observing each person, searching their faces and wondering if any of them were also in recovery and if they could be potential allies.

Cate found that Maggie's description of the mostly rural lifestyle was accurate. Houses were set far back from the main road on large tracts of land, some with large stretches of carefully plowed fields, their uniform lines fanning out as the bus passed by. Its familiarity was comforting to Cate, reminding her of home, her parents, and Charlie. A gentle smile spread across her face at a memory of a long-ago bus ride to school, Charlie playfully teasing her before erupting into his familiar laugh, and tears briefly pooled in her eyes.

As they got closer to the center of town, commercial buildings came into view on either side of the road, including a gas station, a yard ornament store where Cate noticed rows of figures cast in stone, a vegetable stand, and several nondescript single-story brick and stone buildings.

As they approached an intersection, Cate noticed for the first time a wood carved sign reading "Welcome to Graypourt." She could see the edge of the main square several blocks ahead, and her chest tightened. Memories of the previous day flooded back to her, feeling both recent and like they had happened weeks ago.

The bus pulled up to an elaborate bus stop on one side of a large green space in the center of the town. An angled roof shaded a large gathering area with brightly colored benches, some vending machines, and a couple of small tables. Harvey pulled the handle that opened the door, and Cate sensed the other passengers beginning to gather their things. She made sure she had her purse, then stood to exit the bus. She gave Harvey a sad smile, then stepped down and wandered into the gathering area. As she walked under the large roof, she took a few moments to get her bearings.

She turned and watched several of the other passengers coming down the steps–they were all adults and older teens. No familiar faces among them. Some appeared to have the sort of lost, bewildered expression that she imagined mirrored her own. She began to wonder how many others had just recently arrived in Graypourt. Some seemed to be more confident, comfortable and sure of their steps, and she assumed they were more seasoned residents or maybe even natives.

She desperately wanted to reach out to one of them. There were so many questions burning in her mind. How many had landed here unexpectedly like her? What was keeping them here? Did they also have children being held somewhere–or more importantly, could any of them tell her where the children were being held?

She stood there for several minutes. There was no discernable way to tell which of the passengers were just regular residents of Graypourt, which were in the recovery program, or which might be working with Father Matthew. If she chose the wrong person, would they report her to Father Matthew? If he found out she was disobeying him, would he lock her up for good? She couldn't lose what little opportunity she had to try to track down Joey, so the questions just remained trapped in her head.

She took a deep breath and closed her eyes, pressing her fingers together under her nose. Finally, she decided to just start walking.

As she got past the bus shelter, she realized she was at the park, likely where Maggie last saw Anna. There were just a handful of people, some sitting at picnic tables or lounging on a blanket under a tree. Cate felt her chest tighten, and her heart started to pound faster. She scanned the faces and still didn't see anyone she recognized.

There was a modest playground with a swing set, a tall climbing apparatus of rope and steel, and a couple of rudimentary seesaws made of simple wooden planks painted a soft yellow and blue. Its minimalism struck Cate as somewhat nostalgic of playgrounds she remembered from her childhood, but also a little sad. She didn't see any small children, just a couple of teenagers leaning against the climbing tower and a young man and woman listlessly moving back and forth in a pair of swings. They appeared to be in serious discussion, their faces somber and their conversation quiet.

A man was seated at one of the picnic tables closest to the sidewalk, and Cate watched him take a long drag from his cigarette before blowing the smoke out through his bottom lip. He was dressed in a drab, oversized trench coat, his posture slumped as he leaned into his arm resting on top of the table. He sat with one leg crossed over the other, long baggy pants hanging loosely from his legs. Cate caught his eyes and his sad, defeated expression as she walked by. She quickly averted her gaze back to the sidewalk and picked up her pace.

She continued down to the corner. With no other vehicle traffic, she easily crossed to the other side where she found a clothing boutique, a toy store, a small real estate office, and a stationery store. She crossed the next block and arrived at the Mexican restaurant she had passed the day before. She recognized the brightly colored pennants, piñatas, and an awning in the colors of the Mexican flag and reached for the door.

Cate went inside and scanned the room. There was a small bar on one side with a few single guests seated on barstools and a line of booths along the opposite wall stretching into the back half of the restaurant. Closer to Cate were a few square tables, but they were all empty. There wasn't a hostess anywhere in sight, so she grabbed a menu off the host stand and seated herself, choosing a stool at the narrow bar-height counter against the front window. She scanned the menu and tried to muster up an appetite.

A waitress came up behind her, pen and notepad at the ready to take her order. "What can I getcha today, señorita?" she asked in a flat, Midwestern tone. Cate quickly made her selection based on where her eyes landed last and handed the menu to the waitress. "I'll be back with some chips and salsa," she offered before turning to walk away.

Cate allowed her gaze to wander as she took in the surrounding storefronts and businesses across the street. She noted a bar, aptly named "The Bar," a dance studio, and a law office. One large window stretched nearly the entire length of the business directly across the street, identified by large white block letters spelling out "ANTIQUES."

There were a few people walking up and down the sidewalk or entering some of the businesses. It was markedly less active than when she and Joey had arrived, but she just chalked that up to the cooler weather.

The waitress set a small ramekin of salsa and a red plastic basket of chips in front of her. She also delivered a glass of ice water that Cate realized she hadn't ordered, but she smiled at the young woman in gratitude. She opened her straw and dropped it into the glass, taking several large sips. She absently dipped a thin, crispy chip into the salsa and, popping it into her mouth, then reached back to pull her purse onto her lap.

She unzipped the outside pocket and discreetly pulled out the folded sheet of paper, opening it underneath the counter and pulling it toward her into the light. First and foremost, she needed an ally. Someone she could appeal to who wouldn't take her questions and plans back to Father Matthew. Maggie was a possibility, but Cate was going to have to build up her confidence. Plus, after just one conversation, she still wasn't sure how fully she could be trusted. She knew she was going to have to be patient, but every minute she didn't know where Joey was felt like torture. She wasn't convinced that Father Matthew had actually spoken to her parents, but held on to hope that if they truly knew where she and Joey were, they would come looking for them.

She folded the paper back into its compact shape and slid it into its pocket. She closed the zipper and let her purse fall back behind her chair. She scooped another chip into the salsa and raised her eyes back to the scene outside the window.

The skies had turned to a milky gray, a thick blanket of clouds replacing what had been a crisp, sunny blue sky. Cate thought she saw a snowflake or two, then several more flurried across the window.

Now it's snowing?! she thought to herself in disbelief. She knew that Midwestern weather could be wacky, but this was taking it up another notch. Suddenly, it occurred to her that Joey didn't have any warm clothes with him, picturing his teeth chattering, bare arms poking out of the short-sleeved t-shirt he'd been wearing yesterday, crossed over his little chest. It was all she could do to stay in her seat and not run down the street screaming his name.

She vowed to find a kids' clothing store so she could pick up a few sweatshirts and a coat to drop off at St. Ann's. She would demand to see whoever was taking care of Joey so she could be sure that they got to him.

She briefly took her eyes off the scene outside as the waitress dropped off a green oval-shaped ceramic plate. A large bean and cheese burrito smothered in white queso and paired with orange-colored rice and blended refried beans stared back at her. Steam rose from the plate, and her waitress warned her it was very hot to the touch as she set it down with a thick, quilted oven mitt.

"Thanks," Cate said with another grateful smile in the waitress's direction. She simply nodded and left.

Cate shoveled the first bite into her mouth as her eyes rose back to the window. She paused as a woman exited the antique store, her arms piled with artificial greenery and a paper shopping bag with ornaments peeking out of the top. The woman had thick, tightly wound curls, cut just below her chin, circling her head like a bouncy blonde helmet. She wore a denim jacket over a hooded sweatshirt, along with leggings and running shoes, and she had a petite and athletic figure. Cate imagined she had played soccer or ran cross country when she was younger.

Cate took another bite as she watched the woman pull a step stool over to one end of the window and begin attaching the garland to the wood window frame with a large stapler. When she got about halfway across, Cate saw the woman jerk back her free hand, placing one finger in her mouth as she hopped off the stool and set the stapler down. She appeared to swear to herself quietly while shaking her hand, then looked up to mark her progress.

Was this the person who could help her? Cate's heart raced with anticipation and she placed her hand on her chest, hoping to calm herself. She took a few large sips of water, keeping her eye on the woman across the street. She watched her go back inside the antique store, the remnants of her decorating project suspended halfway across the window and piled on the sidewalk below. Finally, her heart seemed to settle, but Cate had completely lost her appetite. She needed to talk to this woman. She turned on her stool to try to make eye contact with the waitress and spotted her leaning against the bar, talking to a young Hispanic man on the other side.

Cate waved at the young man, hoping to get his attention and indicate she needed her waitress. The young woman noticed his gaze shift in Cate's direction and followed his eyes, raising her eyebrows in acknowledgment. She turned back to him to say something before she headed in Cate's direction.

"Did you need something else?" she asked dryly.

"Just my check, please," Cate responded, reaching for her purse.

"Oh! Your bill's already been taken care of," the waitress said matter-of-factly. Cate looked at her, bewildered.

"Really? I don't even know anyone here. Who–?" she abruptly stopped when a familiar face turned toward her from his seat at the bar. Peter.

Cate made a face in Peter's direction, feeling a mixture of confusion and admonishment. She watched him ease off his bar stool, place his hands in the pockets of his jacket, and start walking in her direction.

The waitress, sensing she was no longer needed, made her way back to the bar and the conversation Cate had clearly interrupted.

"Hey," Peter said, shoulders raised and a friendly smile below his twinkling green eyes. "Hope you don't mind me covering your lunch. I know yesterday was a hard day." The sincerity Cate had witnessed upon first meeting him was back in full force.

"That's really sweet, thank you," Cate responded, feeling her cheeks flush. She busied herself with her purse, tossing the long strap over shoulder and turning to push in her stool.

"I'm impressed you made your way into town already," Peter continued, genuine admiration in his voice. Cate quickly took note of his button-up plaid flannel shirt, the sherpa fleece collar of his tan corduroy jacket and his loose-fitting jeans. He looked like he'd walked right out of a ranch in Montana; all he was missing was the suede cowboy hat. "Where ya headed?" he asked.

Cate wasn't sure she wanted company, and she hesitated just long enough that Peter seemed to get the message.

"I'll just catch up with you later, how's that sound?" he asked, taking a step back and giving Cate nonverbal permission to have some space. She once again found herself desperately wishing she could pull Peter into her confidence, but she couldn't ignore a nagging suspicion he was even closer to Father Matthew than he seemed.

"Sure, that sounds good," she said, trying desperately to hide her disappointment. Cate turned and pushed open the door, quickly making her exit onto the sidewalk. The previously crisp coolness of fall had quickly transitioned to a biting cold. She crossed her arms and tucked them in close to her body, her shoulders hunched as she squinted against the brisk wind. Cate realized she was going to have to find some additional layers for herself as well as Joey.

She avoided looking back into the restaurant window, afraid that she would catch Peter's eyes watching her leave. She instead pressed forward to the antique store to see what she could learn about the mysterious blonde woman.

She stepped off the curb and jogged to the other side of the street, pulled open the simple glass-paned door and walked inside, letting it quietly close behind her.

It was deliciously warm inside the antique store, and Cate paused to let her eyes take in the sheer volume of items surrounding her. Shelves of trinkets and collectibles of various sizes, shapes, and categories filled a set of glass-doored bookshelves directly in front of her. To her right, there was a U-shaped desk with a cash register, a pile of plastic shopping bags, and various point-of-purchase items–gumballs, rubber bracelets, and a bowl of small painted rocks. Cate turned to her left and started walking toward an area surrounded on three sides by tall bookcases packed with nostalgic toys, vinyl albums, old quilts and a small collection of coffee mugs with different city and state slogans on them.

She continued down the makeshift aisle, spotting a familiar blonde set of curls crouched in front of a bookcase packed with old pots and pans and other well-loved kitchen items. The head suddenly popped up, and the woman turned toward Cate, a welcoming smile immediately spreading across her round face.

"Oh, hey! I didn't hear you come in," the woman said, brushing her hands off on the sides of the simple white cotton apron she was wearing.

Cate laughed politely. "That's okay–I literally just walked in."

"I'm Michelle," the woman said, confidently offering her hand. Cate took it, noting the short fingernails, rough skin, and firm handshake.

"What brings you in today?" Michelle asked, grabbing a couple of items off a nearby shelf and settling them in the bend of her arm.

"I'm actually looking for a coat for myself–" Cate hesitated before she could finish her thought. She wasn't sure if she could reveal that she also had a son just yet. She quickly tried to recover, saying "... and maybe a couple of sweaters?" She finished with a slight lilt in her voice, inviting Michelle's guidance to point her in the right direction.

Michelle gave Cate a curious glance but seemed to decide not to press her and pointed down the aisle they were standing in. "I think there's a booth or two down that way with a few things that would fit you," she said. "I'm going to take these back up front to get some price tags on them, but feel free to track me down if I can help you find anything," she offered, then turned to head back to the front of the store.

Cate took a deep breath and made her way deeper into the collection of stalls flanking each side of the aisle. Michelle seemed friendly enough, and hope flickered in her chest. She pulled out the list of questions from her purse as she stepped into a small area with a round rack of coats and sweaters.

She paused and looked down at what she had prepared before leaving the house:

1. *Have you seen any children around town today?*
2. *Yes-what did they look like? Who was with them?*
3. *No-is there a school or children's home nearby?*

Cate's heart was pounding as she tried to anticipate how Michelle might react if confronted with these questions from a complete stranger. Would Cate be able to ask them nonchalantly enough so she didn't come off like a weirdo? She needed a back story-maybe she could pretend to be a teacher who was new in town and looking for a job. Or someone looking for distant cousins she'd never met. She folded up the paper and slid it back into her purse, her face and chest prickling with anxiety. She closed her eyes and repeated her mantra several times before beginning to browse the rack in front of her.

It wasn't long before Cate was headed back to the front of the store with several sweaters and a quilted down coat for herself and a couple of sweatshirts and a puffy winter coat for Joey. She was ready now for the inevitable questions that would come when Michelle saw the child-sized items in her haul.

She found Michelle still at work at the U-shaped counter, peeling small white labels from a stack of sheets resting on the countertop. She turned as Cate stepped up to the counter, setting down her pile.

"Looks like you had some great luck!" Michelle commented, beginning to sift through the pile and pulling off each price tag. She looked up to gauge Cate's reaction, and she offered her a polite smile in return. The light caught a small medal hanging from a silver chain around Michelle's neck just then, piquing Cate's curiosity. There was something familiar about the small beveled oval and the raised image of a woman wearing a head covering and long robes, her hands extended at her hips in a gesture of openness and welcome.

"Your necklace is pretty–what is that an image of?" she asked.

Michelle's hand went up to touch the medal as if needing to remind herself it was still there.

"Oh, thank you! It's a Miraculous Medal of the Blessed Virgin Mary. My grandmother passed it down to me ages ago. It's meant to be protective, but I also just love the simplicity of it. I never take it off," she explained.

Cate smiled, the memory of her own grandmother warm in her heart. "My grandma was religious, too," she offered in camaraderie.

"Grandmas are pretty special that way." Michelle offered a soft smile before she went back to ringing up Cate's items.

Michelle didn't mention anything about the children's clothing and quickly typed the amounts into the register. "Okay, looks like $27.13 is your total," she announced, meeting Cate's gaze again in expectation.

Cate pulled out her credit card and handed it over. Michelle's face fell, and she didn't move to take the card from Cate's hand. "Oh, geez, I'm so sorry–we're a little old-school here. We only take cash," she said, offering Cate an apologetic grimace.

Cate's heart sank. She rarely carried cash and definitely hadn't thought to hit the ATM in the rush to get out of town the day before yesterday. She slowly pulled the credit card back and slid it into her wallet, fighting the tears of frustration as she felt her face flush with humiliation.

"Hey, it's okay!" Michelle responded, trying to smooth things over. "Look, if you promise to mention it next time you come in, I'll let you take these items today and you can just pay the difference on your next visit," she sweetly offered.

Cate looked up, her heart swollen with gratitude. "Wait, are you sure?"

"Totally." Michelle answered definitively. "We all need a little win once in a while, am I right?" she added with a polite chuckle.

"Yeah ..." Cate answered with a half smile. This was her chance.

"I'm new here in town and was hoping to locate some family members we've lost touch with. Have you lived here long?"

Michelle slid the plastic bags stuffed with clothes across the counter toward Cate.

"Yeah, I've been here for a while, but I'm not local. What do you know about them?" She focused on Cate with what seemed like genuine interest.

Cate swallowed and cleared her throat. "Well, I don't have a lot of information, but I know they have a young boy–maybe five or six years old, with dark curly hair. Have you seen anyone like that in the last day or so?" Cate wrapped her fingers through the loops in the plastic bags in an effort to mask their trembling.

Michelle's face fell, and her eyes filled with disappointment.

"Sorry, no. We don't see a lot of kids in Graypourt, actually."

Cate felt a cold wave wash over her. "Like, ever? No children at all?"

Michelle shook her head, her mouth folded in an empathetic frown. "There isn't even a school here. I guess families have all moved away to bigger cities."

"There was a festival down the street yesterday ... there were tons of kids–you didn't see them?"

Michelle stepped back and crossed her arms and Cate could tell she was making her uncomfortable.

"No. I wasn't in town yesterday. There was a festival?"

"Yes, right down the street in the big gravel lot where the coal house is."

Michelle didn't seem to be registering at all with what Cate was telling her, and she started to worry that she was going to tip her hand and give Michelle reason to be concerned about why

Cate was pressing her. Something was very off here. She pulled the plastic bags toward her and let them hang from her fingers.

"Okay, well thanks, anyway. I'll um, stop back tomorrow to take care of my bill. Thanks again."

"We'll see you again soon, okay?" Michelle set her hands on the counter and gave Cate a smile.

Cate nodded, fighting back the tears of frustration that threatened to spill out any moment. She quickly turned and pushed her way out the door, eager to get to St. Ann's.

The cold air smacked her in the face as she stepped back onto the sidewalk. She paused by the store window and dug the quilted down jacket out of one of the shopping bags, threading her arms into the sleeves and pulling the zipper all the way up to her neck. She would have to go without a hat and gloves for now, so grabbing the bags, she slid them halfway up her arm and stuffed her hands into her coat pockets.

She started walking in the direction of the bus stop trying to ignore the burning sensation on her cheeks and ears, and the expanding numbness on the tip of her nose. She squinted slightly at the brisk air, noting that the earlier activity on the sidewalks and the park had almost completely diminished. A few people were milling around the bus stop as she got closer, and she tried to recall which direction she needed to go to get to the church.

"Cate! Hey, Cate!" a male voice called from behind her.

Cate turned around to see Peter's familiar figure striding toward her.

"Hey, Peter," Cate greeted him, trying to mask the urgency she was feeling about getting to St. Ann's, as he came to a stop just in front of her. It then occurred to her that Peter might be able to help her get her bearings.

"Where ya headed?" he asked, hands stuffed into the pockets of his jacket, mildly winded from rushing to catch up with her.

"Actually, you might be able to help me," Cate responded.

Peter's face immediately lit up. "I'd love to!"

Cate was instantly grateful for his eagerness and his practically endless desire to be helpful to her. She could use that.

"I have some things to drop off at St. Ann's," she said. "Can you get me pointed in the right direction?"

He squinted slightly, appearing to brace himself for her reaction. "Actually, would it be okay if I just walk you over there? It's not far, and I need to visit with Father Matthew, anyway," he explained.

The cold air was beginning to seep through Cate's jacket, and the skin on the front of her thighs felt like it was being poked with needles of impending numbness, her thin leggings not up to the job of winter weather. She needed to keep moving, and she needed to get Peter on her side.

"Sure, that would be great," she said, and Peter sidled up alongside her as she turned to continue walking.

~ 17 ~

Cate followed Peter past the bus stop and to the corner where she now recognized the street Father Matthew had turned on the day before. They were back in the residential neighborhood and then climbing the steep hill to the church.

Peter was quiet as the two trudged up the road, her body quickly warming with the effort. He reached back silently at one point, extending an arm to offer to carry a couple of the shopping bags. Cate's heart warmed at the kind gesture, and she realized it had been a very long time since a guy had been interested in taking care of her. As much as she valued her independence, she couldn't deny that it felt good to be considered worthy of a little chivalry. They stopped at the top of the hill, waiting for their breathing to return to normal.

"The office is just on the other side of the church," he directed and started walking again as Cate followed. She decided it was easier to let him think she hadn't been here before and quietly followed him past the church toward the office and rectory building. There were a couple of steps and a small landing leading to the office door, which was covered by a small awning.

Peter approached the door and confidently pushed it open without knocking. "Hey, Annie," Cate heard him say before she had even crossed the threshold. "Hi, Peter!" Cate heard a female voice respond. He waited for Cate to join him inside before he pushed the door closed.

They were inside a small front room outfitted with a few basic pieces of office furniture and plain white walls. A petite older woman with short cropped hair, stylish blue fashion eyeglasses and a friendly face remained seated behind a simple wood desk.

"Have you met Cate?" Peter said, turning to Cate with a look of invitation. Cate offered a weak smile and a single-handed static wave. She was apprehensive and couldn't help looking around for any clues that might lead her to Joey.

"How can I help you, dear?" the older woman asked, standing up but remaining behind the desk.

Cate looked down at the plastic bag hanging over her arm, as well as the two Peter was now carrying. "I have some things to drop off for my son–Father Matthew knows where he is staying," she said, gesturing to Peter to hand her the two shopping bags he was holding. She looked up at the older woman expectantly.

"Oh, okay," she said, holding out her hands to take the shopping bags. "Father Matthew isn't in right now, but I can hold on to them until he gets back."

Cate pulled the bags in closer to her body. "No ... sorry, I mean ... there are some warm clothes in here for my son, and I just ..." Her voice trailed off, and she was fighting back the sobs threatening to embarrass her in front of this stranger. She bowed her head and closed her eyes to try to regain her composure.

She heard Peter speak up. "Would it be okay if we just wait here for a bit and see if Father Matthew shows up?"

"Of course you're welcome to," Annie responded, a tentative tone to her voice. "I never know when he's going to be coming in, but you can make yourselves at home in the sitting room." She gestured to a slightly larger room just through the doorway to their left.

"Thanks, Annie," Peter said, moving toward the doorway. Cate offered another weak smile and followed behind him.

The sitting room had a couch, a loveseat, and a couple of armchairs situated around a sturdy wood coffee table. With its dated floral pattern and worn edges, the furniture all looked like it belonged in someone's grandmother's house. Cate's mind went to Maggie's story of her first meeting with Father Matthew and realized it must have happened in this room.

Peter settled into one of the armchairs while Cate took a spot at one end of the loveseat. She set the shopping bags down on the floor by her feet and let herself settle into the thin pillows at her back.

She sensed Peter's gaze in her direction but continued to let her eyes travel around the room looking for doors or hallways, listening for voices, on high alert to anything that could point her to Joey.

Peter finally spoke up. "You're going to drive yourself crazy. Joey isn't here."

Cate focused on Peter, her brows furrowed, her eyes squinted, and her lip slightly curled in indignation. She knew she hadn't told him about Joey, and it suddenly occurred to her that he must be working with Father Matthew.

"How the hell do you know?" she snapped.

Peter looked down at his hands, and Cate immediately regretted being so quick to attack him. If there was a chance he knew where Joey was, she needed to get him on her side. She crossed her arms and felt her shoulders drop as she sighed. "Look, I'm sorry." She sat up straighter, her hands clasped in her lap. "If you have any information about where Father Matthew is keeping my son, please ... say something," she pleaded.

Peter looked up, and Cate was shocked to see his face shrouded in emotion, his eyes glassy and red. It did not look like the face of someone who had assisted in a kidnapping. She apprehensively allowed her heart to soften some, but remained guarded.

"Maybe now would be a good time to share my story," Peter said, his mouth twisting with the effort to hold back his emotions, his hand moving up to pinch his upper lip. "God, it seems like it's been months now, but it's still really hard to talk about," he added, focused on some spot above Cate's head.

"Peter, it's okay–" Cate interrupted, not entirely sure she could handle someone else's pain right now, but he held up his hand to stop her from saying any more.

"No, I really think it will help," he said, composing himself finally with a large sniffle, rubbing his palms across the tops of his thighs.

"Okay ..." Cate answered softly, unsure what she was going to hear or how she would possibly be able to console him.

"A little more than a year ago, my wife and I lost our baby girl–Natalie." He paused here, overcome with emotion, and Cate's heart ached. "She was only a few months old, so of course it was horrible and traumatic for both of us, but my wife–Caroline–it wrecked her. We totally blamed ourselves, and we were just sure that it was something we had done wrong, something we did that caused Natalie to stop breathing. The doctors and nurses tried to reassure us and told us there was nothing we could have done to save her, but it felt like they were just trying to protect us.

"I watched Caroline fall into a deep depression, to the point that she was barely a whisper of the woman I had married. I was completely helpless. We both went to counseling, and I even tried to go back to work. Caroline tried reconnecting with friends, but none of them understood, and we just couldn't shake the feeling that our life was incomplete in a way that was totally irreparable.

"I went out for groceries one Saturday afternoon, and when I came home, Caroline was in an unusually chipper mood and so close to the woman I remembered. She wanted me to join her in bed, and it had been so long since we'd been together, so I did. After–" Peter looked at Cate at this point, slightly embarrassed. Cate nodded for him to go on.

"Afterwards–she pulled me really close and said she was going to be with Natalie. She pleaded with me to come with her. She said she couldn't stand to go without me, and that Natalie needed both of us wherever she was. She said I was the only one who understood what it was like to be constantly reminded of what we'd lost and know that nothing would ever be the same.

"I knew there was no way I would be able to go on without both of them ... living in the house we had so carefully chosen, believing it would be the place where we would build our family. I would never be able to replace my wife, and I would never be able to accept another child." Peter paused and seemed to be gathering strength for the next part of the story.

"We agreed we wanted it to be quick, we didn't want to suffer, and we wanted it to be peaceful. Caroline had just refilled her prescription for sleeping pills, so she had about thirty days' worth. She figured there was plenty there for both of us, and it would be like we just went to sleep together. So, we poured a couple of glasses of wine and had a nice dinner. We got ready for bed like we normally did, then we each took half of the pills in the bottle, and she curled up into my chest." Peter wiped a tear that rolled down his cheek and sighed.

"The next thing I remember is waking up in the hospital. Caroline was in the bed next to me, but she hadn't woken up yet. The nurse told me that we had been found in our bed by our cleaning lady and transported to Graypourt because it was the only hospital that had room to take us. I'd never heard of Graypourt, but my brain was so foggy, I just sort of accepted it.

"When Caroline and I were both fully awake, Father Matthew visited us. He knew about Natalie and said that our parish priest had told him our story when he called to ask about last rites. He told us that we would stay here for a while to rest and recover–like rehab–then we would be able to go home."

"Oh, Peter ..." Cate brought her hands together under her nose, a heavy weight resting on her chest. "Is Caroline here?"

Peter just shook his head and frowned.

"When did she go home?" Cate pressed.

"I'm–not sure ... I mean, I'm not sure that's where she went."

"What do you–" Cate was interrupted when Father Matthew appeared in the doorway to the sitting room.

"To what do I owe this great surprise?" he said as he entered the sitting room, a smile spread across his face. Cate pulled her gaze away from Peter and stood up from the couch. Seeing Father Matthew again made her stomach clench, and her heart pounded inside her chest.

Peter stood up and turned around, "Oh, hey, Father," he said casually, dragging his hand across his mouth with another large sniffle.

"Peter! Glad to see both of you," Father Matthew said, pulling off his coat and hanging it on a coat rack just inside the door. "How's it going?" he asked, stepping farther into the room and taking a seat in the other armchair across from Cate. His casual demeanor felt dissonant and cruel given the story Peter had just shared with her, not to mention all that Cate had experienced over the last day and a half.

"Please–sit down, guys," Father Matthew invited, gesturing to the seats they had just risen from.

Cate glanced over at Peter for guidance and watched him sink back into the armchair, so she reluctantly returned to her spot on the couch.

Father Matthew's expression remained soft and friendly. "How are you doing today?" he asked, in a tone of genuine concern.

"I'd be doing better if I could see my son," she bit back, emboldened with Peter in the room.

Father Matthew winced just slightly, but quickly went back to his softer expression. "I actually have something for you."

He stood up and headed back toward the front room. Cate's heart pounded, and she looked over at Peter in bewilderment. Peter shrugged his shoulders, widening his eyes and raising his eyebrows in interest.

Cate listened as Father Matthew spoke to Annie just out of sight around the corner of the wall.

"Annie, would you hand me that white envelope over there with Cate Elliot's name on it?"

"Oh, of course," Annie's voice was light and helpful. "This one here?"

"Yes, that's it, thank you."

Father Matthew reappeared and walked toward Cate, a lumpy white 9x12 envelope in his hands. He seemed to be carrying it with reverence, and Cate's heart continued to pound in her chest in anticipation.

He stopped in front of her, still holding the envelope with both hands. "I had planned to drop this off to you later tonight, but as long as you're here, you might as well take it with you."

He held the envelope out, and Cate took it from him, setting it on her lap. She could tell it contained a bundle of smaller items that felt like notes or cards through the outside of the envelope. She rested her hands on it, refusing to give him the satisfaction of looking inside while he was standing in front of her. He gave her a small smile and a nod before returning to his chair.

She heard Peter clear his throat and looked over to see him shift uncomfortably in his chair.

Father Matthew turned to him, sliding to the end of his seat as if preparing to get up. "Peter, I have something I need you to look at–do you have a few minutes?"

Peter looked over at Cate, then back to Father Matthew and seemed unsure where his loyalty lay at this moment. "Oh, uh sure, Father. Whatever you need."

Cate pursed her lips in acknowledgment, noting how quickly Peter obeyed when Father Matthew asked.

"Cate, you'll be okay here by yourself for a few minutes?" Father Matthew asked as he stood up and started back to the front room.

"Yes, of course."

"We'll be a few minutes, so feel free to relax and make yourself at home."

Cate nodded and leaned into the back of the couch. She waited a few beats before her curiosity got the best of her and she lifted the open end of the envelope to peer inside. As she had suspected, a stack of cards in their envelopes were gathered together and stuffed inside the larger envelope. She glanced up toward the opening to the front room, but didn't hear any voices so she assumed Peter and Father Matthew had moved to another area of the office.

Cate slid her hand inside the envelope and pulled out one of the cards. A sob caught in her throat as she immediately recognized the handwriting on the front. She would know that scrolling letter C followed by the "atie" in print anywhere. She quickly slid her finger under the flap and tore open the envelope before sliding the card toward her. She turned it over to see a watercolor print of her favorite flower, the wild rose. They grew in abundance in the tall grasses around the farmhouse, and she would pick a handful for her mom every summer. She felt a single tear slide down her cheek, and she wiped it away as she opened the card.

Inside was a note that struck her to her core.

My dearest Catie,

We miss you and Joey so much. It's been awfully quiet around the farm, and it's given me lots of time to think. I've never told you how much I know you suffered after Charlie's accident, how much of a burden that was on you at such a young age. Your dad and I were so proud of the way you stepped up to help around the farm, never giving us any reason to worry or be disappointed. I realize now how heavy that must have been for you to carry—and you did it for us. When Joey arrived, we were so proud of the way you embraced motherhood, and how you threw yourself into being everything Joey needed after his diagnosis. When Anthony abandoned you, I thought my heart would never recover. But once again, you rose to the challenge and have shown us just how resilient you are. You have always carried your burdens with a grace and strength that is a model for all of us. Now it's time to let those burdens go, my darling. You have healing to do, so throw yourself into that with all you have. Joey needs his Mama and we want you to be together. Dad and I love you so much, and we will keep sending encouragement for as long as you need it.

Love, Mom

Cate closed her eyes, shaking with quiet sobs. Her mom's words meant more than anything to her, and she hadn't realized how desperately she needed to hear them. She didn't want to disappoint her parents, who seemed to want her to see this whole recovery thing through. She read several more letters, including one from her dad, one of her coworkers, Joey's favorite teacher, and the sweet older neighbor lady who lived next door to her and Joey. Each one gave her a little more strength and confidence that she could get through this, whatever it was.

Just as she slid the last card back into its envelope, she heard Peter's and Father Matthew's voices as they returned to the front room and greeted Annie. As they entered the sitting room, Cate slid the card into the larger envelope and rested her hands back on top.

"Sorry about that–it took a little longer than I thought," Father Matthew said as he and Peter settled back into their armchairs.

Cate was silent, assuming Father Matthew was looking for some kind of effusion of gratitude or sudden change in attitude.

"There's one more thing that I think you'll be pleased to know." Father Matthew leaned forward in his chair, his elbows resting on the arms and his hands clasped together. Cate braced herself, vowing to hold it together no matter what blow he was about to deliver next.

"We were able to locate some family members, and Joey is on his way home."

Cate felt an icy wave move through her body, and she closed her eyes in an attempt to ground herself and prevent another panic attack.

"How long ago?" Her head began to ache just behind her eyes, and she was sure she was going to be sick.

"Just before you arrived–I just returned from seeing him off, actually."

Cate's stomach lurched–had she really missed seeing Joey by such a small margin?

"I don't understand ... who will be taking care of him?" Cate's voice was strained, and she looked up with a pained expression, her arms now wrapped around her middle, trying to calm the trembling taking over her body.

"One of our specialty guardians is accompanying him and will make sure he's safely connected with family when he arrives at home."

"The only family he knows is my ex and my parents–can't you tell me who he will be staying with?"

"We've been informed of several family members who are ready to welcome Joey and care for him until you are able to join him."

"Is he going back to Anthony?" Cate suddenly felt a wave of heightened panic, knowing he was in no position to care for Joey full time–if he could even bring himself to make the sacrifices necessary to be the father Joey needed.

"No, not yet." Father Matthew was being so maddeningly vague, and these exchanges were becoming exhausting. "We will continue to get updates on how Joey is doing and I'll share with you as much as I can."

Her mind went to the notes and letters, the encouragement and urging to lean into this time of restoration. She still couldn't release the vice squeezing her chest and turned her eyes on Peter, silently pleading with him. She saw his eyes subtly dart over to Father Matthew, who gave a gentle nod.

Peter faced Cate, his face relaxed and his eyes soft, concerned. "Cate, please try not to worry. Pay attention to the people you meet here, learn from them," he said, standing again and making incremental steps in her direction. "I've learned so much already, and it seems like it is the moments when I'm at my weakest that I experience an eruption of grace." He sat next to her on the small couch. "Have hope, you can be confident in that, and open your heart to what this place has to offer you."

Something about the deep tenor of his voice and the intensity of his words touched something deep inside of her. Cate felt the tension in her neck and shoulders soften, the tightness in her chest lessened, and she leaned ever so slightly toward him. He placed his hand on her arm, offering a gentle encouraging squeeze.

"It could be worse–we could be in some sterile institution somewhere. This place isn't so bad."

She closed her eyes and heaved a deep, cleansing sigh. She didn't want to be angry, distrusting, or scared. She wanted to believe with every fiber of her being that Joey was going to be okay. That her parents had found an aunt or cousin to care for him while she was recovering. She realized that she was going to have to make a conscious choice-either try Father Matthew's way or go insane with worry, anxiety and helplessness.

As if he heard her inmost thoughts, Father Matthew spoke up, "You have to make that choice every single day."

Cate blinked, meeting his gaze, and Father Matthew offered an encouraging smile. He then stood up and moved toward the coat rack.

Cate's breath shuddered, and she bit down on her lower lip. She closed her eyes again as a tear rolled down her cheek. She sensed Peter's hand on her shoulder and looked up to see his face shrouded in sympathy. She glanced at the plastic bags of clothes she had chosen for Joey, considered the list folded neatly in her purse, both no longer needed. She pressed her hands over her face, coughing through the sobs as she released a flood of tension.

~ 18 ~

Cate stepped back into the house, the gray evening light casting weak shadows across the kitchen table. She flipped on the overhead light, squinting at the sudden change in illumination. She had never felt this level of exhaustion in all her life. Peter had walked her back to the bus stop from St. Ann's and rode back with her, allowing her to rest her head on his shoulder as she floated in and out of a light sleep. He squeezed her hand as they pulled up to her driveway, his eyes full of empathy. She only looked back briefly, and he gave her an encouraging nod. She had staggered up the driveway and around the back of the house, entering the covered porch.

She peeled off her coat and grabbed a glass of water before heading across the house to the bedroom. She found an extra quilt in the bedroom closet and threw it across the bed before pulling the covers back and kicking off her shoes. She was so tired, she didn't even need to resort to her pills, collapsing into bed fully clothed and surrendering to sleep the second her head hit the pillow.

A knocking woke Cate from what had been deep and satisfying, but dreamless sleep. She stretched, blinking in the mid-morning sunlight coming through the windows. She had forgotten to close the blinds last night, so the bedroom was soaked in muted winter sun. The knocking continued and seemed to be coming from the front door. Cate scrambled to the living room, peering out the front window. Maggie was there, holding the screen door open against her body as she stood on the stoop. Sensing Cate's presence, she turned and spotted her through the window, waving cheerfully.

Cate pulled open the door, and Maggie tumbled in, seemingly eager to get out of the cold. "Good morning." Cate chuckled, amused by Maggie's clumsiness.

"Hey," Maggie said, somewhat breathlessly. "Do you have coffee going yet?" she asked, peeling off her coat and tossing it over the arm of the couch. Cate was startled by Maggie's sudden sense of familiarity after just one conversation the day before, but found it comforting to know that she felt at home with Cate.

Cate ran her hands through her hair, "Um, not yet–I actually just woke up," she said, grimacing with embarrassment. "Let me throw some water on my face real quick, then I can get a pot started." She started moving past Maggie toward the bathroom.

"Take your time," Maggie said, "I've got it!" She made her way into the dining room, and Cate smiled to herself. It felt like there was a true friendship budding, and that was something she needed more than ever. Between Joey's diagnosis and her pending divorce, her friends had started peeling off one by one over the last several years. She had very few left she could count on.

Seated across from Maggie at the kitchen table, a mug of hot coffee between her hands, Cate shared the events of the previous day in all of its exhausting detail.

"What do you know about Peter?" Cate asked, hoping Maggie had gleaned some insight into Peter's connection to Father Matthew.

"He's kind of a broken soul. When he came to help me get settled at the farmhouse, it had only been a few days since his wife had disappeared. He was still kind of a mess and really wanted to talk about it. I let him spill his guts, but I was still so distraught over being separated from Anna and the idea of staying here away from the rest of my family ... so I'm not sure I was much help to him."

"So, he isn't working for Father Matthew?" Cate asked, leaning forward into the table in expectation.

"Oh, gosh no. He's on the same recovery journey we are. What makes you think he's working with Father Matthew?"

"When we were at the office and Peter saw me looking around he immediately said, 'Joey's not here.' I begged him to tell me what he knew, but that's when he shared his story with me about what happened to his baby girl ... it was awful. Then ... Father Matthew told me that he had just sent Joey back home to stay with family while I recover."

Something changed in Maggie's expression that sent a chill through Cate's entire body.

"I ... think I should tell you something."

Cate raised her eyebrows expectantly offering a nonverbal signal for Maggie to continue. She cleared her throat and looked down into her coffee mug.

"So, when you were asking me about Anna yesterday, I wasn't totally honest with you."

Maggie furrowed her eyebrows and frowned apologetically. Cate suddenly understood.

"Wait ... Anna's not in Graypourt, is she?" Cate felt like she'd been stung. That was twice now that Maggie had lied to her.

Maggie shook her head slowly before looking down at her hands.

"Cate, I'm so sorry. Father Matthew had asked me not to talk about Anna yet, but I didn't know that you had arrived here with a kid, too. When you told me about Joey, I wanted to empathize with you but I didn't want to upset you ... and, I hoped maybe Joey would get to stay." Maggie's expression was sympathetic, and her eyes seemed to be pleading for Cate to understand.

Cate couldn't fault Maggie for trying to protect her, realizing she probably would have done the same thing if the roles had been reversed.

"It's okay ... I understand. Maybe Peter already knew that Father Matthew would be sending Joey home, too." Cate saw Maggie's shoulders relax.

"Do you know who is taking care of Joey for you?" Maggie wrapped her hands around her mug and leaned into the table.

"No idea–but I have quite a few aunts, uncles and cousins, including two who live in Kansas City. One is actually a nurse, so I would be comfortable with her caring for Joey. I just wish Father Matthew would tell me for sure. I don't know why everything has to be such a mystery."

"I would never be able to stay here if I didn't think that Anna is back at home with my husband and other kids, but Father Matthew was really vague about it with me, too. I guess I just sort of assumed. Should I be worried?"

Cate didn't want to cause Maggie any reason to panic, so she just nodded reassuringly. "No, I'm sure that's where Anna is. Why would Father Matthew send her anywhere else?"

"Right?" Maggie agreed.

"Yeah ..." Cate averted her eyes to the window, focusing on the small bird visiting the birdfeeder on the other side. "How do you do it? Keep moving forward?"

Maggie looked down again, and Cate saw her swipe her fingers across her cheek before she looked up, tears still brimming in her eyes.

"What makes you think I am?"

Cate's heart dropped. She shouldn't have assumed Maggie was coping, even though she had seemed so chipper when she showed up at the house. She had never felt like she could understand someone as much as she felt she could in this moment. Tears sprang into her own eyes, and she choked out a single sob, bringing her knuckle up to her nose.

"How are we going to survive this?" she asked through her tears.

Maggie shrugged and extended her hand across the table. Cate reached out and wrapped her fingers around Maggie's hand. They sat there for a moment, their sniffles the only sound across the table. Cate gave Maggie's hand one gentle squeeze, then pulled her hand back, taking in a deep breath.

"What is one of your favorite memories with Joey?" Maggie asked, tentatively.

Cate smiled, sensing what Maggie was attempting to do in getting her to focus on a happy memory. "Oh, gosh ... I think one of my very favorite memories was when he was a baby and our eyes would lock. It was like he could see right into my soul ..." Cate's voice trailed off, and she felt the tears spring into her eyes again. She began to wonder if she would ever be able to talk about Joey without crying.

"That's beautiful," Maggie said with a sad smile. "I had that with my first two kids, and it was incredible. Anna never really did hit that milestone, though. What I probably miss the most is just feeling the warmth of her body on mine. A lot of times, it was the only thing that would calm her. Even as she got older–I'd set her in my lap and let her rest her head on my chest or my shoulder, and whatever was going on, she'd relax and stop screeching or crying. It's probably what worries me most now that she's not with me." Maggie's voice caught in her throat, and Cate heard a loud intake of breath as she was overwhelmed with emotion.

It was heartbreaking to see Maggie in so much distress, but Cate felt completely useless to help her. She grabbed a glass of water and set it down in front of her and, just as she had the day before, she eventually regained her composure and sat deflated in her chair.

Cate was reminded then of her college years–that time of her life when her friends became her family. She never thought she would have another opportunity at a season like that, but she began to wonder if it was possible to build similar bonds from a place of shared pain.

"So, what are your plans today?" Maggie asked, sitting up a little straighter.

Cate sighed, grateful for the distraction. She was going to have to figure out some way to keep moving forward.

"Well, I guess I need to get some more winter clothes–a couple of sweaters and one pair of running pants is not going to stretch very far," Cate said, immediately realizing that she was starting to plan for a longer stay. It wasn't what she wanted, as the ache to be with Joey weighed so heavily in her chest, but she was finally understanding that she needed to be prepared for this to take some time.

Cate looked up from her coffee cup, Maggie's wide blue eyes looking at her expectantly. "Do you think you're up for a trip into town?" Cate asked. "I think it could be good for you to get out a little bit, and it might help build your confidence, too."

Maggie's eyes narrowed at the suggestion, but after a brief pause, she answered, "Yes. Let's do it." A wide grin spread across her face as she leaned in for emphasis.

Maggie helped Cate pick up the clothes and other personal items that were still strewn across the bed and floor in the other bedroom, then she relaxed on the living room couch with an old magazine while Cate showered. Cate threw on the same running pants from the day before, with one of her new sweaters–an off-white cable-knit turtleneck that hung just below her hips. She put on her athletic socks and running shoes and grabbed her coat off the hook by the back door as the two women stepped out into the early winter sun.

Once in town, Cate realized she needed to get some cash before they could go to the thrift store. Maggie pointed her toward the local bank just across the street from the park.

Stepping inside was like going back in time. There was one high counter along the back wall with ornate bronze scaffolding and four arched openings evenly spaced across the entire length of the counter. The bank was otherwise empty, with only one clerk behind the counter. Cate stepped up to the counter and was met by a serious-faced older gentleman dressed in a white pinstripe shirt and red suspenders. He had bushy white hair and an equally bushy mustache. His thin, wire-rimmed eyeglasses were perched on the end of his pointy nose, and he considered her over them as he busily sorted paper checks on his side of the teller window.

"Hi," Cate said, hoping a friendly greeting might warm up his sour expression.

"How can I help you?" the man answered gruffly.

"I'd like to cash a check," Cate responded, bringing her purse up to the counter and pulling out her checkbook.

"Do you have an account?" he asked, still not cracking a smile.

"Uh, no, not here, but I have a checking account back at home," Cate said.

"Well, that is obvious given that you appear to have a checkbook," he shot back, a smirk now appearing on his face, causing one end of his mustache to rise up under his nose.

"Oh, right," Cate said with a sheepish laugh.

"Does your friend here have an account with us?" the man said, looking past Cate and directing his gaze at Maggie standing patiently behind her. Maggie's hand went to her chest, and she said, "Who, me?"

"You're the only friend I see here at the moment," the man responded in his sarcastic tone.

Maggie looked at Cate with a sheepish laugh of her own. "No, sorry, I don't," she responded, "but I have gotten cash here before."

"Okay, then you must have an account," he said. "What's your name?"

"Oh, um, Maggie Peterson." Maggie looked at Cate with raised eyebrows while the man flipped through a well-used paper Rolodex that reminded Cate of the one at her grandfather's old print shop.

"Ah! Here you are!" the man said with an accomplished tone. "Maggie Peterson, account holder since August 1." Maggie's eyes widened, and she looked alarmed. "Well, that's when I arrived in town, but I don't ever remember opening an account."

"It's possible someone opened it on your behalf, but the good news is, if you can vouch for your friend here, I can cash her check," the man said, looking at Maggie expectantly.

"Oh, well, okay ... I mean, yes, I can vouch for her," Maggie responded, with a warm smile in Cate's direction.

Cate slid the check across the counter, and the teller slid it into a slot inside a vintage cash register. He punched several buttons, and a second drawer popped open with a loud *ding!*, revealing piles of cash organized by denomination. He counted out several twenties and fives, sliding them back across the counter in Cate's direction.

She offered him a smile and a quiet "Thank you," to which he nodded and returned to his sorting.

With cash in hand and a bank account in her own name, Cate was finally beginning to feel like she was on solid ground.

~ 19 ~

It was only about a block and a half to the thrift store, and as they approached, Cate noticed the garland had all been neatly hung across the large store window, and a friendly plastic Santa stood just to the right of the main door. She led Maggie inside and went directly to the counter, where Michelle greeted her with a smile of recognition.

"Hey, welcome back!" Michelle said, a wide and welcoming smile spreading across her face.

"Hi, Michelle," Cate answered, still feeling embarrassed about how she had left the store the day before. "I wanted to take care of my bill, but I have a little more shopping to do." she added.

"Oh, sure! Go ahead and look around, and I'll just add yesterday's bill to whatever you buy today."

"Perfect ... thank you," Cate said, turning to head back to the aisle she had explored the day before.

"Hey, sweetie, I don't think I caught your name yesterday ..." Michelle called after her.

Cate paused and turned back to face her. "Oh, geez, sorry! I'm Cate ... and this is my friend Maggie," Cate said, placing her hand on Maggie's back. Maggie offered a polite smile and single-handed static wave.

"Very nice to meet you, Cate and Maggie," Michelle responded with a nod and a smile. "Okay, go! You girls have some serious shopping to do!" she said, waving her hand in their direction.

Cate and Maggie chuckled politely and headed toward the back of the store.

An hour later, armed with several more sweaters, leggings, a pair of jeans, a couple of sweatshirts, a stocking cap, and some mittens, Cate made her way back to the counter, laying her items down to be rung up. Maggie had a few things draped over her arm as well and waited patiently for her turn.

"Looks like you had some luck," Michelle said, a satisfied smile spreading across her face.

"Yeah, probably more than I need, but we found some great deals," Cate said, reaching for her wallet.

"So, were you able to get any information about the family members you were trying to find?" Michelle asked, her voice tentative.

Cate scrambled to come up with an appropriate answer, knowing Maggie had no idea what she'd tried to do yesterday.

"Oh, I was mistaken. They must have settled a little farther south of here." Cate tried to look confident and assured in her response.

"Oh, okay ... so, where are you girls staying?" Michelle asked, innocently transitioning to a more innocuous topic, but Cate was still feeling sensitive about sharing intimate details of her situation. She glanced back at Maggie, hoping she might have a better answer.

"We're neighbors out off of A highway," Maggie answered, and Cate offered her a relieved smile.

"Oh, okay! I know a few other people who live out that way." Michelle continued scanning the price tags, finally finishing up Cate's pile. "Okay, darlin', your new total with today's purchases is $68.47." Michelle looked up from the register expectantly as Cate handed her a small wad of cash.

Once Michelle had rung up Maggie's purchases and bagged her items in the familiar plastic shopping bags, she grabbed a postcard off a small stack on the counter and handed it to Maggie with her bags.

"There's a little holiday music jubilee tonight at the community center–you two should come," she said with casual encouragement. "I play guitar, and we have a couple of other gals on bass and keyboard ... we'll just be doing some holiday favorites and a few original songs."

Maggie looked up from the card. "Oh, cool! That actually sounds really fun." She looked back at Cate expectantly and Cate nodded, her eyebrows raised in polite agreement.

"Awesome, I'll see you tonight!" Michelle said with a wave as Cate and Maggie made their way out the door.

Once they got to the bus stop, Cate turned to Maggie with curiosity. This didn't seem like a time for parties, and she wasn't sure she was going to be great company.

"Do you really want to go to this jubilee thing?" Cate asked, testing Maggie's true intentions.

"I've heard about these from Peter. They're meant to be occasional indulgences to give us a break from the healing and recovery process. I guess it's a night to sort of let our hair down and just be together doing something fun."

Cate's brow furrowed, and a wave of doubt and frustration washed over her. She felt like a true reprieve would be the chance to reunite with Joey, not a night partying with a bunch of strangers. She sighed and stuffed her hands into her coat pockets.

"Do you really feel like doing anything fun right now?" she said, fixing her gaze down the road in anticipation of the bus.

"I don't know ... it's been so long since I've just gone out and done something with friends. Part of me really wants to embrace the chance to do that, you know, even if it's just for one night."

Cate looked at Maggie then, sensing the internal struggle she must be having. Cate could only relate at a certain level with the burden Maggie and her husband must have felt in caring for a child with a rare disease. Before Anthony left, there was one babysitter they trusted to stay with Joey so they were able to get out once in a while, and the daycare offered a "mom's day out" around the holidays each year so parents could get their Christmas shopping done. She assumed those kinds of breaks probably hadn't been available to Maggie since so few people knew how to care for Anna. She drew in a deep breath and resolved to put on a brave face for Maggie's sake.

A few hours later, Cate was putting the finishing touches on her makeup, spreading on a thin layer of lip gloss, and giving her hair one last fluff when Maggie's now-familiar knock sounded from the front room. It had been so long since she'd had this kind of freedom, and she had tortured herself for the last hour with self-doubt about doing anything other than figuring out how to get home to Joey. She buried the guilt and reminded herself that tonight was for Maggie.

Cate grabbed her coat off the couch, sliding her arms into the sleeves as she approached the entryway. She put on a smile as she pulled open the door and found both Maggie and Peter standing at the front step.

"Hey, guys!" Cate stepped out and closed the heavy wood door behind her. The winter chill had really settled in now, and she was grateful for her new stocking cap and the mittens she pulled out of her coat pockets. She slipped them over her hands as they walked down the driveway to the waiting bus.

The three friends chatted casually on the way into town, laughter trailing behind them as they climbed down the narrow steps off the bus to the main bus stop. The activity in the center of town was lively and spirited, the crowd definitely more active and celebratory than Cate's earlier daytime visits. Colorful holiday lights twinkled from the roof of the bus stop, and white teardrop cafe lights were strung across the trees in the park. A thin layer of snow was covering the grass, and the overall mood was blissfully festive. She looked at Maggie, noting the dull sadness that had clouded her eyes since they'd met had disappeared, and they sparkled in the colored lights. Cate threaded her hands through the crooks of Peter's and Maggie's arms as they moved down the sidewalk in unison.

It wasn't difficult to find the community center, as the music was already in full swing and wafting through the open door as people entered. Maggie led the trio into the large brick building, and they dropped their coats off at the coat check just inside the entrance to the main hall. There was an all-male folk band currently on stage. Most of the band members appeared to be in their sixties and seventies and were dressed in plaid flannel and denim, their music drawing a similar crowd onto the dance floor.

"Doesn't look like Michelle's group is up for a bit," Maggie shouted back at them, looking up from the paper program she'd grabbed off a table as they passed. Cate had to lean in to hear her over the music, but nodded in understanding.

"Should we grab a drink while we wait?" Peter shouted, nodding toward a well-appointed bar at the back of the hall. There was a large crowd gathered, some leaning against the bar and others standing at cafe tables sprinkled around nearby.

Cate and Maggie both nodded enthusiastically and followed Peter. The girls grabbed a single cafe table a short distance from the bar while Peter went up to order their drinks.

"It's nice having a guy friend, huh?" Maggie said, giving Cate a wink.

"It is!" Cate responded with a short laugh.

"Heeere we go," Peter said as he set down three small glasses of draft beer in the middle of the table.

"Aw, li'l baby beers," Maggie said sweetly as if talking to an infant. All three laughed heartily, and Peter shrugged his shoulders and pursed his lips.

"It's all they had, sorry."

They each took a small sip, and Cate leaned in so the other two could hear her. "If this ends up being really lame, we should head over to that bar across from the Mexican restaurant," she suggested. The other two nodded, Maggie taking her second sip. She seemed eager to dust off this first beer and quickly had the entire glass emptied. Between Maggie's lingering nervousness about being in town and her excitement about the long-awaited opportunity for a night out, Cate understood her need for the extra liquid courage.

"I'll go get round two," Maggie offered, heading back to the bar.

Peter watched Maggie protectively, and Cate let her eyes wander around the room. It was a standard community center hall with painted cinder block walls, high ceilings with exposed support beams, and a simple hardwood floor. Twinkling colored lights were strung across the ceiling, and a small collection of decorated Christmas trees flanked either side of the stage.

The crowd was eclectic, with plenty of other people near their age, older patrons that she guessed were nearing their eighties, and an even larger group of people that seemed to be of her parents' generation. It made her think of them tenderly as tears suddenly burned behind her eyelids. She took a drink of her beer and tried to repress the thought, silently reassuring herself that she would be with them soon.

Everyone seemed to be enjoying themselves, though she did spot a few individuals here and there who were standing alone, swaying to the music but otherwise somber. As she scanned the room, her eyes fell on the familiar confident stride of Father Matthew as he neared their table.

"Evening, guys!" he said cheerfully as he stopped, opening his arms and gently touching Cate and Peter's elbows. "I'm so glad you made it out–is Maggie with you?"

"Yeah, she just went to the bar to grab another round of beers," Peter offered, as Cate tried to soften her eyes so she didn't appear to be glaring at Father Matthew.

"Great—please enjoy yourselves tonight. It's so important to be in community during your recovery."

Cate nodded, forcing a smile, and Peter thanked Father Matthew as he turned and stepped away, moving toward another table.

Just then, she saw Michelle headed their way joined by two other women.

"Hey, friends," Michelle called out as they approached. Her blond curls bounced happily as she flashed her 1,000-watt smile. She was dressed in a festive "ugly" Christmas sweater that had tiny lights flashing on the Christmas tree emblazoned on the front.

"Hey, Michelle!" Cate responded, holding her hand out in Peter's direction. "This is my friend, Peter."

Michelle thrust her hand at Peter, giving him a firm, confident handshake before pulling him in for a generous hug. Peter planted a kiss on the crown of her head and chuckled as he pulled away, looking at Cate with amusement.

"Michelle and I have known each other for a while."

"I see that!" Cate responded with a small laugh, embarrassed at the envy causing an ache in her forehead.

"These are my bandmates, Cora and Jessie," Michelle interjected while facing Cate, gesturing to each woman as she introduced them. The women were stocky, with close-cropped haircuts and no makeup. Cora was wearing a button-up chambray shirt and black dress pants with chunky black loafers, while Jessie wore a plain black t-shirt and faded jeans with black low-top Converse sneakers. Peter gave each woman a fist bump. Turning toward Cate, they both nodded in greeting but appeared tentative and aloof.

Cate and Peter both turned their attention to Maggie as she returned with three more small glasses of beer. "You weren't kidding, Peter, this is literally all they have unless you want some nasty well liquor," she said as she approached, suddenly noticing Michelle and the other two women standing nearby.

"Oh, hey!" Maggie said, wiping her hands on the sides of her jeans.

"These are Michelle's bandmates, Cora and Jessie," Cate explained, and Maggie's eyebrows rose in acknowledgment.

"Awesome, great to meet you both!" she shouted across the table, taking a generous swig of her beer.

The folk band ended their song, and the reverberating absence of music echoed in Cate's ears. She looked up to see the band members packing up their instruments and waving to the small group gathered in front of the stage. There was another group waiting at the bottom of the steps to the stage who looked to be middle-aged men and women, all wearing mostly dark clothing. She wondered what kind of music they were in for next.

Michelle, Cora, and Jessie stuck around through the next band's first set, a moody acoustic rock, and a couple more rounds of beers, then excused themselves to get ready. Cate, Peter, and Maggie were on their fourth round of beers by now, and the familiar warm buzz was beginning to blossom in Cate's head.

"Hey guys, I'm going to go find the bathroom," she said, finally able to speak without shouting over the music.

"I'll come with you," Maggie said, looping her arm through Cate's.

They exited the main hall and navigated a wide hallway where they finally found the door to the women's bathroom. There were several other women at the sinks washing their hands, and Cate and Maggie separated into two empty stalls. Cate sensed the familiar fogginess and fixed stare of drunkenness as she emptied her bladder. She had not intended to let herself indulge quite this much and knew she needed to slow it down when they got back to the main hall.

She exited her stall and had washed and dried her hands but didn't see Maggie. She walked over to the stall she thought she had gone into and spoke discreetly into the gap in the door.

"Mags? You okay?"

"Mm-hmm ... I'll be out in a minute," Maggie said with a loud hiccup. Cate smiled to herself, glad that Maggie was letting go.

"Okay, I'll just be in the hallway waiting for you."

"'Kay, thanks," she slurred back.

Cate stood in the darkened hallway, leaning against the wall with her hands tucked under her lower back. A couple more women entered the bathroom, then she spotted Father Matthew coming down the hallway. Their eyes met, and he smiled as he walked toward her with intention.

"Just the person I was looking for," he said. Cate's brow furrowed in confusion, and she stood up straight.

"What do you mean?"

"Well, tonight is about indulgences, and I realize that means a little something different for everyone."

Cate swallowed hard and regarded him with trepidation. "Yes, it does."

Father Matthew pulled a cell phone from his pocket, and Cate's heart leaped into her throat. She immediately recognized the familiar clear case with the gold glitter, and tears sprang into her eyes. Father Matthew held it out to her, and she looked at him in disbelief.

"Go ahead, you can take it," he said, gesturing toward her with the phone.

Cate took it from him and tapped on the screen, which immediately lit up with the image of Joey's face, frozen in time in a rare wide-mouth grin. It was her favorite photo of him from last year, and seeing it brought a flood of emotions. She sniffled and wiped several tears from her cheeks. Her eyes quickly flitted to the cell signal and Wi-Fi icons, and her heart sank at the SOS staring back at her.

"Still no signal?" she said with dismay.

Her screen was limited to one page, and only a few of her apps were visible. It looked like it had been completely wiped except for her settings, phone, text, calendar, clock, and photos icons.

"Open up your photos and click on the most recent video," Father Matthew prompted her gently.

Cate did as he asked, watching all of her photos populate in miniature. She resisted scrolling through the entire gallery and clicked on the last item, holding her breath as the still image expanded on the screen. She saw a living room awash in sunlight, vaguely familiar to her, but she wasn't able to place it. She clicked on the play button and turned the volume up to its full level. Her hand flew to her mouth as she watched Joey enter the room. The camera followed him to a small upright piano against one wall, and he settled onto the simple wood bench, placing his hands on the center keys.

The song began slowly, the tune unfamiliar to her, but beautifully melodic. Joey's playing was controlled and graceful, and Cate watched in awe as the tempo picked up and his fingers moved expertly up and down the keyboard. Everything else about him was the Joey she knew, but this new skill also made him seem distant and strange to her. The hollow spot in her chest ached to be near him, to know this part of his life. She could no longer control the sobs, and the image began to blur as she continued watching through her tears.

The clip ended and Cate pushed play one more time, watching the entire video as tears rolled down her cheeks. When it ended again, Cate looked up at Father Matthew.

"Joey's guardian mentioned to me this morning that he's taken an interest in the piano. Did you know he wanted to play?"

Cate tried to process the cascade of emotions this new information set off–pride, envy, disappointment, inadequacy. How could she not have known that her little boy wanted to play the piano?

"Um, no ... I didn't know that," she said quietly.

Cate thought about how many opportunities she had wasted to expand Joey's world and introduce him to things that could have made him happy. Her stomach hardened like she had swallowed a large rock. She took a deep breath and released a heavy sigh.

"Thank you," she said barely above a whisper. "Can I keep this?"

"Of course. You can watch the video anytime you want, and you have access to any other photos and videos stored on your phone, too." Father Matthew pulled a charger and cord from his pocket and Cate gratefully took it from him, dropping it into her purse.

"You have no idea how much this means to me. Thank you so much." Cate hugged the phone to her chest in a gesture of gratitude and pleasure. She allowed herself to bask in the glow of this incredible gift and watched the video several more times after Father Matthew walked away until Maggie finally emerged from the bathroom.

She wasn't sure why, but she quickly buried the phone in her purse. She didn't know how Maggie might react since she didn't get a similar gift from Father Matthew. Thankfully, Maggie's current state of mind made her completely oblivious to Cate's actions.

Cate flashed her a smile and offered her arm. "Shall we?"

Back in the main hall, Michelle's band was just taking the stage. They started right in with "Rockin' Around the Christmas Tree," immediately getting the attention of the crowd, whose inhibitions were now well-lubricated. Maggie grabbed Cate's hand and began pulling her toward the stage. Cate had just enough time to reach back for Peter's arm as they passed their table, catching him so he had to reluctantly follow behind, rolling his eyes as Cate threw her head back with laughter.

~ 20 ~

Maggie and Peter lounged on the couch in Cate's living room while she toweled off her hair in the steam-filled bathroom. She knew she was going to make them late, but she had only learned about the assembly when Father Matthew called the house this morning with his daily update on Joey. She'd hardly slept, spending most of the night after they'd gotten home from the jubilee scrolling through her photos and videos, reliving memories from the last six months before they had arrived in Graypourt. Her only regret was seeing the screenshots of text messages from Anthony that she had captured to send to her lawyer.

"Cate! Are you almost ready?" Maggie's voice called from the living room at roughly a three-out-of-five on the urgency scale.

"Sorry! Coming!" Cate called back, her voice muffled through the hollow bathroom door. She tousled her hair a bit more, satisfied that her natural wave gave it just enough style that it didn't look like she'd done completely nothing with it. She flipped her toothbrush back and forth in her mouth as she quickly pulled on jeans and a gingham flannel shirt that hung right at her thighs, slipped into her boots, spit the toothbrush into the sink ,and flung open the bathroom door.

Peter and Maggie lifted themselves from the couch, both failing miserably at hiding their impatience.

"The bus is waiting," Peter said, pulling open the front door and waiting for Cate and Maggie to follow. Cate grabbed her coat from the closet and joined Maggie and Peter on the front porch. They hurried down the driveway, careful to avoid the patches of black ice, and climbed the steps into the bus. Cate shot Harvey an apologetic smile.

"Thanks for holding the bus, Harv," she said as sweetly as she could.

Cate dodged the irritated looks of other passengers as she moved down the aisle watching for the first open seat.

"Sorry ... sorry," she muttered to each person whose gaze she met, finally slipping into a seat next to Maggie.

She leaned over to Maggie, whispering, "So, *why* is everyone so obsessed about getting to the assembly?" she asked, a twinge of sarcasm in her voice.

Maggie shrugged and leaned forward, turning toward the aisle where Peter was seated on the other side.

"Peter ... Cate wants to know why everyone is so obsessed about getting to the assembly," she practically announced, forcing a couple of dirty looks from other passengers who turned to see where the question came from.

Cate sunk down into her seat before turning her head toward Peter in anticipation. Peter leaned forward just slightly, keeping his voice lowered.

"Father Matthew hands out assignments to take care of various things around Graypourt–the assignments are given out at random, so the closer you sit in the front, the better your odds of getting one of the first assignments, which are usually the cushier jobs. It can be the difference between dusting church pews and collecting garbage in the park."

Cate nodded with her eyebrows raised. Work was something familiar, and she knew she could make a good impression on Father Matthew. She felt oddly excited about having an actual job to do and just hoped it would help the time pass even faster. Maybe if she really applied herself, she could expedite her way out of Graypourt.

The bus pulled up to the community center, and Cate could see people streaming into the series of wide double doors with no particular sense of order. Maggie nudged her to get up, so she moved into the aisle and followed the other passengers off the bus and into the parking lot.

There was an air of urgency and anticipation from the group as they moved toward the community center doors. A couple of the other bus passengers moved around Cate, one gently bumping her shoulder as he moved past her. Peter had walked in ahead of them, so Cate stuck close to Maggie, both of them doing their best to keep him in their line of sight.

Once inside, Cate searched the crowded hall for Peter's head of thick brown hair. The hall had a distinctly different vibe from the last time they'd been there for the jubilee. It was bathed in warm fluorescent light, the air thick with body heat. There were people everywhere. About half were already seated, and the rest were either standing in the back scanning the room or moving with purpose down the aisles and rows of chairs.

She felt Maggie grab her arm and start pulling her down one of the aisles between the sea of folding chairs. There was a steady, deliberate hum of voices as people tried to talk over each other and carry on conversations among the din.

"I see him," Maggie called over her shoulder to Cate, weaving with determination through the other people clogging the aisle.

They stopped at a row on their left about halfway toward the front. Maggie kept a strong grip on Cate's arm as they climbed over the people already seated, who pulled up their knees or shifted to the side so they could pass. Cate glanced up to see Peter beckoning them on with his hand, gesturing to the three seats he had secured together.

Father Matthew's familiar figure approached the steps leading up the stage, and he confidently strode across stopping at the podium.

"Good morning, Graypourt!" His voice broke through the hum of chatter and shifting bodies. "Welcome to our semi-regular resident assembly. If this is your first time with us, we welcome you especially warmly and with the highest level of hospitality."

Cate let her gaze wander to the short row of people seated behind Father Matthew and facing the crowd as a few of them nodded in agreement, their expressions soft and filled with kindness. Harvey was there, as well as Miss Henny from the diner and Annie from the office at St. Ann's.

"Today's assembly is an opportunity for you all to find simple purpose here in Graypourt. We know that contributing to the community is a crucial part of your recovery and helps in building relationships with the other residents."

"All right," Father Matthew said, shifting to a more upbeat tone, "Let's get to our assignments!" A soft murmur blossomed as the crowd shifted in anticipation. Father Matthew deployed each of the four people behind him into the crowd, where they lined up in front of each of the four aisles between the rows of chairs.

The room buzzed briefly as new residents leaned over to neighbors or friends for clarification on where they should go or when they would be dismissed.

"First up is the cleaning crew for St. Ann's," at this he paused, and Cate could see the entire first row rise from their chairs and follow Harvey down the aisle farthest from them to the back of the hall.

Father Matthew continued to announce various assignments, from trash pick up at the park to sidewalk maintenance and supply warehouse support. Finally, he came to the row that Peter, Maggie and Cate were seated in.

"Next up is restaurant and retail support." Cate looked down the aisle and saw Annie hold up a hand and gesture to their row to stand up and follow her out. Cate glanced back at Maggie and

Peter as they all rose out of their seats, her skin prickling with anticipation.

They traveled down a wide hallway to a smaller auxiliary hall, where they found a table with the "R" assignments, and each grabbed a sheet with their instructions. They were quickly ushered out into another corridor and back to the parking lot.

"Well, looks like we're about to be gainfully employed," Cate announced to both Peter and Maggie, feeling oddly excited and satisfied. A darkness nagged at her as well, and her smile faded as she slowly realized that this meant she was becoming a contributing member of this community and wouldn't be leaving any time soon.

~ 21 ~

Maggie, Peter, and Cate were gathered around Maggie's kitchen island with steaming mugs of coffee in front of them and heavy snow falling outside the large window over Maggie's kitchen sink. They had all been sent home early from their assignments when the winter weather moved in, and they ended up at Maggie's discussing the best way to spend the rest of the day.

"I mean, there's always laundry," Maggie said flatly.

Cate looked up from her coffee mug and grimaced. "I barely have to do laundry once a week and just washed all my towels yesterday."

"I have a few houses to stop by for Father Matthew later," Peter said, bringing his mug to his lips and taking a tentative sip.

"In this weather?" Maggie chuckled, gesturing with her thumb toward the kitchen window.

"Yeah, Father has a SUV he sends over that handles really well in the snow. His driver has plenty of experience, too."

Cate bristled hearing that Peter had a private driver to take him around on Father Matthew's command. She wondered if it was the same man who'd driven her here from the hospital. Questions suddenly swirled around in her head.

"What exactly is your connection to Father Matthew?" Cate asked pointedly.

Peter looked at her with hurt confusion. "My connection?" he repeated, with a tightness to his voice.

Cate could tell she had offended him, which immediately made her second-guess her intuition.

"Sorry ... I just ... I don't know, it's curious to me that Father Matthew has you running around doing his bidding ..."

"Doing his bidding? Geez, Cate ..." Peter's face darkened, and Cate's heart sank.

Maggie sat quiet and still on the other side of the kitchen island, her gaze locked on her hands, which were splayed out flat on the butcher-block counter. Cate could tell she wasn't going to get any help from her, so she tried a softer approach.

"I think it's great that you're so helpful and generous–I know I appreciate it more than I've said." Cate placed her hand on her chest in a gesture of sincerity.

Peter turned his head and gave her a half smile, and she pressed on.

"I guess I'm just wondering how close you are to Father Matthew."

She paused there, watching Peter's body language. He sat up a little straighter and pressed his palms against the edge of the counter, drumming his fingers a few times.

"You think I'm a pushover?" he said, turning to look at her, his face tight and his eyes narrowed.

"What? No! I'm just trying to understand your relationship with Father Matthew. He seems to really trust you ... and I just ... I wonder what else you might know."

Peter's shoulders seemed to relax, and his face softened.

"Cate ... I don't know anything about Joey. I don't know why you think I do. Don't you know I would tell you if I had any idea how you could get back to him?" Peter's eyes reddened, and Cate felt her throat tighten with emotion.

"You've been here longer than us, and Father Matthew seems to trust you with access to a lot of places in Graypourt ... it just seems like you might have learned something that would give some clues about how to get out of here."

Cate could feel her eyes filling with tears, and she tried to blink them back. She shifted her gaze to Maggie, hopeful that she would jump in and put some added pressure on Peter.

"Cate ... I really don't think Peter knows anything," Maggie said softly, empathy filling her eyes. "I feel like he would have said something to me by now ... I talked his ears off about Anna when I first arrived, and I never once felt like he knew something he wasn't saying."

Cate began to wilt with resignation. She turned back to Peter, feeling small and uncertain.

"Cate, I know what it feels like to lose a child, and I can only imagine how it would feel to know Natalie is at home but not be able to get to her. Please believe me that if I could tell you how to get home to Joey, I would do it in a heartbeat."

Peter's eyes were pleading with her now, and Cate's heart shattered. How could she have been so selfish? Of course Peter would be empathetic to anyone else that had lost a child. She had no reason to believe that he would withhold such important information. Peter cleared his throat and leaned his forearms onto the counter.

"One of my first assignments here was helping out with different maintenance needs at Father Matthew's office and at the church." Peter's gaze was focused on a spot on the center of the counter. "I guess he thought I was decently handy and decided I could be helpful in other places, so it just kind of naturally happened. He would call me when someone new arrived and ask me to look into one thing or another in whatever home or apartment they had been placed in.

"Maggie was actually the first person I met who had arrived in Graypourt with a child." Peter looked up at Maggie, and Cate caught his smile in profile. She looked over to see Maggie returning a grateful smile to him.

"I had no idea what you had been through at that point," Maggie recalled. "I was so focused on my own situation, and you just sat there listening like you didn't have anywhere else to be."

"I mean, to be honest, I didn't have anywhere else to be at that moment ... your house was the only one Father Matthew sent me to that day." Peter chuckled, and Cate and Maggie joined in.

The tension in the room seemed to finally fizzle out, and Cate wrapped her hands around her now cooled mug.

"Listen, the fact is, Father Matthew is just as mysterious to me as he is to everyone else," Peter added. "He's taken good care of me, made sure I have everything I need. Our relationship has evolved a lot since I first arrived in Graypourt, but being available when he needs help doesn't come with any special benefits."

Cate nodded, taking in Peter's sincere gaze. She had to pull her eyes away and refocus on her mug, the shame and uncertainty suddenly overwhelming her.

"Did you say you have a relationship with Father Matthew?" she asked quietly.

"Yeah ... I think that's really all he wants from any of us."

Cate closed her eyes, battling the urge to push back with all the reasons she would never accept any kind of relationship with Father Matthew. Silence weighed heavy over them.

"Soooo ... tell me how your first days went!" Maggie interjected brightly, clearly trying to ease the tension between them.

The sudden change in topic left Cate feeling unsatisfied, but she understood the need to shift focus. They had all started their new assignments the day before, and Cate had been eager to hear how it had gone for them, too.

Cate stood up and went to refill her mug and warm up the now cold remains of her first cup of coffee.

"Mine was good," she started flatly. "I ended up at the Blue Bird Diner with Miss Henny." She eased into a wide smile. "She has me helping out in the bakery, so I set up the bakery case, washed a bunch of pans and trays, and learned how to frost sugar cookies. She let me bring some home for dessert tonight." Cate winked at Maggie, knowing frosted sugar cookies were her favorite.

Maggie leaned forward with wide eyes, slapping both hands on top of the counter.

"Oh my gosh! Yes!" She brought her mug to her lips and took a sip, looking up at Peter.

"How about you, Stretch?" She used her favorite nickname for Peter, meant to poke fun at his shorter stature.

Peter chuckled at the reference.

"It was a pretty slow day at The Bar, actually." He took a sip of his coffee before continuing. "We did a lot of cleaning, and I helped Joe with some of his invoicing and other paperwork. I'll see more customers when I work Friday night."

"How was your day, Mags?" Cate looked at Maggie while reaching for a muffin in the center of the island.

"Meh, it was fine." Maggie laid her hands in her lap as she sat slouched slightly on her stool.

"It's strange to me that Graypourt has a children's clothing and toy store when there aren't any children to take care of." She looked down at her lap, and Cate flinched at the irony of this statement, considering the conversation they'd just had. She also had to agree that her assignment seemed like a particularly cruel and pointless one.

"Caroline worked there just before–" Peter cut himself off, clearing his throat and staring into his mug.

Cate looked at him with concern and anticipation. He gave her a sad smile.

"Sorry ... that was the last place Caroline worked before she left Graypourt."

Cate looked at Peter, her heart aching for him and the loss he felt. She gave him an encouraging nod, then looked over at Maggie, who was listening intently. Peter looked down at his hands before taking a deep breath.

"She really struggled with working there–she hated having to see the little baby clothes and shoes the most. It was torture, really. She tried to ask Father Matthew to reassign her, but he told her she would have to wait until the next assembly. She became really distant and cold, and I thought she was going to spiral again. But then she started to gain more and more confidence the longer she worked there. She started to fully dive in and found a passion for the display window at the front of the store."

Peter looked up at this point, the memory casting a warm glow to his face, his eyes bright and twinkling.

"I remember the Easter display she worked on right before she left … she created little bunnies out of the baby blankets and had buckets of painted wood eggs that she had worked on at home for weeks. It really seemed to bring her peace. Everyone was talking about it and how much joy it brought them–I'd never seen her so happy." He looked down again, and Cate thought she saw a single tear drop onto his shirt.

"She became super driven, like the work was feeding something inside of her, but she was still really distant with me. I felt like she was keeping all of this newfound peace and happiness to herself. So I tried to get her to open up by asking her what had changed.

"She told me that she had just realized one day that when she allowed herself to let go of the pain she had been holding so close to her heart, everything around her softened. Where there had been cold, hard edges and corners, now she could feel warmth, quiet, and light. When she looked at the stuffed animals and little flowered sleepers, she only saw the happy memories with Natalie. The pain just started to melt away. The more she trusted her assignment, the easier the work was.

"But … she said I had become a constant memory of the pain. It broke my heart. I wanted so badly to feel what she was feeling, and it just wasn't happening like that for me."

Cate felt tears burning behind her eyelids, and she instinctively blinked, forcing one to slide down her cheek. She quickly moved to wipe it away. Peter's face was tight, and she could see how hard he was fighting through the pain of this memory.

"I can't ever forget what she said to me that last night after we climbed into bed." Peter's face softened, and he lifted his head, eyes gently closed. "She said, 'I think I've finally accepted that Natalie had to go before us.' She said we weren't being punished … and what an honor it had been to get to love her."

His face fell, and he brought his hands up to cover his eyes and nose, pulling them down over his mouth, then dropping them into his lap.

"She was gone the next morning." Cate watched Peter's shoulders droop then he raised his head and met her gaze, his eyes pools of anguish.

"After everything we'd been through, I couldn't believe that she could leave me all alone." Peter's face collapsed, and he released several coughing sobs. Cate stood up and wrapped her arms around his shoulders, allowing him to rest his head just below her chest. He brought his hands around her waist, holding on as if she was the only thing keeping him afloat.

"Peter, I'm so sorry …"

A sniffle came from the end of the counter where Maggie was sitting, and Cate looked over to see her wiping her cheeks quickly before bringing her napkin to her nose.

"It's so unfair," she said, her voice wobbly with emotion.

Cate released her arms and stepped back, crossing them over her chest. Peter lifted his head and gave Maggie a sad smile.

"What's more unfair? That she left, or that she didn't take me with her?" His voice was raw and vulnerable.

"I think both ... How do you keep going?" Maggie pressed. Cate imagined she must be thinking of Greg and how she might respond if he left her here by herself.

"I guess I keep going ... I stay ... because I still want to believe she's coming back for me."

Maggie raised her eyebrows and frowned in sympathy. Peter turned to Cate.

"Remember when you asked me when Caroline got to go home?"

Cate nodded, returning to her stool.

"I said I wasn't sure if 'home' is where she went because ... well, because I couldn't feel her anymore." He looked at her with a pained look in his eyes. "I just knew that if she was back in our home, I would know somehow. But it's like there's this blank space where I used to feel her–here," Peter pointed to his heart, a tear sliding down his cheek.

Cate's heart swelled with the need to pull him close to her again. Even though she was only just beginning to get to know him, she felt like they had bonded quickly over their shared pain. It was heartbreaking to watch this man fall apart in front of her, and she found herself drawn in by his vulnerability, overwhelmed with a need to take his pain away. It was getting harder to deny it ... she wanted to fill that blank space in his heart.

~ 22 ~

As the weeks passed, the days fell into a familiar rhythm. Cate usually had coffee and breakfast with Maggie, sometimes joined by Peter, usually at either Cate's place or Maggie's. The only exception was Sunday, when Maggie and Peter seemed to prefer to sleep in and wait to get together until later in the day. They went into town a few times each week to complete their assignments, pick up things they needed, or just be around other people, which usually meant hanging out at The Bar.

Father Matthew would stop by Cate's house at irregular intervals, to the point that Cate rarely knew when to expect him. Sometimes he would bring her another note from her parents or a friend, which Cate treasured. Her bedroom walls were now peppered with notecards and sheets of paper as a daily reminder of home and everyone who was pulling for her.

Every time she saw Father Matthew, she would press him for updates about Joey. At first he gave her small pieces of information, but nothing that really satisfied her. The updates gradually slowed until eventually they stopped. Cate would ask Father Matthew if he had spoken to the family members caring for Joey, but he said they had become less responsive. Cate knew caring for Joey wasn't easy, and guilt began to crystallize within her kaleidoscope of emotions. It was bad enough that members of her family had been burdened with an autistic child without warning. She didn't need to put added pressure on them to constantly report back to Father Matthew. Still, she wished they could understand the constant ache in her heart, and how desperately she needed that connection with Joey. She tried to use that desperation to keep herself driven to get out of Graypourt as soon as possible.

As Christmas approached, Cate began to struggle more acutely with the emptiness of Joey's absence, of no longer being responsible for his daily needs or personally knowing how he was coping. She desperately missed her parents and the comforts of her childhood home. The distance was wearing on her, and she was starting to wonder if she'd ever see them again or if she would ever get to go home. She realized how delicate and fragile her resolve really was, and she felt it slowly beginning to fracture.

On Christmas Eve, Cate rolled over in bed, her eyes blinking awake. It had been another dreamless sleep and felt like it had been days since she'd had any dreams about Joey. She woke up with her head clouded in sadness, like a heavy fog.

She rose from the bed, grabbing her robe off the back of the door. It was still early, and she didn't expect Maggie for at least another couple of hours. She moved out to the living room, which was still shadowed in the early winter-morning light. A light snow was falling from the heavy, colorless sky. Cate sunk into the couch, her arm resting on the back, and watched the flakes as they landed on the front lawn, already gathering into soft, white piles. She let her chin rest on top of her arm, a single warm tear sliding down her cheek.

She couldn't stop thinking about Joey, the soft brown curls circling his face, eyes turned down, the thick lashes curling up over his cheeks. She had lost count of the number of weeks since she had last held his hand. She allowed her mind to drift into territory she knew she shouldn't explore–wondering where Joey was right now, who was taking care of him, how he was feeling. She slid deeper into despair.

Her body was shaking now with sobs, hot tears stinging her cheeks. She allowed herself to cough and sputter, allowed the guttural moans she had been keeping at bay to rattle the walls. She was alone, and she felt what little hope she had slipping away. Feeling like a wash rag that had been twisted dry, she fell back into the arm of the couch, letting her eyes drift closed.

A creaking of the front door pulled Cate out of her light sleep. She rubbed her gritty eyes, slow to focus on the figure now entering the living room.

"Hey, sleepyhead." Maggie's chipper voice broke through the quiet stillness as she stepped out of her boots and padded into the room in her socked feet.

"Hey ..." Cate's voice came out gravelly and strained.

Maggie stopped, her eyes narrowing with concern, "Whoa, rough night?" she said, coming to sit on the other end of the couch next to Cate's feet.

Cate pulled her legs in closer and lifted herself into a seated position. She looked down at her hands gathered on her lap and shook her head. "I don't know if I can do this, Mags." She felt the tears spring back into her eyes, her chest heavy.

"Have you had coffee yet," Maggie asked in her comically flat tone. Cate couldn't help but smile, turning to her friend in mock exasperation.

Maggie grabbed Cate's hand, pulling her toward the kitchen and her usual seat at the table. Maggie busied herself with starting the pot of coffee and tossed a couple slices of bread into the toaster. She slathered them with peanut butter and set them on two small plates. She poured two cups of fresh coffee and set Cate's plate and mug down in front of her before taking her own seat.

"Michelle invited us over for Christmas," Maggie said, staring down into her coffee cup. Cate knew she was struggling with the reality of a holiday without her family, too. "No gifts, she said, just company and some good food."

"God, Mags, I am so not in the mood to be around other people," Cate sighed, the heaviness in her chest almost more than she could bear.

"I know, I'm really not either, but when I talked to Father Matthew the other day, he said it would be better if we didn't spend the holiday alone." Maggie looked up, her eyes pained and her face clouded with sorrow.

"Screw Father Matthew," Cate said darkly, immediately regretting it. She was deep in the pit of despair today and struggling to find a way out despite what she knew she needed to do.

"Catie-bug ..." Maggie admonished gently.

Cate sighed deeply, trying to relax her shoulders and ease the tight claw of tension wrapped around her.

"I know ... this is just ... really ... hard." Cate covered her face with her hands, closing her eyes. A sob escaped her throat, and heavy tears rolled down her cheeks once again. She quickly wiped them away, feeling the weight of Maggie's arms wrapping around her. She leaned into Cate from behind, resting her chin on the top of her head. She didn't need to say anything.

"Thanks," Cate said softly, finally feeling the tension easing just enough. "I'll go," she relented, knowing that Father Matthew was probably right. Being alone was the last thing she needed right now. She felt Maggie's weight shift, and she went back to her seat.

Just then, the back door opened into the kitchen and Peter stepped inside. He had already removed his boots, his feet covered in thick winter socks. "Goood morning, ladies," he said cheerfully then hesitated as he picked up on the heavy mood hanging over the kitchen table.

"Hey, Peter," Maggie responded, while Cate offered a weak static wave and half smile.

"What's going on?" Peter asked, concern shadowing his eyes.

"Cate's just having a tough morning," Maggie responded gently, looking up as Peter moved around to Cate's side of the table and pulled out the chair next to her. He settled into his seat and turned to place a warm, comforting hand on Cate's arm.

"What's up, kiddo?" Peter asked softly, using his favorite term of endearment despite the fact that he was barely two years older than Cate.

Cate turned to him, tears welling up again in her eyes, her vulnerability raw and exposed in the company of her friends. "I just can't believe I'm going to have to spend Christmas without Joey," she said, her voice breaking with a flood of renewed sadness and frustration.

She watched Peter look over at Maggie, and they shared a look of understanding and empathy. "Hey, we'll get through it together," he said, squeezing her arm and leaning in closer. Cate laid a hand on top of Peter's, giving it a return squeeze, and looked at him with another half smile and watery eyes. "Thanks," she whispered.

Maggie, the eternal optimist, piped up. "Let's have a baking day!" she exclaimed. "We probably have all the ingredients between our three houses." She stood up from the table and moved to Cate's cabinets. She pulled out a bag of flour, white and brown sugar, baking soda, and vanilla extract. Cate had to laugh at her sudden enthusiasm, and glanced at Peter who smirked and gave Cate a wink.

"I think I might have a few eggs," Peter offered, and all three laughed at his measly contribution.

Later that evening, stuffed full of cookies and the hearty chili they had let simmer all day, the three friends lounged in Cate's living room. Peter had brought in a small stack of firewood from the large woodpile in the backyard, and the fire had been burning for several hours while a light snow had continued to fall for most of the day.

Despite the cozy atmosphere, an unspoken sadness remained suspended in the air. They all knew the next day would be hard without the people they had arrived in Graypourt with. It would be the first major milestone date for all three of them in this new reality they were living in.

"What time did Michelle say to come over?" Cate asked, looking over at Maggie. They all knew what she was really asking was how long they would have to endure Christmas morning alone.

"I think noon," Maggie responded flatly.

"Would it be okay if I sleep over?" Peter asked, his voice barely above a whisper from his recliner in the opposite corner. Both women looked up from their downturned posture, Peter's suggestion striking like lightning.

"Oh my god, that's brilliant!" Maggie exclaimed.

"How have we not thought of that before?" Cate marveled, her face lit up with excitement.

"I mean, we don't have to have regular sleepovers, we are grown-ass adults, but Christmas seems like a good enough reason to not be alone," Peter reasoned, looking from Cate to Maggie.

"It's the perfect reason," Maggie said, eyes twinkling.

Cate claimed the bedroom she'd been using, and Peter insisted that Maggie take the one across the hall. He chose the back bedroom, and they all settled in for the night. Cate had just started to drift off to sleep when she heard a soft knock on her bedroom door. She blinked a couple of times, thinking maybe she was just hearing things, but then heard it again.

"Cate?" Peter's masculine voice filtered through the crack in the doorway. She sat up and stepped toward the bedroom door, pulling it open.

"Hey, everything okay?" she asked, squinting from the overhead hallway light. Peter was in a plain white t-shirt and striped boxers, his arms folded together. Cate felt her face flush at seeing Peter in something other than his regular clothes.

"Yeah, everything's fine–sorry to wake you," he whispered. "The back room is freezing, and I couldn't find any extra blankets in the closet ... do you have any in here?"

"Um, yeah, I think there's a couple of extra blankets in the closet." She ran her fingers through her hair and turned toward the small closet behind her. She pulled the door open and swatted around for the string that would turn on the light. She found it and pulled down, casting a dull, yellow glow on the contents of the closet. Two thick fleece blankets were stacked on the top shelf, and she pulled them both down before turning the light off and closing the door. She turned around, and Peter was just inside the bedroom doorway a couple of feet away. Cate's stomach tensed, a battle playing out in her head between wanting to be vulnerable and needing to maintain control.

"Ah, thank you!" he whispered enthusiastically, stepping forward and taking the blankets from her. They were standing even closer to each other now, and he paused.

"Okay, sleep well," he whispered finally, then moved back into the hallway. Cate went to the door and was pressing it closed when she caught him turning to look at her. He gave her a half smile, flipped off the hall light, and moved quickly into the living room. She smiled to herself and settled back into bed.

$$\sim 23 \sim$$

The bus pulled up to a small stop deeper inside the residential part of town with a hiss of its brakes. The folding doors opened to reveal a single bench surrounded on three sides with clear plexiglass walls and a basic aluminum roof. Cate stepped down onto the sidewalk with Peter and Maggie close behind, briefly pausing to get their bearings before walking the short block and a half to Michelle's house.

Michelle's modest saltbox two-story home stood at the end of a short concrete driveway leading to a single-car garage. A narrow path had been shoveled through the snow leading from the sidewalk to the front stoop. The stoop was decorated with a few haphazardly placed seasonal items that Cate guessed Michelle had picked up from the thrift store. A weathered garland hung over the front door, sagging slightly lower on one side, with a strand of colored lights plugged into an outlet just above the front stoop. A plastic Santa grinned maniacally from his position in the corner against the metal railing, and a tin sign in garish red, green, and white exclaiming "Happy Grinchmas!" hung from a plastic hook near the door.

Cate got to the door first and reached for the doorbell. A handwritten sign taped to the inside of the glass storm door invited them to *Come on in! (doorbell doesn't work)*.

"I guess we just go in?" She turned to Peter and Maggie with a shrug.

"Looks that way ..." Peter agreed, stepping up behind her and urging her forward.

Peter's hand lingered on the small of Cate's back as they stepped across the threshold and into the home's front hall. She caught Maggie's eye as she turned to peel off her coat and saw her eyebrows go up as a cloud of concern moved across her face. Peter didn't seem to notice and continued down the hallway into the kitchen. Cate dropped her gaze, throwing her coat over her arm and following behind him.

Laughter and conversation rolled through the air as they entered the kitchen and open living room. Michelle spotted them from the kitchen counter, where she was dumping a bag of chips into a large red bowl.

"Heyyy, guys! You made it!" she shouted in their direction. There were three or four additional people moving about the kitchen, pouring drinks, pulling a covered plastic container from the fridge or a plate covered by a paper towel from the microwave. The mood was joyful and chaotic, and Cate smiled back at Michelle with a wave.

In the living room, a few more people were scattered around, seated on the overstuffed couch or on dining chairs pulled from the kitchen table or perched on the edge of the brick hearth. A welcoming fire crackled in the fireplace at the other end of the room, and muted winter sunlight spilled in from the large window behind the couch. She recognized Cora and Jessie from Michelle's band ... and Father Matthew. He caught her eye and raised his hand in a static wave, offering a smile. Cate smiled back, though internally she resented his presence, which only stood as a reminder of his control over her situation. She had hoped for the day when she didn't have to pretend to be grateful.

"Make yourself at home! There are drinks in the fridge and snacks pretty much on every surface," Michelle said as she passed them on her way to the living room, balancing the bowl of chips and a stack of three cans of beer. Cate watched as she set the bowl on a large coffee table and delivered two of the beers to Cora and

Jessie before cracking open the third one and plopping down on the couch.

Cate found the whole scene depressing. The unconventional holiday gathering and modern holiday tunes coming from the stereo in the living room. An anemic artificial Christmas tree standing in the corner by the fireplace decorated with a single string of lights and a few randomly placed ornaments. This couldn't feel less like Christmas if it tried. She turned to look at Peter, and he put his hand on her shoulder.

"Thirsty?" he asked.

"Sure," she responded, fighting the urge to turn and walk right out the front door.

"I'll go see what's in the fridge," Maggie offered, moving into the kitchen and dodging a tall, lanky man in an oversized red sequin suit jacket scooping bean dip onto a flimsy paper plate.

Cate and Peter parked themselves next to the large kitchen window, which looked out onto a tired wooden deck. There were a couple of backless stools against the kitchen counter, and Peter pulled them over, sliding one toward Cate. Maggie showed up a minute later with three cans of beer and a plate of assorted snack foods.

"It's better than being alone, right?" Maggie muttered so only Peter and Cate could hear her as she pulled open a small bag of potato chips and stuffed three into her mouth at once.

Cate couldn't help but laugh, her mood immediately shifting as she grabbed a brownie off the plate and took a large bite.

"Merry Christmas to the three amigos!" Father Matthew's cheerful and energetic greeting brought polite smiles to all three of their faces. He leaned back to rest on the edge of the sturdy kitchen table in the center of the room, crossing his arms into a relaxed posture.

"Hey, Father Matthew," Peter said, extending the plate of quickly disappearing snacks in his direction. "Hungry?"

Father Matthew put up a hand and turned his face away. "Gosh, no, I've been shoveling chips and dip into my mouth for an hour already."

"What brings you to this little gathering?" Cate blurted out, doing a horrible job at hiding her annoyance.

"Oh, I try to visit most of the larger gatherings after Mass on Christmas morning, then visit some of our more solitary residents into the afternoon and evening," he explained. "The holidays are tough on everyone here, so I just try to be present where I can. And also, Michelle invited me after Christmas Eve Mass last night," he added with a grin.

Cate fought the urge to ask him where Joey was spending the holiday, looking down at her hands, squeezing her fingers. Father Matthew seemed to sense the darkening mood.

"I know today is difficult. Give yourself some grace," he said, his eyes traveling between the three of them. "Often it is precisely the situations that we cannot control that contribute the most to our growth."

Cate let Father Matthew's words sink in, but she couldn't help feeling like she was being scolded. She nodded, subtly pursing her lips in resignation.

Father Matthew stood up and stuffed his hands into the pockets of his jacket.

"It's time for me to head off to the next get-together. I hope you all find some time to reflect on the grace and peace of this season of Christmas. God bless," he said with a final gentle smile before he turned away from them and walked down the hall to the front door.

Cate sighed, Father Matthew's words ringing hollow given their current circumstances. She grabbed another brownie and took a generous, absent-minded bite.

It had been a long time since the holidays had carried the kind of magic they did when she was a child, even after Joey was old enough to understand what was happening. His autism meant that reactions to gifts were tempered, and he was easily overstimulated. Celebrations were muted, and family gatherings had to be small.

She had spent the previous Christmas managing Anthony's despondent attitude while Joey unwrapped presents at her feet. Her parents had been there for the holiday, providing a welcome cushion for the tension that Anthony was generating on a daily basis. She winced as her heart ached for their familiar and comforting presence. She still longed to be with Joey and wondered who was getting to witness the fleeting sparks of joy that had come to define Christmas Day for her.

She pushed the memory aside and set her hand on Peter's knee, leaning toward him and Maggie, who had pulled a third stool over. She was about to suggest they hit up the local liquor store and head back to her house when Michelle piped up from her spot on the couch.

"Who's in for Pictionary?"

Cate's eyes widened, and a mischievous smile spread across her face. "We are!" she shouted, turning to look at Michelle. She grabbed her stool and set it down next to the couch, rubbing her hands together in mock anticipation.

"Atta girl!" Michelle said, popping up from her seat. She'd already erected an easel and grabbed a cup of markers from the fireplace mantel. Peter and Maggie soon appeared with their stools and settled in near Cate. Teams naturally formed based on who was seated together, and Michelle kicked things off with a series of random shapes on the large pad of paper leaning on the easel. This immediately incited equally random guesses and roars of laughter.

The afternoon passed quickly, and soon Michelle was reaching over to switch on several lamps around the room. She threw another couple of logs on the fire, and a few guests began to say their goodbyes.

Cate had lost track of how many beers she'd had at this point, and the familiar floatiness of inebriation had settled in. She visited the small hall bathroom, running her hands through the cold water and pressing them to her cheeks. She passed through the kitchen, grabbing a bottled water from the fridge, and heard voices from the formal dining room just a few steps away. Stepping through the doorway, she found Michelle seated at the table with two other women. Cate pulled up a chair at the head of the table closest to Michelle and tried to pick up on the topic of their conversation.

Michelle looked pensive. "You know, I've spent my entire life digging my heels in to fight for what I wanted my life to look like," she said emphasizing the "I" in her statement. "But all that time, I was ignoring this little voice in the back of my head urging me in another direction. That voice has only gotten louder since I got here."

"Maybe it's time to listen to it," Cate responded, surprising herself with her boldness.

Michelle turned to look at her as if she hadn't noticed Cate had joined them at the table. "Maybe it is ..." she answered, gently slapping her hand down on the table.

Cate looked from Michelle to the other two women at the table, both of whom were looking back at her with curious expectation. "I'll drink to that!" she threw her water bottle up in the air, a small amount sloshing out onto the table, sending all four of them into howling laughter.

"Merry Christmas, you goofball," Michelle said, leaning over to rest her head on Cate's shoulder. She rested her head on the top of Michelle's, closing her eyes and allowing a pleasant smile to spread across her face.

"Merry Christmas to you too."

The wooden gate creaked loudly as Cate pushed it forward, re-vealing a modest yard adjacent to St. Ann's office and rectory. A narrow path had been cleared through the couple of inches of snow still clinging to the ground, an icy crust that had developed on top of what had been fluffy mounds just a few days before.

The greenhouse stood just a few feet ahead, its milky glass pan-els filling a gap between the rectory and the branches of the trees lining the edge of the yard. A shadowy shape moved across the front greenhouse wall, stopping just before the corner, a full head of hair bent over a solid line stretching the full length of the wall.

Cate approached the simple aluminum door, pulling it toward her as she called out.

"Michelle? You in here?"

Michelle turned toward her from her spot at the long wood pot-ting table, a wide smile spread across her face. Cate took in her hands covered by flowered gardening gloves in a cheerful pink and yellow, a simple tan apron, and rubber clogs. Her hair was tied back on the sides with a red handkerchief, and she was dressed in a plaid fleece jacket, turtleneck, and jeans. Her hands were press-ing the potting soil down into a medium-sized terracotta pot, and three trays of small paper cups were lined up on the table between them.

"Hey, you made it! Grab an apron over there off the wall–I can use you back here." Michelle brushed the excess potting soil off her gloves onto the front of her apron and waited for Cate to fol-low her.

The greenhouse wasn't the tropical humid warm she had been expecting, but there was a heater in the center of the small structure that at least took away the worst of the chill from outside. Cate removed her mittens and pulled her arms out of her coat, unwrapping the scarf from around her neck, and stuffed it into one coat sleeve. She turned and saw several plastic hooks extended from the wall and hung her coat and purse on one of the empty ones before grabbing a matching tan apron from another. She threw the large loop over her neck and wrapped the long tie around her waist twice. She was securing it with a small bow as she moved toward Michelle.

"What is all of this?" Cate directed her question toward the trays of small paper cups that she could now see each had small amounts of potting soil inside.

"Those are about to be the seedlings we'll plant out in the raised gardens later this spring. I'm working on some wild roses at the moment."

Cate's eyes widened and filled with fresh tears at the mention of her favorite flower. "Ohhh," she breathed. "Wild roses are my favorite. They remind me of the farm where I grew up."

Michelle smiled. "I'll hold a few back for you and you can plant some at your house," she offered kindly. "C'mon back, and I'll show you where I can use your help."

Cate followed Michelle around the first of several rows of metal shelving units, which held various pots of mature plants lined up under bright fluorescent lights rigged below each level of the shelving. It was an elaborate setup, and Cate imagined it had to be a huge amount of work to keep all these plants alive and thriving.

"This is amazing, Michelle—how did you get Father Matthew to agree to let you do all of this in his backyard?"

"Oh, this was already here when I got to Graypourt. It's really Father Matthew's greenhouse, but he invited me out here a while ago to help out."

Cate continued to take in all the potted plants arranged on the wire shelves set at varying heights, the lights and cords, plastic liners under the groups of pots on each shelf, and started reading the stakes emerging from the soil: basil, mint, cilantro, spider plants, succulents, kalanchoe and African violets. There was something calming about being among these quiet, unassuming living things.

"It's really beautiful," she breathed.

They had paused in the center of the aisle, and Michelle stood next to her, arms crossed casually.

"Yeah, it's been a great outlet for me. There's something fulfilling about cultivating and caring for a living thing–planting the seed and watching it grow and develop into something so delicate and beautiful, or sturdy and healthy."

Cate looked at her and nodded thoughtfully as Michelle continued.

"Being in Graypourt can feel like ... I don't know, wandering in the wilderness. The greenhouse has been a refuge. A place where I can sort of ground myself, you know? No pun intended." She chuckled lightly.

Cate intimately felt the comparison Michelle made to being in the wilderness, but laughed at the pun, grateful for some levity.

"So, how can I help?" she asked, glancing around for a tool or some other clue as to what Michelle had in mind for her to do.

"See those little tiny gnats bouncing around on the soil? We need to spray these plants down and discourage those little guys from reproducing. They'll easily take over this entire greenhouse if left unaddressed."

Michelle pulled down a plastic spray bottle that had been hooked over the top wire shelf and handed it to Cate.

"Just lightly spray the base of each plant, but don't saturate the soil. A little goes a long way."

Cate started in with a couple of sprays at the base of one of the basil plants. She glanced over at Michelle to see if she approved, and was met with a generous nod, her blond curls bouncing gently.

"Perfect! Okay, I'm going back to the potting table to finish up the seedlings. Go ahead and spray all four rows, top to bottom, then move on to the next aisle."

"Got it!" Cate continued spraying as Michelle turned to go back to the front of the greenhouse.

There was music playing softly from a short distance away, and Cate thought she recognized the angsty ballad from her middle school days. She smiled to herself at a long-forgotten memory of a school dance and a boy she was hoping to dance with. She lost herself in her work, moving along each aisle, occasionally pausing to rest her hand from the repetitive squeezing of the handle. When she got to the last aisle, she realized the bottle was practically empty, and she wasn't getting anything else to come out.

"Hey, Michelle?" she called to the front of the greenhouse.

"Yeah?"

"Where would I find more of the solution that goes in the spray bottle?"

There was a long pause, and Cate peered around the end of the metal shelving to see Michelle walking toward her. She motioned for Cate to follow and led her to a table along the back wall of the greenhouse where there were various tubs, bottles, gloves, bins, and caddies with large spoons, spatulas, and scoops.

"Where does all of this stuff come from?" Cate gestured with her hands toward the shelves of supplies.

"I'm not sure ... I've always just assumed Father Matthew gets it from somewhere. There must be a local garden supply store nearby."

"Have you ever run out of anything? Or had to ask him to buy something you needed?"

Michelle looked thoughtful, then turned to Cate with an expression of realization. "No. Everything I've needed has just always been here."

Cate let that sink in for a moment and observed Michelle seem to briefly get lost in thought.

"So ... does Father Matthew come in here anymore? He must need to restock things once in a while."

Michelle snapped back to attention. "Oh, sure ... not as much as when he first introduced me to everything, but every once in a while I'll show up and he'll be in here putzing around with the mature plants, or promulgating some new ones to give away. He spends a lot of time working on the outdoor landscaping in the spring and summer."

"Oh, right! My very first day here, he told me he was a master gardener at some point."

"Yep, he definitely knows his stuff. I've learned pretty much everything I know about what you see in here from him."

Michelle turned to head back to the front of the greenhouse but paused abruptly and turned back to look at Cate.

"Have you been inside the church yet?" She was looking at Cate with curiosity and some apprehension.

"No, why?"

"I've just sensed that you seem to be looking for a way to find some peace with all of this, and sitting in the quiet of the church has really helped me."

"God, I haven't been inside a church in ages. I used to go with my grandmother when I was younger–she was Catholic, so that's what I am most familiar with. The incense and formality, the standing and kneeling, the funny men up on the altar dressed in long robes. As odd and confusing as it all seemed, I did always feel safe there. Probably because I loved being with my grandma."

Cate found herself getting emotional at the memory of her grandmother and looked down at her hands to try to gather herself.

Michelle laid a hand on Cate's arm. "I'm planning to pop in there when I get done here, so you're welcome to stick around and join me. I should be done in twenty minutes or so."

Cate's stomach clenched, an internal battle commencing in her gut. As much as she wanted to validate Michelle's invitation, she wasn't convinced that the church would bring her any peace at all. If anything, it only reminded her of Father Matthew and his control over her. She felt a cloud pass over her eyes, and a heaviness settled in her chest.

"Um, I'll think about it," she said, then turned to head to the place where she had stopped spraying one aisle over. She heard Michelle's footsteps on the concrete slab as she returned to her place at the potting table.

She rolled Michelle's invitation over and over in her head as she finished up the last aisle of plants and hung the bottle at the top of the wire shelves. She reached for a vibrant purple flower on an African violet plant, allowing her finger to rest just below one of the velvety petals. How was she supposed to just accept that Father Matthew was holding her here? That Joey was being cared for and didn't desperately need her? She felt the anger rising in her chest and took a deep breath, releasing a heavy sigh, but it only temporarily relieved the pressure.

She returned to the front of the greenhouse where her coat and scarf still hung from the hooks on the wall. She quietly replaced the apron and began wrapping her scarf around her neck.

"You taking off?" Michelle piped up from the other end of the potting table. Cate noted that all the trays had been moved to the empty wire shelves behind her and Michelle was sweeping up the excess potting soil from the floor.

Cate swallowed hard. "Yeah, I think I'm going to head back to the house and take a nap. I'm wiped."

"Okay ..." Michelle let her voice trail off, and Cate felt the judgment like a heavy weight on her shoulders.

"I'll see you soon," Cate said, pulling up the zipper on her coat and sliding her hands into her mittens. She shot Michelle a weak smile and quickly pulled open the greenhouse door, then let it fall closed behind her.

~ 25 ~

The coffee shop was warmly lit, and Cate found herself immediately embraced by a waft of fresh ground coffee and the sounds of brewing espresso as she followed Maggie inside. She unwrapped her thick cotton scarf and scanned the room for Michelle's familiar blond curls. Maggie spotted her first, throwing her arm up in an enthusiastic wave, and Cate followed her to a small table halfway through the narrow shop.

She took a seat on the cushioned bench against the wall, and Maggie slid in next to her. Michelle was seated across the table, hands wrapped around her paper coffee cup.

"Hey, ladies," Michelle greeted them with her wide, friendly smile.

"Okay, I am dying to hear your news," Maggie said, "buuuut, I'm dying a little bit more for a vanilla latte."

"Yes, go go go … I can wait!" Michelle said, waving her off.

"We'll hurry!" Cate said, following Maggie to the counter while scanning the menu and reaching for her wallet.

Back at the table, Maggie and Cate settled into the seat and leaned into each other, staring at Michelle in anticipation. "Okay, spill it," Maggie said, pulling the plastic lid off her cup and blowing gently into the foam at the top.

Michelle chuckled and briefly looked down at the table. "Well … I don't know if you remember the girl from the Christmas party with the dark hair, big eyes, beautiful smile?" she said, fishing for recognition.

"Uh, yeah ... the one you were all snuggled up on the couch with when we left?" Maggie said, her voice dripping with sarcasm.

Michelle laughed out loud this time, her shoulders relaxing and her head tilting to the side. "Of course," she sighed. "So ... we're dating!" Her eyes lit up, and she wiggled her hands like a jazz performer.

Maggie squealed and clapped her hands excitedly. Cate's hand went to her mouth, and her eyes were wide with mock surprise. She had seen Michelle and the mystery woman cuddled up on the couch and had assumed there was already a relationship there; she had discussed it with Peter and Maggie half the way home that night. It was still cute that Michelle had wanted to include them in her excitement.

"Things are moving fast," Michelle continued. "She's actually moving in with me this weekend."

"Whaaaat?" Maggie said, leaning forward and placing both her hands on the table.

"Yeah, I know." She looked down, and Cate sensed some apprehension.

"Whose idea was it for her to move in?" Cate asked.

"Oh, it was mine." She looked up now, more confident. "Kelly-sorry, that's her name by the way-she's really been struggling with being on her own, and she's had a hard time meeting people, so I invited her to move in with me."

"How long have you known each other?" Cate pressed, sensing a fragile quality to Michelle's excitement.

"Long enough ... she's been coming out to see the band for a while, and we've partied together a bunch of times. She'll have her own room, so it's not like we're *moving in* moving in."

"But you'll be living with someone you're dating," Cate said, furrowing her brow with a sideways glance. Michelle offered a sheepish grin.

Cate couldn't recall seeing Kelly at any of the band's shows she had attended, and she was pretty sure the Christmas party was the first time she'd seen her and Michelle in the same room, much less intimately connected. She swallowed her skepticism with another sip of her mocha.

"So, tell us about her–how did you guys meet?" Maggie asked.

"We met at The Bar. She had just wandered in by herself and looked like a lost puppy. I immediately pulled her over to our group, and by the end of the night, she and I were the only two still there. There was a pretty immediate physical attraction, but the more we talked, the less I wanted to be apart from her. I invited her to one of our shows, and we grabbed a drink afterwards. It wasn't long before she was partying with my larger group of friends, coming by the house, and spending the night.

"It evolved pretty quickly, but Kelly fills a gap in my life I've been missing since I arrived in Graypourt. My life was kind of a mess back then, and I hurt someone I cared about a lot back home. I pushed her away and never got the chance to apologize. And this is so stupid, but I left my little dog behind ... Wyatt ... I just hope that someone is taking care of him." Michelle's voice caught in her throat, and she looked down at her hands. "So, Kelly just ... makes me happy." Michelle looked up, quickly wiping a tear that had rolled down her cheek.

Maggie reached across the table, and Michelle took her out-stretched hand. Cate offered her an understanding smile and added her hand on top of Michelle's.

"So, when do we get to meet her?" Maggie asked excitedly, sitting up straighter and taking a sip of her latte.

"Actually, she should be here any minute," Michelle answered, looking toward the door. As if on cue, a petite woman who appeared to be in her late thirties or early forties walked through the door. Her dark hair was cut in a cute bob styled with loose curls, her large dark eyes and wide smile brightening her round face the moment she spotted them. She waved tentatively and strode over to their table.

"Hey," Kelly said a little breathlessly. She wore a black leather jacket over a thick black turtleneck sweater, tight-fitting jeans and stylish ankle boots. Michelle looked up at her affectionately and stood to greet her with a light peck on the cheek and a friendly hug. She reached over to the next table and slid an empty chair over next to hers, which Kelly quickly settled into. She busied herself pulling her purse over her head and removing her coat, hanging both over the back of the chair.

"How was work?" Michelle asked, making casual conversation.

"Oh, yeah, it was fine," Kelly responded, letting her shoulders sag just slightly and giving Michelle a resigned smile.

"Kelly works for Daylight Ministries out of the community center," Michelle explained to Maggie and Cate. Both raised their eyebrows and nodded, impressed.

"Babe, these are my friends Maggie and Cate," she said, turning to Kelly.

"You were both at the Christmas party, right?" Kelly said, resting her forearms on the table and clasping her hands together.

Maggie and Cate both nodded, smiling politely.

"So, how long have you been together?" Kelly asked looking from Maggie to Cate and back again.

Cate nearly choked on her coffee, covering her mouth with her fist to keep it from spraying across the table. Maggie's eyes were saucers.

"Oh, no, no, we're not dating," Maggie said emphatically ending with a nervous laugh.

"Oh! Okay, just friends, then?"

"Yes, just friends," Cate further explained. "I mean, we're both attracted to men."

"Ohhhhh ... okay! Sorry, I just assumed. My bad!" Kelly chuckled, and Michelle was looking at her in disbelief.

Cate shifted in her seat and tried not to look at Michelle.

"I met Cate and Maggie at the thrift store," Michelle explained. "They've been to a couple of our shows, too."

"Got it, got it," Kelly said, clearly eager to change the subject. "So, do you both live here in town?"

"We're a little farther out–on A Highway," Maggie responded.

They visited a while longer, talking about living in the country, the inconvenience of the bus, and their favorite songs performed by Michelle's band. They avoided discussion of how they all ended up in Graypourt, which seemed like a deeper conversation for another day.

"You two really should come out and volunteer to serve breakfast sometime," Kelly suggested, leaning back in her chair and throwing her arm casually across the back of Michelle's chair.

Cate looked over at Maggie, and they both nodded. "I'd love to," Cate said with genuine interest.

"The guests are always so grateful to just see a friendly face and get a warm meal," Kelly added. "I'll let Michelle know when we have another volunteer opening."

Eventually, Cate and Maggie finished their drinks and Cate started wrapping her scarf around her neck, signaling to Maggie she was ready to go.

"We'll see you girls again soon ... it was great meeting you, Kelly," Maggie said, sliding out from her spot in the booth and standing next to the table. Cate gave Michelle a friendly squeeze around the shoulders and moved to follow Maggie toward the door. Kelly moved around the table to sit on the bench, and she and Michelle leaned in to continue their conversation.

On the way to the bus stop, Cate couldn't stop thinking about Michelle's story about what had happened right before she arrived in Graypourt. She turned to Maggie with a pained expression.

"Do you think Michelle is really happy?"

Maggie looked at her in confusion. "What do you mean? She seemed happy to me."

"I don't know ... that story she told about pushing someone away, and missing her dog ... it didn't sound to me like she's resolved any of those feelings."

"Oh ... yeah, I see what you mean."

Cate's heart felt heavy, and she knew she had to get Michelle to dig deeper. To figure out how to move past whatever burden she'd carried with her to Graypourt.

~ 26 ~

Before arriving in Graypourt

Michelle eased the white Jeep Wrangler into the barely two-car garage and pulled the key out of the ignition, letting her hand flop into her lap, bracing herself for what was going to come next. Helen's silver Honda–the silver fox, she called it–sat ominously still between Michelle and the door into the townhome.

She grabbed her water bottle and turned to her wirehaired canine companion. "This is it, Wyatt–time to face the music." Wyatt's small pointy ears perked up at his name, and he tilted his head to one side. She opened the door, and Wyatt hopped over the console into the driver's seat and down to the garage floor behind her. She could hear his little claws and jingling tags trailing her to the door.

The door swung open into the tiny living room, the galley kitchen and adjoining dining area straight ahead of her. Late afternoon shadows cast a gray tone over the room as Michelle set down her water bottle and tossed her keys onto the breakfast bar. She absently sifted through the small stack of mail, knowing she was just delaying the inevitable. She heard Wyatt lapping up what was left in his water bowl and closed her eyes, sighing.

She could hear Helen moving around in the bedroom, then the toilet flushing and water running briefly in the bathroom sink. Michelle moved to the refrigerator and pulled out a bottle of beer, twisting off the cap and tossing it into the sink.

Helen appeared just then from the hallway, running her hand through her shoulder-length brown hair, eyes downcast. The tension was suffocating.

"Hey," Helen said, leaning onto the back of the sofa, arms crossed, eyes set like glassy stones pointed directly at Michelle.

"Hel, don't be like that. I tried to explain that this has nothing to do with anything you've done."

"Maybe explain it to me again," Helen said icily. "You're so willing to just throw the last three years away like they never happened and you don't think it has anything to do with me?!" Her voice got louder and screechier as she talked.

"That's not what I said." Michelle set the bottle down on the counter, tucking her chin, eyes fixed on Helen's face. She moved closer, standing between Helen's long legs and wrapping her arms around her thin frame. Helen shoved her away, standing to her full six-foot height, several inches taller than Michelle, arms still crossed.

Helen had every right to be upset–Michelle knew that. She had come halfway across the country to move in with Michelle, leaving behind her close-knit family.

"I know there's someone else. Just tell me ... please," Helen said, a tortured look on her face that said she didn't really want to know the answer.

"Hel, I promise, there's no one else. I told you that a hundred times already." Michelle stepped closer to Helen again, taking both of her hands. "I just need some time to figure shit out." She dropped her hands abruptly and went back to her bottle of beer, taking a long swig.

Helen was glaring at her. "Oh, sure. Okay. Well, while you're 'figuring shit out,'" she said, making air quotes with her fingers, "What the hell am I supposed to do, Shell? Just disappear?" Helen's chin began to quiver, her face crumpling into tears. She angrily swiped her fingers across her cheek and turned her back on

Helen to look out the sliding glass door onto their small concrete patio.

"I'm going to April and Jenny's," Helen said, her voice low and gravely. "They said I can stay with them until I find another place to live, or ... decide to go back home."

"Helen, I don't want you to leave ... just stay in town. I have a feeling ... I mean, I hope we can still work this out."

"The world does not revolve around you!" Helen screamed, whipping around, fists balled up at her sides. Wyatt barked sharply at the sudden commotion.

"I am not going to just wait around, displaced from my own home, my own bed ... there is no way you care at all about me if you would ask me to do that." Helen was really sobbing now, verging on that hyperventilating kind of crying that was impossible to stop. She walked briskly to the bedroom and was back a moment later, a large duffel bag thrown over her shoulder. "You can go to hell!" she growled through her sobs, pointing a long, bony finger aggressively in Michelle's direction. She spun around and threw open the door, slamming it closed behind her.

Michelle tipped her beer back, finishing the bottle with two final gulps. She set it on the counter and turned to the cabinet above the fridge where they kept the liquor. She pulled down the handle of scotch, poured two fingers into a rocks glass, and tipped it back, letting the alcohol slide down her throat with its familiar burn. She winced and coughed, then poured a second shot. It was the only way she knew to numb the constant nagging in her brain. The voice telling her that there was another path for her, something else she was meant to be, but never giving any clear answers to her questions about what exactly she was supposed to be doing.

She pulled the flyer out from under its magnet on the fridge, the glass of scotch still cradled in her other hand. It advertised a traveling nurse program she had heard about at the hospital where she worked, including a presentation of heart-wrenching stories of people in desperate need of medical care in economically distressed communities. She crumpled up the flyer in her fist, tossing it in the sink. She emptied her glass and grabbed her keys off the counter. She sensed Wyatt trotting behind her, expecting to join her, and she turned to him. "Not this time, Wy-wy." He stopped, taking a seat on the matted carpet. Michelle pulled the door open, swaying ever so slightly, and stepped into the garage.

***

When Michelle opened her eyes, she had to squint at the bright fluorescent light glaring just above her head. She sensed quiet activity immediately to her left and slowly turned her head to find a nurse standing at a computer terminal parked next to her bed.

"Hi, Michelle, how are you feeling?" the nurse asked somewhat absently, not yet looking at her.

Michelle struggled to find her voice, but finally choked out, "Um, okay ..." Her throat was like sandpaper.

The nurse finally turned to her and touched her hand. "I'm going to give you some time to fully wake up, but I'll be back soon."

Michelle nodded slowly, grateful to be relieved of the pressure to be fully responsive. She was still fighting her heavy eyelids and the instinct to give in to what she recognized as anesthesia-laced sleep. She struggled to remember anything that had happened before she woke up. It seemed just out of reach.

A few moments later, as her surroundings were taking on a more concrete quality, the white exam room curtain was gently pulled aside, and the nurse returned with a man that Michelle immediately recognized as a priest. The nurse silently took her position at her work station, and the priest approached Michelle's bed, his face soft and kind. She was instantly on guard.

"Hey, Michelle," he said. "I'm Father Matthew."

~ 27 ~

Cate stepped up to the wide front porch of Maggie's farmhouse, loaded down with several fleece blankets and two bottles of red wine, and let herself into the front room. The bitter cold had started to break, and Maggie had invited some friends over for a bonfire in her sprawling yard.

She made sure the door was closed, knowing that the old house was drafty enough as it was. She made her way down the narrow hall into the kitchen, immediately spotting the pile of folded fleece blankets covering the top of the kitchen island. She added her blankets to the pile and set the two bottles of wine on the counter. The house was quiet, so she helped herself to a glass of water from the sink.

She had just leaned back against the counter when a creaking sound above her signaled movement on the second floor. She set her glass down and headed back down the hall to the main stairs. At the top of the stairs, she turned down the hallway toward the bedrooms. The open doors cast shafts of muted daylight across the wood floors, but it was the closed door at the end of the hall where Cate knew she'd find Maggie. She gently knocked with a single knuckle to avoid startling her friend, but no one came to the door. She heard a toilet flush, so she waited a moment more before knocking again. Finally, Maggie pulled open the bedroom door.

She stood in the doorway, staring back with glassy eyes, puffy eyelids, and red cheeks. "Hey," she said, her voice a little raspier than usual.

"Mags, what's wrong?"

Maggie's face crumpled, and she brought her fist just under her nose. Cate stepped forward, wrapping her arms around Maggie's body, which was now shaking with fresh sobs.

"I miss them so much," she squeaked out between sobs.

"I know, it's okay ... let it out," Cate soothed.

Maggie pulled away from Cate and sunk onto the edge of the bed. Cate leaned against the doorframe, arms crossed, and waited for Maggie to catch her breath.

"It just hit me like a freight train this morning, and I can't stop crying." Maggie looked up at Cate, wiping her fingers across her cheeks while fresh tears pooled again in her eyes.

"Was it a memory, or just generally feeling alone?" Cate fished for something she could grasp or relate to in order to help her friend cope.

"I just started thinking about the holidays, the birthdays, the everyday moments I'm missing out on ... and we're trapped in this ... prison." Maggie brought her hands together under her nose again, tears spilling down her cheeks.

Cate felt her own chest begin to constrict as hot tears pressed against her eyelids. She felt Maggie's frustration so acutely herself and had no way to comfort her. Anger began rising from her gut, and she stood up straight, dropping her arms.

"I'm so sorry, Mags, I wish there was something I could say to make you feel better."

Maggie dropped her hands in her lap and looked up at Cate with a sad smile. "Thanks, babe. You're an amazing friend–I'll be okay." She sighed. "Let me wash my face, and we can head down to start getting everything together." She stood up and swept her hand down Cate's arm as she walked past.

Cate's heart ached with understanding of the helpless and broken feeling that lived inside of them now. She tried not to think about how much she missed her parents, her coworkers, her friends. She just wanted her old life back, to return to that sense of normalcy and familiarity. She briefly covered her face with her hands, then looked up and stared at the bathroom door.

Time passed so strangely in Graypourt, and she had no idea how long it had been since Maggie last saw her husband and other two children. She really didn't talk about them much other than to share their names and ages, or the activities they were into–almost like she'd never left them at all. Cate got it. Sometimes denial was the only way to cope–and behaving like you still had control was the only way to hold on to hope.

She let her eyes wander around the room when something on the bedside table caught her eye. It had a bright-pink case and the black, vacant screen faced up toward the ceiling. She peeked at the bathroom door, open just a crack, then moved toward the small wood table. She picked up the phone and tapped on the glass. She gasped at the image that appeared–a portrait of a family, clearly shot by a professional photographer, their faces in various stages of laughter as if someone had just delivered a hilarious joke.

She spotted Maggie right away, and next to her was a tall, handsome man with short blonde hair and a healthy, athletic build, his arm wrapped around her waist. A teenage boy stood on the other side of her, clean cut with a clear, handsome complexion. A girl who looked to be around eight or nine years old was standing just in front of her husband, perfect French braids falling from her head past her shoulders. And there was Anna–seated in a child's wheelchair, her head lolled to one side, her eyes wide and a half-grin spread across her face. They made a beautiful family, dressed in coordinating outfits of navy, yellow, and brown, the sunny fall landscape surrounding them like a warm hug. Cate suddenly felt Maggie's loss that much more acutely and quickly set the phone back down on the table as guilt overwhelmed her.

She walked over to the bathroom door, rested her shoulder against the doorframe, and leaned toward the small gap between the door and the frame. "Mags–have you ever seen anyone leave Graypourt?"

The bathroom door opened fully, and Maggie turned to face her from her spot in front of the sink where she was drying her hands on a small towel. "What do you mean?"

"Like in their car? Or by bus?"

"Um ... not since I got here. From what I hear, people just leave kind of unannounced, without any fanfare. One day they're here, and the next they're just ... gone."

Cate nodded, her mind going to Peter's story about his wife. "And ... does anyone ever come back?"

Maggie stared back at her and seemed to be searching for an answer, but her face was blank. "Let's ask tonight–maybe someone else who has been here longer can answer that." Maggie tossed the towel on the counter, and Cate stepped away from the doorframe. Maggie grabbed a hair tie off her bedside table and brushed her hair back into a low ponytail. As realization hit her, she turned toward Cate.

"Cate, don't be mad ... Father Matthew gave it to me, but it doesn't have any service. It's basically just so I can look at old photos and videos of my family."

Cate walked over to her friend and gently placed her hands on her arms. "It's okay ... I have mine, too."

Maggie's shoulders relaxed, and a smile spread across her face. "Oh, thank goodness! I was so worried that you would feel like I was getting some kind of special treatment–"

Cate interrupted her. "Seriously, I'm glad you have yours, too." Cate dropped her hands back to her side. "Mine is the same–just photos and videos I had on there from home, my calendar, clock ... the most basic apps."

"I guess it's better than nothing," Maggie said with a shrug, and Cate nodded.

"You have a beautiful family," Cate said softly.

Maggie nodded, her face crumpling with another wave of emotion. She recovered, wiping a fresh tear from her cheek and looked up at Cate. "I want to see your photos, too! Will you show me next time I come over?"

"Of course."

"C'mon ... everyone will be here any minute, and I literally have done nothing to get ready."

Cate followed Maggie back down to the kitchen, her mind still calculating and questioning.

Peter was the next to arrive, immediately jumping in to help gather up the blankets and carrying them outside, where he threw one over each chair facing the large stone circle where the fire was just beginning to take shape. Maggie and Cate started setting the snacks up on the weathered picnic table nearby when they heard the crunching of gravel as the supply bus pulled up at the end of the long driveway.

Another half dozen of their friends exited the bus and started walking toward the house. Maggie waved, and several of them waved back or raised the bottle of wine they were carrying. Cate spotted Michelle and Kelly; Max, a buddy of Peter's from The Bar; Leo, the bartender from the Mexican restaurant; and two other women close to their age who had recently arrived in Graypourt, Emily and Renee.

The friends all greeted each other–the girls moving in for friendly hugs, the guys preferring fist bumps or enthusiastic handshakes–and everyone settled into a chair around the fire, which had now grown.

Maggie went back into the house and Peter followed, so Cate settled into one of the plastic Adirondack chairs, tucking the fleece blanket around her legs. Michelle and Kelly were chatting with Max, and Leo was chuckling at something Emily had said. Cate leaned back and turned her head toward Renee in the chair next to her, admiring her rich ebony skin and poofy bob hairstyle that framed her face perfectly. Renee had a confident air to her, even under their current circumstances, and despite her distress over her daughter who had been separated from her the day they arrived in Graypourt.

"Hey, friend." Cate reached over and patted Renee's hand, which was gripping the arm of the chair she was seated in.

"Hey ..." Renee responded with a sigh. "This is really nice ... I definitely needed this," she added.

Cate sat up. "I'm getting a glass of wine, do you want anything?"

"I'd take a vodka and diet coke," Renee answered. "There's a bottle of Tito's on the end of the table by the marshmallows."

"Got it." Cate lifted herself out of the chair and made her way over to the table. Maggie and Peter emerged from the side door of the house, and Cate was surprised at the envy that suddenly ballooned in her chest. Maggie was laughing, and Peter had a knowing smirk on his face like they shared a private joke. Happiness was such a rare commodity, Cate couldn't help feeling like she was being cheated out of what they had. She quickly brushed it away as Maggie's eyes met hers and lit up.

"You will never guess what Peter just did." Maggie set down the bowl of chips she was carrying, talking through her continued laughter. The balloon in Cate's chest deflated as Maggie pulled her into their private moment. "Peter was fighting with the bag of popcorn and could not get it to open, and he was pulling so hard that when it finally came apart, popcorn literally went everywhere ... seriously, I'm going to be finding popcorn in my kitchen for days!" Cate joined in Maggie's laughter as Peter approached the table and set down the four two-liter bottles of soda he was carrying.

"Yeah, we won't be having kettle corn tonight ..." Peter added, and the three of them dissolved into giggles.

Cate mixed Renee's drink in a plastic cup and poured herself a generous cup of pinot noir before returning to her seat. Maggie and Peter settled into the remaining open chairs.

She looked across the fire pit and noticed Michelle looking down at her lap, arms crossed and a somber look on her face. Kelly was in an animated discussion with Max, just then tossing her head back in a generous laugh. Michelle looked up and caught Cate's eyes, and offered her a tight smile. Cate definitely sensed something was awry and offered Michelle a caring smile in return. She discreetly jerked her head toward the house, a questioning look on her face. Michelle briefly averted her gaze to her lap, but quickly met Cate's eyes and nodded.

Cate stood up and threw her blanket onto the seat of her chair. She walked the short distance to the side door to the house and entered into the quiet of the kitchen. She settled into a stool at the center island just as the screen door opened and Michelle stepped inside. Cate searched her face for any clues about what was bothering her, but she kept her eyes downcast as she came over and sat on the stool at the far end of the island.

"What's going on? Are you okay?" Cate pressed, keeping her voice soft.

Michelle sighed and cleared her throat. "Sorry, I'm just a little off today. I wasn't going to come, but Kelly laid it on thick and made me feel like I would offend Maggie if I didn't show up."

Cate scoffed. "No way ... Maggie would have understood."

Michelle just stared at her hands. "I just haven't been myself lately."

Cate couldn't ignore the foreboding in Michelle's voice, and her chest tightened in anticipation of what she was going to share with her. She finally nodded, encouraging Michelle to continue.

"So, I was over at the greenhouse again the other day and decided to go sit in the church for a little bit. I was sitting quietly, when I was suddenly overwhelmed by this intense feeling of guilt and a sense that I wasn't being totally honest with myself. I was so uncomfortable and put my face in my hands to try to make the feeling go away.

"After a couple of minutes, I heard someone moving around on the altar, so I looked up, and Father Matthew was walking down the steps toward me. He sat down in the pew right in front of me and leaned his arm over the back of the seat. He asked me how I was doing. I think he could tell that I was upset, but I didn't feel like getting into it with him so I just told him I was doing okay.

"He obviously knew I wasn't being truthful with him, so he asked me if I was sure. I started bawling and told him I was really struggling to figure out what I am doing here and what he wants from me so I can go home." Michelle paused here, and Cate sensed she was reliving the emotion from that moment. She patted her arm and waited until Michelle was ready to go on.

"So he sat there and listened and let me babble on, and I finally calmed down. I was hoping he would give me some clue as to what he's waiting for me to recognize or understand, but he just said, 'Trials are a necessary part of the experience in Graypourt, but it is also where you will find your freedom.' He also said something really strange that he's never mentioned before. He said he isn't here to condemn me, but that he wants more for me. After that, he patted my hand, then said he had to finish getting ready for Mass and went back to the altar. I was so confused and angry. I feel like he is never going to tell me what I need to know. It's been hanging over me ever since."

"I'm so sorry, Michelle. That would be so frustrating. It sounds like he's just telling you to suck it up and accept that this experience is designed to be traumatizing and demoralizing. How is that helpful?"

Michelle looked at her with a pained expression. "I know, right? I thought he was supposed to be helping us, and it felt like he completely dismissed me when I was trying to reach out to him."

"Do you think he's trying some tough love on you?"

Michelle took in a deep breath and released a long sigh. "I don't know ... maybe. I just wish there was some way to move past this feeling."

Cate felt terrible that she didn't have any solid advice for Michelle or some way to make her feel better. She had seemed in good spirits at the coffee shop, so Cate wondered if Kelly had anything to do with this new mood she was in.

"You have Kelly now ... have you tried talking about it with her?"

"A little. She tries to cheer me up, but doesn't really have any answers. She's in the same boat as we are."

"Let's go back out and try to make the best of this time tonight. It has to be better than being alone and wallowing in your frustration." Cate tilted her head to try to get Michelle's attention and meet her gaze. She finally looked up and offered Cate a half-hearted smile.

Cate stood up from her stool and was relieved when Michelle followed. She put her arm around Michelle's shoulders and walked her to the door. They returned to their chairs, and Cate pulled the blanket back around her legs. She threw a quick glance at Michelle as Kelly handed her a can of beer with a concerned look on her face. Michelle took it with a soft-spoken "thanks" and cracked it open.

The bonfire cast a warm orangey yellow glow on the faces of the group, a clear night sky and a dome of stars above them. They were playing a game where each person had to complete the next part of the story without stopping in a sort of stream-of-consciousness challenge.

"Joe traveled through the mist, steering his boat carefully to avoid the floating logs and debris when the mouth of a cave appeared out of nowhere ..." Max trailed off, signaling the next person's turn.

Cate picked up the story. "A twinkling light caught his eye, and he rowed toward it. Suddenly, a giant serpent rose out of the murky water, towering above him, its mouth opened wide bearing long, white fangs ..." She paused and looked toward Renee.

Renee quickly swallowed her drink, sending a ripple of laughter around the circle. "Joe was shocked when the serpent started singing his favorite song, 'I don't know what they want from me ... it's like more money we come across, the more problems we see ...'" She sang the tune in perfect pitch, and the group fell right into the chorus along with her, ending in a round of laughter and cheers.

No one seemed to have a better way to continue or end the story, so the game came to a natural close. The fire continued to pop and crackle, and Peter added a few more logs which immediately caught, the added heat soothing in the lingering quiet. Cate sensed an opening and felt now was as good a time as any to satisfy her curiosity about some of the things she'd been questioning since arriving in Graypourt.

"So, I don't really know all of your stories. How did everyone end up here?" Cate let her eyes move around the circle, hoping to catch someone who seemed interested in sharing. Max's eyes were fixed on the fire. Then he suddenly looked up and met Cate's gaze.

"Sure, I'll go."

Cate gave him an encouraging nod and a sympathetic smile. He took a long swig of his beer and tossed the can into the fire. Leaning forward in his chair, intensity burning in his eyes, he rubbed his hands together and cleared his throat.

"I'm here because of ultimate betrayal," he began. Cate's heart thumped, suddenly unsure if she truly wanted to know everyone's story.

"My brother and I lost our parents in a car accident when we were both in college. I only had a year left, so I was able to graduate and get my degree, but my brother just couldn't seem to stay motivated and ended up dropping out. We didn't really have any other family, so we moved down to Florida. My degree was in business, and my brother had a passion for cooking and was actually really talented.

"We opened our restaurant–Brothers Brew Pub–and barely survived our first year. But we had some incredible regulars and investors and ended up with a really solid ten-year run. Our regulars helped to keep things stable, and we would get a nice influx of vacationers during tourist season. But when the pandemic hit, we just couldn't make ends meet and were at the point where we were going to have to make some really tough decisions.

"Danny–my brother–he came to me one day and said that he had a way for us to stay open and ride out the pandemic. At that point, everyone thought it would only last a few months, so a temporary solution seemed reasonable. He told me to trust him, and even though I was the one with the business degree, I stupidly did.

"In the end, the temporary solution that Danny had come up with was money laundering for a local drug trafficker. The longer the pandemic wore on, the more obvious it looked when we would invest in improvements to the restaurant or Danny would pull up in a hot new car. I just couldn't do it anymore. I told Danny I wanted out, and he panicked.

"He chose them. He sold me out and told them he was afraid I was going to become a problem and he needed their help to ease me out. Of course, there's only one way that works.

"I was in the office one night after we had closed, wrapping up receipts and stuff from the day, and I heard a noise. I knew there wasn't anyone else in the restaurant, so my hackles immediately went up. Next thing I knew, a skinny South American dude in a black suit was standing in the office doorway. I barely even had a chance to react before he pointed his gun at me and started shooting.

"The next thing I remember is waking up in the hospital in Graypourt. Father Matthew said I'd been transferred here after several months in a coma. A good Samaritan had apparently heard the gunshots and found me slumped over my desk and got me to a hospital in Florida, but they couldn't keep me any longer. I haven't heard a word from Danny, so I assume he's too spineless to reach out. He probably thinks I want nothing to do with him. So ... here I am." Max ended with both hands extended, a look of resignation on his face.

"That is so intense ..." Kelly piped up from her chair on the other side of the fire.

"What's your story?" Max asked her, leaning back into his chair and taking the fresh beer Leo handed him from the small cooler by his feet.

"Oh, geez–it's definitely not as exciting as all that. Um ... so, my whole life I've had a bunch of food allergies. Wheat, dairy, nuts ... it's always been a major issue I've had to manage. My parents are older and from a different generation that didn't have to deal with food allergies, so they haven't always been super supportive, and we've been estranged for quite a while. I've become a total expert in reading labels, and I rarely eat out at restaurants because there are so many risks of cross-contamination.

"Since I'm so limited in where I can go and what I can eat, my circle of friends is pretty small. It's partly why I started Daylight Ministries–I get why some people just can't interact with the world the same way as everyone else.

"So, I was dating this new chick, and she was really sweet, but not the sharpest knife in the drawer. I hadn't really been seeing her long enough to fully explain how serious my food allergies are. We were having a movie night, and she wanted to bring brownies over. I gave her the very specific brand of mix that I knew was safe for me to eat and told her that she could not put anything extra in them or I would get really really sick.

"She seemed to totally get it and promised me she would be super careful. So, what I didn't know is that she was a huge fan of almonds–especially the chili-flavored ones. She had been snacking on them while she was making the brownies, and enough of the oil from her fingers contaminated the brownies that I had a major allergic reaction halfway through the movie.

"I knew immediately what it was, and tried to get to the cabinet in my bathroom where I keep my EpiPen, but it happened so fast this time that I blacked out before I could get there. The next thing I remember is waking up at the Graypourt hospital. Father Matthew told me that once I fully recovered from the anaphylactic shock, I would need time for emotional and spiritual healing.

"My circle of people who understand my situation is small enough that Father Matthew is able to keep them updated on my progress ... but so far, I have no idea when I'll be able to go home." Kelly's voice caught, and she coughed as if to cover up her emotions.

Cate saw Michelle reach over and take Kelly's hand, which she seemed to welcome while leaning her head back against her chair with her eyes closed. Cate was starting to regret having set this chain of sharing in motion, when Emily piped up next.

"I just got married," she blurted. "My husband, Nate, is seriously the very very best person I know." She put her head down and pressed a bent finger under her nose. Cate didn't think she was going to continue, but then her head popped up again, and she stared into the fire with a determination that caused everyone to sit up a little straighter.

"I wish I could relive our wedding day over and over. Family and friends that we hadn't seen in years, some since we were just kids, showed up. It was truly a "this is your life" kind of event for both of us. We are both elementary school teachers, too, so a bunch of our students came with their parents–it's just the kind of thing that only happens once in a lifetime. We were so grateful for every moment.

"We had so carefully planned our honeymoon during our summer break from teaching. We rented this beautiful RV, a gift from our parents, and planned to hit as many national parks as possible before we had to report back for the new school year. We started in Maine at Acadia National Park and kept making our way west. The last one I remember is Great Smoky Mountains National Park in Tennessee. We stopped at this sweet old wood mill, and it was right at sunset, so we grabbed a blanket and snuck into the nearby woods and had some of greatest sex of my life–"

Emily paused here, realizing she'd lost herself a bit in her story. She took a deep breath and cleared her throat.

"I think it was a few days later as we were making our way across the Midwest that everything changed. Nate was handling most of the nighttime driving, and we were really trying to push through because I was obsessed about seeing the Grand Canyon before we turned around to go home.

"I had drifted off and just remember starting to wake up because the RV was making this strange jerking motion and bouncing over these huge bumps ... I couldn't immediately make sense of it, and then I just blacked out. When I woke up, I was in the Graypourt hospital. Father Matthew told me that there had been an accident, and Nate and I were both thrown from the RV. I had mostly recovered from my physical injuries while in a coma, but ... I'm like Kelly ... I need to stay here and complete my emotional and spiritual recovery before I can be released to go back home.

"Father Matthew hasn't told me where Nate ended up but keeps promising me he will reunite us as soon as he possibly can. I just feel like I'm holding my breath ... I'm not a complete person without him," Emily choked on a sob, and her shoulders shook as she completely broke down.

Maggie popped out of her chair and knelt in front of Emily, grasping both her hands while she sobbed. It didn't seem like the right time to ask Emily about the rest of her family or how they were being kept apprised of her whereabouts and her condition. It was a heartbreaking story.

"I'll pass," Renee snapped. Cate reached over and patted her arm, intimately familiar with the overwhelming combination of emotions that accompanied being separated from your child.

"Same," Michelle said flatly. Cate saw Kelly shoot Michelle a look of hurt confusion, probably since she'd just poured her own guts out.

"I'm not sure any of you gringos wants to hear how I ended up here," Leo piped up from his chair next to Max on the other side of the bonfire. His soft voice and Hispanic accent had a lyrical quality. The fire gave his dark skin an amber glow, and made his eyes appear almost luminescent.

Maggie had taken Emily inside the house, and Cate was beginning to think this would be a good time to stop. She pulled her hand back from Renee's arm and was about to let Leo know that they could revisit his story the next time they got together, but that seemed unfair. If Leo wanted to share, he should have the opportunity just like everyone else. She caught his eye across the flames licking the air above the pile of burning wood.

"Go ahead, Leo, of course we want to hear your story." Cate watched him crack open a fresh beer and take a long drink.

"I was just trying to start over," he began. "I made some bad decisions in my teens and had to get out of Mexico. My cousin knew some kids who were drug mules and could help me take the train across the border. It was a horrible trip, and I thought I was going to die at least once a day.

"By some kind of miracle–*alabado sea Dios*–I made it and decided to continue by train to the North, where my papa had some family. I couldn't buy a ticket because I lost my passport, so I had to keep hitching a ride where I could. The kids I had ridden with in Mexico told me about this guy at one of the truck stops who was friendly to immigrants and would let a few ride with his truckload sometimes.

"I actually found him, but it was in the middle of the day, so he couldn't risk letting me into his trailer. He told me to wait until dark and one of his buddies would be passing through and might let me hitch a ride with him. So I camped out behind the truck stop with a few migrants who were headed to California to look for work, and they invited me to come along with them.

"We had to wait until the middle of the night for the truck that would take us to California. It was so hot inside the trailer, and there was hardly any water. I didn't think there was any way I'd actually make it to California, but a few days later, the driver opened up the trailer and we all tumbled out in the middle of some remote desert. He dropped a case of water at our feet and told us good luck.

"We were making our way through the desert, and I got to the point where I literally couldn't take another step. I stopped under a tree while the rest of the group continued on, and I fell asleep. When I woke up, I was in the hospital here in Graypourt."

"Holy shit, man," Peter said. "You've got some serious balls to take that kind of risk. Did Father Matthew give you any idea how long you have to stay here?"

Leo squinted through the smoke that was blowing in his direction from the fire and cleared his throat.

"He just said that I'll be here until he thinks I'm strong enough to go home. But I really don't want to go back to Mexico. I'm not sure where home is for me anymore."

Cate watched Peter just nod, and a quiet fell again on the group. Maggie and Emily returned to their seats and settled in under their blankets. The fact that everyone had been told they were required to stay seemed to beg the question Cate had posed to Maggie earlier that day.

"If you've been here awhile," she started, meeting the faces of those she knew had some history in Graypourt, specifically Peter, Michelle, and Leo. "I want to know more about the people who have left."

A silence fell over the group, and Cate immediately regretted casting an additional sour tone on what had been such a raw and intense moment of sharing. Max seemed to read her mind.

"Man, Cate, and we were having such a good time ..." he said sarcastically, draining the rest of his can of beer and tossing it into the fire.

"C'mon, we could really use some hope. I know you all don't plan to stay here forever ..." she pressed, determined to satisfy her curiosity.

Peter stared down at his hands, and Cate thought he was going to mention Caroline, but he looked over at Michelle. "There was that weird situation with Erica ..." He trailed off, seeming to give Michelle the opportunity to pick up the story.

Michelle's eyes widened and searched the faces that were now all waiting for her to continue. She cleared her throat.

"Yeah, um, Erica was here when I arrived in Graypourt and sort of took me under her wing," she began. "She showed me around and introduced me to a bunch of people, and we became friends." Michelle paused and seemed to be collecting herself for the next part of the story.

"She ... battled some demons." Michelle looked down at her hands in her lap, picking at one of her nails. "I never got the full story, but there was a darkness to her that she couldn't seem to let go of. She started to really lean into this tendency she had to cast doubt and anxiety on everyone she interacted with ... and she started to drag me down with her." Cate could tell Michelle was struggling with something and looked over at Peter with concern. He was zeroed in on Michelle, though, willing her to continue.

Michelle sighed, "So, Father Matthew approached her one night when we were all hanging out at The Bar. He pulled her into a corner, and it looked like they were having a pretty heated discussion, which was really unusual. Erica was throwing her arms up in the air, and Father Matthew was pointing his finger toward her chest. She basically stormed out of the bar, and we never saw her again." Michelle crossed her arms and raised her shoulders as if she was suddenly chilled.

"Do ... you think Father Matthew did something to her?" Leo asked.

"No, I don't think so," Michelle quickly responded. "He came over to us after Erica left and apologized for making a scene and asked us to rally around her and try to help her see that there is still hope. He really seemed to want her to find peace." Michelle's voice was clouded in sadness. "And there wasn't ever any evidence that anything bad happened to her ... all of her stuff was still at her apartment–she was just gone."

"But that doesn't really prove that she left Graypourt," Cate interjected. She didn't mean to be so skeptical, but Michelle's story only seemed to increase the level of mystery and her curiosity.

Michelle looked at her with irritation. "Then you explain where she went, smarty pants."

"Well, I suppose Father Matthew could have gotten rid of her, that still seems likely, or she ... took care of herself," Cate's voice trailed off, and she glanced over at Peter. That familiar dark cloud passed over his face, and he stood up, his blanket pooling on the ground at his feet. He turned and strode back toward the house, hands in the pockets of his jeans.

"Cate ..." Maggie quietly admonished, standing up and following Peter into the house.

Cate looked around the circle, an uncomfortable quiet now hanging heavily in the air. The hum of the supply bus and crunching of gravel broke the silence, and the rest of the group began collecting their things. Michelle and Kelly started down the driveway, Kelly's arm wrapped around Michelle's shoulders, rubbing her hand along the side of her arm. Renee stood up and looked at Cate with sad eyes.

"Take care, Cate," she said, absently folding her blanket and dropping it onto the seat of her chair. Cate glanced up with a half smile, averting her eyes toward the dying fire.

The rest of the group left in silence, and Cate watched as they all climbed up into the bus, the folding doors closed, and the bus pulled away, trailed by a white cloud of dust.

~ 29 ~

Cate sensed the side of the bed sink near her knees, and she allowed her eyes to flutter open. Peter was there, seated on the side of her bed, the morning sun casting a buttery glow on the side of his face. He gazed down at her with kindness, moving to rest his hand on her leg. Cate smiled and sat up, wrapping her arms around his neck and resting her head on his shoulder.

"I'm so sorry, Peter. I didn't mean to hurt you."

She felt Peter's hands on her back, and she pulled away to look into his eyes. But instead of Peter's face in front of her, it was a woman, so beautiful it took Cate's breath away. She appeared to be a little older than Cate, with large expressive eyes, strong cheekbones, and flawless skin. Her dark hair fell in soft waves just above her shoulders, and she had a classic, sophisticated air about her. She flashed a playful smile, and Cate felt her long, thin fingers gripping her arms.

"You want to get out of here?" the woman said, her voice low and raspy, but her delivery confident and strong. She stood up and moved toward the bedroom door. There was a magnetic quality to this woman, and Cate sat up on the side of the bed. She followed her into the hallway and through the living room to the front door. The woman wrapped her fingers around the brass doorknob and turned to look at her.

"Ready?"

A tickle at the back of Cate's head made her look back into the living room. Joey stood in the doorway at the other end of the room, his wide brown eyes pooled with tears.

"Mommy?" he whimpered.

"Let me bring him with me," Cate pleaded with the woman.

"Let him go," the woman said. "He doesn't need you now."

"What do you mean?"

"You don't belong here, Cate ... you've done your time. You've suffered and sacrificed and you didn't deserve that. Joey is being cared for, so now is your chance to live the life *you* want to live. I'm giving you permission to walk away and finally get to do all the things you've always wanted to do ... to take back control. If you're ready to finally be free, then come with me," she said confidently and convincingly. "But he can't come with us."

Cate felt like she was being torn in half. She looked at Joey standing in the doorway, small, vulnerable, pleading. She looked back at the woman, whose face was calm, patient, assured–as if she had no doubt Cate would choose to join her. Something was squeezing her heart, and she gasped for breath. She turned away from the woman and ran across the room, fell to her knees, and threw her arms around Joey's warm body. She felt him melt into her as she held his face in her hands and kissed the top of his head, tears streaming down her face.

She held him for another moment, her eyes closed, then she felt Joey's presence begin to fade, the solid reality of his body dissolving into a cool mist. She opened her eyes and looked down at her arms, now empty, but still tingling with the sensation of his body like a limb that had been cut off. She turned back to the front hall to find that the woman had also disappeared. Defeated, she curled into a ball on the floor where Joey had just been standing.

~ 30 ~

Cate gasped and felt her eyes snap open, revealing the early dawn quiet. She brought her hands out from under her pillow and covered her face. Her chest felt heavy with the memory of the dream, and she rolled onto her side to look out the window, grounding herself back in reality. She needed to see Peter, apologize, and make sure he wasn't upset with her.

She threw on her favorite oversized cable-knit turtleneck sweater, leggings, and slip-on tennis shoes. Maggie had started calling it her "Cate 'fit." She ran a brush through her hair and applied deodorant, then grabbed her denim jacket on her way out the back door.

The sun was just cresting the horizon, a strip of fiery orange and yellow merging with the indigo sky as night transitioned to day, and frost still clung to the grass that had barely begun to green again. She knew Peter would be up, putzing around in his kitchen and waiting for the coffee to finish brewing. Maggie wouldn't be over for a couple more hours, and Cate had come to savor her one-on-one time with Peter on these rare mornings when they met at his house.

The gravel crunched quietly under her feet as she made her way the half mile down the road to Peter's place. She crested the final hill and saw his simple, single-story white farmhouse come into view. She walked down the long driveway and bypassed the covered front patio to head toward the back of the house.

She eased open the back door into Peter's large country kitchen, aware that he might not be especially excited to see her this morning.

"Knock, knock," she sang, stepping across the threshold. Peter was at the counter with his back to her, pouring ground coffee into his coffee maker. Cate quietly slipped off her shoes, leaving them on the rug by the door, and stood still with her arms folded around her middle. She observed Peter's broad shoulders and back, his casual but confident stance. He wore a dark-blue t-shirt and golf shorts, ever the prepster, but his hair still had its early morning scruff. He turned toward her, and she took note of the day-old stubble across his upper lip, chin, and jawline.

"Hey," she said apprehensively.

"Morning, kiddo," Peter answered with a sideways glance and a weak smile, moving to fill the carafe with water from the sink faucet.

Cate waited for him to turn off the water and set the carafe in place, pressing the start button. He turned toward her and leaned back into the inside corner of the counter, his hands resting on the edge by his side.

"Peter, I am so sorry," Cate said, her voice catching in her throat.

"I know." He stood up and walked toward her, and she met him halfway across the kitchen, wrapping him in a hug. She pulled back, and he kept his hands on her arms. He tucked his chin and smiled, his eyes pools of kindness.

"Let's sit," he said, gesturing toward the aged oak table by the large kitchen window.

The coffee maker beeped, and he poured each of them a cup, walking Cate's to the table and setting it down gently in front of her.

"How did you sleep?" Cate asked, sinking into the oak dining chair and wrapping her hands around her mug.

"Oh, fine ... I helped Maggie clean up and was in my bed by 11:30 or so."

Cate felt a pang of guilt that she had left so abruptly after watching the bus pull away, ashamed and embarrassed that she had caused the gathering to end on such a sour note.

"Sorry I didn't stay to help."

"It's okay–we understood. Did you get much sleep?"

"Sort of ... I had a really bizarre dream."

"Really? What was it about?"

Cate described her dream in detail, taking a sip of her coffee while she waited for Peter's reaction.

"What did the woman look like?" he asked.

"She was a little older than me, maybe early thirties. She had beautiful eyes and strong cheekbones–she kind of reminded me of a classic movie star. Her voice was sort of deep and raspy."

Peter paused. He was staring at her, and she sensed he was thinking hard about what he was about to say.

"I think that was Erica."

Cate's blood went icy cold, and her heart leapt into her throat.

"What? Why would she appear in my dream? I've never laid eyes on her!"

"I–don't know ..." Peter leaned toward the table, looking at Cate intently. "Erica's dangerous, Cate. You need to avoid inviting her back if you can help it."

"Back? Back from where?"

Peter leaned back in his chair. "Back from wherever the heck she went."

Now Cate leaned forward into the table. "What do you mean, she's dangerous?"

Peter's cheeks reddened, and he looked down into his mug. "She ... seduced me," he finally said, his voice tight and quiet.

"Seriously?" Cate swallowed hard.

"Yeah, it was right after Caroline disappeared, and I was a mess. Erica just showed up here at the house acting like a friend, but she was being really affectionate. It just started out as a hug but then she leaned in for a kiss, and I shoved her away."

"Oh my god ..." Cate took another sip of her coffee, fighting the conflicting feelings swirling around in her head. If asked, she wasn't sure she would be able to honestly blame the girl.

"That wasn't the worst of it, though, it was the horrible things she said after I pushed her away."

Cate raised her eyebrows, her eyes widening in anticipation.

"She kept screaming at me that I needed to just let Caroline go, that she obviously didn't really love me if she could just disappear without a word. She kept repeating what Caroline said about how I reminded her of the pain of losing Natalie. She said how selfish Caroline was, and that I didn't need that in my life. I was so broken already, I actually started to believe her." Peter's brow wrinkled, and he bit his bottom lip. Cate saw he was fighting against the pain of this memory, and she felt tears begin to burn behind her eyelids.

"Peter ..." Cate reached across the table, offering her hand. Peter reached back and gave her hand a squeeze before releasing her and wrapping his fingers around his coffee mug.

"She was trying to separate me from everyone–you know, like a lioness seeks out the weakest member of the herd. She kept telling me that everyone I'd met in Graypourt didn't think I could hack it here, especially now that Caroline had left. They didn't think I was strong enough or would be able to find a purpose without her ..."

Peter looked up at Cate. "... It was like she was reading my freaking mind."

The blood drained from Cate's face as she realized that what Erica had said to her, as much as she hated to admit it, eerily reflected her feelings, too.

As Peter continued, his gaze was bouncing around the room, like he was searching for the next phrase on the ceiling, the walls, the cabinet doors. "It was everything I'd been telling myself since Caroline disappeared. And hearing her say it out loud made it feel true–like if everyone else thought the same thing, who was I to argue with them?"

Peter was really rolling now, and Cate tried to be as still as possible, practically holding her breath to avoid distracting him. His gaze settled on the mouth of his coffee mug.

"Eventually, she broke me down so much, I really felt like I had nothing left to lose. She moved in again, and this time I ... let her kiss me. We started drinking wine, then one thing led to another and the next thing I knew, I woke up next to her in my bed."

Peter looked up at her at this point, the pain in his eyes almost more than Cate could stand. She folded her lips over her teeth, trying to keep her emotions in check, her brow creased with the effort. She desperately hoped he wouldn't ask her what was wrong. She knew she wouldn't be able to be honest with him without risking their friendship. She nearly sighed with relief when instead, he looked down and continued.

"I wish I could say that I was totally horrified with myself, but her hold on me was so strong. She said things that made me feel like I had taken control of my situation and had given into my natural need for comfort and companionship–that was something she knew Caroline and I had struggled with ever since losing Natalie. She made me feel masculine ... and powerful."

Cate cleared her throat, her heart pounding in her chest. "So ... how long did you stay together?"

"The night she stormed out of The Bar, I followed her. I'd never seen her that upset. She was screaming and yelling about how unhinged Father Matthew was, how weak and pathetic. That she didn't belong here and she was going to leave. She begged me to come with her. She was crying and pawing at me, like some kind of wild animal. I was torn–I think I had become so dependent on her validation and the way being with her made me feel. I tried to get her to tell me where she was going, but she just kept saying that it would be better than here. Something was stopping me, and I wouldn't commit one way or the other. So I followed her back to her apartment, we had sex and fell asleep. The next morning, she was gone."

Cate finally felt like she could breathe again. Something Peter had said at the bonfire came back to her just then.

"If you and Erica were so close, why did you ask Michelle to tell the story at the bonfire?"

"No one knew that Erica and I were sleeping together," Peter admitted. "They actually thought Erica was with Michelle."

Cate swallowed hard to avoid spraying coffee all over Peter's dining room table.

"What?" She laughed uncomfortably. Did Erica have any limits at all?

"Yeah, it wasn't my finest hour ..." he said, tipping his coffee mug back and draining what was left.

Cate looked down at her hands, her fingers fanned out on the table, and laced them together before looking up and clearing her throat.

"Do you think she's watching me because I'm getting closer to you?" Her heart was racing, and she felt her eyebrows rise in anticipation.

"I don't know," Peter answered darkly.

~ 31 ~

Joey's face stared back from the smooth glass surface of her cell phone screen, the photo another one of her favorites from his toddler years. He was sitting in a miniature folding chair, his head tilted back toward the sun. It had been a scorching-hot day, and he had been begging Cate to go outside. She had finally given in, even letting him play with the garden hose, the cold water running over his feet, creating a huge mud puddle at the edge of the patio. He had wandered over to his chair to dry off, and she had caught him in a moment of pure relaxation. She sighed, fighting against the feeling that she had abandoned her child, reminding herself that he was with family and they would be together again soon.

She gently placed the phone back in the drawer of her bedside table and stood up from her seat at the edge of the bed. Kelly had been asking them for weeks to sign up to volunteer at Daylight Ministries, and Maggie, Peter, and Cate finally all had a shared day off to take her up on it.

Cate pulled the windbreaker over her shoulders, peering through the front window for the supply bus. She slipped into her running shoes, the familiar feel of the cushioned footbed taking her back to the time before Graypourt and her favorite jogging route at the park by the hospital. She shook off the memory yet again, pulled open the door, and pressed past the screen door and down the concrete steps.

It was still the frosty predawn hours of the morning, and Cate pulled the windbreaker tighter around her body as she hurried down the driveway.

The bus came to a stop with a loud hiss of its brakes, the door folding open on the side facing her house. Maggie appeared around the front of the bus, head tucked and shoulders raised. She had her hair pulled up into a messy bun, poking out the back of her baseball cap, and her hands were stuffed into the front pocket of her hooded sweatshirt. She looked up at Cate with the bleary eyes of someone not quite awake for the day.

"Hi, Mags." Cate threw her arm around Maggie's shoulders with a friendly squeeze, then followed her up the steps into the bus. There was a new driver at the wheel this morning, and Cate flashed him a friendly smile before moving down the aisle. She spotted Peter a few rows back, seated behind Michelle. Maggie slid into the seat next to Michelle, immediately laying her head on her shoulder, and closed her eyes. Cate chuckled then took the seat next to Peter.

He patted her knee and planted a brief, friendly kiss on her cheek. Cate patted the top of his hand and smiled. They had all grown so close, like a small family, though Peter's gestures had started to cause a flutter in her belly. She sensed there might be deeper feelings developing, but it was too complicated and messy. He was still holding on to Caroline, and after what he told her about Erica, Cate just knew they couldn't go there.

The bus rumbled down the gravel road to the paved country highway and into the heart of town. They pulled up to the community center, and everyone exited the bus onto the paved lot where Kelly was waiting to welcome them.

"Hey gang," she called out to the twenty-five or so volunteers. "Welcome to Daylight Ministries!" The group clapped with enthusiasm, eager to exercise this new sense of purpose in a place where most of them felt they had little control over their circumstances.

"We'll be serving breakfast this morning to some of our fellow Graypourt neighbors who for one reason or another just need a friendly face and a warm meal," she explained. "Some aren't comfortable in restaurants, and some haven't accepted or adjusted to life in Graypourt, and this is a simple way for them to be in community."

Cate glanced over at Maggie, and they exchanged sympathetic looks. Cate could imagine how horrible it felt to be so trapped by your depression that going out to eat at a restaurant or shop at a store would be unthinkable. She felt a new sense of purpose in serving a community that was probably desperate for any positive human interaction.

They entered a thick aluminum door into a narrow hallway that led to a large industrial kitchen. It was already bustling with activity as the first wave of volunteers readied the ingredients and equipment for food prep. Kelly started tossing out cloth aprons to the new crew as they crowded around the stainless-steel counters in the center of the kitchen. She introduced several members of the first wave of volunteers, who appeared to be well seasoned in their duties. They offered friendly waves on their way out, and Kelly began to assign people to specific tasks in setting up the various breakfast items.

Cate and Maggie were on oatmeal-serving duty and pulled the loose plastic gloves over their hands before doing a quick inventory of their station. Cate was stirring in one final pitcher of milk while Maggie added the cinnamon and raisins when Kelly clapped loudly a short distance behind them to get everyone's attention.

"Okay, everyone," Kelly announced from the center of the kitchen, "doors are opening in two minutes–remember to make eye contact and ask each guest if they are interested in what you are serving before you put it on their plate or tray. This helps us to honor their dignity and treat them as guests. Thank you for serving!"

Peter wandered over to Cate and Maggie's station from where he had been setting up the dishwashing area, peering over their shoulders in mock supervision. Cate swatted him back with the hand towel she had draped over her shoulders, and he laughed.

"Work hard, ladies!" he sang, then moved along to where Michelle was ready with her set of tongs to serve the sausage patties. Kelly stood next to her with a large serving spoon over a warming pan of scrambled eggs. Cate watched as they laughed at something Peter said, then forced herself to look away.

"Here we go ..." Maggie said as the metal double doors parted and the first guest approached the counter.

Cate's heart pounded faster at the sight of the sea of faces–some elderly, worn down by time and circumstances, their eyes filled with gratitude and longing. Others were more middle-aged, their faces hardened and dark, unapproachable. She even spotted an older teenager or young adult, it was hard to tell for sure, her face thin and pale, her hair hanging in long, stringy strands just past her chin. She was initially overwhelmed, thinking about all the pain these people seemed to be carrying, but she took a deep breath and pushed it away. She smiled as the first guest approached their station, dipping the serving spoon into the oatmeal while Maggie handed her a small plastic bowl.

"Good morning! Would you like some oatmeal today?" Maggie asked sweetly. The older gentleman smiled and nodded, offering a quiet "yes, please" as he held out his weathered, knobby hand. Maggie handed him the small bowl, pausing to be sure he had a good hold on it, then he moved along down the line.

The group served more than 150 weary and hungry neighbors, emptying every last bit of food they had prepared. When the last guest had been served, Kelly quickly moved to begin cleaning up.

Cate watched Michelle go over to Kelly, literally patting her on the back, her wide smile apparent even from her profile. Kelly turned to her and swatted her hand in the air as if rejecting Michelle's praise. Michelle placed her hand on Kelly's shoulder, her body language increasing in intensity. Kelly nodded and appeared to finally accept what Michelle was offering before turning to her cleaning with earnest.

Kelly dismissed all the volunteers, and the final crew entered the kitchen. Cate followed Maggie toward the door, coming up behind Michelle as she was untying her apron and dropping it into a white plastic laundry basket.

"That was sweet of you to recognize her hard work," Cate said as she stepped up beside Michelle, lifting the apron over her head.

"Oh, you saw that?"

"Yeah, I couldn't hear what you were saying, but I could tell by your body language that you had to really sell her to accept your praise."

"Well, I shouldn't have. She was complaining to me last night that she feels like this is such a thankless job. She said she puts in so much work, and really has a gift for this ministry, but she doesn't feel like anyone ever recognizes it. She doesn't want to look like a jerk for asking for it, but I guess she felt comfortable letting me know. I knew if I didn't validate her, I was going to hear about it later."

Cate suddenly felt guilty for missing the opportunity to share her admiration and appreciation for Kelly as well. She understood Kelly's desire and Michelle's motivation to avoid conflict with her partner. It made her a little uncomfortable, but she allowed herself a small grimace in an attempt at empathy.

Peter was staying behind to lead the dish crew, so Maggie and Cate turned and waved goodbye. He raised a soapy gloved hand before greeting his new crew members as they approached the industrial dishwasher.

The rest of the serving crew stepped out into what was now a sunny spring morning. The supply bus idled in the same place where it had dropped them off, but Maggie turned to Cate, placing her hand around Cate's arm.

"Coffee ... stat!" she announced and pulled Cate toward the sidewalk that would take them into town.

Michelle was just a few steps ahead of them heading toward the bus, so Cate called to her.

"Michelle! Come get coffee with us."

Michelle hesitated briefly before joining them, falling into step on the other side of Cate.

~ 32 ~

The coffee shop was just beginning to fill up, and there were still several open tables. Cate threw her jacket over a chair at a table near the front window and went to join Maggie and Michelle in line.

Their friend Emily was working behind the counter this morning and greeted them with a broad smile.

"Hey, girls! What can I get you this morning?"

"Hey, Em!" Cate smiled back. "How's the job going?"

"It's a nice distraction," she said with a sad smile.

"Hang in there." Cate offered a sympathetic smile before turning to Maggie. "What are you having, Mags?"

They ordered, then moved to the other end of the counter to wait for their drinks. Balancing mugs and saucers, they settled into their seats. Maggie yawned, quickly moving to cover her mouth.

"Sorry," she mumbled, and Cate and Michelle chuckled.

"Kelly has that whole process down to a science," Cate said, hoping Michelle would have some extra ammunition to pass along to Kelly when she had the opportunity. She was legitimately in awe of well-executed activities.

"Yeah, she's ... great," Michelle responded flatly.

"Whoa, do I sense some trouble in paradise?" Maggie finally perked up, sitting a little straighter in her chair.

Disappointment flashed across Michelle's face as she looked down into her coffee cup. Her reaction to Cate's earlier question made a lot more sense now.

"What happened?" Cate interjected, sitting back in her seat to give Michelle some space.

"Nothing ... that's the problem. Kelly hasn't done a damn thing wrong. I'm just freaking miserable."

Michelle took a sip of her coffee but still wasn't making any eye contact.

"I'm constantly on edge, so I snap at her all the time, then I feel terrible so I find little ways to apologize, but I just feel ... unsettled."

Cate furrowed her brow and glanced over at Maggie, who stuck out her bottom lip in sympathy.

Michelle was slumped in her chair, her face sullen and dark. She was turning her mug back and forth on its saucer, and Cate leaned forward, resting her forearms on the table around her coffee mug.

"Does Kelly sense anything is wrong?" Maggie asked, still sitting back in her chair.

"I'm sure she does, but she hasn't said anything to me yet ... I just see it on her face." Michelle took a deep breath and sighed, leaning forward to rest her elbows on the table, placing her face in her hands. She paused for a moment, then sat back in her chair.

"I just can't seem to break out of this cycle ... this is exactly how I felt right before I ended up in Graypourt. I sent my girlfriend away because I needed space, left the house totally buzzed, and I think I fell asleep at the wheel. The next thing I remember is waking up in the Graypourt hospital.

"Father Matthew told me I needed to stay here and recover until I was ready to go home ... but it's not like I have anything to go back to. I'll just be stuck in this same cycle of broken relationships and disappointment." A tear slid down Michelle's cheek, and she angrily wiped it away, finally looking up and meeting Cate's concerned gaze.

Cate thought back to their conversation in Maggie's kitchen and Michelle's feeling that she wasn't being totally honest with herself. It seemed like she was really struggling to pull herself out of this dark place, and Cate found herself once again questioning Father Matthew's approach. If Michelle's freedom was tied to the trials she would experience here in Graypourt, what was it she was supposed to endure?

"Don't worry about me, I always seem to figure out how to keep moving forward. I don't want to give up on Kelly yet–we have such a good time together when I'm not being a total jerk."

If honesty was where Michelle was struggling, Cate wondered if maybe she could help. "So what is it that's holding you back in this situation?"

Michelle looked at her thoughtfully, then glanced down at her hands wrapped around her coffee mug. "I just want to be someone ... to make a difference in the world. Leave my mark, you know?"

Cate felt now they were getting somewhere. "Okay, so if you could do or be anything, what would it be?"

Michelle looked at her quizzically with a half smile. "Are you psychoanalyzing me, Elliot?"

Cate chuckled. "No ... just wondering if maybe there's something you are ignoring or pushing off because you're ..."

"Afraid?" Maggie chimed in tentatively.

"Okay, ladies, what is this?" Michelle narrowed her eyes and furrowed her brow, folding her arms across her chest.

"We just want to help," Cate offered sympathetically, glancing over at Maggie, who nodded and leaned forward.

Michelle's face softened with a sad smile. "I know ... and you're sweet to try. I've been in this cycle most of my life, though. I don't think there's any other way for me to exist."

"Of course there is–people break cycles all the time," Cate said confidently. "Also, you never answered my question ..."

Michelle sighed dramatically, unfolding her arms and leaning on the table. "If I could do anything ... it would probably be to run a free medical clinic in a remote African or South American village."

"That's ... pretty specific," Maggie said, a sense of awe in her voice. "I feel like maybe you've been thinking about that for a long time."

Cate smiled, trying not to appear smug, but a satisfied pride was rising in her chest.

"Bingo," she said.

It was Saturday, and Maggie was coming over later to help Cate pull the weeds that had popped up in her flower beds on the side of the house. A cleansing spring rain had just ended, and she pushed up the bottom half of the small window over the kitchen sink to let in the fresh air. She saw the supply bus rambling up the road and figured Maggie must have ordered a few things.

She ran a damp washcloth over the counter, scrubbing a spot of dried pasta sauce before taking it over to the sink to rinse it out. She heard a soft knock on the back door and shut off the water.

She knew it couldn't be Maggie or Peter since they rarely knocked anymore before walking into her house, so she glanced at the small trio of windows near the top of the door. Whoever it was was too short to be seen or was standing at the bottom of the steps. She tentatively pulled the door open.

Michelle stood at the bottom of the steps into the house, her eyes puffy and red. Her blond curls hung limply around her face, and faded red blotches covered her neck and chest. Her arms were crossed, and she didn't immediately make eye contact.

"Michelle? Are you okay?"

She looked up at Cate and slowly shook her head back and forth, her face sullen and eyes pooled with tears.

"Get in here ..." Cate stepped back, pulling the door wider and Michelle shuffled in, standing awkwardly in the doorway between the kitchen and dining room.

Cate pushed the door closed, and wrapped her arm around Michelle's shoulders, guiding her gently through the dining room and to the living room couch. Michelle didn't say a word, and sunk back into the couch with a quiet sniffle. Cate grabbed a box of tissues from the bathroom and sat at the other end of the couch with one leg folded underneath her so could face Michelle. She set the tissues in between them and waited quietly for Michelle to decide she was ready to talk. Michelle grabbed a tissue from the box and balled it up in her hand while resting her knuckle under her nose.

"She moved out," she finally said, her voice rough and gravelly.

"Oh, Michelle …" Cate sighed sympathetically. "Do you feel like talking about it?"

Michelle looked down at her hands, absentmindedly pulling the tissue apart in her lap. She sighed, then turned her body so she was facing Cate.

"I got home from my shift at the thrift store yesterday, and she was just sitting on the couch watching TV when I walked in. When I saw her sitting there, all I felt was dread. She looked up at me with these puppy dog eyes. She popped up off the couch and came over to give me a hug, and I just pushed her away. It was like I couldn't stand to be touched.

"She was so hurt. I couldn't even look at her. She just started yelling at me, asking me what was wrong and why I was being so cold. She wanted to know what she had done wrong, how she could fix it … it was awful." Tears rolled down her cheeks. She grabbed another tissue and held it over her nose, blowing gently.

Cate laid her elbow on the back of the couch and rested her head on her hand, waiting to see if Michelle would continue. She ran the tissue over her nose and sighed, shifting her weight just slightly to lean more heavily into the back of the couch.

"I felt terrible and tried to smooth things over. I made her favorite spaghetti and meatballs for dinner, and we shared a bottle of wine. We went to bed and … made up." Michelle's eyes flicked up to meet Cate's, and she responded with raised eyebrows, nodding in acknowledgment.

"It was a bad idea ... when we woke up this morning, I just felt that same sense of dread. It hadn't gone away, and now I had to break her heart all over again." Michelle's gaze was locked in on her lap, and she ran the tissue across her nose. She finally raised her head, taking a deep breath and clearing her throat.

"She got up and went to the bathroom to shower, and I just sat there in bed rehearsing what I was going to say when she came out. She was just wrapped in a towel and started walking toward the dresser, and I asked her to wait. I told her that we needed to talk, and of course she was hurt again because I think she knew what was coming. I tried to tell her that I care about her, but that I was afraid if we kept going the way we were I was only going to hurt her more. She started yelling at me again and I listened, but I knew it had to be over.

"I told her I would step out so she could get her things together, but that I needed her to be moved out by the time I get back. Which is why I'm here ..." Michelle trailed off and looked at Cate with an apologetic frown.

"Wait, she's moving out now?" Cate said, widening her eyes and raising her eyebrows.

"Yeah ..." Michelle turned and leaned into the back of the couch.

"So, you must have figured out what you're supposed to be doing here!"

Michelle gave a forced laugh. "No, not at all. I have no clue what I'm even qualified for that would make an impact here. I just can't keep dragging Kelly down with my hopelessness. I just can't be the person she needs me to be."

"Has Father Matthew been any help?"

"No, and I think I've realized that I'm holding onto such resentment over being so dependent on him ... for everything."

Cate was surprised that this had only just now occurred to Michelle when Cate had been feeling this since the moment she woke up in the hospital and learned Father Matthew had separated her from Joey. She felt a shadow pass over her eyes again, and anger rose in her chest.

"I hate that he is the only person who can send us home," she said darkly.

"I don't know if it's worth fighting it anymore ... I think I've realized that I need to just let go and stop trying to figure it out. It's been so exhausting, and I feel like I'm spinning my wheels."

Michelle looked up at this point, and Cate noticed a clarity to her eyes and a softness to her face. She couldn't believe Michelle was just going to give in.

"I think what I decided this morning before I finally asked Kelly to move out was that I need to sort of clear the deck, start with a clean slate, and just wait to see what comes next. As upsetting as it's been to lose Kelly's companionship, it's also been oddly liberating."

"Liberating? Michelle, that makes no sense. We're completely trapped here."

"I know ... it doesn't make sense, but honestly, Cate, my way just isn't working–it never has, really. I'd be happy for a little while, but it never lasted. No relationship ever truly satisfied me. I always felt like there was something missing. So, I don't know–maybe trying Father Matthew's way isn't the end of the world. I feel like all I have left is to trust that I will get what I need as long as I'm living in Graypourt, and ... I don't know ... maybe all of those other things I want ... just aren't meant for me."

Cate looked at Michelle with skepticism and, as much as she tried to hide it, pity. She felt like Michelle was giving up. The only way Cate could rationalize it was to assume that it was because Michelle hadn't been separated from a child and, as far as Cate could tell, didn't have anyone waiting for her at home. There was nothing else motivating her to move on from Graypourt.

Michelle sighed and looked up at Cate with that same clarity in her eyes.

"You know ... maybe the key to going home is accepting the longing for what I thought I wanted ... and just embracing the trying moments of this whole experience. What if giving in to them, instead of fighting to make them stop, is what will make going home that much more powerful?" Michelle's eyes were misty, her expression filled with wanting.

Cate offered a sympathetic frown. "Michelle ... give it some time. You'll figure it out."

"Well, I guess time is all I have left."

Cate felt this like a punch to her gut. She knew Michelle had been here longer than her, and it didn't give her much confidence to hear her punctuate that fact. She tried to gather her strength and do what she could.

"Okay, well, stay as long as you need to. I was just picking up a little bit, then Maggie's coming by to help me pull some weeds in my flower beds. I actually have tulips coming up!" Cate leaned toward Michelle with a wide smile, hoping this might lighten the mood.

Michelle turned and looked at her with a tired smile. "That's awesome! I might just close my eyes for a little bit, if that's okay?"

"Absolutely! Do you want to lay down in the bedroom across from mine? That way you can just close the door and rest?"

Michelle nodded and pulled herself up off the couch. "Yeah, that sounds great." She flashed another half-hearted smile and headed toward the bathroom. Cate set the box of tissues on the end table and went back to the kitchen to give Michelle some privacy.

She heard the bedroom door close lightly, and the silence sent a chill through her body. She rubbed her hands up and down her arms and turned toward the window over the sink to watch for Maggie.

~ 34 ~

Cate didn't hear much from Michelle over the next several days but thought of her often, hoping that the transition back to living alone and her newfound liberation was going okay. It was her second day off for the week, so Cate was trying to stay busy until Maggie got home from her assigned day at the children's boutique.

The phone rang with a shrill clanging sound from the direction of the kitchen. Cate finished hanging up the bath towel on the metal bar next to the shower before making her way across the house. She had learned the phone would continue to ring until she picked it up, so there was no real reason to rush.

"Hi Father," she said into the receiver cradled in her hand.

"Hello, Cate!" he answered enthusiastically. "How's it going?"

"Oh, fine. I was just folding some laundry and getting a few things put away. What's up?"

"Well, I wanted to ask you a favor."

Cate's first reaction was to laugh. Father Matthew sure had a messed up sense of humor if he thought she would be open to doing him a favor given all he had taken away from her, put her through, and asked of her already. She leaned back against the counter and closed her eyes. Despite all of that, he had returned her phone to her in a sense, so she buried her cynicism and tried to be open-minded.

"Sure ..."

The back door swung open just then and Maggie stepped into the kitchen.

"Heyyyy, la–" her hand flew up to her mouth as soon as she spotted Cate on the phone. Cate waved her in and put up one finger to indicate she wouldn't be long.

"Hi Father!" Maggie called as she turned toward the dining room. Cate stifled a laugh and collected herself as she waited for Father Matthew to reveal his favor.

"Hello, Margaret ..." Father Matthew's voice responded into her ear with an air of playful admonishment.

"Sorry, Father ... go ahead." Cate crossed one arm over her midsection and focused on the floor in concentration.

"I'd like you to say a prayer with me."

It was a simple request, and prayer wasn't completely foreign to Cate. It was something she recalled with fondness, the memory of her grandmother's perfume, the silkiness of the skin on her arms as she leaned against her in the church pew during Mass. So Cate was surprised when her stomach clenched and her throat tightened. She didn't understand why such a simple request would cause such a negative reaction.

"Cate ... are you there?" Father Matthew sounded more concerned than irritated, and Cate tried to shake off her hesitation. She thought about what Michelle had said and realized she wasn't about to let Father Matthew's righteousness get to her. No way she was going to give in and give up on Joey. She cleared her throat.

"Sorry, Father ... I don't think I'm up for that today."

Father Matthew was quiet, but she could still hear him breathing on the other end of the line. Her Midwestern "nice" was severely conflicted, but she wasn't budging.

"Okay," Father Matthew finally said, sadly and softly. She could tell he was disappointed, but Cate was proud of herself for standing up for what she wanted to get out of this experience.

With a gentle click, the line went quiet, and Cate set the receiver back in its place on the wall. She let her hand linger there for a moment as she processed Father Matthew's reaction. It surprised her how quickly he'd backed off, and she couldn't help but feel a little ashamed for declining his offer. She allowed her hand to fall to her side and went to find Maggie in the other room.

She was seated in one of the recliners, flipping through an old magazine that sat gathering dust on the bookcase next to the chair.

"Hey ..." Cate said, still thinking about the call.

"How's Father Matthew?" Maggie asked with an edge of sarcasm.

"Um, he's fine."

"Oh, yeah? What did he have to say?"

"He wanted to pray with me." Cate looked at her as she settled into the couch, folding both legs underneath her.

"Oh. What did you say?" Maggie seemed to be trying to decipher Cate's feelings about it, searching her face for any clues.

"I told him no."

Maggie winced, slowly replacing the magazine on the bookshelf and turning back to focus on Cate.

"Peter's working at The Bar tonight," she shared, hinting that they should plan a visit.

Cate was grateful that Maggie seemed to pick up on her need to pivot to another topic.

"We should go see him—what time can you leave?" Cate leaned into the arm of the couch.

"An hour ago ..." Maggie said with wide eyes.

"It's three o'clock." Cate chuckled.

"I know ... it was a long day at the children's boutique, and I just need to unwind."

"Okay, let me freshen up a little bit, then we can head over. Do you want a pre-game glass of wine while you wait?"

Maggie's eyes lit up, and she nodded like a child being offered a cupcake. "Yes, please! But I can get it ... go get dressed!"

It was finally warm enough to ditch the leggings, and Cate pulled out a denim skirt she'd picked up at the thrift store that hit her mid-thigh and an oversized blue gingham dress shirt, which she half-tucked under the waistband of her skirt. She slipped on a pair of white tennis shoes and grabbed her purse off the bed. She stopped in the bathroom to run a brush through her hair. When she first arrived in Graypourt, it fell just below her ears, but it had grown and now rested at her shoulders in soft waves. She brushed on some blush and lip gloss, rubbing her lips together with a quiet *pop*.

"Okay, let's roll," she said when she reached the kitchen. Maggie tipped her wineglass back one last time and set it gently in the sink.

The bus pulled up to The Bar, its brick facade and unassuming wood door now a familiar part of their life in Graypourt. Cate and Maggie walked inside, letting their eyes adjust. The only light came from the large picture window at one end of the room, flickering wall sconces evenly spaced along the other three walls and the backlighting from the shelves of hard alcohol lining the wall behind the bar. There was already a lively happy-hour crowd gathered. There were just a few open seats at the bar, and most of the tables were occupied with at least a couple of guests.

Peter spotted them and waved from his spot behind the bar, pointing to the table near the window where several of their friends were already seated. They both waved back in acknowledgment and made their way across the bar.

Emily and Renee were seated on one side of the table, and Maggie went around to offer friendly hugs, taking the last chair next to Emily. Cate settled into a chair between Leo and Renee, noting Kelly's absence as she greeted everyone else at the table. Max was working behind the bar with Peter, and Cate tossed him a wave as she caught his eye.

Peter came by with a couple of pitchers of beer and set them down in the center of the table. He held the tray against his side and leaned on the back of Cate's chair. She ignored the fluttering in her stomach as usual and resisted the urge to look at him with the admiration she was trying hard to suppress. She nonchalantly grabbed one of the pitchers and filled the glass in front of her.

"What shakin', gang?" Peter asked, searching the faces around the table.

"Just letting off some steam, Stretch. How are you?" Maggie said, filling her pint glass. Cate looked up to see Peter's reaction to Maggie's favorite term of endearment for him, her smile laced with amusement and anticipation. He shot Maggie a look of mock exasperation before he turned and went back to the bar.

Cate turned her attention to Michelle, searching her face for some sign of how she was coping with her return to single living. She was pleasantly surprised to see her relaxed shoulders and a look of confidence and contentment on her face. Michelle seemed to sense Cate's attention and she turned with a friendly smile.

"Hey Catie-bug!"

"How are you, friend?" Cate leaned on the table to try to get as close as possible without crowding Leo and to be able to be heard over the sounds of competing conversations, music, and typical bar noise. He seemed to pick up on her signals and offered to switch seats.

"Thanks, amigo." Cate smiled as she quickly slid into his chair when he offered it to her. "You look so good, Shell."

Michelle smiled gratefully. "I am good ... really good."

"Wow, that's great. I guess your new approach is working?" Cate took a generous sip from her beer mug, a twinge of envy prickling in her chest.

"Well, I had a dream last night and ... I think I know what I'm supposed to be doing here." Michelle took a drink from her pint glass and set it down, turning to look for Cate's reaction.

"So ... are you going to tell me what that is?" Cate's eyes widened, and she lengthened her neck in Michelle's direction expectantly.

Michelle chuckled. "I want to start a community health clinic here in Graypourt."

Cate sat up, quietly smacking her hand on the table. "Get out! That's an awesome idea!"

"Yeah, I mean, the hospital is the only place we can go if we need medical care, and I figure there are probably enough people with minor illnesses, injuries, or health concerns who don't necessarily want to go to the hospital. I've sketched a whole layout for the community center, a triage process and schedule."

"Shell! I'm so proud of you! When do you think you'll be ready to open?"

"Well, soon ... and I was hoping you would help me." Michelle narrowed her eyes and grimaced.

"Wait, really? Did you know I was a nurse back at home?" Cate asked her incredulously.

Michelle nodded. "Father Matthew might have mentioned it to me the other day after I was at your house. I know I can do this if you help me."

Cate's heart swelled.

"Count me in."

$$\sim 35 \sim$$

Maggie set a fresh cup of coffee in front of Cate and settled back onto the barstool at her kitchen island.

"So, you and Michelle are going to pitch her idea to Father Matthew today?" Maggie kept her gaze focused on Cate while taking a tentative sip of her coffee.

"Yeah. I'm really impressed with how organized and prepared she is–she was definitely made for this."

Maggie paused, and her face softened with a wistful smile. "That's one of my favorite quotes–Joan of Arc, right? Or was it Esther?"

"Oh, I don't know … I'll take your word for it," Cate answered with a wink.

"So, what will you be doing?"

"I think she wants me to be in charge of triage. So I'll check patients in, prioritize them based on how severe their need is, and direct them to an open exam room if they need to be seen. I can also give out over-the-counter medications like ibuprofen or bandages, stuff like that."

"Nice! I'd love to help, too, if you think there's something for me to do."

"Oh, I have no doubt there will be a job for you. I'll know more about what other roles we need to fill after our meeting today." Cate's eyes flicked up to the clock on the wall. "Shoot–I still need to get showered …"

She hopped off her stool and set her mug in the sink. She wrapped her arms around Maggie from behind and gave her a quick squeeze and a friendly peck on the cheek.

"I'll see you this afternoon!" she called on her way down the hall to the front door.

"Bye, Catie-bug!"

The bus pulled up to the corner at the bottom of the hill leading up to St. Ann's. Cate followed Michelle down the steps, and they began the two-block climb up to the church.

"The leaves are budding," Michelle observed, her eyes traveling to the treetops on both sides of the street.

"Yeah, and the flowers are really coming in now, too," Cate added, pointing to a collection of tulips, daffodils, and crocuses in one front yard as they passed.

"I've always loved spring."

Cate felt the sun warm on her cheeks and drew in a deep breath. "Me, too."

They were hitting the steepest part of the climb and quieted to concentrate on their breathing. They reached the walkway up to the church, and each took one side of the divided concrete path. At the top of the steps, they passed through the open gate and paused for a moment to gaze up at the arched doorway and twin spires of the church rising above them.

"So pretty," Michelle sighed.

Cate wasn't used to Michelle being this content and pensive. She turned and marveled at her face, relaxed and serene, like she didn't have a care in the world.

"Have you been taking medication today?" Cate asked.

"No, why?"

"I've never seen you this relaxed."

"I know ... it's pretty great." Michelle gave her a peaceful smile, then turned and started walking toward the church office.

Cate followed Michelle into the small entryway where Annie was in her usual spot at her desk.

"Well, hey, ladies!" Annie welcomed them with a broad, friendly grin. "Let me go let Father Matthew know you're here."

They watched Annie go through a nondescript door, which she quickly closed behind her, leaving Cate and Michelle alone in the entryway. She came back out a few moments later, followed by Father Matthew.

"How are two of my favorite people?" he said, his signature wide smile lighting up his piercing blue eyes.

"Hi, Father," Michelle said while Cate gave him a friendly static wave.

"Let's go into the sitting room." He walked in front of them through the wide doorway into the next room. Michelle and Cate followed, taking seats on the couch across from Father Matthew, who was seated in one of the high-backed armchairs. He crossed his legs and sat back casually in the chair, his hands clasped in his lap.

"So let's hear about this exciting plan of yours," he said, his eyebrows raised expectantly.

Cate watched in awe and admiration as her friend detailed her plans for the free medical clinic, watching how her eyes twinkled as she leaned forward from her spot on the couch and gestured with her hands for emphasis. Cate found herself wanting something that would make her feel the same. Excited, motivated, passionate. But she couldn't push past the thick, heavy lump in her belly or the stubborn frustration of being controlled, held captive, and kept from her child. She felt the familiar dark cloud settling over her. Her excitement for Michelle shifted, and the dreaded envy rooted in her competitive nature began to snake its way around her head.

She caught Father Matthew's eye, and he seemed to see the change in her expression. *Please don't say anything, she thought. To-*

day isn't about me ... please don't make this about me. She forced a smile and averted her eyes back to Michelle just as she wrapped up her pitch. She couldn't help but offer celebratory applause, her pride and admiration returning to the forefront of her mind.

Michelle turned to her with an appreciative laugh, clapping her hand on Cate's shoulder and gently giving her a shake.

"I could not have gotten to this point without this girl right here," she said, looking at Cate with grateful and misty eyes.

Cate's eyes flitted to Father Matthew, and he nodded, giving her a fatherly wink of approval.

"You two seem to make a pretty good team," he said, sitting forward, hands clasped in thought. "I like this idea ... a lot." He sat up straight, then leaned back in the chair. "Whatever you need, we'll make it happen."

Michelle gasped and brought her hands together under her chin, then looked over at Cate with wide eyes and an even bigger smile. They hugged, then Michelle turned back to Father Matthew.

"Thank you so much, Father." Michelle pulled the yellow legal pad out of her backpack, tearing off the sheets that had the handwritten list she and Cate had worked on, carefully organized by category. She handed it over to Father Matthew, and he skimmed through it, flipping each page gently as he absorbed the long list of items. He set it down on his lap and focused on Michelle, his eyes filled with pride.

"Well done, Michelle. I'm on it and will let you know when everything is ready. How else can I help?"

Michelle looked over at Cate, and Cate gave her a nod of encouragement.

"We were hoping to also get a small panel van ... so we can make house visits to anyone who isn't able to get to the community center." Michelle's hands gripped her knees, and Cate saw how she started bouncing one foot at the heel.

Father Matthew's face took on a more serious expression, his brows furrowed and his mouth turned up on one side.

"Let me give that one some thought, okay?" he tucked his chin and smiled just slightly.

Michelle nodded, and Cate felt her heart sink. That had been an important part of Michelle's mission, and she thought Father Matthew owed her that gesture of trust. She looked down at her lap and waited for Michelle to bring the meeting to a close.

"Okay, well, thanks again, Father. We'll just wait to hear from you then?"

All three of them stood up from their seats, and Father Matthew tucked the list under his arm.

"You got it–it won't be too long." He held out his hand, and they each accepted his handshake. Michelle nodded, pressing her hands to her thighs. She picked up her backpack and threw it over one shoulder, then moved toward the doorway into the office. Cate followed close behind, offering Annie a small wave and a polite smile.

"Oh, bye, ladies!" she chirped from her desk, her blue-rimmed glasses perched at the end of her tiny elfin nose.

Cate caught up with Michelle, who seemed to be moving at a racehorse's pace toward the gate. She just caught her swiping a hand across her cheek before trotting down the concrete steps to the walkway.

"He'll come through," Cate said, wrapping an arm around Michelle and pressing her free hand to her shoulder. Michelle wiped another tear off her cheek and sniffled.

"I hope so ..." she sighed, letting her eyes travel up to the blue sky, where cottony clouds floated by, briefly covering up the sun.

~ 36 ~

Cate carried the final box down the narrow steps of the supply bus, stepping carefully and keeping her eyes on the ground to avoid tripping and breaking her neck. The box of medical supplies wasn't heavy, but it was awkward to carry, and she was relieved to finally set it on top of the pile they had stacked near the side door into the community center.

Maggie stood a few feet away with her clipboard, occasionally glancing up to count boxes or check a label.

"Everything here?" Cate asked, shielding her eyes from the bright afternoon sun as she waited for Maggie's response.

Maggie made one last checkmark and met Cate's glance.

"Yep! All here!" She gave Cate a thumbs up and a satisfied smile.

Cate turned to the open door of the supply bus, meeting Harvey's expectant look.

"All set, Harv! Thank you!" she called with a grateful smile and a friendly wave.

"All right, kids–good luck to you!" Harvey returned the smile. He pulled the lever to close the folding door and the bus pulled away toward the road.

Cate grabbed the dolly and began stacking the first few boxes to take them inside where they would be storing everything. She saw Maggie tuck the clipboard into her backpack that was resting on the ground and pull a second dolly over to begin loading up boxes.

"Careful, Mags, there are a couple on the bottom that are super heavy."

"Okay ... we can save those for Peter," Maggie said with a playful grin.

Cate laughed, her eyes flitting up to the gathering clouds off to the south. Peter was wrapping up his early shift at The Bar and had said he would join them as soon as he got off.

"Let's hope he beats the rain," she said with a twinge of apprehension. "C'mon, let's get this first load inside."

Maggie followed her, pulling the dolly behind her. "Where did Michelle wander off to?"

"Good question ... it seems like she went inside a while ago."

The side door was propped open just a crack with a small wood block, so Cate set the dolly upright and pulled the thick metal door open toward her. She leaned back against the door and let Maggie go past with her dolly before following her inside. She let the door go and heard it settle against the block with a hollow thud.

She followed Maggie into the small office they had been offered to store their supplies until they were ready to open the clinic. She was already pulling boxes into one corner, and Cate joined her to add the stack from her dolly.

It had been several hours since the last Daylight Ministries volunteers had left, and the community center had a quiet stillness to it at this time of day. They brought in a second load of boxes, and there still was no sign of Michelle.

"I'm going to see if I can find Michelle," Cate said, her face etched with concern.

"I'll come with you." Maggie set her dolly upright next to Cate's in the hallway outside the office and followed her toward the kitchen. The hallway was dark except for the emergency lights near the ceiling, and they carefully made their way into the dimly lit kitchen.

"Everything's pretty buttoned-up in here–let's check the main hall," Cate said, moving past the stainless-steel island and around the buffet counter. They pushed through the swinging door into the large hall, the high cinder block walls rising up to the exposed metal infrastructure of the ceiling. Just then, Cate noticed some movement near the bar at the back of the hall.

"Is that Michelle and Kelly?" Maggie said quietly as she stepped up to stand next to Cate.

"Sure looks like it." Cate paused, observing Michelle's blond curls peeking out from the open doorway behind the bar, Kelly's wide eyes now focused on them. She watched Kelly nod in their direction and Michelle spun around and stepped into the bar area, partially hidden behind the counter. Cate could tell even from a distance that Michelle was embarrassed, but Kelly just seemed to be irritated as if they had been interrupted.

"Hey, guys!" Michelle called, her voice a little higher pitched than normal. "Just give me one more minute and I'll meet you outside."

"Okay ... everything all right?" Cate called back, concern on the edges of her voice.

"Yeah! Yep ... everything's good." Michelle gave them a thumbs-up and Kelly crossed her arms, a tight smile carved into her face.

"Okay, we'll see you outside in a minute." Cate and Maggie reluctantly turned around and went back the direction they had come from.

"That did not look good," Maggie said, expressing the exact thought swimming around in Cate's head. She looked at Maggie and nodded, her eyes narrowed and pursed her lips.

"Yeah, probably not what Michelle needs right now," she sighed as they got back to the spot where they had left the dollies.

They made several more trips before Michelle finally emerged from the side door and walked toward them, a sheepish grin on her face.

"I am so sorry, you guys. I did not mean for you to unload all of this by yourselves."

Michelle stopped when she reached the last pile of boxes and bent down to move one onto Maggie's waiting dolly.

"Careful, those are the really heavy ones," Cate warned. "What was that all about?" she pressed as Michelle slid the box onto the dolly.

Michelle stood up, looking at Cate with a contrite expression, her lips folding into a frown.

"After I propped the door open, I went into the kitchen to grab a glass of water, and Kelly was still in there, closing everything up."

"Breakfast ended hours ago ... what was she still doing here?" Cate's brow furrowed, and she wrinkled her nose in mild disgust.

"I think she was waiting for me."

"Aw, Shell ..." Maggie sighed, stepping around Michelle so she was facing her, crossing her arms and standing next to Cate.

"She said she wanted to talk, and she had to organize some things at the bar, so I followed her over there. I really didn't think it would last so long."

"It's okay," Cate said, stuffing her hands into the pockets of her shorts. "What did she want to talk about?" Cate knew she was being nosy, but she didn't want anything to derail Michelle's plans and felt somewhat responsible for keeping her on track.

"Well, at first she was just mad. She wanted to rehash the whole argument we had before she left, and I just wasn't going to engage with her about it. I think once she realized I wasn't going to go down that road with her, she sort of backed off. She asked when we thought the clinic would be opening. She told me how proud she was of me for taking this leap and how much happier I seemed to be. She started asking me a bunch of questions about how the clinic would work, and I was actually excited to share all the details with her.

"I followed her back behind the bar where they store all the extra booze, napkins, that kind of stuff, and I was just blabbing on and on. I didn't even realize that she had turned to face me ... then she kissed me." Michelle dropped her face into her hands, then let them drop and lifted her eyes up to the sky with a loud sigh.

Cate felt anger and frustration simmering in her belly, and she crossed her arms while she waited for Michelle to continue. She started mentally preparing her response if Michelle expressed any consideration of getting back together with Kelly.

"Is that what we walked in on?" Maggie piped up, mildly amused.

Michelle laughed. "Uh, yeah."

Cate had to laugh at that point, too, briefly putting her hand over her eyes.

"Anyway ... after you guys left, I told her that we can't get back together. I said that even though I might selfishly want to be in a relationship, it's become a distraction from what I feel like I'm being pulled toward. That I have felt that way for a long, long time–before I came to Graypourt and way before I ever met her. I know deep down in my heart that I need to give the clinic my full focus and attention.

"I told her that I really hoped we could be friends, though, and how much I enjoy spending time with her–that our connection is still really important to me."

"How did she take it?" Maggie asked, her expression more serious.

"Um ... she was sad, but then she sort of relaxed and gave me a hug. She said that if friends was all she could get, she would take it in order to keep me in her life."

Cate's heart swelled with pride and admiration. She knew that Michelle was made for this mission she was embarking on, and it was so satisfying to see her fully committed to it. It made her think of Joey–how difficult life had been after his diagnosis, how much she had doubted herself, but how she chose to get up every morning and just be the best mom to him she could be.

"I'm proud of you," she said with a nurturing smile. "You just have to keep choosing to stick to your mission every single day. You can do this."

"Thanks," Michelle said, her eyes misting up. She took a deep breath and cleared her throat. "Also, great news–Kelly wants to make the clinic part of Daylight Ministries. She has some really great ideas about where guests can hang out after breakfast if they want to wait while we get the clinic set up, then they can move right into their appointments. She also thought we could even triage while they eat, just going through the dining hall and checking who needs to be seen."

Maggie dropped her arms and brought her hands together, letting out a small gasp. "That's amazing!"

Michelle's smile lit up her entire face. "It really is. I think we're on our way, friends."

~ 37 ~

The large open hall of the community center was divided with rows of temporary exam curtains. At the far end by the main entrance, a line of folding tables and chairs had been placed just inside the main doors, clipboards lined up for patient forms.

Maggie stood ready to check in members of the community with various medical needs from common colds to sprained ankles. Peter was stationed outside to assist anyone who required a helping hand, a wheelchair, or transportation to the hospital. Cate was assigned to a separate station where she would triage each person as Maggie handed her the form they had filled out, directing them to an exam area or dispensing any medication they might need.

Father Matthew had provided all the medical staff with light-blue scrubs, dropped off at the community center as they were setting up that morning. Cate had watched Michelle's eyes well up when she opened the box and took in the sight of the unexpected gift. Cate had to admit, it did make them all look a lot more professional. She couldn't help but smile when she saw herself in the mirror of the community center bathroom, feeling a little like her old self.

They heard the bus pull up to the community center, and the low hum of voices from the line of people stretching from the main entrance around the corner of the building. Michelle stepped up to Cate's station, confident and in control. She held a small stack of half sheets of paper and a clipboard.

"That should be our volunteers. I'm going to meet them at the side door–do you want to come hear the instructions?" she asked.

"Yeah, absolutely." Cate set the package of bandages she was holding in one of the supply bins stacked behind her chair and walked around the table to follow Michelle.

"Mags, come listen to the volunteer instructions," Cate called to Maggie at the check-in tables. She popped up out of her seat and fell into step next to Cate.

The volunteers were already streaming down the hallway and into the kitchen by the time the three of them arrived. Michelle stood on one side of the stainless-steel island, and the small crowd quieted. Cate had helped with volunteer recruitment, so she already knew that the group included other nurses like her, a doctor, a couple of pharmacists, and a handful of non-healthcare professionals. She and Maggie went to join Peter and the rest of the volunteers now standing quietly between the doorway and the island where Michelle was waiting.

Peter raised his eyebrows and threw his arm around Cate's shoulders. She leaned into him, and she felt him squeeze her arm. She patted his hand before shifting out from under his arm and turning her focus to Michelle.

"Hey, everyone, welcome to the Graypourt Free Medical Clinic. Thank you for volunteering this morning. It looks like we have a big crowd today, so put on an extra layer of patience," she announced. "Once you have your assignments, we'll go into the hall and I'll direct you to our different stations."

Each person stepped up to the island and gave Michelle their name. She checked them off the list and handed them their instructions, including the station they were assigned to. Cate marveled once again at Michelle's natural ability to organize, coordinate, and literally think of everything. Michelle led the group into the main hall, her blond curls bouncing as she walked, and pointed out the numbering system on the exam curtains, the check-in table positions, and the triage stations. The group dispersed, and everyone took their places. There was a nervous excitement in the air as Michelle went to the main door, pushing the bar that released the doors. She propped both open, and Cate heard her welcoming their first patients.

"Welcome, everyone! Please come in a single file, then you may line up behind any of the five check-in locations at the first table. Our volunteers will instruct you on where to go after that. If you or anyone in your group need assistance, we do have a few available wheelchairs."

Michelle went quiet after that, and Cate didn't see her come back into the hall, so assumed she was making her way down the line of people to see if there was anyone who needed more urgent care or should be diverted to the hospital. Only a moment later, the first residents entered the hall and approached the check-in table. The Graypourt Free Medical Clinic was officially open.

The stream of people entering the community center remained steady for a full hour, and it was satisfying to realize that they were truly meeting a need. Cate hardly had a chance to do much more than respond to the patients who were directed to her station or the volunteer nurses who came to request basic supplies. Finally, the initial crush slowed enough that she could take a breath and look around.

Patients were exiting a few of the exam rooms and getting in line for the prescription medication station. One person hobbled out on brand new crutches and two others were being pushed out in wheelchairs. She handed over a box of bandages to an older woman who had a number of cuts on her hands, Cate guessed from gardening. She gave her a friendly smile and told her to come back next week if the cuts hadn't improved.

She watched the woman walk toward the exit, and her eyes fell on a petite figure tucked away in a corner of the large hall, leaning against the wall with her arms tucked behind her, watching and observing, but keeping her distance from the activity. Cate initially was concerned and stood up from her chair to go check on her. She paused, noticing the serene and confident expression on Michelle's face. She watched in awe at Michelle's ability to make herself small, humble and completely at the service of others.

It would have been so easy for Michelle to remain at the center of the activity, barking directions, micromanaging her volunteers, yet she chose to stay in the shadows instead, reflecting the light back to those who were doing the work and those being served.

Cate smiled, surprised at the flood of emotion that overwhelmed her as she quickly wiped away a lone tear that rolled down her cheek.

~ 38 ~

A loud cheer erupted from the small crowd gathered inside The Bar as they all raised their glasses when Michelle came through the door in a shaft of early evening sunlight. She put her hands up to her face, her fingers meeting just above her nose, the corners of her smile just visible on either side of her hands. Her bright-blue eyes crinkled at the sides as she seemed to fight back the emotion from the sight of such a huge wave of support and celebration.

Cate stepped away from the bar and wrapped Michelle in a huge hug, bending gently from side to side in an added gesture of affection. They pulled apart and Maggie followed with her own hug, which then opened the floodgates as others came up to love on Michelle. She was crying in full force now, tears streaming down her cheeks through her wide smile and the occasional laugh when someone approached her with yet one more hug.

Finally the crowd settled, and Michelle was able to move toward the long table Peter had arranged for the volunteers so they could all sit together. Father Matthew had joined them as well, seated toward one end while they insisted Michelle have the seat of honor at the head of the table.

"You guys, this is too much," she playfully admonished. Cate and Maggie had had a flower arrangement delivered, filled with all of Michelle's favorite spring blooms, so large it completely blocked her from view when she took her seat. Cate swooped in and offered to move the flowers over to the bar, and Michelle thanked her with a small chuckle.

"Speech, speech, speech, speech ..." several members of the group began chanting. Michelle's cheeks flushed and her eyebrows folded in, her eyes widening. The group refused to relent, so she stood up slowly and reluctantly, clearing her throat.

"Okay, here's all I'm going to say," she started with a smile. "If ever you feel a nudge or pull or even a really powerful shove to make the world a little bit better ... don't ever, ever say no." She raised her glass and the rest of the group followed with a chorus of "Yeah! Whoo hoo! Preach, sister!"

Cate saw Father Matthew gazing at Michelle with such pride and admiration it actually moved her to tears. This man who had made life so hard for them, separated some of them from their children, and kept them from their families, really did seem to want to see them restored in some way.

The group ordered a smorgasbord of appetizers, and most stayed through several rounds of drinks before people began to peel off in twos and threes. Eventually, the last people left at the table were Cate, Maggie, Peter, Michelle, and Kelly and her new romantic interest, Grace. They stayed through one more round of drinks, then Kelly and Grace said their goodbyes and left. Cate could see that Michelle was fading. Her eyelids were getting droopy, and she was spending more time stifling yawns than making conversation.

"I think we should call it a night," Cate offered, hoping Michelle would take the opportunity to make her exit.

"Yeah," Michelle responded with a long, deep yawn. "I'm beat."

Peter made sure they had taken care of their tab, then the group stepped out into the cool spring evening air. The earlier rain storm left behind a mild humidity, and small puddles of water had collected in the pockets and cracks in the concrete.

"Oh! Your flowers!" Maggie said, running back into the bar and returning a moment later carrying the large arrangement with both hands, her entire head and shoulders blocked by the voluminous blooms. "Maybe we went just a little overboard with this ..." she said, and the entire group burst into laughter.

"Here, I've got it," Peter said, taking it from Maggie's hands. He held it in front of his chest while they made their way down the street and past the park to the bus stop.

When they turned the corner, Cate spotted a figure sitting at one of the round tables under the large overhang at the bus stop. She immediately recognized the black shirt and pants, the well-manicured hair and chiseled jawline of Father Matthew. He looked up as they approached and smiled warmly.

"Hey, guys! Finally headed home for the night?"

Michelle yawned again, quickly moving to cover her mouth, and everyone chuckled. "Yes, I'm wiped out. In a good way, though," she added.

Father Matthew leaned his arms on the table, directing his eyes at Michelle. "It's good to celebrate our accomplishments, and this was a big one. How do you feel?"

"Honestly, I probably would have been just as proud of myself without all the fanfare. It was so incredible to see how many people we helped today, their faces full of gratitude and just ... peace." Michelle crossed her arms, stifling another yawn.

Cate caught Peter glancing down at the flowers, and a guilty feeling prickled in her chest. Maybe they weren't necessary, and now she was embarrassed that she and Maggie had gone so over-the-top with it.

"I also feel bad taking so much credit," Michelle added thoughtfully. "I definitely didn't do this by myself, so I'm really happy everyone who volunteered and, of course Cate, Maggie and Peter, could celebrate, too. This accomplishment is just as much yours." She gestured with her hands in the direction of all three of them.

"Awesome, so I can keep this ridiculously large arrangement of flowers?" Peter said dryly. Everyone burst into laughter, and Peter set the vase down on the table nearest to him.

"Wanna know what I'm most impressed by?" Father Matthew said, standing up from his seat. They all looked at him expectantly. "I'm impressed that you were able to set aside your own wants and desires in order to bless so many others. You weren't trying to get anything out of it for yourself, just following an urging in your heart. That takes a very strong spiritual maturity."

"She surrendered."

Cate said it so quietly she wasn't even sure she had said it out loud. No one reacted, staying focused on Michelle, and Cate assumed they didn't hear her. Then Father Matthew nodded at her discreetly, the smallest of smiles playing on his lips. She looked over at Michelle just as the bus turned the corner and rumbled up to the bus stop, unable to define a new and different kind of anxiety beginning to bloom in her chest.

Cate ran a brush through her hair and pulled it back into a ponytail. She brushed her teeth, drying her mouth on the hand towel hanging from the ring attached to the wall by the sink. She straightened her shirt, a light knit short-sleeved cotton in a cheerful yellow, and tucked one corner into her linen shorts.

Spring was in full bloom now, and the weather had turned to a more predictable pattern of mostly sunny and warm. She was due at the bakery in a few hours, but she had agreed to meet Maggie, Michelle, and a few of the other girls at the coffee shop before their shifts all started.

She walked through the house to the kitchen just as Maggie came through the door from the back porch.

"Hey, Mags," Cate said nonchalantly. She grabbed her purse off the kitchen table, throwing the long strap across her body.

"You ready to go? I think I heard the bus stopping at the house up the road." Maggie wore her usual knee-length linen shift dress, this one with a collar and three-quarter-length sleeves in a bright pink. Her blond hair fell in long waves over her shoulders, and she had on her favorite cork-and-leather sandals.

"Yep, let's roll." Cate flipped off the kitchen light and pulled the door closed behind her. She followed Maggie down the sidewalk and around the side of the house to the driveway. The tulips and daffodils had matured weeks ago, leaving their long, headless stems behind. Cate had planted petunias and geraniums, which were flourishing now, and she smiled to herself at this simple pleasure that also gave her the tiniest sense of control over her environment.

They climbed up into the bus, greeting Harvey as they turned down the aisle to find their seats. Peter was in the third row, and Cate assumed he must have the early shift at The Bar again today. He was looking at something in his lap as Maggie took the window seat across the aisle from him, and Cate took the one next to her on the aisle. Peter looked up and smiled, leaning forward to greet Maggie as well.

"Hey, ladies, how are you this morning?" He flashed his familiar smile, and Cate's belly fluttered as she smiled back.

"Good! Did you have to stay late last night?" Maggie asked, leaning forward just slightly to see him.

"Yeah, and I have to go back again this morning."

"Geez, does anyone else work at that place?"

"Yeah ..." Peter sighed. "We've had a few no-shows lately, so Max has been giving me more hours since he can actually count on me to be there."

Maggie grimaced. "Sorry, dude."

Peter shrugged and turned his attention to Cate, his expression shifting ever so slightly to something softer, more affectionate. "You working at the bakery today?"

"Yeah, I have the lunch shift today, so I don't have to be there until 10:30."

It had been a few days since she'd seen Peter, and being in his presence after some distance always stirred up the feelings she tried so hard to repress. It was easier when she saw him more often and could get used to his eyes on her, the warmth of his smile, and the gentle way he spoke to her.

"Whatcha reading?" she asked, diverting her gaze to the book open in his lap. She knew Peter was a voracious reader and always seemed to be at least halfway through some large tome of a novel, usually historical spy fiction.

His face immediately brightened, and he lifted the book to show her the cover, using his finger to mark his place. "Oh! This is a new one I picked up at the library this week. Spy novel ..." he said, flashing the boyish grin that always made her blush.

"Of course," she chuckled. She turned away then to watch the scenery go by out the window, and when she looked back, he was focused on his book. She wished she had a camera then to capture the way the light highlighted his nose that rounded right at the tip, how his hair fell across his forehead, his lips protruding just slightly when he was reading. She quickly turned back toward the window before he sensed her watching him, laying her head back against the seat and letting her eyes gently close.

The bus pulled up to the main stop at the park, and Maggie nudged Cate out of her light sleep. She blinked a few times, letting her eyes adjust to the light again, and stood up to step into the aisle. Peter stood up at the exact same time, and they collided, making Peter drop his book. Cate immediately bent down to pick the book up from its landing place in the aisle and came up just inches from Peter's face, their noses practically touching.

"Thanks," he said, taking the book from her hand. "You okay?"

"What? Oh, yeah, I'm okay."

"Okay."

Peter stepped down the aisle, angling himself around Cate.

"Arrrre we going?" Maggie said over her shoulder.

"Oh, yeah, sorry ..." Cate finally made her feet move and paused when she got to the gathering area under the canopy. Peter was already making his way down the sidewalk to the corner where she knew he would turn to head down to The Bar.

"You good?" Maggie asked, her brows furrowed and a questioning look in her eyes.

"Yeah, just tired." Cate smiled, and they started down the sidewalk to the corner. When they reached the coffee shop door, Maggie pulled it open toward them and walked inside. Cate paused with the door open and briefly looked over her shoulder across the street just as Peter walked into the main entrance of The Bar. She sighed and entered the coffee shop, letting the door ease closed behind her.

Emily and Renee were already seated at a table, chatting with Kelly and Grace who were in the booth seat next to them. Cate and Maggie waved and got into line. Iced lattes in hand, they sat down in two of the chairs across the table from their friends.

"Good morning, you two," Renee said with her familiar bright smile.

"Good morning!" Maggie said, and Cate smiled and took a sip of her drink.

"Where's Michelle?" Cate asked, searching the other girls' faces.

"No clue," Renee answered.

Emily shrugged and Kelly said, "I haven't talked to her this week at all."

"Weird ... I talked to her two days ago after we wrapped up at the clinic, but she was too tired to join us at The Bar," Cate recalled.

"I hope she's not sick," Emily said with a sympathetic frown.

"Me, too." Cate glanced toward the door, hoping Michelle would appear, but it stayed frustratingly still. "If she doesn't show up, I'll check in on her at the thrift store when I get off work."

Cate was the first to leave since she had the earliest shift of the group. Michelle hadn't shown, and concern was heavy on her chest as she pulled open the door to the Blue Bird Diner, the familiar smells of melted butter, sugar and dough washing over her.

Miss Henny was busy with a customer, but one of the other employees, Sue, greeted her as she passed through the bakery. She waved as she walked through the dining room, moving quickly past the table where she and Joey had sat their very first day in Graypourt, and pushed through the swinging kitchen door. She pulled her apron off its hook near the walk-in cooler and tied it around her waist. Miss Henny appeared around a corner from the main counter and flashed Cate a warm, friendly smile.

"Hey, Catie-bug!" She had picked up on Maggie's pet name for her and had gotten into the habit of using it almost more than Maggie did.

"Hi, Miss Henny." Cate tried to veil the concern that was becoming increasingly hard to ignore and offered a weak smile back.

"What's wrong, hun?" she asked in her signature soft Southern drawl. Miss Henny busied herself pulling several ingredients down from a shelf and lining them up on the stainless-steel counter.

"Oh, nothing, I think I'm just tired."

Miss Henny paused then and gave her a look that told Cate she wasn't fooling anyone, but she chose to let it go and not press her on it.

"All right, then, how about if you mix up a batch of dough for the donuts, then I'll get you going on frosting."

Cate moved through most of her shift in a fog, distracted by her emotions and the growing urge to make her way down the street to the thrift store, where she hoped to find Michelle healthy and exactly where she was supposed to be.

Finally, the lunch crowd thinned, and the post-rush clean up was done. Cate tossed her apron into the laundry basket by the office and passed through the dining room to the door. She waved to Miss Henny but didn't look to see if she waved back, and she pushed out the door while the bells tinkled above her.

She walked urgently the short half block to the thrift store and went inside. Her eyes immediately landed on the checkout counter, where an unfamiliar older man was standing. He glanced up as she approached the counter, her heart rate picking up.

"Hi, is Michelle working today?"

The man shook his head, his expression and tone flat. "Nope, she was a no-show."

Not "she's out sick today," but "she was a no-show." That definitely did not sound like Michelle.

"Okay, thank you." Cate tried to hide the tightness in her voice and quickly turned to leave. She paused briefly on the sidewalk, not quite sure where to go next.

She found herself at the bus stop and climbed up into the waiting bus. She briefly met Harvey's gaze but couldn't bring herself to smile or do anything other than avert her eyes and slide into the first available seat. She stared blankly out the window, watching the now familiar scenery and the increasingly rural landscape as they got closer to the house.

She flashed Harvey a sad smile as she stepped down onto her driveway and plodded up to the sidewalk along the back of the house. Once inside, she threw her purse down on the kitchen table and pulled open the fridge, staring blankly into the cold, gaping space. She pulled out some lunch meat, cheese, and mustard, grabbed the loaf of bread from the cabinet, and slapped a sandwich together. She leaned back against the counter and took a slow absent bite, barely even tasting her food as she chewed.

She had a foreboding feeling, and her intuition was setting off signals like a five-alarm fire. Why wouldn't Michelle show up for work? It was out of character, but Cate reminded herself that there were a hundred simple explanations–she could be sick, or she might have twisted an ankle, or was in some kind of depression fog. Maybe the guy at the thrift store just had his story wrong and Michelle had let the owner know she wouldn't be in today.

She heard the squealing of the spring coming from the covered porch and set what was left of her sandwich down on the counter just as Maggie walked through the back door.

"Hey," Cate said solemnly, swallowing her food.

"What's wrong?" Maggie hung her purse on the back of one of the kitchen chairs and helped herself to a wine glass from the cabinet.

"I'm really worried about Michelle." Cate's brow furrowed, and she wrapped her arms around her waist.

Maggie grabbed the open bottle of red wine from the counter and helped herself to a healthy pour.

"She wasn't at the thrift store?"

"No, some older guy was working and said Michelle was a no-show today."

Maggie took a long sip of wine, narrowing her eyes toward Cate as she swallowed.

"That doesn't sound like Michelle."

"I know. I don't know what to do, though. I can't call her, and I don't want to take the bus all the way to her house just to find out she's perfectly fine and just took the day off. Something just doesn't feel right."

"Well, maybe we should just sleep on it tonight and you could go see Father Matthew tomorrow. It's your day off, isn't it?"

"Yeah ... okay." Cate gave Maggie a weary smile and stepped around her to pull another wine glass out of the cabinet.

"Hit me," she said, holding the glass out toward Maggie.

~ 40 ~

Cate stepped down from the bus into the small stop near Michelle's neighborhood. It was early, and there was a quiet stillness blanketing the street. She had hardly slept all night, flipping from side to side while she watched the numbers change on her bedside clock.

As she made her way around the corner and down Michelle's street, it was barely on the light side of sunrise, an early morning chill still hanging in the air. She pulled her cardigan more tightly around her body, turning up Michelle's familiar driveway and front walk.

At the top of the steps, she pulled open the aluminum storm door and knocked on the heavier wood door to the house. She knew Michelle would be up, considering her legendary status as an early bird. When no one came to the door, Cate knocked a little louder, then wondered if maybe Michelle had hopped into the shower. She went back down the steps to the driveway, planning to go around to the back deck, when she heard the storm door creak open behind her.

Cate spun around expecting to see her friend, a wide smile breaking across her face, but a stranger stared back at her from the open doorway. She was looking at a younger man, she guessed in his late twenties, heavyset, dressed in baggy sweatpants and a large short-sleeved t-shirt. His hair was tousled, and his eyes had the glassy look of someone who had just woken up.

"Ken I help you?" he grumbled.

"Oh, um, sorry ... I was just looking for my friend, Michelle?" Cate stepped closer to the concrete stairs leading up to the landing but stopped when she noticed the man shrinking back just slightly. He sniffed loudly, running a large, meaty hand under his nose.

"Yeah, I don't know who that is ... I just got here last night."

Cate's memory flashed back to that first disorienting morning waking up at the house in Graypourt, and shame washed over her for disturbing this poor man. The feeling was quickly replaced by confusion and the early prickling of panic firing in her head. She felt her heart rate pick up, and her chest tightened. She closed her eyes and tried to take several deep breaths. When she opened them again, the man was staring at her in bewilderment.

"I'm so sorry to have bothered you," she mumbled, then turned and jogged back to the corner and all the way to the bus stop. She collapsed onto the wood bench, covering her face with her hands, her stomach a hard knot.

Where is Michelle?

When the bus didn't show up after a few minutes, Cate decided to just start walking. It was only about a mile to the park, and she needed some time to think before confronting Father Matthew.

She finally came to the familiar turn onto the street leading up to St. Ann's. She immediately climbed the hill toward the church, making her way up the walkway and through the gate at the top of the steps. She bypassed the church and made a beeline to the office, entering with purpose.

She was surprised to find Annie was in her usual spot at the desk and wondered if she ever slept. Annie looked up over her blue-rimmed glasses perched on the end of her nose.

"Well, good morning, Cate! My, you're up and at 'em early today. How can I help you?"

Cate tried to catch her breath but gave up waiting for her heart and lungs to calm down and just launched in.

"I need to see Father Matthew," she gasped. "Michelle was a no-show at work yesterday, and no one I know has talked to her in the last two days. Something doesn't seem right."

Annie's face darkened, and she stood up from her chair. "Okay, dear. I'll let him know you're here. Go ahead and have a seat in the lounge."

Cate sunk into the cushions at one end of the sitting room couch. The air was still, and Cate squeezed her fingers, trying to calm her racing heart. She closed her eyes and took some deep breaths, feeling her shoulders and back start to relax.

"Hi, Cate." Father Matthew entered the lounge and took a seat in one of the high-backed chairs, leaning back and crossing one ankle over his knee. "Annie said you were asking about Michelle."

Cate sat forward, resting her palms on the edge of the cushion. "I think something's wrong," Cate said, her voice starting to shake again.

"Why do you think something's wrong?" Father Matthew's face was calm and sincere.

"She didn't show up for work yesterday, which is really unlike her. When I went to her house this morning, a strange man answered the door. I haven't talked to her since clinic on Wednesday, and I can't seem to find anyone else who has talked to her since then, either." Cate was breathing hard, her fingers gripping the edge of the cushion.

Father Matthew set his foot on the floor and leaned forward, his elbows resting on the arms of the chair, and brought his hands together.

"Michelle's been allowed to go home."

The blood drained from Cate's face, and her whole body went ice-cold. It was like someone pressed a pause button on time, and Father Matthew's image wobbled in front of her. She closed her eyes and took a deep breath. Then another one.

"Cate ... come back to me. You're safe." Father Matthew spoke calmly from his chair a few feet away. Cate opened her eyes, and the world seemed to settle.

Michelle was gone. She had been allowed to go home. This was a good thing, right? She should be happy for her. So why did she feel so gutted?

"Why didn't she say goodbye?" she finally breathed. This didn't make sense. She and Michelle were close. They were partners in the clinic, and she knew how much work Cate had put into making that happen. How could she just walk away?

"I can't answer that for you," Father Matthew responded, his voice sympathetic and nurturing. "I can promise you, though, that she cared for and respected you very much. If she could have, she would have let you know she was leaving."

Cate shook her head. She wanted it to make sense. No, she needed it to make sense. She stood up, steadying herself as the blood returned to her head.

"Thanks, Father. I have to go," she mumbled and moved quickly through the lounge and out the office door. She exhaled, only then realizing she'd been holding her breath. She reached the gate and trotted down the steps to the top of the hill leading to the street. Then something made her turn around.

The water trickled and gurgled over the flat slate stones next to the sidewalk, and a bird's shrill mating call sounded from the mass of tree branches above her. Something about the way the church stood so solidly against the cerulean-blue sky drew her in. She needed something solid. She moved toward the steps, taking each one slowly, and passed through the gate.

Rustic brick was laid in large a circular pattern leading up to the doors of the church, and a simple cross of white limestone was set into the center. A modest black rubber doormat with white lettering had been placed just in front of the double doors. Cate paused to read what it said–"Mercy to all who enter here"–and she pulled the simple wood door open toward her.

She was in a narrow, circular vestibule, and a small wood table with long spindly legs stood waist-high centered between her and a second set of double doors. There was a small basket of Rosaries on the table, and she was reminded of her grandmother. She could still hear the gentle clicking of the beads between her fingers, her voice making soft incantations as she prayed. Cate moved around the table and pressed her palm against one of the doors, which gradually revealed the main part of the church.

The distinctive sweet scent of Easter lilies immediately got her attention, and she gasped at the shafts of sunlight streaming through the row of stained-glass windows to her left. A matching set of stained-glass windows lined the opposite side of the church, their jewel tones casting a kaleidoscope of color across the floor.

Cate let her gaze wander up to the modest arched ceiling, which ran the full length of the church. She took in the warm oak wood floors and pews. The walls were painted a warm white, the edges of each arch and architectural feature outlined in a dark brown. Cate moved down the center aisle between the rows of pews toward the altar. Potted Easter lilies were arranged in generous groups on either side and across the floor in front of the solid marble altar, flanked by voluminous potted ferns. She stopped a few rows from the front and gently settled into the solid wood pew.

She sat there for several minutes, eventually allowing her gaze to rise to the highest point of the arched ceiling. The cross hung there, solid wood with the familiar slumped form of a thin man affixed to it. His arms were outstretched, his ribs visible under his skin, his sinewy muscles stretched across his shoulders and biceps. She was struck by how broken and weak he looked, and she realized how much she could relate. A sob caught in her throat, and she brought her hand up to her mouth to keep it from becoming a full on wail.

She pulled down the padded kneeler and rested her full weight on her knees.

She knew she'd been avoiding this. The church had piqued her curiosity from the moment Father Matthew had brought her up here with Joey that very first day in Graypourt. It had been calling to her, beckoning her to come inside.

"Okay," she said out loud with a sigh. "You have my attention now. I'm listening."

She heard the door leading into the church whisper open, hard-soled shoes coming down the aisle toward her, closer and closer. She didn't move and didn't turn around to look. She already knew who it was. She felt a solid presence approach the end of her pew and settle onto the seat next to her.

"Cate, I'm sorry that you didn't get to say goodbye to Michelle," Father Matthew said softly and sincerely.

Cate still didn't look at him. "This whole place just feels like one never-ending chain of goodbyes."

Father Matthew sighed quietly. "I know that you recognized her ability to surrender her own desires so she could fully become who she was meant to be. She was finally able to say yes to her true calling. You've done that, too, you know."

Cate turned to look at him now, narrowing her eyes and furrowing her brow in confusion and disbelief.

"When you became a mom, you accepted your true calling–you said 'yes' to being Joey's mom, no matter how difficult that was. Even when Joey's father walked away, you stayed. And you're still fighting to be Joey's mom every day."

"Then why can't I go home?" Cate asked tearfully.

"Because everyone's journey is different. You are not yet the person you are meant to be."

Cate stared at him incredulously. "I'm doing everything you've asked me to do. I helped Michelle start the medical clinic. I haven't protested or asked for anything. What else do I have to do to prove to you I'm the person I'm meant to be?"

"It's not something you earn, Cate. No one is keeping score. You can get there, but you have to trust me–and trust the process."

Cate glared at him, hatred and anger burning in her chest. "No. This is over ... now. I'm going home," she practically growled.

She stood, angrily kicking the kneeler up, and exited the pew at the opposite end. She turned to look back at Father Matthew.

"I'm going home to my son."

"That's not possible on your own. You don't have to accept my help, but this will end very differently if you continue to fight it," he said, his arm stretched across the back of the pew, his face maddeningly calm and controlled.

"Is that a threat?" Cate snarled.

Father Matthew looked down at the seat in silence. After several breaths, Cate understood she was being dismissed and turned angrily toward the back of the church.

Cate slammed her palms into the double doors, hearing them bang against the walls. She pressed past the main door out of the church and ran down the steps onto the divided walkway and into the road. She didn't stop jogging until she was back on the main road through town, her chest heaving and tears blurring her vision. She wiped her eyes and ran her arm under her nose, purposefully walking the four blocks to the diner. She needed to go back to where this whole nightmare started.

The streets were quiet, most people not yet reporting to their assigned positions. She could see a few early birds sipping coffee inside the coffee shop, but she kept going.

She walked past the diner and crossed the street, stopping in front of the wrought-iron gate that she and Joey had passed through on their way into Graypourt. The narrow courtyard could be seen through the bars and decorative scrolling pattern. She wrapped her fingers around the bars, closing her eyes and resting her forehead against the cool, hard metal. Her stomach tightened and a heaviness settled in her chest, tears burning behind her eyelids. She opened her eyes and lifted her head, letting her hand travel down to the small round knob that would release the gate's closure. The metal warmed in her hand, and her heart was racing.

If I can just get to my car, I can be on my way back to Joey ... she thought.

She turned the knob and felt the latch catch, the gate loosening from its frame. She pushed it toward the alley and stepped through the opening. The other end of the narrow corridor was hidden in shadow, blocked from the early-morning sun by the leafy branches hanging over the wall. She got as far as the iron cafe tables before her entire body went cold.

A woman stepped out from the shadows, and Cate immediately recognized her. Her familiar large, expressive eyes, strong cheekbones, and classic sophistication. Cate tried to control her breath, but her heart was racing, and her hands immediately began to tingle.

"Hey, Cate." Her voice, though low and raspy, dripped with a sugary sweetness, like a decadent dessert you wanted but knew you shouldn't have.

"Erica." Cate hated how shaky and uncontrolled her voice sounded. She needed to be tough with her, but she couldn't stop thinking about Peter's warning. She was desperate to know what Erica was doing back here, hiding in the shadows. How had she returned?

"Where are you headed?" Erica asked, a sharpness to her question.

"I, um, I was going to go back to the motel to see if my car was ready to be picked up." Cate knew she was failing miserably at trying to sound casual, and she crossed her arms to try to stop her body from trembling.

"You okay? You seem a little freaked out."

"Yeah, yeah, I'm okay." Cate bit her lip, desperately willing herself to calm down.

Erica moved a few steps closer to her, her arms hanging casually by her sides, her movements confident and controlled.

"I can help you get back to your car if that's what you want." She stopped, resting one hand on the back of a wrought-iron chair, her body language calm and patient.

Cate resisted even considering accepting Erica's help, though after her interaction with Father Matthew it was becoming more clear she wasn't going to get what she wanted by following his direction. So far, everything Father Matthew had suggested had only taken her farther from Joey and the way home. She was on her own.

"Oh, thanks ... but I actually know where I'm headed. I can get back to the motel just through this gate here." She walked past Erica toward the end of the alley where the green wood door would open into the motel courtyard. As she stepped into the shadows, she felt her knees weaken. Her heart leapt into her throat, and she felt the blood drain from her face.

The garden door was gone, and a blank brick wall rose up to meet the leafy branches hanging over the edge.

She took a few staggered steps in retreat and turned to face Erica.

"You can't go that way." Erica spoke calmly and directly, leaning against the back of the chair she had been standing next to, arms crossed.

Cate shook her head, a sob rising up from her chest and tried to beat back the panic flooding her brain. She felt herself stumble backward before a wave of nausea and lightheadedness slammed into her. Then the world went dark.

$$\sim 41 \sim$$

Cate pressed the balls of her feet into the wood floor of the wide covered porch, the swing moving back and forth easily beneath her. She felt Joey's warmth next to her, his narrow shoulders under her arm. She leaned down and let her lips rest on the top of his head, smelled the sweet and sour scent of his hair. A large hardcover book rested on their laps, and Cate's gaze landed there as Joey turned the page.

An illustration of a vibrant yellow butterfly was centered on the page, and below it read, "Blessed are the poor in spirit, for theirs is the kingdom of heaven."

Cate rolled over, her lids parting and her eyes slowly adjusting to the bedroom awash in morning sunlight. She was back in her bed in Graypourt and as the details of her dream began to crystallize, gratitude washed over her like a soft wave. To feel Joey next to her and to so vividly interact with him made her heart swell. She stretched and pushed herself up to a half seated position, her head and shoulders resting against the pillows.

Confusion flooded her senses.

She gasped as the memory of what she had seen in the alley returned to her. She didn't know how she had gotten back to the house or any sense of how long ago that had been. Erica's hollow, saccharine voice still echoed in her head. She felt her body go cold again with the realization that she could not leave Graypourt the way she and Joey had come in. She closed her eyes and breathed deeply, desperately trying to ground herself before the panic set in.

The weight of her sadness settled like a dark shroud, and questions rained down on her. How much more was she going to have to endure before Father Matthew finally let her go? Would she ever see Joey again? Why was Erica there? Was she back in Graypourt?

She leaned her head back against the wall and repeated her mantra. Finally the questions dissolved, her heart rate slowed, and her breathing returned to normal.

She swung her legs off the bed and stood up slowly, testing her strength. She glanced down, noting she was still wearing the same zip-up and joggers she'd left the house in yesterday morning. As she moved toward the bedroom door, something caught her attention, resting against the small digital clock next to her bed.

She picked up the small white envelope, the size of a notecard. Her name was the only thing written on it, in handwriting she didn't immediately recognize. The envelope was sealed, and she ran her finger under the corner, carefully tearing it open across the top. She pulled out the card, revealing an illustration of a bright-yellow butterfly on a white background, and below it read, "Blessed are the poor in spirit, for theirs is the kingdom of heaven."

The card dropped to the ground, and Cate grabbed her hand as if it had been burned. The image was the exact same one that she had seen in the book she had been reading with Joey in her dream. It stared up at her from the bedroom carpet, the phrase below it like a riddle taunting her. She reached down with a shaky hand and forced herself to pick it up. She unfolded the card and found a note in the same handwriting as the front of the envelope and began to read.

Cate,

I know you've been struggling to understand why you are here in Graypourt. It will be revealed to you a little more each day, but for now, be assured that you are on a journey of recovery, restoration, and renewal.

This journey will prepare you to be reunited with Joey, but only if you follow every single step of the road map provided to you.

The first step is often the most difficult for everyone. You first must allow me to lead you. Allow yourself to trust me, forget everything you believe about relying on your human instincts, and learn to depend on me. This is what it means to be "poor in spirit." This step is the seed from which all the other lessons will grow. It means laying down everything you are attached to, recognizing your limitations, becoming humble and small, and being open to everything I offer and ask of you.

I will not force you. You have complete autonomy to choose to follow me ... or not, but you cannot go home the way you arrived. The only way out of Graypourt ... is through.

This journey won't be easy, and there will be many temptations to walk away, but as our relationship grows and matures, you will be amazed at what we can accomplish together. You are not here because you have earned it, but simply because you are worthy. I hope you know how desperately I want you to succeed.

If you accept, join me at St. Ann's at 8 a.m. where we will begin.

In faith,

Father Matthew

Cate stared in disbelief at the words, reading the note several times and trying to come to terms with what Father Matthew was asking of her. She didn't want to be completely dependent on anyone. It felt like a cruel and insurmountable task, and it went against everything she believed about how to achieve a fulfilling life. Could she really have gotten it all wrong? She sank back down onto the side of the bed, the note hanging loosely from her hand.

Father Matthew said she had a choice, but she had to allow him to lead her and do everything he asked of her, if she was ever going to see Joey again. In her mind, he had left her no choice at all.

She felt a shift inside of her, overwhelmed by the sensation of her body simultaneously sinking and cracking open. Suddenly, everything Michelle had said to her that day on the couch fell into place. This was no longer about what she wanted–she had to let go.

She glanced over at the clock–it was already 7:15. She was going to have to hustle if she wanted to make it to St. Ann's by 8:00.

She shuffled into the bathroom and, after using the toilet, washed her hands and splashed cold water on her face. She patted it dry with a hand towel and steadied herself on the counter with both hands, forcing herself to look in the mirror. Her hair hung limply past her shoulders, and her skin looked pasty and dull. Her hazel eyes were glassy, her eyelids slightly puffy. The spray of freckles across her nose and cheeks had faded, and her lips were dry and pale. She looked like she'd been through hell.

If she was going to do this, she wasn't going into it like a wounded animal. She quickly showered and towel-dried her hair, dressed in a comfortable pair of underwear and her favorite bralette. She pulled on a pair of white linen pants and a fresh floral top. She glanced over at the clock, and it was already 7:40. Sweat beaded on her upper lip and under her arms, but she swallowed back the growing anxiety rising in her throat.

She slid into a pair of leather sandals and put dainty gold hoops in her ears. She quickly swiped on some blush and brushed her teeth. The bus was pulling up just as she stepped into the living room, and she quickly rushed out the door and down the driveway.

She gave Harvey a nod before making her way into the aisle. She quickly scanned the first few rows of passengers, expecting to see Maggie or Peter, when her eyes landed on the last person she ever thought would be there.

"Hey, Cate! Have a seat," Erica patted the seat next to her, and Cate felt her knees nearly buckle underneath her. The bus began to move, and she settled into the seat across the aisle, desperately hoping Maggie or Peter were on the bus somewhere and would come to her rescue.

"Aw, you don't feel like sitting with me?" Erica asked with mock disappointment and a pouty lip.

Cate gave her a tight smile. "What brings you back to Graypourt?"

"Oh, I come and go all the time. Comes with the perks of freedom, I guess you could say."

"You get to leave Graypourt whenever you want?" Cate asked incredulously.

"I do ... Headed to St. Ann's?"

"Yes, how did you know?"

"Father Matthew has asked you to become 'poor in spirit,' right?"

Cate's heart was racing as everything she knew about Erica fell into place. "Is that what made you get so upset with him just before you left the first time? Back when you were with Peter?"

Erica smiled, sending a chill down Cate's back. "You and Peter are pretty close, huh?" she cooed.

Cate immediately regretted mentioning Peter's name. "We're friends," she offered casually.

"Mm-hmm, right," Erica said with a wink. "Anyway ... yes, I saw right through Father Matthew's little game. I bet he told you that the only way to gain your freedom is to become totally dependent on him."

Cate nodded, her armpits prickling with new beads of sweat.

"It's a lie. He's just a control-hungry dictator, building up his little army of followers so he can keep his precious kingdom going. I'm the one who is truly free." Erica leaned closer to Cate, resting her hand on the empty seat next to her. "Don't give in to him."

Cate averted her eyes down to her lap, willing herself to stay committed to the reason she was going through with this.

"Do you have any kids, Erica?" she asked, meeting her eyes with confidence now.

"God, no. I was never mothering material–no woman should be forced to be something she's not."

"Well, I have a son–a five-year-old boy, Joey. He has autism, which I certainly wouldn't have chosen, but I wouldn't trade a single second of the life I had with him." Cate felt her chest tighten, her face warmed and tears pooled in her eyes.

"Mm, and where is he now?" Erica asked, an icy cruelty etched across her face.

"You know he's not here," Cate said, her eyes narrowed. "He's with family who are taking care of him until I can get home."

"So you've been told."

"Accepting this recovery is my only chance to see him again–you even said so yourself when you visited me the first time."

"I only said he couldn't come with you."

"Wait ... do you mean ... can you take me to see him?" Cate felt her resolve begin to crack.

"Let me work on that ... I'll get back to you." Erica sat back in her seat then and Cate swallowed hard, feeling as if she'd passed some kind of test.

Finally, the bus pulled up to the main stop at the park and Cate stood up to leave. "Have a good one," she said, glancing down at Erica who hadn't moved from her seat. Erica gave her a tight smile before turning to direct her gaze out the window.

Cate started up the street toward St. Ann's, turning back to see if she spotted Peter or Maggie coming off the bus, but they didn't seem to be on board. She began to wonder if maybe Father Matthew had only invited her, and a sadness settled in her chest at the thought that they might not be getting the same opportunity to reunite with their families. She pressed forward, finally coming to the hill that led up to the church.

As she reached the divided walkway, the bells rang out, signaling the top of the hour. Cate had heard them before, but never this close, and the sound had a solemn gravity she hadn't noticed until now. She took a shaky breath, stepping through the iron gate onto the brick courtyard leading up to the church doors.

As she pulled the heavy wood door toward her, organ music and choir voices filled the small entry space as she navigated around the small table with the basket of Rosaries. The doors leading into the church were propped open, and there were people scattered randomly in the pews all the way to the front row. As she made her way down the aisle, two heads turned to look at her. Cate's hand went immediately to her mouth as a small whimper slipped from her lips.

Peter's and Maggie's eyes lit up, and they stepped farther into their row to make room for Cate. She immediately leaned into Peter as his arm came across her back, and she reached out to squeeze the hand Maggie extended to her.

"I can't believe you guys are here!" she whispered quietly. "Did you get notes from Father Matthew, too?"

They both nodded with misty eyes and Peter said, "We've been waiting for you." Cate's eyes immediately welled up. This was it. This was how she would get through—with friends and the support of everyone she loved. She placed her hand in Peter's, letting him lace his fingers through hers and give her hand a gentle squeeze. Cate's heart swelled, knowing that she was on her way home.

"Hang on, baby. Mommy's coming."

Epilogue

A suburban Midwest apartment

Anthony rolled on to his back as he slowly became more aware of the pounding in his head. He brought his hands up to his face, attempting to rub the grittiness from his eyes. His mouth felt like it was stuffed with a cotton sock, and he moaned at the heaviness in his stomach. Another late night with his coworkers at the Corner Bar, and here he was, nursing yet one more hangover.

He forced himself to a sitting position on the edge of the bed, waiting for the phantom boat he was sitting in to stop rocking. He allowed his eyes to open just enough to see daylight trying to push its way between the thin aluminum blinds of his bedroom window. The pounding in his head intensified, and he shuffled into the small apartment bathroom, grabbing the nearly empty bottle of ibuprofen off the counter, clumsily twisting off the childproof lid and dumping four round tablets into his palm. He grabbed the small juice glass next to the sink and turned on the faucet.

With the ibuprofen slowly dissolving in his sour stomach, Anthony shuffled into the kitchen for a cup of coffee. As he waited for the Keurig to fill his only coffee cup, he thought he heard his cell phone vibrate on the bedside table. He grabbed his coffee mug and gingerly made his way back into the bedroom. When he picked up his phone, he noticed several missed calls and fourteen unopened text messages.

"The heck ..." he muttered.

The first text he opened had just come through while he was in the kitchen getting his coffee. It was from an old friend he hadn't spoken to since he and Cate had split up. They had been "couple friends," and it just wasn't doable once one couple's relationship fell apart. The friend lived just a couple of blocks away with his wife and family, and they ran into each other occasionally at the grocery store or gas station, but it always felt forced and uncomfortable. The fact that he was texting him now set off alarm bells as Anthony's heart began to pound in his chest.

"Turn on Channel 9," it said.

The hair on the back of Anthony's neck stood on end, but he quickly took the few steps necessary to pass through the small kitchen into the front room where his couch and TV were. He set his coffee cup down on the end table and grabbed the remote, quickly scrolling to the right channel.

"An accident this afternoon on a rural Midwest highway has taken the life of a young mother and her five-year-old son ..." the female newscaster's voice said. The screen showed a mangled dark-blue sedan on the side of the road, multiple emergency vehicles parked in front and behind, lights flashing.

Anthony took the two or three steps to the coffee table just a few feet from the television. He collapsed onto its smooth, hard surface, knocking an empty beer can onto the worn carpet. He rested his elbows on his knees, placing one hand over his mouth and nose, and he listened to the newscaster continue.

"It appears a semi crossed the center line, and the mother and her young son were killed on impact."

The pieces fell together as Anthony's phone slipped from his hand onto the carpet. He choked over several sobs and thought he might be sick to his stomach. He ran into the kitchen, gripping the edge of the counter and folded his fingers over the edge of the sink.

"Oh God, what have I done?..."

Just outside his apartment door, on the wooden railing with its peeling paint overlooking the parking lot, a vibrant yellow butterfly landed, softly opening and closing its delicate wings.

Acknowledgments

This book is the culmination of 40+ years of cultivating a dream, the providence of God's perfect will and plan for me, and the incredible people he has brought into my life. So first and foremost, I want to thank God for bringing me to this moment. There are so many people to thank for their love, encouragement and courage to challenge me when something didn't sound quite right: my family, especially Christopher, Thomas, Andrew and Maddy who have all contributed an idea (or many!) or praise at some point. My parents, who nurtured this dream from day one, and have pitched in to help any time I've asked. To my dad for lending his artistic talent when I approached him with the crazy idea of designing the covers for the Blessed series. My editor, Amanda (The Engaged Editor), who also served as a book coach and teacher and along the way, became a friend. To my First Edition Book Club ladies whose input, insights and questions have unequivocally made this story what it is today. Thank you to the Mid-Continent Public Library and the Story Center team at the Woodneath Library who have provided incredible support and encouragement during this entire process. Lastly, I'm so grateful to Father Jacques Phillipe, who said yes to writing the book that inspired the Blessed series, *The Eight Doors to the Kingdom*, with its beautifully accessible and grounded meditations on The Beatitudes. May I always be a reflection of God's merciful love, as well as someone who never forgets to be poor in spirit because it is in surrender that we truly find our freedom.

Ashlie Hand is a life-long storyteller and writer who has spent the last 40 years nurturing her craft through journaling, short stories, magazine and newspaper articles, speeches and social media in the academic and nonprofit world. She is a devoted wife, mother of three, and practicing Catholic living in the Midwest.

Website | ashliehand.my.canva.site
Facebook | Ashlie Hand Author
Instagram | ashlie_hand_author